The Romantic Collection

Paul John Hausleben

The cover photograph "Odyssey of Romance," the cover design, and cover concept by Paul John Hausleben
All other photographs by Paul John Hausleben
Logos, artwork, and designs by Paul John Hausleben

Published by God Bless the Keg Publishing LLC
Henrico, Virginia, U.S.A.

ISBN: 978-1-7330927-1-5

Dedication

To the journey. To hot tea in the afternoon, to soft music, to the gentle taste of wine, to the harsh bite and then the smoothness of whiskey, and to the gentle waves arriving onto the shores of our lives.

The Romantic Collection

Paul John Hausleben

Contents

Acknowledgements

Many thanks to my family and friends. To Mr. Harry M. Rogers Junior and an extra round of thanks to Lopez for her awesome introduction and her kind words, for enduring my photography, and most of all, for the nudge and then the gentle push on this one.

"No matter where I go, what I do, or when I think – I will always bring you with me. Now, until the end of all time."

Paul John Hausleben

August 2022

Notes from the Author

"You are a fantastic romance writer, Paulie."

In the chess match in my mind and hidden within my vivid imagination, I moved my queen to D6 and froze on my next move. Although she had recently asked me to teach her the game of chess, I thought about how it was a good thing that I have not yet taught my lovely companion the game of chess. I can outmaneuver her.

I winced and painfully listened to the words; I blinked and looked at my nearly empty Manhattan glass and then looked for the bartender and, with my eyes, I begged for a quick refill. Luckily, this was a gin-joint that I often frequented, and the bartender was intuitive. She was on top of her game. I downed the rest of the cocktail and drained it and gave her a thumbs up.

"I despise writing romance."

My companion slowly leaned in.

Her dark, but magnificent eyes flashed at me while she carefully studied my face. With a little sexy growl to her voice and a challenge to my comment to her compliment, she asked, "So why do you do it?"

Oh no! In a daring move, she just moved her rook to H5! Very tricky! Apparently, she knows the game!

I was stuck, once again, staring at the board for my next move. And stuck staring at her captivating eyes, her dark features, lovely face, and beautiful hair. The lowlights of the bar cast a gentle glow on her hair and her eyes glowed in the lights.

I stumbled for words but knew the answer. The refill arrived, along with an accompaniment of Heavenly Angels. Strumming harps. Golden harps. I took a sip. This bartender was the best-Manhattan-mixer-chick in the entire world. I know . . . editor bullshit . . . too many nouns in a sentence. Just go away, editor. I am treading water here.

"Because the stories require romance. I write enveloped within human emotions, and love is the most powerful of human emotions. It is unavoidable. As much as I despise romance, it is a necessary ingredient in my writing recipes."

My companion took a sip of her hot tea and laughed.

"Okay, good answer, so answer me this. Why do you never write a happy ending romance?"

Oh, oh. On the spot. Her bishop just moved to A6. I fiddled with a slide of my rook hidden behind a wall of pawns, and the queen and the knight. Safe move.

I protested with an unnerving wiggle in my voice, "Ah, well, not always. I write some happy endings. I do." I nodded my head. I then pondered the statement and, in my mind, I quickly scanned my many volumes of work. "Okay. You *might be* correct. I don't write happy endings. Mostly. I often leave the endings unhappy or hanging and allow the reader to decide how it ended."

My companion laughed, and she rolled her eyes.

"C'mon, now. Ah, Paulie? Where the 'River Bends and Curls.' Your only romance novel. An amazing book. One of your best. I love Renee Gorman. Everyone loves Renee Gorman. She is snarky, confident, brilliantly smart, sexy, gorgeous, and the perfect match for Henson. Renee was head over heels in love with Henson, and Henson was the same with Renee. She is one of your best characters ever! The story, and the ending, tears your heart out. Why, oh why, did Henson not stay with Renee and end up with Binky? Binky ditched Henson. He took her back. Huge mistake."

Checkmate.

I took another sip of the glorious Manhattan and answered, "Cuz, Henson is a dope and he is a chump. Romance is for chumps. It never ends happily in real life.

Why should it end up happy in fiction? Love is difficult. Relationships are difficult. It is easier to go through life without all those burdens. Isn't it? I mean, okay, well, maybe not, but romance is painful, and it never ends up happily."

The bartender lifted a suspicious eyebrow toward me and my cocktail. She was looking to maximize a tip, but I think she was also looking out for me.

Perhaps.

My companion flashed her lovely eyes at me again, and the glow in her eyes quickly turned from seductive and sexy to a hint of anger, and she wiggled her glorious backside into the barstool to dig in a bit. She tugged at her blouse to reveal just a hint of her glorious chest.

Oh no. I feel a protest coming. Glorious backside wiggles and a hint of glorious chests always mean trouble. In many ways.

"Paulie, you are wrong! Love and romance *always end* happily. As in ever after!"

"Does not. You are an incurable romantic. Besides, love and romance are two entirely different things."

"I admit that I am a romantic! Incurable. And you, Paulie, are not. You are a pain-in-the-ass. I challenge you here and now to write a happily ever after romance story. Not a half-ass, kinda, sort of, happy ending as many of them end. Or as many them do end, in outright heartache. I want an unquestionable, clear-cut, happily ever after ending story, complete with fireworks and starry eyes."

"Challenge accepted."

Damn those Manhattans. They are my Achilles' heel.

"Additionally, Paulie, you should publish a book of the best of your romance stories and add this new story to it."

Check. Game over. My king is a loser. The dope deserved to be captured. I suck at chess.

Therefore, this collection was an idea over cocktails and tea, then a project and now a reality. We combed the stories for romance, and I downed more Manhattans to dull the pain of reading my own romantic words.

Seriously, all humor-laced writing pushed aside now, I thank my lucky stars every day for the wonderful people who hang out with me, care about me and our work, give me great advice and push me to be better. They enjoy my books; they dive in, take the stories and the characters personally, and continually challenge me to write some more, to try new angles and swim within a sea of words. It means so much to me. More than I can ever say.

Therefore, the best of my stories of blessed (along with not so blessed) romance all exist here, along with one brand new novelette and some other meanderings. Inside of two covers. Not all of them, but most of them. I admit that I reluctantly compiled this collection, but now that I completed this collection, I am very pleased with it.

In addition, yes, I wrote a somewhat annoying, happily ever after story for my drinking companion. I hope that she enjoys it.

In fact, I hope that all of you enjoy these stories as much as I enjoyed the experience of writing them. Some of them might be retreads for some of the readers. Some might not be so.

Regardless, thank you for reading them. Forgive me for taking a slight pause in my writing world, but for now, I need to practice my chess game.

August 2022

Paul John Hausleben

Prologue

From "Christmas Cocktails"

Fred Kelleher was not exactly sure why he was so nervous. He patted the pocket of his suit jacket to make sure it was still there.

It was.

Just as it was, the fifty or so previous times that he patted the same pocket. Fred had planned this evening out ahead of time, and he felt as if he had not missed a single detail. In fact, he was sure of it.

It was Christmas Eve and the love of his life, Miss Marlene White, sat opposite of him, at their favorite table, in the quiet corner of their favorite restaurant. A restaurant where they went on their first date, shared their first kiss, and a restaurant where Fred was sure they fell in love.

Everyone was in on the plan. Gregory, who was their usual server, Hal the bartender and Gladys, the night manager. The plan was perfect. The setting was immaculate. Hal perfectly dimmed the lights in the nook where they sat. From their table they could look out the windows and see the snow gently falling upon the streets of the city. The Christmas candle in the holly and berry Christmas centerpiece in the center of their table flickered, danced, illuminated their faces, and added to the already glorious ambience.

Marlene, as usual, looked stunning. Her hair was perfect, the black dress that she wore enhanced her amazing figure and the white pearl earrings in her ears matched the white pearl necklace around her neck. Gregory stood on the sideline, just far enough away to watch the scene unfold and still attend to his other two tables. Gregory was carefully watching from afar, and he knew the plan and carried it out to perfection. First, a round of cocktails, a bourbon Manhattan in a cocktail glass with ice for Fred and a rye whiskey sour for Marlene. When he dropped off the first cocktails, he would also drop some bread, the menus, and then leave the two lovers alone for about ten minutes. The first cocktails usually go quickly and when they finished the first round of cocktails, Gregory would drop two more without Fred requesting the refilled drinks. Gregory would disappear without taking their meal order, and Hal and Gladys would team up to make sure there were no interruptions. Fred wanted two rounds of drinks to soften his nerves. . ..

Gregory dropped the second round of cocktails on the table and Marlene laughed and nervously giggled while commenting, "My dear, Fred. My goodness, I barely finished my first drink. I might get a bit tipsy too soon here and look a bit foolish!"

Fred knew that it was the perfect time and with a gentle shake of his head, Fred said, "You could never look foolish. You are the most gorgeous woman in the world." Marlene blushed while taking another sip of the drink and she giggled again, this time at Fred's comment of praise and adulation. "I think there is something uniquely special about Christmas cocktails. Don't you agree, Marlene?"

"I do. It might just be the glorious atmosphere here, but I have to say that they taste extra marvelous tonight. Hal is always wonderful at mixing cocktails, but tonight, I think that he added some extra Christmas magic to the Christmas cocktails."

"He might have and I brought some magic along too." with those words, Fred moved quickly as Marlene's eyes danced in the candlelight and she searched for the meaning of Fred's words. Without hesitation, Fred reached for the box in his pocket, took it out, jumped out of his seat and dropped to one knee in front of Marlene. Marlene gasped as Fred slowly took the box in his hand and opened the lid, revealing the stunning diamond engagement ring inside.

"Will you marry me, Marlene? Will you be my wife? I love you with all of my heart and soul and want to be with you for all of eternity. Every Christmas Eve, every Christmas, every birthday, and every day in between. Good days and bad days. I want to be with you forever." Fred remained on his knee and his eyes searched Marlene's face for her answer. For a few seconds, Fred thought about how he might have made a major mistake because it seemed to be taking a long time for Marlene's answer to arrive. In reality it was not, it was just the shock of the situation, which stalled Marlene's words.

"Yes! Yes! Yes, of course. I will marry you, my beloved, Fred. I too, love you with all of my heart and soul and I will love you now and forever."

Upon hearing her words, Fred breathed a sigh of relief, took the ring, and gently slipped it on Marlene's finger. While they kissed, the entire restaurant erupted in joyous applause and heartfelt congratulations.

For sure, it seemed as if Marlene was correct, because there might have been a little extra magic in those Christmas cocktails.

Then again, at Christmastime, there always seems as if there is magic in the air and love in our hearts.

Christmas love and magic in the air, seems to make quite a Christmas cocktail.

The Rock

From "The Spring Collection"

I sat on the front steps of the parsonage of Reunion Lutheran Church, staring out into an early spring sunset. For me, there is not too much in the world that can exceed the majesty of a glorious sunset, while it is announcing the pending darkness of a spring evening.

Oftentimes, it is indescribable.

To a great extent, sunsets are almost incomprehensible. The colors, reds, oranges, yellows, shifting clouds and the reflections of light.

With a sunset, we exemplify God's great creation and broadcast peacefulness that this day has ended, and darkness will fall, but tomorrow we can start anew. It is the end of the day and somehow, a promise too. A promise of hope for a new start tomorrow. In my opinion, there is nothing quite as magnificent as the beauty of the glory seen in a soft, golden sunset. I have always enjoyed sitting and watching the sunsets. Not only to admire, and to enjoy the beauty of them, but to capture my thoughts at the end of the day. There is something very calming to my soul about watching sunsets, and in fact, it has been a fascination of mine since I was just a small lad. If I live to one hundred years old, and I watch a sunset every single day of that long life, then it still will not be long enough to comprehend it all.

Here at Reunion Lutheran Church, we were all very lucky. The church sat nestled in an enclave of natural beauty. It was an unusual property, a magical setting, a setting carved out of the woods in northwestern New Jersey. The trees, peace and serenity, were magnificent. The setting often made me think that the leaders of this church had to be steered by the hand of God, in order for them to have been so fortunate to find a property of such beauty and peacefulness, to build their church upon this very special location.

My mind traveled back to the first moment that I arrived here, with my wonderful wife by my side, holding her hand tightly as we began a journey into the next phase of our young lives together. A journey filled with hope, love, God's plan, and our own dreams and desires. It had been worth it all to be the pastor of this wonderful church, which despite the challenges, truly lived up to the name on the charter, the name Reunion Lutheran Church. In many ways, the church reunited not only many people's lives that grew up here with this church, but it also reunited my family, friends, complete strangers, and my own soul. In fact, this church accepted me while I was still a young man, when I was struggling with my past life and with my doubts, and the church gave me back my purpose and then laid perfection upon my soul.

It had to be part of the plan because in my mind, no other explanation could be true.

I sat here on the front steps, enjoying the glory of the sunset in front of me and enjoying the sunset, yet reflecting rather pensively on where I was right now in my life, marriage and career. Reflecting on how far I had come, how much we had left to do and what brought me to where I was right now.

My wife had set out earlier with our two children on some shopping excursions and it would be a bit more time before they returned. Therefore, here I sat and relaxed, thinking deeply, taking a few moments out of my harried life to enjoy God's creation and to reflect and ponder while I waited for them to return.

I leaned back and felt it in the front pocket of my vest, while I stretched my long frame backwards on the cold concrete of the parsonage steps.

There it was in the pocket of the vest, just as it has been for a very long time.

I felt the rock.

I reached into the pocket, grabbed the rock, and pulled it out. I studied it, felt it in my hands, rolled it around, and then smiled. It was just a rock, a small, round rock. Nothing special, no brilliant colors, no vibrant lines, cold, dark and dull, but it was not the appearance of the rock, which made it special.

It was what it symbolized to me.

After all of these years, the rock was still the same, and the memories it brought to me were not only joy-filled, but in many ways painful too. While I sat there holding the smooth, little, rock in my hand, I returned once again to another front stoop and another set of front steps, a place of my boyhood, a place where I often, just as I did tonight, sat, watched sunsets and passed my time.

A special place, called 182 Belmont Avenue.

"What are you up to there, Paulie boy? Sitting out here again, eh? Watching our world go by, eh?"

I was somewhat startled by the voice, as well as the disturbance, to the haphazard peacefulness from the foreground of the city noises on the busy street in front of me. The traffic whizzing by on Belmont Avenue in front of me had some type of mesmerizing influence upon me. It was a bit hard to explain or describe. One would not think that a busy city street full of trucks, buses, traffic and blaring horns could lull anyone into complacency, but I imagine the many years of watching and listening to the same scenes and noises had somewhat dulled my senses.

I looked up to see my grandfather standing on the sidewalk in front of me. I had no idea of how long he had been actually standing there watching me.

I smiled and answered him, "Hello, Gramps. Yes, sort of, well, somewhat daydreaming, I guess. You know, thinking about things at the end of the day. I am not sure what I am thinking about but, I am thinking."

He smiled back at me, waved his hand a bit, tugged at his trousers, and took a sip from the bottle of Big Boulder beer that he held in his hand. He was dressed in his usual wool sweater, with a crisp white tee shirt underneath it. His trousers were just a bit too big for him, but he pulled them up when he moved a bit in my direction. Despite the somewhat cool weather creeping in as the sun started to set, my grandfather only wore his favorite English wool sweater. I only wore my favorite light vest, which covered a tee shirt emblazoned with the logo and name of my favorite rock-and-roll band. A grandfather and grandson, cut from the same mold. We were both impervious to the cold or a chill of the late afternoon and early spring evening.

"Do you mind if I join you there on the front steps, Paulie boy? I would like to share a bit with you in your meandering thoughts and pensive ways tonight. You do not mind now, eh?"

I nodded and smiled while motioning for him to come ahead and sit next to me. I admired his English accent gently framing his words with a golden lace. The echo of his voice; I can still hear in my mind many years later, in fact, all of my waking days.

His many years of living here in the United States had done very little to fade his accent, which he acquired from his native land. I was indeed quite happy that he retained it, since it was a part of my own heritage.

In actuality, as my grandfather settled in next to me, this was a scene that we had replayed countless times over in our lives. We had viewed many a sunset and passed many early evenings sitting together upon these same front steps. In fact, ever since I was old enough to remember, he and I sat here together while we were both thinking and watching.

Gramps settled in next to me. He wiggled a bit, looked over and smiled at me, while taking another sip of the beer he had in his hand.

After a period of a long silence, he asked me, "So have you read a bit more from the book I gave you? What story are you up to there, Paulie boy? What is our favorite detective up to these days?"

I smiled, reached down next to me and pulled up the leather-bound book, a book containing the adventures of a certain detective, who lived at a famous address of Baker Street in London, England.

"I forget the name of the story, Gramps, but it is the one where the snake comes down the bed pull and he gives it a bash with his walking stick. Love it. What a great story!"

Gramps laughed at my enthusiasm, and he patted me on the back. He joyfully told me, "Ah, yes. The speckled band story. Indeed, it is a good one. I knew you would like them. However, I have to say, they are all great stories. One after another, from a great mind, a storyteller. . .."

Gramps looked at me and he seemed to be admiring how I held the leather-bound book tightly in my hands while I studied it.

He continued to speak, "Are you writing anymore, Paulie boy? I rather enjoyed the story about the time bomb of troubles and mayhem that Ronzo created. I know that I told you how much Chadwick down at the bookshop enjoyed the draft that I allowed him to read. Chadwick knows books and authors better than any person whom I know of. You have a talent. I dare say that, I hate to see you stop writing. You are a captivating storyteller too. You watch everything, and you capture it in your mind. I find it quite remarkable. I marvel at how you will use it later on, not only for you to entertain us, but to allow it to escape in your mind and touch others with what you have experienced. Not too many people can do that, Paulie boy. I must say that it is a gift. A very special gift that you have. You do know that. Do you not?"

I shrugged my shoulders and did not answer him. I was actually writing many stories but keeping them all in my mind. My mind never stopped; I just did not think they were good enough to put down on paper. I smiled at my grandfather, put my head down and then glanced over at him while he studied me with his eyes over the rim of the beer bottle he was sipping.

I finally answered him with an honest reply, "I write a little here and there, Gramps, but mostly, I just enjoy sitting here thinking. You are correct, in that I am capturing the entire world, and keeping it close to me, in order to write about later on. Right for now, work, reading, and hockey are what I mostly do. When I am not playing hockey, I am thinking about it. Watching the shooter's eyes, playing my angles, keeping my body square or in the right position. I play it all over in my mind. When I am not doing that, then I think about what I will write, and I watch the world go by here on Belmont Avenue. Besides, the stories I have in my mind, I am not sure that anyone would be interested in them. I rather sit here, when I am not hanging with Harry or Jeff, or playing goal, and watch things go by. It gives me ideas. I think someday, maybe, way down the road, the stories will come out of me. Until then, I gather what I need. Does that make any sense, Gramps? Or am I a little strange?"

Gramps put his beer down and he laughed a bit at me. He shook his head. He shifted off to speaking in his second language of Welsh, as he described me a little in the Welsh language, "Paulie boy, you are a rhyfedd (weird or strange is what he categorized me as) one! All goalkeepers are, in football or in hockey. You goalkeepers are all the same. You are complex and a very deep thinker, but I do understand. The best writers are the people who gather what they need. Use it all later on in your life. Sir Arthur did that very same thing, too. He was a medical doctor before he became a writer. The medical practice served him well to conjure up adventures."

I nodded in agreement, but did not comment. We sat in silence for quite a long time, neither of us saying much.

We watched two cars stop for the red traffic light at the corner. The driver's doors flung wide open, the two drivers of the cars both jumped out. They met in the roadway and argued and screamed at each other in Spanish, and shook their fists in each other's faces. Obviously, they knew each other and the argument must have boiled over from a previous adventure, and it now was going to culminate on the street corner in front of our house. Gramps and I carefully watched the wild scene unfold.

"Bloody well, those two chaps might create a bit of a tussle for each other, Paulie boy. Perhaps, a spot of too much cheap wine, eh?"

"I suppose so, Gramps. Let's see how it goes."

Was this just another scene to provide more wild adventures for inspiration later on down the road? Who knows?

Car horns blared, obscenities screamed out of many car windows, traffic snarled, and life went on around the two irate combatants. Even though neither Gramps nor I understood Spanish, we managed to follow the general gist of the conversation. The two men settled their differences with a few shoves here and there, yelled a few more words at each other, and happily, they resolved this one without a gunfight, fist fight, a knife fight, or other potential assorted methods that were all too common in our old city neighborhood.

Northern New Jersey, home to the most amazing

varieties of life in which you could ever imagine! Mobsters, street life, tortured souls, happy people, sad people, natural beauty and urban decay, all within a step or two of the front door of our home. It is one of the unique places on the face of this Earth, yet I would not trade growing up here for a million dollars.

As we watched the scene dissipate, I turned to Gramps and said, "That is why I sit here, Gramps. So many scenes unfold before my eyes. Some are happy, some sad, some terrible and some enlightening. I have seen it all pass by the front steps of our house here. It is better than any movie or television show in which you could ever imagine."

"Only because you absorb it, and put a positive approach on it, Paulie boy. You have a huge heart and are a magnet for people and happenings. Your mind needs to absorb it all and capture it forever. You are very much the same as I am. In England, as a young boy, I would wander the meadows outside of Sherwood Forest, listening to the whispers of the wind in the meadows, retaining the stories that the wind told to me, whilst it whistled through the dry grass that leads up to the edge of the forest. There, the wind gave up on the meadow grasses and focused on moving the mighty limbs of the forest. The whispers became a howl, and I understood that the wind was, as our lives are. Sometimes, we need to whisper, and sometimes, we need to howl. Something as simple as the wind, invoked my imagination. Retain it all, Paulie boy. It will serve you, and others well, someday down the road."

Gramps had been studying my eyes as he spoke to me, as I was studying his. He now moved his focus away and leaned back more into the stairs.

He shifted his position on the stairs, and I imagined that some beer was now influencing his speech, as he became a bit deeper in his thoughts.

Gramps then tapped his chest with his right hand as he spoke again, "All that you need to do, is keep your heart open, stay strong and tough as you are, and imagine that everything is speaking to you. Understand your potential to imagine, retain and share it with others. You will be a great storyteller someday, maybe, not a great author, but a great storyteller. There is a difference. I for one prefer to read great stories rather than eloquent and glorious, flowing prose. After all, in the end, a grand story is what the reader desires most. Your ability to imagine and create, well, it is limitless, Paulie boy. It will touch people's lives."

I smiled at his profound words and captured them in my memory banks forever.

My grandfather watched me out of the corner of his eyes and I watched as he chugged the last of his beer. He placed the empty bottle next to us on the steps; he then slowly stood up and walked over to the small section of grass between our sidewalk and our home. Gramps seemed to be studying the mixture of grass and dirt, and his actions were a bit puzzling to me. I did not say a word, but I studied him while he poked at the ground with his feet. He then seemed to spot what it was that he was searching for, reached down and picked up a small stone that his foot had uncovered on the ground. He picked it up, turned and walked back to where I was sitting, all the time holding the rock in his hands. His amazingly clear, blue eyes sparkled as he walked over to me and he held the rock in his hand. Most people would call it a stone because it was too small to be a rock. Yet, held tightly in my grandfather's powerful hands, I would never say that he picked up a meager stone.

Therefore, it was a rock.

Forever more, it would be a rock. In Welsh, we would say, "Am byth." Forever.

"Here, Paulie boy. What is it that you see?"

I studied the rock for a few moments. It had some dirt along the edges. It was small, but solid, not colorful, rather dull, and it was nothing very special. I reached out, took the rock from him, and held it in my hands. I turned it over repeatedly in my hands and then I smiled at my grandfather.

Finally, I spoke, "I see the spot on the ground, in which you and my grandmother first stepped on, when you first came to America from England. Perhaps, this rock was part of the actual ground where your feet first landed. It was underfoot as you stepped off together, arm-in-arm, hand-in-hand, together into a journey of the unknown. The rock did not break or give way and it helped to lead you. It became a little smoother, but the rock remained solid and powerful. It was here before you came and will be here long after we are gone. It is part of a new life, a symbol of hope, a part of the pathway to where we all are right now."

I looked up and Gramps put his hand on my shoulder, and he squeezed it tightly. I could feel the power in his hands. He was a powerfully strong man, both in emotion and in physical prowess. A man of unparalleled strength. His grip was strong and deep.

This was, however, not a grip of control; this was a grip of encouragement, a sign of his love.

Gramps smiled widely as he told me, "Bloody amazing! You see how well, in which you can imagine, Paulie boy. Wonderful! Study for now. Then you can write when you decide the time is right. However, please, someday write. Most of what I have learned in life, I learned by reading. It is a gift that we all can take advantage of and share."

"I will, Gramps. I promise, someday."

Gramps looked at me, smiled a bit and said, "I do, however, think that is a stone you are holding there, Paulie boy, because rocks are larger."

I shook my head and replied, "Sorry, but with respect, you are wrong, Gramps. It symbolizes you. You are too powerful to be just a stone. I have to say that what I hold right here in my hand is a bloody rock!"

Gramps laughed aloud, loosened his grip upon my shoulder, and waved his hand in the air at me.

"Oh, bloody well! Please, do not let your mum hear you say that bloomin' word. She will blame me for teaching you! Then a rock it 'tis. Good night, Paulie boy. And, my dear Paulie boy, please remember that sometimes, you will need to whisper and sometimes, you will need to howl. The rock will remind you of that, and you are smart enough to know when you need to choose between the two. Cheerio for now."

"Cheerio, Gramps. Thanks for the rock and the chat."

I brushed off the dirt from the edges of the rock, spun it and placed it in the front pocket of my vest. It fit perfectly in there, smooth, solid, it felt good. It reminded me of my grandfather and I thought about how I would keep it.

The spring gave way to a hot summer, then the seasons passed quickly and soon I found myself still sitting on the front steps of our home on another spring night.

Watching and waiting, gathering information as the world flashed before my eyes.

I was now about nineteen years of age, or thereabouts, tall, strong, lean, and powerful. Long hair, down past my shoulders, a solid growth of a blonde and red beard growing upon my chin and face, and I was now on the cusp of manhood. Yet, I remained blind to so many things, all the information gathering was far from complete.

Other than my best friends, Harry M. Redmond Junior, and Jeff Porter, my hockey teammates and a few on and off again girlfriends, I was a loner. I enjoyed being alone; I found nothing wrong with it. I was able to pass the time on my own. I read books on the front steps and in my bedroom at night. In and amongst the pages were where I escaped to far-off lands. Enjoyed wild adventures, fought wars, confronted pirates, sailed the high seas, solved crimes, sought pretty women, and I captured their hearts too. It was easy to imagine that I was driving down lonely country roads in fancy convertibles with the top down, all while never leaving the front stoop and the front steps of my own home.

It was magical.

I read, The Bible too. In fact, I read anything that I could. Gramps was correct. All we need to learn in life, come from true experiences and from reading. It all unfolds for us; we just need to absorb and retain all of it.

Sometimes Gramps joined me on the front steps, and sometimes, I remained alone. I often took the rock out of my vest pocket and rolled it around in my hands, while I watched and thought, or read.

I spoke to neighbors who passed by, chatted with strangers, petted dogs on their head, spoke to our resident stray and oftentimes, pet cat, Pussface when he decided to stop by and hang out with me. Sometimes, my faithful pet fox terrier, Skippy, would sit with me and he too watched the world go by our front door. I knew when to run back in the house when I heard some random gunfire or other trouble emitting from the darkness of the neighborhood. I refused to partake in the illegal drug deals occurring in front of my eyes; the lure of their promise to escape to far-away places had no appeal to me. I had my dreams of a hockey career, my words, and books for that!

It was amazing what scenes unfolded here on these gritty streets, right before my eyes.

Then in the late spring, when the summer was closing in, and the heat seemed to be creeping in closer and closer, my world changed a bit. The trees had now all bloomed out, and the leaves were proud and fresh upon their branches. The large maple tree in front of 182 Belmont Avenue now had left a deposit of dried, brown spinners chasing all around in front of me as a reminder of the lateness of the spring. The usual vest that I wore to fend off just a touch of the spring evening chill, was almost ready to return to the confines of my closet, because I found sitting there on the front steps that the nights were not quite as cool as they had previously been. Yes indeed, my world changed a bit, because it was on one of these late spring evenings that she came by.

I noticed her one night, looked up from my book and watched her pass by me. She looked at me and smiled, and I smiled back. I did not say anything to her, but I caught her eyes, and then admired her from a distance, when it was safe to steal a glance, without the embarrassment of her catching me.

You know, I was checking her out.

My goodness, she was gorgeous!

She walked by me, and I could not help but to notice how well she was dressed. As she wiggled by the front steps, wearing a pretty blouse with a light sweater over it, along with tight bellbottom pants, I could see streaks of red wisps in her blonde hair and most of all; I caught a whiff of some intoxicating type of perfume that was floating around her.

Oh, how in such a short period of time, the scenery had dramatically changed.

The usual roar of trucks, city buses, guys yelling at each other, car horns blaring, and the occasional gunfire in the distance all no longer mattered.

She had smiled at me and I had smiled at her. I found myself captivated, and as a result, I purposely arranged my daily timetable to ensure that I was sitting out on the front steps at that same time each night, which I had seen her first pass by me.

One night passed, and she did not walk by, then two nights, then three. Perhaps she was just passing through; maybe, she did not live close by. After all, I had lived here for a very long time and I had never seen her before. On the other hand, perhaps, she was new to the neighborhood.

A million different scenarios ran around in my mind. All I knew, and all that I could recall, was her smile. Her smile had lingered upon my mind's eye, and the image of it was a bit difficult to overcome. With one simple walk by me, on a late springtime evening, she had cast a spell upon my heart.

One night, about a week or so after I had first seen her, I looked up from the book that I was reading, and there she was, strolling down the sidewalk in front of me. I felt my heart jump in my chest and my throat close up. Playing it cool, I leaned back and casually flipped the pages of the book. There you go, Paul, make as if you do not even see her.

Yet, it was impossible. Our eyes locked and I could not prevent the wide smile that came upon my face.

It just came over me.

She passed by and she smiled widely at me, melted my heart with one smile, and mouthed a gentle, "Hello" to me. I was too love struck to answer, too much in awe of her beauty even to murmur a single word. She wiggled by and continued on her way.

In a flash, she was gone. I had blown it!

Geez. I could not even begin to imagine what a bum I was.

Now, it was not that I was uncomfortable around young women. I had a few gals chasing me here and there, and even at my young age, I had chased a few back. A friend of my sister, Maureen Zipperelli, had taken a bit of a fancy to me since we were very young, and even though she was older than I was, we had shared many special moments together. It was not as if Maureen and I were dating one another exclusively, but time would tell. Maureen was great fun to be with, she had an amazing personality, and one more thing stuck in my mind whenever I thought about Maureen Zipperelli, and that fact was that she was knockout gorgeous too.

I also had a long-time and long-distance romance and pen pal relationship with a gal named Debbie Boatwright, but that is a story for another time and place. Debbie sure was a pretty gal, too. When you are young, well, you know how it is. . ..

"Beautiful lassie, eh?"

My grandfather's voice echoing from behind me had made me jump off the steps, and in shock; I almost dropped the book that I had been reading.

Gramps had caught me gawking at the young woman!

"Yeah, yeah, yeah, she is Gramps," I humbly admitted. There was no sense in denying that I had admired her.

Especially from the rearview. . ..

Gramps laughed at my embarrassment. He turned the corner from behind me, patted me on the back, and he said, "Don't blame you! She is quite the lovely young woman. Do you know what I think, based upon that brief encounter? Next time she will stop, Paulie boy. I will bet upon it. You are a handsome lad. I agree with my sister Alma that you look very much like our Cousin Percival. Percy does not have all that longhair and a wispy beard upon his chin, but you look like him. He is a handsome man and has had all the women in town chase him around for years. He never settles down with any of them. Instead, he allows them to continue to chase him. Nothing wrong with that. You share his position in sports too. He was a football goalkeeper. Unlike your skills, Percival was a poor one at that!"

Gramps stood in front of me, while I sat on the front steps, he stomped the ground a bit, waved his hands in the air as if he was duplicating a soccer goalkeeper waving at a shot towards him, while allowing the shot to go by him into the goal net. I laughed at his demonstration. As a goalie myself, I felt the pain of allowing a goal.

Gramps continued to speak, "I hear you are quite a bit better at the position than your relative is, even if it is in a different sport. More and more, as time goes on and you grow older and more powerful, I see touches of your father in you too, and that is an exceptional thing, Paulie boy. Your father is still a very handsome man, and he might be stubborn as an ass, but he is a good man. A harder working chap does not exist on this good earth. My Joanie, she picked a good one in that father of yours. I am quite proud of him and love him as a son."

I nodded in acknowledgement of the description of my father. Gramps leaned back, pulled at the sleeves of his sweater, and he smiled at me. Gramps seemed to be transporting to another place within his mind.

He smiled, sighed a bit, then said, "Young lassies. Eh? Pretty, cute, yes. Enjoy and be smart about it! Please, be smart, Paulie boy, a young woman as beautiful as she is, or that, other woman . . . what is her name, eh? It escapes me a bit now and then. The gorgeous, Italian lassie?"

"Maureen Zipperelli is her name, Gramps." I helped Gramps with the memory of the name of the captivating and quite alluring, Maureen Zipperelli.

"Yes, indeed, Maureen. She is a beauty. What a beauty she is, Paulie boy. You do attract them. It is best not to let her catch you with another lassie, because that might ignite a bit of fireworks. She has been after you for years upon years, Paulie boy. I suppose that she can be a bit emotional and difficult to control. The gorgeous ones always are."

Gramps laughed and tugged at his waistline again to pull his pants back up a bit.

"Young lassies can also bring you a bit of trouble, too. They can peddle their wares, flitter about, captivate you with their beauty, and lure you into a spot where it might be a bit difficult to control. You are very smart. You will remember my words and when the time comes, you will make the correct decision."

He winked at me, and I understood very clearly where his advice was coming from.

"What is it that your father always says? He does have quite a few of those, New Jersey street-wise statements that he blurts out here and there. Statements that are actually quite profound and are meant to teach, meant to coach, and often are, spot on in their meaning." Gramps looked at me as if he wanted to see if I could recall the words and lessons that my father gave to me about relationships with young women.

I did, and smiled as I relayed it as proof that I paid attention, "Five minutes of pleasure has to be measured against a potential lifetime of pain."

Gramps laughed and nodded, but after our laughter faded, his face changed to a more serious look as he said, "On the same subject, you are only young once, and as long as you keep your wits about you, and remain smart, then enjoy it all. This young lassie will not stop for most young men. When you are that beautiful, then you can select whom it is that you want to stop for in life. Yet, she will stop for you. I can tell. She might be a bit older than you are, Paulie boy. Time will tell, be careful, and keep your wits, eh? Say, I am going to the corner for a six-pack of Big Boulder beer. Would you enjoy a cold soda?"

I smiled. Gramps was so cool.

"Sure, thanks."

A few days later, my grandfather's prediction came true.

While I was sitting at my usual front step post, she passed by me and, after an alluring smile and a nod of her head, she turned around quickly and she stopped.

I had just set upon clandestinely admiring the rear view of her, and I did not expect her to stop and whirl around so quickly. I was quite sure that she caught me gawking at her backside!

My heartbeat increased, my face turned red, and I watched while she slowly walked over to the sidewalk in front of me and asked, "Is that all you do with your life? Do you always read and only smile at the gals as they walk by? Or can you actually speak?"

"I speak and I read and I do other things and, well, I watch too." At this point, since I figured that she had caught me gawking at her beauty, that a dose of honesty could not hurt me.

She tilted her head a bit; her body swayed and leaned in closer to me.

Her mouth turned into a bit of a seductive smile, and her voice lowered as she asked, "Oh, yeah, huh? What is it that you watch? Never mind answering, because, I think I have an idea of some of the things that you might check out here and there."

She stood up straighter, smiled, and posed a little by tilting at the waist a bit and placing her right hand upon her hip.

Well now, I was not quite ready for this type of dialogue, and I found my tongue tied up in knots. I made a mental note to read a bit more of the romantic stuff, because I needed to steal some sappy material for use in real life. There was no doubt now that she obviously had caught me in my rather poor efforts to conceal my admiration of her beauty while she passed by.

"Do you have a name?" She asked.

After a few stops and halting starts, the words finally came out with a forced and rather dumb sounding laugh, "Sure, sure, sure. Paul. Paul John Henson. How about you? I am quite sure that you have a name too."

"I like your humor and style. Very subtle. Yes, I do . . . Kyra. Hello, Paul John Henson. Nice to meet you. My full name is Kyra Lovell. I see you read an awful lot when you are not watching certain things, or actually or more specifically, watching and admiring female body parts. So, what do you read?"

Oh well, I was now proud that I had not fudged the truth at all and confessed up to my gawking.

I held the book cover up for Kyra to see it. The book cover had the name of the great detective emblazoned upon it in large block letters. Certainly, it was not hip or cool, and not the type of book that one would expect a long-haired, hippie young man to read, but I did not care. I marched to my own drumbeat, and I never really cared to lockstep with what other people did.

"Oh, I see. Very impressive . . . Sherlock Holmes. So, the classics are what you usually read."

"I do read the classics quite often, but I read all kinds of books. My grandfather gave me this one. It is a leather-bound edition. He brought it with him from England. He was born there."

Kyra walked closer to the front steps. Now that I was interacting with her and studying her closely, I surmised that she was around twenty-two or twenty-three years old, and in my heart and in my mind, I hoped that I could appear to be a few years older than what I actually was. While she stared at me, I noticed that her eyes were green. Deep green, sparkly, yet very warm. Her eyes were wide, and she laced the lashes of her eyes with some type of eyeliner to enhance them, her hair was blonde, it hung down in gentle curls to her shoulders and in the setting glimmers of the waning sunlight, I could detect some red highlights. She was tall for a woman, and I could see that she wore low-heeled shoes with soft bottoms. They were the perfect pair of shoes for walking, and perfect shoes for a tall woman to wear. Kyra Lovell had a long neck, a thin face, with perfect features. Kyra wore tight, black, bell bottom hip huggers, which clung to her amazing figure. She wore a white blouse, and on top of the blouse, she wore a black knit sweater. She left the sweater open and unbuttoned, and with her blouse being a rather tight fit on her, it was impossible not to admire her petite, yet shapely and perfectly formed breasts. Around her neck, she wore a thin gold chain that only enhanced her long neck.

She was gorgeous.

"Oh, I see. England . . . that is very cool. What is your favorite story of the great detective's adventures? Mine is the one where the criminals put an ad in the newspaper for red-haired men, in order to lure the banker out of his office, so they can dig the tunnel under his office into the bank vault."

I now, officially, became a mess. Suddenly, waves of emotions captured me, and I encountered all types of difficulty in forming even simple words, huge troubles with speaking, and in formulating simple sentences. In fact, I became speechless!

A love struck, babbling fool.

A gorgeous gal and she read and knew the stories of the great detective!

A rare and precious find. She was a gem.

I finally managed to find some words deep within my mind, take my focus off her smile, her hair, her eyes, and her other attributes and say, "I forget the name of the story, Kyra. It is the one where the snake comes down from the bed pull and he gives it a bash with his walking stick. Love it. Great story!"

Kyra smiled, but she did not answer me. I had a feeling that she actually knew the name of the story, but did not want to reveal it to me.

I recovered enough to gain a bit of ground and asked her, "So, I have lived here forever, and I have never seen you around here before. Did you just move into the neighborhood? Are you living close by?"

Kyra walked even closer to me and she leaned up against the wall next to the front steps of our house. Her green eyes now reflected a bit of the spring sunset lowering rapidly in the sky. I could tell that she was very keen on my interest in her.

"I am staying close by here, over on North Tenth Street, at my grandmother's house. She has not been feeling well. My home life over in Great Falls is complex right now, and in a little turmoil, so I came to stay with my grandmother for a few weeks. I start a new gig in college in a few weeks, my final year. I transferred in from a college in New York and I plan to finish here in a college down in south Jersey.

Near Philadelphia. I am a literature major. Things were not the greatest in New York, and being a Jersey girl, I decided to return home."

"I see. That explains it. Well, I hope it works out for you. Literature, eh? And that also explains the interest in books and Mr. Holmes, eh?"

I felt a bit deflated; she was quite a few years older than I was, and she was heading off for a new life. A life where I knew that I did not exactly fit in. Kyra stopped leaning on the wall. She pulled her sweater around her, as it was obvious the night air was growing colder. She smiled at me.

"Thank you, for the well wishes. Yes, it does explain some of it, not all, but some. I love to read, and my plans are to teach and write someday."

Kyra studied me carefully; she was deeply looking at me, almost as if she sensed my deflation at her plans.

She took a few steps and waved in the air to me while saying, "Well, I guess that I will continue my evening walk. It has been nice meeting and speaking with you, and while I do not want to pull you away from such an engrossing evening of your own, the neighborhood is a bit rough around here. Would you care to join me? You know . . . would you like to walk with me?"

I closed the book and smiled. An invitation, an opening and now, do not blow it, Henson! You usually mess up these types of situations. Think hard and do your best not to blow it. I stood up from the steps, bent over and placed the book on the step next to me, and noticed how intently Kyra studied me.

"Oh my, I did not realize how tall and athletically built that you are. You did not look so tall and muscular sitting there on the steps. I think that you will be quite a protector of me!"

"Kyra, I can assure you that no one, actually messes with us around here. My family has been here so long, we, along with my buddy Harry and his family over on John Street, we are the anchors of the neighborhood to some extent. Newcomers might test the waters, but all the older residents, they know better than to test us in foolish ways. I will be glad to walk with you, and I can assure you that, you will be fine."

"I imagine so. You are quite imposing. I never thought you were as big, as tall, and as strong as you look right now while standing there. When you sit, you must slouch."

I think I surprised Kyra by my height and size. Or she was turning on the flirting big time. Perhaps it was a bit of both.

I reached down, grabbed my book, and picked up the rock, which I usually kept in my vest pocket. I had set it aside while I was reading, and must have forgotten about it, until I stood up and noticed it. I saw Kyra's eyes study me while I grabbed it and placed it back in my vest pocket. I was now officially doomed, since she now knew that I was a whacko.

"Why do you have a stone that you keep in your vest pocket, Paul?" Kyra asked the question which I knew would be coming.

"It is not a stone. It is a rock. It helps me to think, to imagine, and to create. I am a bit on the rhyfedd side. That is the Welsh word for strange."

Yes, I was a doofus and blowing this big time. Geez, a stupid rock.

What a dorky and goofy thing to have.

After spilling the explanation for having such a silly item to carry around with me, I immediately looked up at her and brushed the long hair from in front of my face. I was studying her face for a reaction. I was sure that she would laugh at me and recognize that I was just some weird young guy, sitting on the front steps of his house while dreaming endlessly. Kyra did not answer me right away, but she watched me as she started out first to walk up the sidewalk and head north on Belmont Avenue. To my surprise, instead of dismissing me, she smiled at me.

"You speak, Welsh?"

"Very little . . . some, well, I dunno. I guess a little more than just some. Just what I picked up from an aunt of mine and from my grandfather . . . a few words here and there."

"I see. And what do you create, Paul?" Kyra asked as she walked ahead of me with a few steps. I was still fumbling with my book and placing the bookmark in the pages.

"Oh, not much right now. I wrote a draft of a book consisting of three short stories a bit ago. Now, I just study things, compile adventures and scenes, until the bug bites me to write again."

Kyra stopped dead in her tracks; she turned and smiled as she studied me. Her hair, her eyes, her beauty was riveting.

It sent a shudder down my spine.

"Really? I would love to write well. My writing sucks. It is a weak point for me in my studies. Of course, being a lit major, I read and write, and I try so hard to write well, but I cannot ever come up with storylines to write something decent. Characters are easier. I just do not know where to place them in the stories, nor do I compose any meaningful dialogue. My goodness, what a surprise it is to me that you write. You are full of surprises, Paul John Henson. I would love to read what you have written and I hope that perhaps, someday, you would share it with me."

I did not answer her, I guess the writing did take her by surprise, but right now, the last thing that I would want to do is to show her some draft of my short stories. She knows great literature, not my hokey writing. I did not want her to read my silly short stories about life in this old neighborhood. It would be very embarrassing.

Kyra still stood and smiled at me, and when I had no reply or reaction, she pointed towards my vest pocket and pronounced, "And by the way, that is a stone, not a rock there, Paul."

She waited for me to catch up to her. When I did reach her side, she reached out towards me, and to my profound and complete surprise, she took my hand and pulled me along as we continued to walk. It was without the slightest hesitation that I took her hand, and she gripped my hand rather tightly. I was now close enough to catch another whiff or two of her perfume, some type of magical scent in which lured me to a place that I had never been before, and now embedded into my senses forever.

In the spring evening we walked, we talked, and we shared conversation. It was a conversation of a deep level. We spoke of writing, and of literature, of how to create a dialogue between characters and how to create story settings. Her intelligence was amazing, her thoughts were captivating for me, and the discussion took me to a new level.

Somehow, it seemed as if I had known Kyra Lovell for my entire young lifetime.

What a profound connection.

Suddenly, this early spring evening had turned into quite an exhilarating situation. I only just met this woman.

Geez, even though we were only casually dating, and we had no formal agreement or commitment, Gramps was correct. In the fact that Maureen Zipperelli would be a bit ruffled if she saw me right now with Kyra Lovell. What a tangled web we weave sometimes!

"So, other than reading, writing or pardon my correction, but studying for future writing, and observing the asses of women who pass by your front steps . . . what else is it that you do, Paul John Henson?"

I laughed. Kyra Lovell was indeed honest and I could tell she was a reader and literature major. Her vocabulary was quite extensive, and to be honest, very appealing.

"I play hockey. Kinda started out on the street, then

roller hockey leagues and now I am playing on the ice rinks. I am a goaltender. Currently, I am in a part-time goalie clinic over at Ice Land in Great Falls. I want to play professionally someday."

Kyra stopped walking; she dropped my hand and put her hands on her hips.

"Ice hockey? Ice skating? Very cool. You write books, read all the time, sit on the front steps, I must say that you are indeed, whatever that word in Welsh for strange was that you said, Paul! However, that makes sense now, and it does explain your athletic build and body. You have a remarkable physique."

"Thanks, at least, I think. I do dabble in quite a bit of different things."

"I'll say, and you are what, eighteen or maybe nineteen? I am twenty-three by the way, in a month and just a few days, I will be twenty-four."

Kyra looked at me for an answer. I would not lie to try to close the gap between us.

"Nineteen. 'Be twenty in November. I graduated from a vocational school. I am a journeyman electrician and electronics technician. The service shop should promote me to master someday soon. Just need more field time now, already passed all my exams with close to one hundred percent scores on 'em all. I hope that they promote me soon."

Kyra waved to me to take her hand, and I did so, while once again, we resumed walking.

"They will. It does not surprise me that you passed all the exams with such a high score. Very nice. A tradesman. Very sexy, a man with a tool belt. By the time that you are twenty-five, you will be quite the amazing man, and I must say, quite a catch for some young woman too. I think that you are already quite the catch."

We stopped walking for a moment and while still holding hands, she studied me. I stood taller. Her eyes looked me up and down, and I knew what was going through her mind. Part of playing the position that I played in hockey, was to remain confident, and I knew what you projected forward, came back to you. A weak posture, sitting back on your skates, a lack of challenge, all of them combined to allow a shooter to think right away that you would allow a goal. I learned to project confidence by standing in the net playing goal, walking through tough neighborhoods and by passing through life, and it was a powerful lesson. A lesson that Gramps and my old man both taught me, and we all used well.

Kyra finally spoke, and I relaxed.

"You are a fantastic looking guy, amazing looking, in fact. That hair, wow! My goodness, you must have all the women fainting. Paul, I want to say. . .."

I abruptly cut her off. Embarrassed a bit, or perhaps actually playing it cool, would be a more accurate description.

"I think that we should keep walking," was all that I said, and this time, I took the lead and gently held her hand. We walked together, hand-in-hand and as we did, I decided to project some of that confidence. I held her hand tightly, and we continued to walk all the way to North Tenth Street.

Just to ice the scene, and not be a complete idiot, I added, "You are gorgeous, Kyra. Stunning and pretty amazing looking. You are gorgeous."

She only gripped my hand tighter and did not say a word.

We spoke about seemingly hundreds of subjects in five city blocks, and by the time we made it to her grandmother's house, the sun was set and darkness, framed upon a backdrop of smutty city streetlights, was all around.

"This is my grandmother's house. Right here, Paul," Kyra said as she let go of my hand, turned, and faced me.

We had stopped in front of a narrow, small home, tucked back from the street a bit. I had passed this house a million times or more, during my times wandering all over the old neighborhood. Previously, I had never given it a second thought. Now, it would embed in my mind forever. It had a small fence lining the front yard, which was a strip of land about six feet wide, leading to a small wooden porch. It was a typical Paterson, New Jersey home. It was neat, clean, and well maintained. I looked at the home, spotted a light glowing in the front window, and then I looked back at Kyra. I was making my first move to reach out, shake her hand and say goodbye. When she gently reached out, she took my face in her hands, stood on her toes and kissed me.

She tasted better than candy, her lips were very sweet, and her kiss was soft and passionate. The smell of her perfume made me weak in the knees. I was too stunned to say a word; I leaned in and, well, enjoyed it.

I had swapped many spits with Maureen Zipperelli, and; I am not ashamed to say, shared a bit more than just a few kisses with Maureen, too. I had enjoyed a few kisses and such with other young women in my short nineteen years, but I never shared a kiss quite like that kiss was.

Kyra let go of me, stood back, smiled and without speaking a single word, she opened the gate, went up the stairs, turned the knob to the front door and she disappeared into the house. I stood there in front of her grandmother's house for a long time, while recovering my sense of awareness and collecting my thoughts.

Geez! What the hell just happened to me? That was the only thought that came into my mind. I had stolen a kiss with some gorgeous, older woman on a fine spring evening and I had not a single regret.

It was exhilarating!

I reached into my vest pocket, grabbed the rock, and held it in my hand. I tossed it up and down and caught it in my hand while I began to think.

This was going to make one helluva story someday!

Most every night, I sat on the steps watching and waiting for Kyra to come by, and most every night she did. We walked, we went to the local park and sat on the benches and talked for hours. We spoke about books, stories, and people, and joked about the simple things we saw and observed. She laughed easily and often, and her mind was keen, her words were poignant and carefully selected. I took her to the Paterson Diner where we had dinner, chased down with coffee, tea and snacks, and we sat and talked for hours about nothing that was very special. Or so it seemed to be nothing special.

I never did, despite her gentle prodding, share the draft of the book in which I wrote. For some reason, I was too embarrassed to do it. Her magical use of the English vocabulary floored me, and I felt my writing was too simple, too quaint and uneducated, in order to compete with her ability to link glorious words into sentences.

We laughed, we joked, and we kissed, and we shared some magical times together.

I knew that our time grew short, however; I just did not realize that it would come so quickly. The springtime was waning now and the end of the month of May loomed closer; the days grew longer and the evenings grew much warmer. Spring was now becoming a memory.

One rainy Saturday evening, I was sprawled across my bed, reading a hockey magazine. I was being lazy. Harry and Jeff were both busy and not around, so I was goofing off and killing time reading an article, in which I had already read a few hundred times before.

I had an intense hockey practice and hard skate earlier in the afternoon and I was a bit sore. It was time to relax and recover.

I heard the front doorbell ring, but I knew the old man was in the living room watching television and he would answer it. Usually, a ring at the front door at this time of night meant it was just a neighborhood bum seeking a few coins or a handout. Even Skippy, my faithful fox terrier, did not get up from the foot of the bed to check out who was at the door.

It was that kind of evening.

I was a bit stunned when the old man appeared in the doorway of my bedroom and he smiled at me.

He looked at me for a second or two and finally said, "Better get off ya lazy ass and get your act together there, twenty-seven. Some really gorgeous twigeon is at the door, bundled up in a raincoat and hat, and she is asking if you are home."

I looked up, tossed the magazine aside, and sat up.

"Really? Do you know who it is?"

"Nah. Geez, man, what the hell do I look like, a detective? How many ya got chasin' ya now? Damn. I think she is that cutie ya been walking with from the other block. Better, not let Maureen spot ya with her. The fireworks from that explosion would be a son-of-a-bitch. But, if I were you, I would not keep her waiting too long. Maureen is a hot little numbah, but this gal, whoo wee. She is amazing."

"Yeah, okay, I got it, Dad. Thanks!"

I nodded, jumped up, ran in the bathroom, washed my face, brushed my teeth, took the hair tie out of my hair, combed my long mop of hair, smoothed my clothes out, and ran to the front closet. I pulled an old ball cap off the top shelf and my trusty vest and almost ran to the front door. As usual, I was dressed in my rock-and-roll tee shirt and canvas sneakers. My attire seldom changed, but later on in my life, it would suit me well.

"Hey there, Kyra. Geez, I did not think you would be around tonight. You know, with the rain and all."

She winked at me and waved as she quickly descended the front steps, where she stopped at the base of the stairs to make sure that I was following her. If it were even possible, Kyra Lovell looked even more captivating than she usually did, wearing her raincoat and a hat, her smile shining through the raindrops.

"Does the big, strong, tall and handsome, hippie goalie melt in the rain?"

I smiled at her description and question.

"No, not at all."

"Then, let's go! A walk in the rain is the ultimate pinnacle of romance!"

Kyra was correct. We walked in the rain for hours and hours. Around and around the city blocks we went until we were both close to being soaked to the skin. While we walked, we talked, and we shared in one another's magic. When we once again finally reached the front of her grandmother's house, instead of remaining on the front sidewalk, Kyra dragged me by the hand to the front porch.

"Here, let's get out of the rain now," Kyra explained as we walked up the three short steps leading to the porch and stood in the darkness together under the cover of the porch. I knew the same scene that we had replayed repeatedly during the past three weeks or so would be different this go around. I could tell by the look in her eyes and the huskiness in her voice that something was different.

Very different.

I was young, only nineteen, but I already had a strong sense of when the look in a young woman's eyes had become different towards me. This was not a casual look in her eyes; instead, this was a very intense stare.

Kyra unzipped and removed her raincoat, pulled her hat off and she placed them on the seat of a rocking chair sitting on the porch. Underneath, she had on her usual blouse and sweater, and of course, she wore those glorious, tight-fitting dungarees.

"There, time to get out of those wet things," she said as she walked over to me and slowly and seductively unzipped the zipper to my vest, removed my hat and placed it over the top rail of the rocking chair. She then reached up, moved wayward wet strands of my long hair out of my face and then despite her height, she did as she always did, and stood up on her tippy toes, took my face in her hands and kissed me. This was a longer, deeper, and more intense kiss than we had ever shared. After our kiss, she rested her head against my chest and relaxed, while I wrapped my arms around her and she wrapped her arms around me, too. Even in the dim light of the front porch, I could see her close her eyes, and heard her exhale a gentle sigh, while she nestled into the folds of my chest. As she rested upon me, we remained enfolded in each other's arms, while we gently rocked back and forth, not speaking a single word but simply enjoying each other's warmth and closeness.

Kyra's hands wandered from my back to my chest, where she lingered with her hands, for some time, while exploring my chest with her gentle touch. Her breathing changed to deeper breaths, almost gasps, long and deep breathing, all the while growing increasingly deeper.

We shared an intense stare, and I marveled at how, even in the dim light of the porch, her green eyes sparkled and glowed.

Kyra softly spoke, "Oh, Paul, you are a remarkable man. Tell me, how a woman does not fall in love with you? I guess that question is too late because I have fallen in love with you."

I did not answer her because the truth is that I would not know how to answer her. Now, it was my time to breathe deeper and while she explored my body with her hands; I studied the look in her eyes. As they grew even more intense, her breathing remained deep and hard, even with a shudder or two between breaths. Her hands worked some magic in various locations on my body, and I am not ashamed to say that parts of me reacted. Kyra then her hands slowly glided around me and she placed her hands upon my backside. There, she slid her hands inside the rear pockets of my dungarees, and once again, she rested her head upon my chest.

Kyra then whispered to me, "Paul, I leave tomorrow. Tonight, is my last night here in Paterson. My grandmother is not home. She will not be home until late tomorrow. I would like very much for you to come in and we can say goodbye together. We could share one, last very special evening together, in each other's arms."

Waves of emotion and pangs of seduction came over me, shaking my body, rippling through my soul. I knew what she meant; I just did not know exactly how to react.

While pushing the long hair out of my face, I bent down; we kissed again, deeply and powerfully. We held each other, and I, too, allowed my hands to wander. My hands first gently wandered from her face, to her neck, to gently caressing her lovely breasts and then I began rolling my fingers and hands over the hardness of her nipples. After releasing her breasts and while kissing her, I held each side of her glorious backside and I firmly pulled her body into mine. When I pulled her into me, even while kissing, I could hear her throat throttle with a slight gasp at the power of my grasp. In a somewhat out of character and bold move for me, I now held her glorious body next to mine with a seductive yet a powerful clasp.

There was no doubt that I held her so tightly that our souls welded together. We were so close, and so tight, that I could feel the hardness of the nipples of her breasts tucked against my chest. I could feel every inch of her body next to mine, and I was certain that she could feel every inch of mine too. It felt glorious, and the smell of her perfume, combined with the feel of her body next to mine, was magically intoxicating, and it was difficult not to wither in the grips of her beauty. When I felt my soul and willpower collapsing, I then remembered the words of my grandfather.

They echoed in my head and resonated into my inner being.

"Young lassies, can also bring you a bit of trouble too. They can peddle their wares, flitter about, captivate you with their beauty, and lure you into a spot where it might be a bit difficult to control. You are very smart. You will remember my words and when the time comes, you will make the correct decision."

I knew what to do. It was not going to be easy, but I knew what to do.

While still holding her closely, I looked into her eyes, smiled, and told her, "Kyra, I would love to, but I can't. Believe me, when I tell you that you are gorgeous and captivating. Our exploring hands only make this decision even more difficult. You are a woman beyond description. However, I am not about that. Commitment is a word that I know all too well. I write books, ya know, and study the use of words. That is just not, where I am at right now in my life. Someday, it might be my style, but not right now."

As soon as those words left my mouth, I wanted to retract them. While shaking my head to display my disagreement, I corrected my words, "On second thought, it might never be my style."

I took both of my hands, gently held each side of Kyra's face while looking in her eyes, and I told her, "You are a one-of-a-kind beauty, with a diamond for a personality and gold for your heart. Yet, try as I might, I can't light a flame like that, then walk away, and try to forget you for the rest of my life. You are unforgettable, and after sharing a special night, then I might never let go of you. Instead, I would rather remember these special three weeks for what they have been, not what they might have been. I want to keep them as a special dream in a nineteen-year-old, young man's heart."

I let go of her face and once again hugged her tightly. She wrapped me in her arms and rested her face against my chest while she listened to me.

"Kyra, dreams do not cost anything and they allow me to whisper my greatest secrets and wishes to the sunsets every night. Dreams just might be God's greatest gift to us. If I pretend, and put this moment into retrospect, then it is easy to say that despite the fact that you are older than I am that we are both way too young. It is a fabulous excuse for my actions and my decision. Maybe it is correct and maybe it is not. Yet, I rather keep the dream close and then someday, when I choose to write this story, then I might be able to finish this story, in the way that I wanted it to end . . . not how it actually did end."

Kyra smiled a wide and glorious smile. A smile of understanding, a smile of love.

She kissed me long, deeply and profoundly, one last time and she whispered gently in my ear, "That is not what I wanted you to say, but rather it is, what I expected you to say. Mature beyond your years, you are. Amazing. Only a powerful and special young man would turn down an invitation such as this, in a manner such as what you just did. You will someday, Paul, fill some very lucky woman's heart with joy and with love. I too, will dream, dream of you. You are going to write a great story about this someday, Paul. Promise me that someday, you will write this story."

She looked at me for confirmation and I nodded to indicate that I would, and then I mouthed, "I will."

For a brief second, Kyra looked away, and then returned her eyes to mine.

She continued speaking with tears in her eyes and just a hint of a smile on her face, "I will read that story, with tears in my eyes, and joy in my heart. I too, will never forget the last three weeks, or ever forget you. You are so correct, when you said that we are both going to always remember this time for what it has been, and not for what it might have been. You are too special to describe or to forget.

There are no words. Other than, perhaps, one word . . . love. I love you. No question that I do. I will never forget you. Ever."

She started to let go of me to turn and to walk away, but she stopped, leaned back into my arms, and spoke in a low voice, almost a whisper, "By the way, you were right and I was wrong. Very, very wrong. That is not a stone, which you carry around with you in your vest pocket. It *is* a rock."

With a lingering handhold that slowly and somewhat painfully faded away, Kyra let go of me. I watched as she turned, picked her rain garments off the rocking chair, walked away, put the key in the lock, opened the door and disappeared forever.

She never looked back.

I grabbed my hat off the chair rail, reached into my vest pocket, grabbed the rock and held it in my hand while putting the hat on my head. I tossed the rock up and down and caught it in my hand while I began to think. I zipped up my vest, adjusted the hat on my head, and walked back out into the rain and into the night.

Yes, indeed, this was going to make one helluva story someday.

Spring gave way to summer, and the night air was warmer now.

June weather was quite unpredictable.

The seasons changed, but I did not. As usual, at the end of the day, I sat on the steps of 182 Belmont Avenue, reading, watching the world go by. Watching another incredible sunset in front of me.

This was going to be a special one. I could tell by the colors. Red, gold, a touch of yellow, but it was the whispers of red, which made it special.

Hockey season ended a week or so earlier, and now, if I was not out with Harry or Jeff conquering the world, I was here on the front steps gathering all that I required for use later on in life.

On the other hand, was I?

All of it was passing by in front of me, the cars, buses, trucks, taxicabs with horns blaring, all of it. I loved every minute of it.

Yet, somehow, I secretly hoped that she would magically appear in front of me, smiling, with her green eyes glowing in the early evening, the whiff of that perfume and all the rest of her magic.

"Eh, so whatcha up to there, Paulie boy?"

The voice of my grandfather echoing from behind me made me jump once again. I turned and looked at him, placed the book that I was reading down on my lap, and smiled at him. He stood in front of me now, his blue eyes wide open, his white hair crisply tucked on his head, not a hair out of place. Even at his advanced age, my grandfather was a powerful man and his large barrel chest, with his ample muscles, displayed sturdily underneath his sweater.

He wore a smile a mile wide.

"Reading, Gramps. As usual, I am reading and watching our world go by us."

"I see. Visiting Baker Street again, eh?"

"Nah, not tonight. Tonight, I am in a garden and reading some Kipling."

"Oh my, a good one. The gardener story. Mind if I join you?"

I patted the stairs next to me. I watched as Gramps settled in next to me with a bit of a groan and a creak of his legs. He carried a Big Boulder beer with him, and once he sat down, he took a long swig of it.

We sat in silence for a long time.

Finally, he spoke to me, "You have been quiet as of late, Paulie boy. The pretty lassie is gone now I guess, eh? Off to university."

I did not answer him. Instead, I only nodded.

"You fell a bit hard, eh? It will not be the first time,

Paulie boy. I hate to tell you that it will never be easy. I think, by looking at your face, that you had to make a difficult choice. A very tough choice, eh? Maybe, what I had warned you about, Paulie boy. Have you reached a point that you are now wondering if it is a deep regret or not? If I had to bet, you spoke in a whisper and not a howl, eh?"

"Definitely, a whisper. As far as the regret part of this goes, I am not too sure, Gramps. I kinda think that she was special. Maybe, one of a kind. And yes, it hurts like bloody hell. She was more than just beautiful, it was her laugh, her conversation. Damn, just the words she could put together, geez, she made me jealous. I could never construct sentences like that. She will be a great writer someday."

Gramps looked over at me and he spoke a bit softer. I could tell that he felt my conflict and pain. I had a feeling he had been here too, at some time in his life.

"Oh, I see. And, you will write many great stories too. Don't sell your talents too short, Paulie boy. The young lassie might have the benefit of the university education, but you have this front stoop and these amazing front steps with the window to our world all in front of you. I have to admit, I have no glorious words to make you feel better. Nevertheless, I do hope that you recall what your father and I taught you so long ago, when you were just a young lad, shining shoes and earning a few coins. I hope that you do recall that afternoon in the Widow's Pub when that crazy, drunk bloke went a bit on the wild side and then he regretted his actions. Do you recall that lesson, Paulie boy?"

I leaned back and smiled while I closed the book and set it aside. The lesson was very clear and bold in my mind. It would be there forever, just as so many lessons that Gramps and my parents taught me would be.

I answered him boldly, "Sure do, Gramps. I will never forget it. Not that one. Regrets are for fools. Regrets are only foolish doubts of decisions that we made. They serve no purpose. They only cause us angst and worry. Make a choice, be a man, then move on. Never doubt."

Later on, in my life, I would use that lesson a few times more.

Gramps smiled at me. He took another swig of beer and patted me gently on the knee.

"Good show. I am very proud of you. You should be proud of yourself too. It takes quite a bit to admit what you passed up and to stand up proudly for your actions."

"I guess, but still . . . it hurts."

"It does, I am sure of that. Yet, you are very young, strong and remarkably handsome and you have my word that there will be many other young lassies that will come along, my dear Paulie boy. You will fall in love and out of love. You will find some special lassies, and eventually, you will make the correct choices. You are too smart not to make them."

I reached into my vest pocket and pulled the rock out. I tossed it up and down while Gramps watched me.

We did not say a word for a very long time. Instead, we studied the sunset.

Gramps finally handed me the beer bottle, and he said in a low whisper, "Here, Paulie boy, take a long sip and do not tell your mum, eh."

I set the rock aside, took the bottle, tilted it back, and took a sip. It tasted cold and good. I handed it back to Gramps, took the rock once again in my hands, and held it tightly.

"Ya know something, Gramps? Someday, I have to think that all of this will make one helluva story."

He smiled at me, reached out, took my hand, and squeezed it tightly.

I felt his power, his encouragement and his love, as he told me, "Well then, Paulie boy, my suggestion is that someday, you write it, eh?"

I saw the headlights of our jeep pulling into the church parking lot and I knew that it was my wife and children returning from their day of shopping. I returned to where I was, back to reality, back on the front steps of the parsonage, and I left 182 Belmont Avenue behind once more.

Or did I?

I never did write that story in the manner in which I hoped that it would have ended, but I did keep my promise to Gramps and to Kyra, and I wrote it. The storyline and plot were a bit different. The characters changed to the point where only Kyra and I would know of whom I based them upon, but I wrote it.

Wrote that story and a whole helluva a lot more of them too.

I never searched for Kyra Lovell to see if she became a writer, or a teacher, or if she fulfilled her dreams. I often wondered if she ever sought me out and if she ever read any of my material. Who knows? Yet, I know that I have no regrets about anything I wrote or anything that I ever did. Regrets are only foolish doubts of decisions that we made. They serve no purpose. They only cause us angst and worry. Make a choice, be a man, then move on. Never doubt.

I held the rock tightly in my hand and thought deeply about the decisions that I had made in my life.

I lost my beloved grandfather when I was about twenty-five years old. Gramps was well into his nineties and he was still strong and powerful. His death was not a sign of his weakness; instead, it was the pinnacle of his strength. He died, as he lived, strong, proud and brave. I was lucky enough to be with him and hold his hand during his last moments in this world.

I felt his strength.

I felt his power and his love. He was a really cool guy, and I loved him with all of my heart.

Not a day ever goes by that I do not think of him, or wish that he were right here with me. To sit with me on the front steps on a warm spring evening, to feel his power, tap his wisdom and capture his advice. He taught me more than I ever could imagine. He encouraged me to write stories, of which I never dreamed that I could ever create. He taught me the power of words and the joy of books.

If I could be half of the man that he was, then I would be proud.

I squeezed my hand tightly around the rock in my hand. I opened my hand and studied it. Dull, colorless, yet full of power, solid, strong, and forever.

Am byth.

Yes indeed, no way was this just a stone.

It is, was, and always will be, the rock.

THE END

Breeze

From Greetings from 182 Belmont Avenue
The Essential Collection

This morning, the morning after our hockey game in Monmouth County, I missed the team bus for the ride back to our home area in Great Falls, New Jersey. I did not miss the roll because of tardiness, or sleeping late in the hotel room, or because I celebrated our hard-fought victory, of three goals to one, and sucked down too many beers with my teammates, or any other factors within my control. In fact, I did not have much time to celebrate the win at all. I missed the bus because I had to sit in the local hospital's emergency room until all hours of the night and early morning to receive medical attention. Five more stitches to add to my growing stitch count accumulation. This time, right inside of my left eyebrow. A slap shot from the point went through a screen and I was down on the ice and did not see the puck until it came through some legs and shin pads and BAM! The puck nailed me right dead on in the mask. That horrible feeling of warm blood running down my face is a feeling that I have felt a little too often in my career. It was late in the game, only three minutes or so left, and my back-up goalie came in and shut the door the rest of the way. When the cagey team trainer, a man we lovingly named, "Equipment Joe," even though his real first name was Kenneth, could not stop the bleeding with all the usual tricks; then I knew it was a deep cut. When he proudly announced that he could see my skull bone through the cut and that I needed to head to the hospital, then I knew it was going to be a long night. Technically, he was not our team trainer, our team was bare bones and on limited finances. In reality, he was equipment manager, scorekeeper, ice skate sharpener and repair technician, and general all-around logistical man. And, yes, he applied medical attention as best as he could. In addition, he made sure we had cold beer in the locker room after the game. There are priorities in the ice hockey world.

Ah, the life of a semi-professional ice hockey goalie. All this for seventeen dollars a game. At least, the team paid for the medical attention and the train ride back home. I keep telling myself that someday, when I am playing goalie for some team in the big time and fulfilling my lifetime dream, of playing professional ice hockey, that this will all be worth it. Someday. Until then, we labor onward and reach for our dreams. Right now, I was sitting on a northbound train heading up the New Jersey coastline, rolling back to Newark. It was early Sunday morning and once I arrived in Newark, I would call around and see if anyone wanted to pick me up from there. Maybe Harry was hanging around, but chances are that he was sleeping in from his date last night with Joyce and the odds were not good to see Harry roll to Newark. If Harry had a rough night, then maybe Ronzo, or the old man, would be available to pick me up and bring me back to Paterson. If not, there are plenty of buses and it would only be two more bus rides to the street corner right outside of my home at 182 Belmont Avenue. Mass transportation in New Jersey was awesome if you lived in the cities. If you were not living in or near the larger cities, then it could be an adventure.

I enjoyed riding the train, especially so after such a long night. My hockey gear and equipment were on the bus and Equipment Joe would make sure it was safely stowed in the locker room at our home rink. I was not in a rush to pick it up because we did not have any practices or games until the middle of next week. We played out of Long Island and at some point, I needed to ride out or take another train and a bus to pick up my jeep which was parked in the parking lot at the arena. However, I had tomorrow off from my regular job, so once more, I was not in any rush to pick everything up.

All I had with me was a duffle bag with my wallet, some cash and other valuables in there, and my precious goalie ice skates stuffed in the bag too. My skates were my lifeblood, and they only traveled with me. Luckily, I had stuck a book in my bag for the ride home. A book by Sir Arthur Conan Doyle, about some detective guy who solved a helluva lot of crimes and mysteries. Now, I sat in a bench seat in a car at the end of the train and had my nose in the book.

If not for the book, then the gentle rock on the rails might have put me to sleep; in fact, I felt droopy right now while reading the book and my eyelids grew heavy when I heard a woman's gentle voice ask me, "Did you have an auto accident?"

I looked up from the book and since I was half-dosing and half-reading, I stalled a bit in my response. In fact, I could not even identify who had asked me the question. The train car was not crowded, but it was not empty either. I sat alone on a bench seat. The area next to me was unoccupied and directly across from me was an elderly man and I might have been half-dosing but this chap was out like a light. Next in line was a young couple, and they were immersed in love and then a middle-aged man with large joules and immense layers of his own body, which folded all around him as if he was sitting inside of layers of skin. Then, my eyes wandered to the bench seat to the far right of mine, on the opposite side of the car from me. Ah, ha, there is the woman who asked me the question. She smiled a wide smile at me as if she was waiting for me to find her, and then she waved a little wave in the air.

"Yoo hoo, yes, over here," she said.

She was very cute. In fact, extremely cute.

'A hippie chick,' I thought, and while I was a part-time athlete and a full-time electrical and electronic technician, one would rather easily assume that I was a hippie. My appearance would certainly give one that impression. Here I sat, with long blond hair, with red highlights that touched my shoulders, a full beard, black jeans, black canvas sneakers and a rock-and-roll tee shirt emblazoned with the logo and the name of one of my favorite rock-and-roll bands, The Electric Light Orchestra. I did not possess the typical appearance of an ice hockey goalie, but then again, goalies are always a little different and odd. I marched right in step with that label.

Even sitting on the bench seat, I could see that she was petite in her build and frame and her flaming red hair was not only striking, but it was perfectly suited for her face. She tied her long red hair into two woven braids that currently draped across the front of her chest, just past her breasts. The white frills of the neckline of her long dress, touched the edges of the braids and the dress was printed in a flower pattern, with flowers of various types, and soft, muted colors such as yellows and soft greens and dull pinks and violets, all sewn together in a haphazard pattern, not unlike a patchwork quilt. I would think that it was homemade, as was the macramé-type bag that she sat at her feet. Feet that had open-toed sandals on them, very worn, open-toed sandals. It was now, right around mid-April, the hockey season was almost over and while it was not cold outside, it was hardly open-toed sandal weather. It was instantly apparent to me that this chick did not care much about the temperature or the weather; she most likely wore these sandals year-round. The color of her toenails was striking, too. Not because of the color, but of the fact that each toenail was a different color. Leading me along that her attire, the bag, and maybe even her sandals were homemade was the fact that winding out of the aforementioned bag at her feet and into her hands was a long string of red yarn mixed with a white yarn. In her hands, she held two knitting needles that she worked the yarn with into some type of long cloth material. Over her eyes were black-framed eyeglasses, perfectly suited for her face. A lovely face too, in fact, all of her was quite lovely. Even sitting down, I could tell that she had a nice figure. . ..

"I see the bandages over your eye there and thought how, you do not seem to have any other injuries, and that you might have hit your head on a steering wheel or something," she giggled a little and then her face turned a little red in an effort to match the color of her hair, and she continued, "but if you hit your head in a violent auto crash or something similar to that experience, then perhaps, you would have some more injuries." Upon finishing speaking, her mouth turned up at the corners and then she screwed her mouth up like a corkscrew and let it unwind a bit before saying, "Sorry. I am nosey. You were reading, and I interrupted you. It is just that you . . . have such a beautiful face . . . it is a shame that you have that bandage there. Your hair is amazing and your beard too. Sorry. I am gawking and babbling at a stranger on the train."

I still sat there without saying a word, while studying this quirky young woman and her antics and struggles for finding the correct words. Yes, she was babbling, and yes, she was nosey, but damn, she was cute.

No one else on the train even glanced over at us or administered us any attention. It was not as if she was shouting at me, but she was a little distance away and the rattle and banging of the train was not exactly quiet.

"It is okay. It was not a car crash. I am a semi-professional ice hockey goalie and I took a hard shot off my goalie mask in the game last night. Just some stitches. Five, to be exact. They had to shave some of my eyebrow off, but it will heal fine. Maybe a little scar. I have a few scars, in fact, more and more each day. It is a part of the game."

Her eyes widened under her glasses and her mouth turned into a perfect letter "o" shape. A capital letter "O."

"Woaahh now, an ice hockey goalie! Fooled me. Geez, I wouldn't have ever guessed that one. Maybe, you are a rock-and-roll star, yes, a lead vocalist for a band, but a hockey player. No way. You look like a hippie. Like me."

She rolled up the yarn onto the knitting needles and then carefully folded the cloth she was working on and stuffed it all into the bag at her feet. "Okay, if I come over and sit by you? All this yelling back-and-forth kind of sucks for everyone else on the train and us too."

Her eyes remained wide as she proposed the seat change. I looked around at our neighbors and none of them actually even knew we existed. The old gent was snoring his brains out, and the young couple needed to rent a hotel room.

"Sure. Come on over," I said and I patted the seat next to me. She quickly grabbed her bag, stood up, and she quickly scampered over to me and nearly jumped in the seat as she landed with a "thud." Yes, she had a nice figure. I caught a glimpse of her parts and pieces as she moved across the aisle. This young woman was certainly intriguing and cute. Very, very cute.

"Hi," she said as she proudly stuck her hand out to me and said, "Breeze Connelly is my name and you are?"

I gently took her hand and grasped it while staring at her beautiful green eyes underneath her eyeglasses. She had a sprinkling of freckles around her nose and upon her high cheekbones.

'Green eyes, red hair—Irish heritage,' I supposed.

"Paul John Henson is my name. Most people simply call me by my uniform number. Twenty-seven. Is your name, really, Breeze? As in not a nickname, like twenty-seven is?"

"Yup, Breeze is the name. Two e's in there. Two n's in the last name. No middle name. My parents are hippies, too. Like we are." She pointed at me, then at her, and continued, "They said they smoked a ton of bad weed in the sixties and dreamed up really cool names and since they both loved gentle breezes, they picked out Breeze for my name. They wanted a little red-haired girl who was calm and gentle and loved taking walks. As with a breeze. So, that is my name."

I thought about how her parents nailed it with her name. She leaned in and studied me, and then looked at the bandage and shook her head.

"Wow! Up close, you are even better looking than you were across the aisle. A woman can lose herself in that hair of yours there, Paul John Henson. I am resisting the urge to run my fingers through it. I am not calling you by your uniform number. I think that is rather foolish. Then again, my name is Breeze, so am I even qualified to say that?" She laughed at her own quirkiness and went off again. "And you have all your teeth. Don't hockey players lose them? Especially goalies? I am hardly qualified as a hockey expert here, because I have only seen the game once, but doesn't the puck knock your teeth out, or a stick, or an angry player from the other team knocks them out of your head in a fight. Hockey players fight all the time. Do you fight? You don't seem mean." I laughed a little as she stuck her hand in her mouth and bit down on her fingers as if to mimic chewing in order to emphasize teeth. Before I could answer, Breeze dove in once more, "I mean, I guess they could be false teeth. Are they? Sorry, I am prone to babbling, but I have to get all these thoughts and questions out of my head. They come in waves in my head, as if they are ocean waves rolling to shore. It is not too often that a girl meets a knockout hunk of a man on a train. A man . . . who is also a hockey player. You know?"

She leaned in while studying my teeth as I answered and now I needed to play with her a little, so I folded my lips over my teeth to cover them and mumbled, "Yup, all of them are gone. Lost to a hockey puck. All false choppers now."

Breeze leaned back and blinked, and with her standard giggle and the now familiar wide-eyes opening underneath those thick frames, Breeze spoke between giggles, "No. They are not false. But you have a great sense of humor and a great smile and a few great . . . other things too."

"Breeze, honestly, no, false choppers here. They are real. Actually, I lost one wisdom tooth and one molar way in the back of my mouth to a puck in a game last year, but you can't see them and it does not matter much. And, I am not mean and I seldom fight. Unless, I have to."

"Oh good. Mean people suck. I lost my wisdom teeth last year. However, a doctor took them out. It was a plan to do so. No pucks for me. I guess you save on extraction bills. What the hell color are your eyes? They are captivating. Are they gray or blue or what? WAIT!" Breeze slapped the bench seat with her hand as if she recalled a thought. Her quirkiness was contagious. "They are chromatic, something or others. I read about eyes like yours in a book. They change colors and your eyes can be two different colors." I nodded my head and laughed again while she went off into quirky land once more. "Woaaah, you are sooo interesting. I mean, meeting you on the train is so cool. I bet that puck thing hurts when it hits you. Wow. You are brave and rough and tumble but now that I am close to you, I can see the muscles and the build and stuff. What a hunk you are."

I did not know how to answer her as the train conductor called out for a stop and the train slowed.

"Perth Amboy. Next stop, Perth Amboy."

We were working our way up the coastline.

"Rough and tough but, nevertheless, you are not mean."

"No, I am not mean, and I have to say that I might be stupid rather than brave to play goalie, but I love it. Hockey is my life right now. Someday, I want to play in the big time. It is my dream. I must tell you that you are quite an attractive young woman, Breeze."

She wiggled her backside a little deeper into the seat when she heard my words and her voice moved to a gentle whisper, "Thank you. I don't have a boyfriend." Her words layered out of her mouth with a tone that implied dual meanings, and the last letters floated out in a strange manner as if to ask me if I had a girlfriend.

"I don't have any gals in my life right now, if you want to ask."

"Oh, hell yeah, I was going to ask that question, all right! Not sure how or why a hunk of a man such as you, Paul John, does not have a current gal, but hey, sometimes a gal needs to play her cards right and win a game or two of luck and fate. Whatcha reading?" Breeze pointed at the book that was still in my lap.

"Sherlock Holmes. I read a lot of classics."

"So cool. Holmes the great detective. I bet I am a great detective too and can guess that you are on this train to meet someone in . . . Newark."

"Impressive. You are halfway there to being a great detective, Breeze. The Newark part is correct, but I am not meeting anyone. I missed the team bus back to Long Island because I was in the emergency room until late, so the team put me on the train. Haledon is my destination. Right on the Paterson line. I am going to call my best buddy to see if he can pick me up in Newark, otherwise, I will take a bus to Paterson's City Hall stop and then one more bus to the Borough of Haledon on the number fourteen bus. It stops right outside of my home on the mainline roll."

With a nod and a very coy smile, followed by a push of her eyeglasses at the bridge of her nose, Breeze said, "I am not actually much of a detective at all. I cheated. In this life, it is best to be perfectly honest because the truth never hides for very long when you share your heart with someone. You used the train ticket as a bookmark. I read it.

Even upside down." She then laughed and placed her hand on mine. When Breeze did so, her warmth floated through my hand to my soul. "I live in Newark. A few blocks from the Newark Penn Station stop. I was visiting my parents and my grandparents in Long Branch. I grew up there. At the Jersey Shore. I needed to show them my new dress."

She jumped up, posed for me, and spun around while allowing me to study her dress. It was gorgeous and so was Breeze. The dress clung to all the correct places, her large breasts bounced a little underneath the cover of the frills, and the dress gently wisped at her ankles and danced across her body alluringly. Her long red braids of hair floated behind her while she spun around and then they gradually caught up with her and with a flip of her hands, she pushed them around until they rested upon her chest. Still, no one even glanced at us. It was as if we were now within our own little world here in this nook on the train. Breeze sat back down, and I caught the fact that her face blushed and she seemed slightly embarrassed by my study of her dress and, specifically, of her body.

"It is a gorgeous dress and you look stunning in it, Breeze."

"Thank you. I made it myself." She reached down, picked up her bag and proudly announced, "And this bag too, and my sandals," Breeze picked up her feet one-by-one to show them for me and then she reached down and tugged at a string of yarn around her neck and pulled up a delicate hand-woven thread of yarn that tied off to a small seashell. Breeze held it in her hand, leaned in, and admired it. It was gorgeous. "I made this too. I am a seashore gal through and through. I also made my bra and panties but I think that I would get in trouble if I showed you those. At least, if I showed you . . . here." She paused for a second or two and added, with a wink of her eye, "Maybe later." Breeze pulled at her neckline and dropped the seashell back down into her dress.

"They are . . . all . . . gorgeous, Breeze. You are very talented," I sheepishly stuttered, trying hard to ignore the thoughts in my head as to what her homemade bra and panties might look like. A change of subject was in order, "And what were you making before we began chatting?"

"A scarf. A long red and white colored scarf without tassels on the end of it. I don't like knitting tassels. They are a pain-in-the-ass," Breeze answered without hesitation.

The conductor's next announcement was for the North Elizabeth train station, and the train slowed and stopped. A few people jumped up and got off, and the elderly man finally woke up and rubbed his eyes. He looked around, but only glanced at us for a second or two, before picking up the newspaper in his lap and opening it up to study it. The young couple stopped exploring each other and began to gather their things and adjust their clothes. Most people on the train seemed to be preparing for Newark. It was only a few train stations away now.

Breeze was not the type of person who remained quiet for too long. She spoke with a change of enthusiasm in her voice. The sultry voice was gone and now her voice came out singsong, light, and airy.

As if it drifted upon a breeze.

"They are awesome, aren't they?" Breeze pointed at the logo on my shirt. "I mean, E.L.O. The new album is beyond fantastic. It is about a time traveler who goes ahead in time and ends up in outer space living on some planet and then he wants to return home to Earth. Have you heard it?"

"I have not. I need to buy a copy and give it a spin or two. They are one of my favorite bands. The concert last summer was astounding. The laser show, the flying spaceship over the stage, the entire scene and experience at the concert was fantastic."

Breeze leaned back in her seat and sighed.

Her words echoed a lament, "Damn. I missed it. Next time. I want to get a tattoo of the E.L.O spaceship. Maybe right here." She leaned back and made a circle with her two thumbs and forefinger just below her belly on her dress. "Maybe right here or in my pubic area. I think that would be so cool. Do you think the artist could duplicate the colors of the spaceship?" I shrugged my shoulders while remaining very captivated by Breeze, and I marveled at how she effortlessly moved from one subject to another. "I have a few tattoos. Two on my shoulders and one on my back, but they are of flowers and a rose . . . wait, a rose is a flower, right?" Breeze did not wait for an answer, but instead, off she went speaking as if the words were a lullaby. "I love plants. I also have a tattoo of an oak tree on the base of my spine, right above my butt. I would show you, but once more, it might not be the best idea that I ever had to do that right here. Do you like tattoos, Paul John? Do you have any? Do you think that trees and plants have souls? I think they do. I need to find out if they do or not."

Bounce, bounce, bounce, from one subject to another. Some subjects were light and airy, and the other subjects were deep, intense, and profoundly thoughtful. Her name was so perfect. Breeze. I tilted my head to study her lovely face and lowered my voice a little while somehow resisting the urge to kiss her, and she must have sensed the connection because Breeze blinked at me, curled her lower lip into her top lip, and gently bit her lower lip. A kiss would serve two purposes, one it would stop her from babbling, and two; it would satisfy my urge to see how she tasted. I had a feeling that she tasted amazing. As if her lips were laced with sweet candy or mint and I bet that her lips were soft, gentle, and warm.

My voice came out with my best Paterson twang hanging on every word, "I like tattoos but I do not have any. I enjoy all types of art and yes, trees and plants have souls. All living things have souls."

Breeze did not comment on my answer. She only blinked a few times to tell me that she was deep in thought about my words. By now, I was used to how her thoughts jumped around in her head.

This woman did not stay silent for too long.

"Say, uh, Paul, would you like to come by my apartment and listen to the new record? I don't have a car or I would drive you home. I walk or take the train or the bus everywhere. I work at a gift store in Newark. My work is only a few blocks from my apartment. I mean . . . we could . . . listen to the music and talk and . . . talk and do . . . stuff. You could use my phone to call your friend."

Once more, Breeze did not even pause in order to listen for my answer to her invitation.

"My apartment is not much of an experience. It is very small. I mean, tiny. Just a small nook in this world of madness. It's all that I can afford."

"Sure. I would love to listen to the new record with you and talk and we could. . . .." I trailed my voice off on purpose and added the finishing touch. "Do stuff."

The duplicity of the meaning of the words hung like leaves on an oak tree inside of the train. Maybe a specific oak tree that I had in mind. She smiled widely and studied my face very carefully, as if it was a moment in paradise for us.

For once, Breeze did not speak. Her eyes spoke for her.

The stop for Newark Airport sailed by and then the announcement for Newark, Penn Station, floated into the air.

"This is it," Breeze said while we gathered up our things. It was then that I realized the book was still open in my lap. I grabbed my duffle bag, unzipped it, and dropped the book in there. I followed Breeze down the main aisle of the train and the herds of people who all seemed as if they were getting off here in downtown Newark. We stepped off the train and Breeze turned in the direction of the main platform and then turned right to a step of steps.

"This way, Paul. It is quicker."

Breeze stuck her hand out, and I grasped it. Her tiny hand eclipsed within my large mitt, but once more, I felt her warmth. We climbed the stairs, and I tried hard not to study her perfect backside as she stepped in front of me.

I miserably failed in my quest.

The day was cool, and the sunlight was bright and the sky cloudless. Her red hair glowed in the sunlight and the dress whipped around her ankles. Her sandals flapped on her feet while we walked down the city street. The large and tall buildings of Newark loomed all around us, along with the diverse blend of storefronts and restaurants and the people on the streets . . . and this entire world whizzed by us. I did not see much of anything other than this gorgeous woman holding my hand.

"We can stop at this corner liquor store coming up here on the right side of the street and pick up some beer if you want. I drink red wine and something tells me that you are anything but a red wine kind of guy." Breeze stopped in her tracks and she studied me. Her quirkiness never wandered very far from her. She let go of my hand and waved her hands at me, as if to encompass my presence.

"Geez, my goodness. You are a huge man. I mean, huge as in large. I had better be careful here, because my mind is wandering now. Anyway, I had no idea how tall you are. You did not seem so tall while sitting on the train. How tall are you, Paul John Henson? Do you slouch down or something?"

"I am not exactly sure. I might slouch. I am around six feet five or so. At least, before the hockey season, that is. That is what Equipment Joe measured me at."

"Do you shrink as the season goes by? This hockey stuff seems to take a toll on your body."

I was not sure if Breeze was serious or not, however, since the delivery of her words seemed to be serious in tone and nature, I answered her factually.

Yet, I shrugged my shoulders to add a disclaimer to my

words and said, "Maybe, I shrunk. I will need Equipment Joe to measure me. His name is not even Joe. He is our all around, does everything, guy for our team. He tried to close my cut last night before deciding that it was hopeless and he sent me to the hospital."

"Paul John, you are such a deadpan with your humor. People don't shrink until they grow old. I was only kidding."

We began walking again and Breeze took my hand and tugged me along again while we made our way down the sidewalk.

"I am glad that Equipment Joe could not fix your cut."

Now, it was my turn to stop walking, and I still held her hand but stopped and rather gently spun Breeze around to face me.

"Sorry?" I asked.

A smile rose across her face, and she adjusted her macramé bag on her shoulder while stating, "Duh. We never would have met Paul John, if you did not go to the hospital. You are brilliantly intelligent. After all, you are a man who reads Sherlock Holmes books on a train to Newark, but sometimes, things do not land with you, as they should. I don't think you struggle with your relationships with women, because sexiness oozes out of your every pore. I think it is more as if you do not realize how hot you are, Paul John. Or, you choose not to believe it. Self-doubts, maybe."

I stood there without answering her until the words and the famous proclamation of my best friend, Harry M. Redmond Junior, resounded clearly in my head. The words that I have heard since Harry and Paul first met when we were ten years old.

"My best buddy in this world, Harry, says that I act like an old lady," I confessed. Breeze stopped short, and she dropped my hand while covering her mouth with her hand to hold back her outburst of laughter. Breeze bent over and held her arms around her body to prevent the laughing from escaping.

"Please, go ahead and laugh. I can take it."

"Sorry, Paul. Harry sounds like an astute judge of you. I think you are conservative . . . for a hippie. Like in . . . I bet you don't touch or partake in any weed."

"I don't. An athlete . . . you know."

"I totally understand and promise to keep mine under wraps. I have to say that your friend might be onto something, but it is a large part of your appeal. Something tells me when it counts . . . you are anything but an old lady. Tell me, how long have you been besties?"

"Since we were ten years old. We are as close as brothers are."

I spotted the liquor store on the street corner right in front of us, and this time, I reached out, grabbed her hand, and pulled her in the direction of the liquor store. It was time to assert myself.

"Let's get that beer. Red wine gives me a headache."

"Okay, very manly action here and now, in your sudden assertion and the change of direction, Paul John. I like. Very much so. Are we going to run?"

"No, not necessary. I doubt that the store is short on a beer supply."

Breeze tugged at me to indicate that we should stop walking. She pulled at me, in order to pull me in closer, and I spun around and loomed over her as we studied each other's eyes.

"Good. Because I only run for red wine and for quality time spent with a very special man. If you understand my meaning."

I smiled and this time, I was not going to be an old lady. Her lips begged me to kiss her. I leaned down and tilted my head, and she did the same to meet my lips. And damn, I kissed her. As in toe curling and explosive. And yes, she tasted better than the sweetest candy could ever taste.

After we kissed, I whispered to her, "I do understand and I promise that I will keep that in mind." With another gentle tug on her arm, I pointed us in the direction of the liquor store.

When a man hustled by us and commented, "That the two of us should go and get a hotel room," I completely shattered the old lady image by yelling unabashedly back at him, "don't need one. She has an apartment."

We climbed the stairs to her apartment that was on the third floor of a typical brick walk-up, row-style downtown New Jersey, or any other big city apartment and I squeezed at the six-pack of Big Boulder beer tucked under my arm and tightened my grip on my duffle bag. Breeze fumbled with the key and after fiddling a bit with it, she turned the lock and opened the door.

"Please give me the beer, Paul. I will put it in the fridge," Breeze said as I handed it off to her.

Her apartment was small but tidy. It was as I expected. It was all about Breeze. All the walls were a bright white. No other colors. Dainty curtains hung on two living room windows that faced the main street, curtains laced in fringe and dotted with flowers. Homemade, no question. Furniture was sparse. The living room only had one small loveseat and one table, with a lamp made from a wine bottle. The lamp had Breeze's handwork stamped all over it.

I set my bag down on the living room floor next to the table. I leaned in to inspect the lamp while Breeze hustled off to, "I will be right back after I put the beer in the refrigerator and I use the bathroom. Make yourself comfortable, Paul. I have loose-leaf peppermint tea too. I can brew some for later. It is very soothing to your soul."

While she danced away, I stood there and studied the rest of the small apartment. I bet it was no more than five-hundred square feet or thereabouts. In the living room, there was an old tube-type radio sitting on a wooden stand

and a record player on a metal table with two speakers sitting on the floor next to it. A small rack of vinyl albums sat next to the right side of the speakers, and that was about it for the living room.

Inside the rack, I recognized the spaceship logo on a number of the album covers. . ..

The floors were all old hardwood floors covered by woven macramé throw rugs. Homemade, no doubt. There were homemade curtains on the window over her bed, which was just behind a small curtain wall. At my height, I could see right over the wall and the bed had a homemade quilt on it, with a pattern that was not unlike the dress that Breeze wore. Perched upon the headboard were two noticeably homemade pillows. The pillows had bright cases made of cloth with prints of various flower patterns on them. Obviously, Breeze loved flowers.

I tried not to dwell on her bed. It was a queen size. It just barely fit in the nook of a bedroom. Despite my large size and height—I would fit in it. Despite my best efforts, I was losing this battle with my inner thoughts because I dwelled.

There was a small kitchen with a tiny refrigerator tucked into a nook, a small set of cabinets, a half-table tucked in a corner with two chairs and a hallway off the kitchen that must lead to a bathroom. Everywhere was Breeze. There were small oil paintings on the walls, and I studied them and surmised that they were the results of the amazing handiwork and artistic efforts of Breeze Connelly. There were flowers, gardens, and trees and while they were simple—they were beautiful. The place was immaculately clean and orderly. As if no one ever lived in it. My beloved and dear mum, who waged an eternal and perpetual war against dust and dirt, would give Breeze a gold medal for her housekeeping efforts.

Breeze returned, and it seemed as if she glowed even brighter. I gasped and caught my breath because her trip to the bathroom brought a refresh of sorts. Her hair was no longer in braids and she had set it free and loose. It hung in great waves and seemed to surround her very being and illuminate her entire presence. The sunlight gleamed through the small kitchen window. It chased a shadow across the floor, and while it did so, it covered her in waves of light. My goodness, this woman was stunning. Beyond this world and into a few new ones somewhere beyond the setting sun.

"What?" Breeze asked while she studied my face.

"I need a . . . a beer, please, Ah, yes, a beer. Please. Breeze. And a glass. I am a beer snob and need to pour a beer into a glass. I cannot drink it out of the bottle."

Breeze laughed and waved her hand in the air, "Okay, not a problem. I am poor and do not have much money to spare, but I have glasses, Paul. That is not snobbish. That is a preference."

"Oh, and I need another kiss," I boldly proclaimed when she walked by me to turn into the kitchen. That kiss came without any hesitation from either of us. Our lips crashed into each other's lips and we lost each other for a few minutes. Deep, passionate, and intimate. Her hands wrung through my hair and her gentle moans in my mouth were like a sob. I too ran my fingers through her long hair and finally, I had to break away for fear of losing myself forever.

Our lips escaped from each other's lips and I sensed how her body groaned in disappointment.

I gasped, "Thank you" to Breeze and immediately after speaking the words, I knew that my words caused me immense embarrassment.

"You are welcome, Paul. But for what?" Breeze asked, while she leaned away from me.

I paused, leaned back and stuck my hands in my pockets, and shrugged my shoulders.

I conjured up an admittance of my feelings, "I have

kissed many women, honestly, even made love to a few too, but never have I been kissed like that."

"And I am not a virgin, but I am hardly experienced in the love department, but I too, never have been kissed like that either. I felt my toes curl." Breeze paused in her thoughts. She gathered her words, cleared her throat and spoke, "Honestly, I never do anything like this, Paul. You know, meet a random man, invite him here, and kiss him and . . . well . . . you are just so very, very special. There was no doubt in my mind as to how special you were when I first put my eyes on you. I did not want to lose the opportunity." Breeze turned and spun and then looked over her shoulder and smiled at me while allowing an admittance of sorts to escape her lips too, "My toes curled and some other parts reacted too and I felt yours react too. Redemption is amazing because I was not wrong in my lustful supposition about you." She pointed to the kitchen and added, "I will get you the beer and the . . . glass. And a red wine for me and maybe an ice pack. Please, the records are in a rack next to the record player. In the living room. Please, find the record and load it. Time. Time is the name of the new album. It has a paint drip and the world on the cover. It is super cool stuff."

With those words, off she went to the kitchen, and I attempted to recover from her honesty.

I muttered an "okay and a thank you" and ran my fingers through my long hair. I was blowing this big time. How could I fall for a chick in a few hours? On a train to Newark. With a damn bandage on my eyebrow and five stitches in my head. Geez, this life is full of twists and turns.

I wandered off to the living room to find the record album, and I heard Breeze's voice from the kitchen, "You say that you play hockey on Long Island? What is the name of your team?"

"The roosters. The Long Island Roosters."

"Really? The roosters! Oh yes, ducks and roosters and such. Long Island stuff. What colors?" Her voice was closer now, and I had found the record. I removed the record from the album jacket, lifted the dust cover to the player and began to load the record onto the turntable when Breeze appeared in the living room. She held a full beer glass and a long-stemmed glass of red wine in her hands.

Her beauty made me lose my words and maybe pieces of my mind, too.

"Huh? Colors."

"Your team colors, Paul? The Long Island Roosters?"

I laughed and dropped the record onto the spindle of the player and hit the play lever.

I said, "Oh, yes, sorry. I lost you there. Red and white."

Upon hearing of the team colors, I heard her mumble a single word, and she did so with a gentle smile upon her face, "Fate."

I did not understand why she said the word, but continued speaking about our hockey club, "Our logo sucks. It is so stupid. A dopey looking cartoon of a rooster. And the fan club does this cockle-doo-doo chant that drives me nuts. But the fans are loyal and love the team."

She handed me the glass, and I took a long and glorious sip of the beer. More of a gulp. It tasted cold and glorious.

"And what do you work at between these hockey adventures?"

"I am an electrical and electronic technician. I reached the master level last year."

"Oh wow, very cool. A man with a tool belt. Sexy stuff."

Breeze sat down on the love seat and patted the seat next to her in an indication for me to sit next to her.

Her voice waltzed out into the air, "But you love it. Don't you? This game that beats the hell out of you and knocks you all over the place has captured your soul."

I sat down on the love seat and deeply sighed. The music began, and it was an electronic synthesizer vibe and it was immediately appealing.

"I do. My dream is to play in the big time, someday. I think that I already mentioned that to you. How did you know that hockey is a huge part of my life?"

"Because, you don't have a girlfriend. No man that looks and acts as you look and act and is brilliantly smart and funny and all the things that you are would not be without a serious woman for too long. No ordinary woman could compete with hockey for your heart."

I was going to protest, but Breeze intercepted my words, "I am going away to college in Vermont in August. Vermont is perfect for hippies. I am going to study horticulture. I plan to learn if plants and trees really do have souls or not. My parents are both college professors and they are all for me to fulfill my dreams. Maybe, in the search for plant's souls . . . I will." Breeze took a long sip of the red wine and then ran her finger over the rim of glass and licked the wine off her finger. Damn, this woman was melting my heart. Breeze turned and set the glass down on the table next to the love seat. I took another sip of beer and set my glass down on the floor next to the love seat.

"They have souls, Breeze. Believe me, they do."

The music was amazing. We leaned into each other, I put my arm around Breeze, and we snuggled into the cushions and lost our dreams in the music. She leaned her head on my shoulder and I leaned into her. Her scent was glorious. Better than fresh strawberries, topped with whipped cream, and better than roses. Better than sweet peas on the first warm spring day and better than all things fresh and new.

Her silence now was somewhat startling but understandable. It was a magical moment.

About halfway through the record, Breeze jumped up, and she grabbed my hand and pulled me to my feet.

Her enthusiasm caught me by surprise but I pulled it together because this was Breeze, and she never settled for too long.

"I love this song. It has a cool reggae groove to it. Do you want to dance? Do you dance, Paul?"

I jumped to my feet and proudly proclaimed, "I do. I Love to dance. Let's dance."

"Cool. The name of the song is 'The Lights Go Down' and it is so soothing and has a perfect vibe to it. Jeff is a musical genius."

As the music began and she felt the groove and vibe, Breeze stood in the center of the living room. She took her glasses off and set them on the end table next to her wineglass. She then closed her lovely eyes and began to sway to the music. Her body moved gloriously, her hips swayed, and her shoulders moved slowly to the music. I stood next to her while capturing the beats of the music. When she opened her eyes and smiled at me, she extended her arms and wrapped them around my shoulders. I did the same to her and absorbed her warmth. We slow-danced to the music and Breeze tucked into me.

I heard her chest rumble as she whispered, "Damn, you are a marvelous dancer. You are so tall and large and huge. Your eyes are so beautiful that they make me melt. The scent of your skin is unique, and it is pure man."

I did not comment, but knew what she felt. I felt the hardness of her breasts welding into my chest. We danced, and the song seemed as if it went on forever. When the song ended and the next song began with a techno-electronic beat, Breeze reached under my tee shirt and pulled it off and over my head and she tossed it aside. Breeze then ran her hands up and down my bare chest.

"My goodness, Paul, your muscles are like iron."

"Too bad my head is not like iron," I quipped while touching the bandages on my wound. "I feel like a bit of an idiot standing here like some wounded soldier, especially with you looking like an angel."

A smile formed at her mouth; however, it quickly faded,

and her face turned serious. Her eyes sparkled, and her breathing turned heavy and deep. Once more her hands worked up and down my bare chest, and then her fingers roamed and danced upon my bare skin. My body reacted and certain parts reacted rather intensely to her touch.

"You could never be an idiot. Your wounds only add to your sexiness. Never, have I ever felt or held, or seen a man like you. I want to lose myself in you. I need to fall into you. I need to be careful because it might be forever."

We kissed long and hard and I gently ran my hands over her breasts, felt their fullness, and held her desire in between my fingers.

We slowly melted as one onto the floor.

Before too long, there were haphazard piles of our clothes spread out on the floor. All Breeze wore was her seashell necklace and all that I wore were bandages and stitches.

Soon, Breeze had covered every inch of my body with her magical hands and I had done the same to her, and now, I was officially falling in love with a hippie chick that I just met a few hours earlier today.

After a number of long sessions of lovemaking and incredible passion, and between gasps for air, I rolled onto my back and stared up to the ceiling, while Breeze snuggled in next to me.

I finally managed to say, "Geez, this is one helluva record and dance. Ah, the record ended a long time ago, Breeze."

Breeze laughed and said to me, "It did. Not my fault. Your stamina is to blame. Amazing stamina. Hockey players might need to be outlawed to unsuspecting females unaware of the side-benefits of their lovers playing the sport. It is one helluva record, and yes, this is one helluva day. That was beyond words to describe, Paul. You took me to a place that I never even imagined existed. Ever. We fit together perfectly. We melted into one person. You are simply amazing, in every way. I could easily lead you to my bed now and we could take this to a level that we could never return from but . . . Paul, you know and I know that we will not do that."

Breeze slowly stood up, and she reached out her hand. I grasped it as we both stood and joined our hearts, as well as our naked bodies. Once more, her magically roaming hands danced over my body. I leaned back, and she pulled her hands from my body while I studied her eyes as she grabbed both of my hands and held them in a gentle and loving clasp in front of our bodies.

She smiled at me and said, "Our dreams would pull us into different worlds. I would rather leave the magic as it is. Magical. Unknown but all knowing in what it entails. You have your world and I have mine. You have your dream to play hockey and I have my search for souls. Paul John Henson is not a onetime fling. You are forever, and unfortunately, a random breeze has not opened the door to forever right now for either of us. We crossed into each other's worlds because of fate. All because of a train ride. Because of magic, and now, it is best to allow reality to invade our lust and intercept our love before it enters our dreams."

Breeze kissed me again, and it was deep and passionate and toe curling. All of our kisses were toe curling. After she kissed me, her words once more floated as if they were part of the air.

On a breeze.

I remained silent and carefully listened to her words.

"I could easily fall in love with you, Paul. Perhaps, I already have."

Breeze shook her head and a slight smile invaded her mouth.

Just at the very edges of her mouth.

"Whom am I kidding? Damn. I already have. I will regret this moment forever and cherish it too. I am tempted to open the door leading to forever and allow the two of us to fly beyond our dreams and go off together somewhere only for us. But that would be foolish. Instead, let's remember this day forever. This takes our breath away. All of this does. To think, it was a simple train ride. Many amazing kisses mixed with a shared passion and the perfect feel of our bodies welded together. Some wine, some great music, some beer, and us. Some time. Just like the record. Time. It will be magical forever."

Regretfully, I knew that Breeze was correct. Reality needed to invade our lust and intercept our love before it entered our dreams. She would have to go her way and I would go mine.

I lowered my head, touched my forehead to Breeze's forehead, and whispered, "Let's finish that beer and wine and turn that record over because it is skipping on the label now. You are amazing. You are wise for the both of us, and your words drill into my mind and soul. Fate is awesome, but it has side effects that rather suck too. We have plenty of time left to share this one moment in time and we can listen to music and talk and talk and not do any other . . . stuff. Maybe, when the wine and beer run out, we can have some of that peppermint tea that you mentioned."

While still touching foreheads, Breeze nodded, but she kept her head down. I gently lifted her chin and wiped away the streams of tears that rolled down her face.

I did not want to see her sad, therefore, I broke the mood, "By the way, your homemade undergarments are beautiful and amazing and I love the tattoos. Especially the one right above your perfect backside."

Her laughter filled my soul now and forever.

"You ain't so bad yourself, there, big guy. Or, ah, huge guy. Geez! Hard to handle, you are, Paul! For a few days, or maybe even a week, I will be sore and sensitive in all the right places and it will be an amazing reminder of our love. You are a dream. Glorious expectations fulfilled in a world that usually lets a person down. I need to go to the bathroom and dress and clean up. I will be back in a minute or two."

"Okay, I need to use the bathroom, too. I will go after you do."

Breeze gathered up her clothes from the floor, picked up her eyeglasses from the end table and slipped them on over her eyes.

She took a few steps and turned around, looked over her shoulder as she often did, and asked, "Oh, yes. By the way, what is his real name?"

I was beginning to dress while Breeze stared at me, shook her head, and sighed a little.

"Who? What?" I was somewhat puzzled, as well as distracted by the glorious view standing in front of me.

Breeze stared intently at me and then mumbled, "Damn, a once in a lifetime view. What a body you have. I must be crazy to enter reality into this day. I should have kept my glasses on in order to see you clearer. Anyway, this Harry guy, he might be right, but he is sooooo wrong too. I now have firsthand knowledge and I know better." Her eyes rolled and then she explained a little further, "Equipment Joe. His real name is?"

Oh, yes, back to reality. Back to this time. This *was* Breeze, and she jumped around quite a bit. I rewound my mind and recalled the earlier conversation.

"Kenneth. His real name is Kenneth.

"Weird. However, all this hockey stuff is. Be right back."

The last views and the time spent with Breeze embedded into my mind forever.

Equipment Joe tossed a package on the bench next to where I dressed into my goalie equipment. It was the final regular season game of my rookie season with the Long Island Roosters. I had played quite well in the net for the Roosters this year and the future was bright. It was going to be a long way to climb, but I was in it for the long haul. I was digging in hard, and nothing would derail my dreams.

"For you. It was at the front desk," Equipment Joe said as he pointed at the box and then he turned to attend to the collection of hockey sticks for the game.

My teammates looked up at me and I shrugged my shoulders. Everyone returned to dressing and mentally preparing for the game and ignored me. Goalies were notoriously weird anyway. No one seemed to care. We had an important game to play. A game with playoff implications.

I first removed the card taped to the exterior of the box, slid my finger under the flap and pulled out a card. The card was simple. All it had was a flower on the cover. A simple but elegant flower.

Breeze loved flowers.

I opened the card, and it was blank except for a few handwritten sentences. With a heavy heart and with love captured within my mind, I read the words.

'I would write to you from college, but why mess up perfect? Let's just keep it as it is. Perfect. Magical forever. Stay warm. Stay perfect as you are. Love always, Breeze.'

Next, I set the card aside and opened the box. I pulled out a red and white homemade knitted scarf. It had the number twenty-seven embroidered into it with white numbers. No tassels.

It was then that I recalled her words on the train, "A scarf. A long red and white colored scarf without tassels on the end of it. I don't like knitting tassels. They are a pain-in-the-ass ass."

I now understood her mumbling of the single word of "Fate" in her apartment.

The scarf was beyond fantastic.

My best friend on the team and my key defenseman, Big Joe Starost, wandered over and pointed at the scarf while I ran my fingers over the amazing yarn.

It was perfect. I felt the glorious yarn in my hands and it felt amazing. Just as smooth as her hair and her skin and as amazing as the feel and look of her naked body was.

"Woaahhh, team colors, there super-goalie. Is it a gift from a fan, twenty-seven? It is amazing. Very cool," Big Joe Starost said as he studied the wonderful gift.

I looked up at Big Joe and smiled while saying, "Yeah. A fan. It is from a fan." I felt the yarn once more and then I carefully folded it, placed it back into the box along with the card, and secured it in my locker.

Sitting back on the bench, I tugged at my left skate and pulled the laces up tight while mumbling, "It will be magical forever. Yes indeed, forever. On a breeze."

We won the hockey game. The Roosters qualified for the playoffs, and our hockey club was making a run for the league championship.

Even though it was almost forty degrees when I dressed and left the arena, I wrapped the scarf around my neck.

It is best to be prepared because, after all, you never know when a random breeze arrives in your life and it blows open the door leading to forever.

THE END

On a Breeze

A Sequel
From Greetings from 182 Belmont Avenue
The Essential Collection

The words from the newspaper article burned into her eyes and then slowly filtered throughout her mind and then they plowed full speed into her heart. Her eyes immediately filled with tears.

While crumbling the newspaper up and stuffing it into her macramé bag at her feet, the words came out in a painful groan, "His dream, his dream is dead . . . how awful. I know that he will bounce back. He is too strong and resilient not to recover. I only knew him for one glorious day but I feel as if I know him better than I know any other person in this entire world."

Still, the words from the newspaper burned into her mind and the thoughts of how he must feel right now surrounded her despite her best efforts to resist them.

'Local sports hero finally retires from his long professional ice hockey career after suffering debilitating knee injury. During his last game in the net for the Norfolk Navigators, right before his call up to the Boston Bears hockey club. Damn. Terrible luck.'

There was a photograph of him playing the position of goalie. His longhair tied behind his head, his long body and powerful frame leaning on the top of the net, with his goalie hockey mask tucked onto the back of his head, while taking a drink of water from a bottle. A stupid, blurry, black and white newspaper picture made her heart flutter. How she wished that she never read that article. In an effort to bury the memory of the words, she reached down in her bag and picked out the yarn and the handwork that she began last night. The handwork that she began after the children were in bed and her husband dozed off in his chair while watching television.

Her husband often dozed off early.

Especially on a Saturday evening, when all she longed for was passion, for love, and for a lover to hold her in his arms, just as *he* did so long ago.

Instead. . ..

It was a Saturday night of handwork for her.

She was knitting two scarves for the children. One blue for their son and one pink for their daughter. She never knitted using the color red or white. Ever. Not since that special red and white project. Her watery eyes would not tolerate the burn of the colors enough in order to allow her to see the work. She feverishly tugged at the yarn and worked it to begin the next row of work. She looked out across the park from the bench that she sat upon and watched as her husband pushed their two children on the swings. First, he pushed their son, then their daughter. He was a good man and a wonderful father, and together, they created the most amazing children. Children that she would die for without even blinking an eye. Children that were her entire world.

She met her husband in the final year of college. She was just a few credits away from her horticulture degree and he was studying chemical engineering. They dated for a year or so and when they graduated from college and were on firmer ground, they married. Her husband was loyal, he was steady, handsome, and charismatic, and when they met, she had not seriously dated any men since that fateful day. No man ever excited her, measured up, or managed to erase *his* memory from her mind. She loved her husband, or at least, she thought that she loved him. In her own way, she did. He was very stable, and she required stability. Her hippie ways could cause some instability in her life. He had a solid job, earned a rewarding income, and she worked part-time in a local garden center when the children were off in school.

She was still searching for the plant's souls.

Someday she will find what she was looking for in the world.

Her husband, when he was not too tired and had the time for her and the desire, was an adequate lover, but he was awkward and unsure in bed and their lovemaking sessions were rather short-lived. While there was passion between them, there was no fire, no burn, and certainly no melting into each other as there was *with him.*

With a shake of her head, to erase all of these crazy thoughts, she worked even harder at the yarn and when her children waved to her; she dropped the handwork and waved in return.

There was her reason to enjoy her life and not dwell on the past.

This was unhealthy to continue to think of him and of that one glorious moment in time.

After all, she made the decision. It was her choice and despite telling her own mind a million times over or even more that it was the correct decision, the pain never left her. The what if? The love that she felt in her heart was undeniable, even after all of these years, and it was wrong to feel that way. Unfair to her husband, unfair to her children.

She picked the yarn up and with a deep sigh; she gazed out across the majestic trees that surrounded the park. The sun was dipping close to the horizon, and soon the day would wane. The sky was glowing with some orange colors mixed with gentle reds and blues. Another day done, and soon, the shadows of the night will call. Call her into his arms, into his scent, into a life and a dream that will never be. She knew in her heart that he would be fine.

Knowing the passion that he held for his dream, she knew that his pain will follow him but she will invisibly reach out through time and space to embrace him, send her love, her warmth, and her comfort. No man in this world is stronger than he is. She had followed his career from afar. Hockey was not her bag, but she made it an interest in order to follow his movements and to cheer his success. He was so close to the big league. It was a tragedy, or maybe; it was part of a plan. Who knows?

Time would tell, and the plan would unfold.

No man could capture her heart as he did and some lucky woman will finally capture his heart. It was her hope that their lives will be glorious together. That was her only wish for him.

Her husband stopped the swings and the time to go home was near. It was dinner time now. She wrapped up the yarn and quickly wiped away the tears from her cheeks. Her children were running to greet her with wide smiles and laughter, and she needed to get it together and not spoil the mood of the day.

Her tears needed to hide. Forever. She needed to go on in her life and forget him.

Still, how will she go on and forget him?

She quickly admitted to her soul what she always knew, because she never could. She never would even try to. He was her one true love. It was painful to admit and guilt filled her for a few seconds, but it was the truth.

Did he ever think of her? Did he too live with the memories of one simple moment of love in time?

Time. Their time.

Each of us has limited moments in time and they shared the most amazing moments together and now the memories of that day haunted her and enthralled her too. He still made her loins ache, his love molded her soul, he taught her true love, and he made her whole. She vowed to hold him in a special place within her heart and within her soul. All the rest of her life. A secret place, and a place that she could only visit during special times, times when she needed to see him once more. A place where the door to forever occasionally opened and she could sneak a peek inside.

"Mommy! Mommy!" The children cried as she kneeled down to embrace them and feel their warmth and love. She buried herself in them as she absorbed their love.

"Hi. It is time for us to go home now. It was fun, but we are all hungry. Do you want to eat out or eat at home?" Her husband asked.

"I think we should go for pizza. How about that, guys?" The children bounced up and down in delight at the prospect of pizza and ran off while holding hands in front of their parents in the direction of their car.

"On the sidewalk, guys. Please do not get too far ahead of us," her husband yelled to the children.

He reached for his wife's hand as she slung the macramé bag over her shoulder and once, she had it positioned; she gently grasped his hand.

"Are you doing, okay?" He asked, while studying her eyes.

"Yes, I am fine. Why do you ask?"

"Oh, okay, nothing really. You just seem far away right now. That is all."

"No, no, no. I am here. This has been a glorious day."

"It has been. Pizza was a great idea to cap it all off. You do have brilliant ideas."

"Thank you," she said as she let go of his hand. Her eyes spotted a trash can tucked in the corner of the parking lot and she reached into her bag and pulled the newspaper out and neatly folded it, reverently ran her hand over it and deposited it into the trash can.

Her husband pointed at the trashcan and asked, "Is that today's newspaper? I haven't read it yet."

"It is," she wiped away the long strands of red hair from

her face as a gentle breeze picked up while the sunset closed off the light, "trust me, it is all full of bad news. You do not want to read it. It will spoil the mood."

She tried not to feel as if she just tossed parts and pieces of her soul into the trashcan along with the newspaper.

"Oh, okay. I guess, honey. I guess." He said while he nodded his head and reached out for her hand and once more, they walked hand-in-hand to where their excited children waited for them next to the car.

"You sure that you are, okay?"

"Never better." After proclaiming her status, she stopped next to the car door, looked at her children and then at her husband and she spoke in a voice just above the whisper of the breeze that was picking up and welcoming in the night, "I love all of you with all my heart and soul."

The children looked up at their mother, and her husband, first, looked at the children and then with a look of puzzlement on his face, mixed with happiness, he studied his wife, shrugged his shoulders and said with a smile, "And we love you too."0

"We love you, Mommy!" The children happily broadcasted in unison.

"Where did that come from, honey?" Her husband leaned into her and asked in a whisper while they both made sure the children were secure in their car seats before they settled into the front seats of the vehicle. She did not answer him right away.

Once she had settled into the passenger's seat and her husband settled into the driver's side and he started the car, she rolled down the window as the car began to roll away. She allowed the gentle breeze to flow through her glorious red hair. It felt glorious on her face, and the breeze invaded her essence. The breeze was as if it brought with it a memory of a glorious love that will never die or ever leave her soul.

It was a breeze of love.

Finally, the answer to his question arrived. Her husband had been patient, perhaps, because he sensed his wife's pensiveness.

"Oh, I dunno. Maybe it arrived on this glorious breeze that just swept in as the sun faded away. It feels so wonderful. Doesn't it?"

Her husband did not answer his wife, unless a gentle nod counted for an answer. He kept his eyes on the road but stole a glance at his wife, too.

"I simply had to release the words from my heart and from my soul. Yes, I think that the love floated in on this evening's glorious breeze. I think that love on a breeze is the greatest love. It fills your heart and your soul, and on occasion, it blows open the door leading to forever and magically walks into your life."

THE END

The Gypsy

From Tales of the Quiet Stranger in the Black Hat

"Ohhhhhhh . . . Miss Wainwright! I foresee a great event coming for you in the very near future! A new horizon, a new man perhaps . . . or something else. The glass is foggy yet, and the visions are not yet clear. It is a vision in the making, a new adventure or a new person. No, no, let's look deeply into the mysterious glass! I think that it might be a new business venture!"

The gypsy, or as she was known on the main drag in this small city by her glowing neon sign in the small storefront window, "The Great and All-Knowing, Ms. Lolita," waved her hands over a crystal ball glowing in front of her on a table.

While Ms. Lolita waved her hands and focused into the magical glass, she occasionally rolled her eyes back into her head and leaned back into her chair. Ms. Lolita, then, in a seemingly deep trance-like state, leaned back in, in order to stare once again deeply in the crystal.

The crystal that held all the secrets within its glowing mystery!

What the unsuspecting customer, the humble, extremely wealthy and slightly naïve, Miss Wainwright did not notice, was that while Ms. Lolita leaned back, rolled her eyes and then refocused on the glowing crystal, Ms. Lolita occasionally picked her eyes up and she was actually studying Miss Wainwright's every move and her every motion.

The "gypsy" fortune teller was carefully studying body, eyes and facial language for a "hit" or a twitch, or some type of signal from Miss Wainwright, based upon what the all-knowing Ms. Lolita had just spoken to her.

'Geez, shit, no hit yet. All this stupid battleaxe does is to stare endlessly into the glass. Okay . . . here, let's try this one.' Ms. Lolita thought to herself, while she leaned back for another round of "magically enhanced," observations after searching Miss Wainwright for clues.

The mysterious and powerful Ms. Lolita leaned in and with her left foot carefully concealed underneath the red tablecloth, she carefully pressed down with her foot on a pedal located on the floor. While she waved her hands wildly over the crystal ball, she pushed the lever and the mechanism attached to the pedal, made the table slowly rise into the air. Slowly, gradually, it rose in the air, all while Ms. Lolita was vigilantly watching Miss Wainwright for some type of clue.

Ms. Lolita feigned her deepest, trance-like state, and she spewed ominously in her patented indecipherable babble of her supposed trance.

"Ohhwowe, bammlota, zooombaki, kilita, HUCKENY!"

"Oh, my, Ms. Lolita! The table is rising." the naïve spinster, Miss Wainwright somewhat, shakily observed.

In strict accordance with Ms. Lolita's instructions, despite the intense pressure of the power of the magic, Miss Wainwright managed to keep her folded hands firmly upon the now levitating table.

After all, we would not want to risk a shattering of the magical spell.

Ms. Lolita continued with her deepest trance; she reached over and threw some magic sawdust into the air. She turned the hidden knob under the table to float more burning incense into the air, all while still babbling on and on in her best incantations.

Slowly, Ms. Lolita relieved the pressure on the table

lever. The table descended back down to the floor and she leaned back intensely, still studying the crystal ball.

"Let's give this another shot now," the phony gypsy thought to herself.

She spoke once again in English, after a dramatic roll of her eyes, in order to recover from her trance, "I see a man now. He is clearer within my visions . . . dark hair, maybe . . . a little bald in the front."

Here we go now . . . pay dirt!

"Oh yes, that is the man you mentioned last week when you read my palm. I think it might be the man who services my automobile, he was very nice, and he seemed quite interested in me too," Miss Wainwright had shown a chink in her armor and now that was all, Ms. Lolita required to move in for the kill shot.

"Yes, it is! The man whom I foresaw in your palm last week. The man at the automobile service center. He smiles easily. He is handsome, single, and he is interested in you. I see him studying you as you walk away. He is admiring your fabulous figure. I think it might be a love for you that I foresaw."

"Oh my, how embarrassing. I did not realize he was watching me so intensely. He *is* a handsome man!"

"What is it that will happen to us, Ms. Lolita?"

Ah, sorry. Not quite so fast, Miss Wainwright. Unfortunately, it does not work that way. Magical transmissions from far-off lands and spheres outside our normal realms do not come so easily, nor do they come so cheaply either.

"Ooh, no! The visions are growing darker and darker! You must have some inner mind blockage, Miss Wainwright. It is some hidden, dark secret deep within your spirit, which is preventing me from seeing the entire picture, and the ball is . . . fading."

As Ms. Lolita spoke the words, she slowly rotated the hidden knob under the table to shut down the light underneath the glowing magical predictor of all fate, as well as shutting down the intensity of the incense control.

Incense is not free either.

"Oh my," Miss Wainwright fretted at the sight of the disappearing glow of the powerful crystal, "I thought I had cleared my mind of all those thoughts. It must be so deep inside of me that even I cannot detect it."

With that, Ms. Lolita stood up. She walked over to the light switch and snapped on the overhead lights in the small store. The lights flickered to life and the remaining smoke of the burning incense danced and floated in a magical haze within the room.

"I am sorry, Miss Wainwright, but we do grow closer and closer to the truth. I think for our next session we will combine the power of the crystal ball with the palm readings and even try some hypnosis. Perhaps then, we can clear these deep and profound blockages from within your mind."

"Oh, I agree. Whatever you suggest, Ms. Lolita, will that session cost some more money for my fee?"

Ms. Lolita whipped up her best regrettable frown and changed her voice to convey an air of phony sympathy, "I am afraid to say that it will. I will need to bring in an assistant to help me with the hypnosis. We will need to combine my powers with the Great Randolfski. He is, after all, world-renowned. I will need to check his availability and call you with the payment amounts as soon as I hear back from him. That way, you can bring along a check and we can pay him for his services. My meager services and abilities, well, they pale in comparison to the Great Randolfski."

"Oh well, I understand. Oh, my, I will need to retain the services of such an expert! Yes, I agree—whatever it takes, here, here, here, is a check for today with a tad extra for your insight. I will be back next week, or should I come sooner and more often?"

"Well, Miss Wainwright, I think we should go with every other day, at least until all of us together manage to clear these obstacles. I regret that we must cut this short now. I do have other appointments."

Ms. Lolita took the check from Miss Wainwright, slipped it down inside her brassiere. She then gently grabbed Miss Wainwright by her hand and guided her out the front door. All the time, Ms. Lolita was consoling her as to how to cope with her pressure and stress, until they could meet again and finally, for the last time, they could discover together the secrets of her somewhat shrouded future.

When the door closed behind Miss Wainwright and the confused spinster had pulled away in her expensive luxury automobile, Ms. Lolita reached over, turned the key in the door and turned out the blinking neon sign in the front window. She rested her head upon the door and sighed deeply. Bilking lonely spinsters out of their life savings was a bit exhausting.

A curtain along the side of the reading room parted, and a tall, lanky man appeared. He smiled from ear-to-ear and he held in his one hand a bottle of whiskey, and in his other hand, he held two glasses. A lit cigarette dangled precariously from his lips.

"Here, all-knowing one, you look as if you need a drink. I need to prepare. After all, the Great Randolfski needs to be on top of his game too! I have a grand entrance to make next time. I loved that part where you told her the man at the service center was checking her out as she walked away. A woman, who looks like a half-eaten pear, wears blue wigs and has eyeglasses as thick as soda bottles. Ha! I do not think so! Now, you on the other hand, let me reach down inside that marvelous chest of yours and claim not only that check, but some other things too." He lifted his eyes seductively towards Ms. Lolita as a prelude to some slightly, uninhibited intentions that he harbored.

The man set the bottle and the two glasses upon the

table and pulled a chair over to sit down. He took the cap off the bottle and poured two drinks in the glasses. Ms. Lolita shook her head and slowly walked to the table to join the man.

She spoke softly, almost as if she was afraid of someone else listening in, "Yes, well, it was not easy this go around. I think I overdid the incense, but I could not get her to crack. I think I am losing my touch after all of these years of dealing with these kooks who wander in here."

Ms. Lolita pulled the chair out, sat down, and she took the glass in her hands. She tilted the glass back and took a long swig. She pulled her blouse down, as well as her brassiere, exposed her breasts to the man, removed the check, and handed it to the man with a coy smile.

"Here is the check. As far as the rest of the probing down there—it will have to wait until later. I am exhausted. Steve, can you please look at that lever for the table? I told you last week that it was hard to push down. I was turning blue in the face, trying to hold that stupid table up."

"I see that you are full of love. I will look at it first thing tomorrow, Ann. I promise. You know Ann, no pressure here. However, we have to get this dough from this old bird. We need the thousand bucks by next week, or you know it is not gonna be pretty."

Ms. Lolita, or now, specifically, or more factually, Ann Lolita, nodded her head, waved her hand and spoke softly while motioning to Steve to refill her glass.

"I know, I know, I know, I will get it. I wish you would stop playing those ponies. You get us in trouble all the time and soon, they will all be calling for the money you owe them. Don't worry, together, we will soon have her forking over her house, her car notes, everything. I promise. Just like that other weirdo. What was his name? I let him stare down my blouse all the time, and he handed the money over right and left. Too bad, he keeled over before we hit the big payoff!"

She smiled, threw down the next shot, and she then waved to Steve.

"Now, come to think of it, I feel refreshed! How about a bit of that probing, big guy?"

That night, after a bit of a whiskey-induced frolic or two with Steve and some smokes from a lot more than just the incense that floated around the store, Ann sat wide-awake in a chair in their bedroom.

Steve snored loudly; sound asleep in the bed in front of her in the darkness. She often wished she picked a better boyfriend than this particular one on this go around, but he was loyal, and a great con man too. He was not that bad looking, a worthy partner for a roll or two in the hay, and he did make her laugh on rare occasions. She could do without his habit of betting on the horses and numbers too much and wasting their money, but overall, he was not too bad.

She had worse. . ..

Ann sat in the darkness, dragging deeply on a cigarette, thinking where this all went so wrong, where her life went so far astray that she could not even remember what her goals were or where she originally started out.

Ann Lolita was gorgeous, a beauty queen, the star of the show. She was captain of her cheerleading squad in high school; she could have her pick, anytime, anywhere, of any of the young men. Ann had an attractive figure, with a slim waist that gradually flowed into gentle curves and hips that rocked young men's worlds. She had wonderful features, olive skin, unblemished by a mark or flaw, gorgeous black hair tumbling down over her shoulders.

Queen of the prom, queen of hearts.

Somehow, it all went away, lost in a maze of time.

Besides her physical beauty, she also had other talents. She was highly creative, an artist, above all, she always was an artist. Even as a little girl, she could pick up a pencil and draw people, animals, landscapes, anything. No formal training, no effort, all miraculous, God-given talent. She could draw anywhere, any time.

Remarkable talent. . ..

She was indeed a phony gypsy! She actually grew up outside of Hartford in Connecticut, a family of Italian Americans, her mom was a schoolteacher, and her dad worked as a mid-level executive in a Connecticut utility company. She grew up happy, with a nice house, no brothers or sisters. She was an only child, but she was happy. All of her teachers in school encouraged her to go on to pursue the arts in a university, and she did. She went off to Philadelphia, to a university there, which had studies focused upon the arts as well as general studies. Ann took theatre, art, and drama classes. Her drawings won awards, glowing reviews and seemingly endless praise of her remarkable skills. Her professors posted them in the university's galleries and she was on her way.

Then, in her junior year at the university, in an off-campus drama production of which she had a supporting role in, she met him. He was there watching, observing, keeping an eye on local talent. An agent, a man of the world, a man with connections. Ann had caught his eye, and after the play, he spoke to her, filled her head with glory and entranced her with dreams of Broadway, Hollywood, television, the big lights, the red-carpeted runways! He was older, but extremely good-looking, smooth talking, and to be honest, rather ill intentioned.

He captivated her. After ample wine, romance and dining in fancy restaurants, rides in fancy cars, a few nights of bedroom antics and passion, he lured her away, and she left school to a howl of protest from her professors, her friends and her parents. She left behind the drawings, the art, the hope and the dreams.

Sadly, Ann Lolita left the largest part of her soul hanging on walls in those galleries.

Now, her new agent did have connections, and he did manage to obtain a few minor acting roles for Ann. They crisscrossed the nation, first in New York City, then Atlanta, then to Chicago, and finally, just when the money ran out, they ended up in California.

Along the way, he also picked up a bad drug habit and Ann, in frustration, left him and went out on her own to pursue the dream.

A dream which never came.

A few more minor roles, a number of attempts of working her way to the top by seducing various executives in key positions, all failures and all too soon; the dream was dead.

Lost in a dusty memory, along with her drawings.

Ann finished her cigarette; she snuffed it out in the ashtray and watched as the smoke from the dying flame spiraled around the tray. Even in the dim light of the bedroom, she could see it there, whispering gently into the air. Sadly, signaling to her, of how her dreams were dying embers now, too.

She leaned back, sighed and thought how strange this life is. How did a chance encounter of sorts at a carnival turn into a career as a con artist? She reached for the pack of cigarettes and the cigarette lighter, and she lit one more.

'One more smoke and I will go to sleep,' she thought.

As she lit the cigarette, she could clearly see herself entering the tent of the gypsy fortune teller set up in the corner of the carnival. There, in some type of quiet desperation, she was seeking to know her future, her destiny. Her dreams were now dead. But could this strange woman from another time or another place, or another spiritual plane, be able to advise her of which direction to go?

After dropping a few dollars in the jar, the old gypsy rattled some beads, chanted some magical incantations, "Ohhwowe, bammlota, zooombaki, kilita, HUCKENY!"

She waved incense in the air and threw sawdust into the sunlight to see what patterns it would create when it landed on the table.

Patterns to foretell what lies ahead for Ann.

That is how far we fall sometimes in this life, to where we no longer follow our hearts and we are willing to allow sawdust falling from the sky to guide our instincts and directions.

Now, Ann was an artist and an actress, and while she had fallen from the grace of her previous glory, she still was very good at what she did.

The old gypsy did have some points that she was correct about in Ann's past, but nothing of any significance, and as far as her future predictions, Ann did not buy any of it.

No one *in this world* can tell of a complete stranger's past or foretell what lies ahead for them.

She could tell a fellow actress when she met one.

She came away from the tent at the carnival, far from enlightened as to what her future held. Or perhaps, she did come away with her future.

She entered the tent as Ann Lolita and left as, "The Great and All-Knowing, Ms. Lolita."

Sadly, she never drew a sketch or picture again. Her bitterness would not allow her creative spirit loose.

Now, she lived a life that in her heart, she knew, was nothing more than a slow and quiet torture. She sat there in the quiet darkness and she snuffed out the cigarette in the ashtray. Ann watched as the glowing embers of the dying cigarette faded in the darkness, along with her own spirit that largely had faded too.

The next morning was the same as all the others. Or was it?

Ann turned the key in the front door of the storefront; she flipped the switch on for the neon sign in the window and watched as it flickered to life. It was the middle of April and the weather seemed to be decent enough, sunny and cold right now, but it was sure to warm up by the afternoon. Ann looked out the smoky front window of the store and wiped away some residue of the smoke from the incense that covered the glass.

"I really do need to clean this glass someday," Ann spoke aloud as she walked away. She lit some candles, turned the incense burners on, and sat down at the table.

Steve was behind the curtain, but she knew he would not work on the lever today. Right now, even without seeing Steve, Ann knew that he had the newspaper open and he was circling the selections for the horse races later on in the day.

After all, that was her "gift" to be able to predict the future.

Right after noontime, he would slip away, walk down to the bar on the corner and with the local bookie, place more bets for horses that will not win. In addition, all too soon, they would be calling for the money he owed them, in fact, in a day or two. . ..

The day passed along slowly, a few young college students stopped by for a palm reading or two for fun, a curious businessman searching for false hope stopped in for a reading. He was obviously having an extramarital affair, and he was wondering if his mistress would eventually marry him, when his kids were finally grown and he could safely leave his wife.

All the usual drivel.

Miss Wainwright would be in for her big moment tomorrow afternoon; therefore, Ann did not expect too much from this particular day. It was all business as usual.

On the other hand; she thought it was.

Out on the streets, in the bright sunlight of a glorious April morning, the distinct click of metal tips of highly polished boots on a hard surface, mixed and echoed with the traffic rolling along the main street. The boots clicked loudly, because the man who wore them walked along the sidewalk at a rapid pace. He moved quickly and effortlessly through the crowds of browsing window shoppers; he maneuvered between dog-walkers, mothers pushing babies in strollers and shoppers carrying their newly purchased goods.

He walked by the outdoor fruit and vegetable market and ignored the shouts of the shopkeeper, peddling the fact that early season strawberries were on special this glorious April morning.

The man did not move his eyes to acknowledge anyone or anything. He was dressed all in black, with sharply creased black trousers, a black shirt, and all he wore, as an overcoat of sorts, was a black leather vest, in which he left unbuttoned except for the last button just above his waist.

On his head was a black hat with a wide brim, which he pulled down close to his ears, but you could still make out some of his facial features.

A neatly trimmed, black beard framed his handsome face and his facial features were striking, with a neatly trimmed moustache that lined his mouth. His clothes were made of the finest materials. Not a single item was out of place, not a hair on his head or his face, untrimmed or even slightly askew.

He walked with an air of confidence as he strode along. Everyone who noticed him could tell that this was a gentleman that was used to traveling around, and you could easily see that he was comfortable in many different surroundings.

He had dark, black, piercing eyes. Eyes that focused straight ahead, his face was void of all expression; he had no emotions, and an aura of an ominous presence followed along behind him.

It seemed as if he had a mission, a mission of which nothing could derail.

He was the quiet stranger in the black hat.

The quiet stranger strode along until he reached what

appeared to be his destination. He stopped in front of the small, dingy storefront of, "The Great and All-Knowing, Ms. Lolita."

He stopped, and he spun around a few times as if he needed to adjust or somehow confirm his final direction and destination. His dark eyes spotted the sign in the window and for a few seconds, he stared at the sad, blinking, neon sign proclaiming her so-called talents to the entire world.

He adjusted his hat, pulling it down a bit more in the front of his face, in order to shield his eyes just a bit. He lowered his head, moved quickly and with a turn of the knob of the front door, he stepped into her lair.

When she heard the door open, Ms. Lolita looked up from her table and within seconds, she identified the potential of this particular customer. It was what she did because within seconds, she could analyze a potential bilking opportunity. Ms. Lolita seldom, if ever, missed her targets; yet, this time . . . she might just meet her match.

'Okay,' she thought, 'handsome, extraordinarily so and his eyes are so dark, and he has a tall, lean, powerful frame. My, he astounds you! He is well dressed in the finest clothes, a hat that must be worth a fortune alone, and look at those boots. Wow! This boring day has suddenly taken a surprising turn. This handsome man has some extra money to burn. My, he is so immense in stature. . ..'

She watched as he stood there for a second or two while she studied him. He looked around in the dark store, scanned the surroundings and then he settled his eyes upon her seated at the table.

She felt a cold shiver. His eyes and stare seemed to go right through to her soul. An aura of an ominous presence seemed to have come along with this handsome stranger.

Time to crank it up, Ann!

Do not allow this sucker to get away.

"Welcome stranger! Welcome to the reading room, a

room that unlocks the secrets of your future, as well as the mysteries of your past. Come in, come in, sit, and let Ms. Lolita allow you to be in touch with your own inner spiritual awareness of your past, and let me reveal to you, your future fate!"

The stranger stood and stared at Ms. Lolita; however, he did not say a single word.

Ann thought to herself, 'Wow, . . . good-looking guy, but he might be a weirdo. I hope Steve has not left yet to place his pony bets. Although, this immense man would crush poor Steve with one sweep of his arm.'

After what seemed as if it were a lifetime, the stranger finally walked over to the table, he reached inside of his vest, took out a crisp, fifty-dollar bill and without saying a single word, he placed it into the jar on the table. He pulled out the chair, sat down opposite Ms. Lolita, and stared directly into her eyes.

Dark, piercing, black eyes, a large, yet lean frame. This was a big, powerful man and his ominous stare extremely unnerved Ann. He continued to send cold shivers up and down her entire body, and if he had not dropped that fifty-dollar bill in her jar, she decided that she would have asked him to leave.

There was something very strange and unnerving about this customer. And even with all of her experience, she could not place what it was with this man or what was so different about him.

Still, fifty bucks just bought a bit of her time, so she cranked it up, "What is it that brings you in today, dark stranger dressed in black, shall I read your palm, or look into the crystal ball, or perhaps, something deeper or darker?"

The quiet stranger in the black hat still did not speak, but with his right arm, he slowly reached out across the table and held his right hand out over the table, over the top of the crystal ball. While never unlocking his eyes or stare from Ms. Lolita, he slowly and gracefully turned his palm upside down in front of Ms. Lolita.

"Oh yes, read your palm, unlock the mysteries of life for you, quiet, dark stranger!"

She leaned back in her chair and rolled her eyes back as she started her usual, tedious act, and when she reached under the table to turn the knob for the on switch for the incense, she pulled back in shock, because the quiet stranger had met her hand under the table.

He already had his hand on the knob! He moved so fast! How did he put his hand under the table? How did he reach so far! It seemed as if he never moved a muscle!

Ms. Lolita's face erupted in shock, and she pulled her hands back and noticed the quiet stranger still held his other hand out in front of her. He still did not speak, but his eyes went from her eyes to his palm, and then back again. He was indicating to Ann for her to look at his palm.

She breathed deeply. She sighed, while she slowly and apprehensively, reached out to take his hand. When she did, she felt an incredible warmth emitting from his palm; it filled her with a glow, a strange sensation of pain and sorrow leaving her body. Ann shook it off quickly, flipped the reading glasses hanging on a chain around her neck up to her eyes, and she stared in. As she did, she saw the quiet stranger move his legs, and she felt the table rise! He must have his foot on her lever!

How could he even reach it? How did he know it was there?

She went to pull her hand away and end this charade, but the stranger held her hand tightly and finally spoke, in a low, yet melodious voice, "No, look at my palm, Ann. Just as the old gypsy did with you in that tent years ago, in the carnival. Read it!"

How did he know that? She trembled in fear now, but his grip was strong. She felt for a moment, as if she should cry out and pull hard to escape his grip, but her fear, for some reason, slowly subsided and she forced herself to look down at his hand. When she did, she gasped in shock, because to her horror, she saw it had no lines, it had no marks, and it was smooth and unblemished.

She dropped his hand in continued awe and shock, but he quickly took her hand back and gently grasped it, as if to assist in steadying her and to calm her. She felt faint. The room was spinning, and she felt her chest heaving, while she took deep breaths to prevent from fainting.

While she leaned in, she finally managed to whisper, "Just who the hell are you? What do you want?"

He gently let go of her hand, let the table back down, folded his hands in front of him and placed them on the table.

He spoke again, in his low, deep melodious voice, "Ann Lolita, born in Hartford, Connecticut, April twentieth, in the year 1955 at three ten in the afternoon. You have a loving family, your father was successful in his career, your mother is a loving woman, who taught children, and she loves you with all of her heart. Your mother cherishes the pencil drawing of your first puppy that you drew when you were seven years old. Your mother still has it in her drawer, in the top, left-hand corner of the roll-top desk in her living room. The drawer with the silver handle with the red inlay. You recall, which one I mean. Where she also keeps for safekeeping, the good luck charm of her own dear mother. Life ran over you, evil men swayed you and you gave up your passion in disillusion, in heartbreak, in a tent in some shady carnival."

He took a little breath, pierced her with his eyes, pointed with his finger and said, "You need to return to your passion, give up this sham of a life, and return to Miss Wainwright, all the money you have bilked her out of and share with the world, your gifts. You have too much love, beauty and talent to give to this tired, old world. Only when you share them, will you be set free."

Ann did not know what to say. She sat there in horror and at first, she thought to call out to Steve for help, but she realized that he was already gone to place his bets, or he would have already rushed in to try to save her.

Save her from . . . what?

To save her from the truth?

To save her from her own past, or from her own dreams and desires?

Truth that remarkably somehow, or someway, this quiet stranger in the black hat has the insight to know and the courage to tell her.

How does he know? No one *in this world* can see the future or know the past!

He stopped speaking, smiled, and slowly outstretched his arm again over the table. He motioned with his eyes for her to take his hand. It seemed as if his mission now was to comfort her. Ann now had tears rolling down her cheeks, but she reached out and took his hand.

Instead, he flipped her hand over and studied *her palm.* "Number one, two, seven, Glenbrook Road. There is an art gallery and cultural arts center there. It is operated by a man whose last name is Jenkins. He is looking for an artist to sign to a contract. Mr. Jenkins is getting on in years and he is looking for a partner to work for him, he loves art, particularly, black and white pencil drawings. He longs to display quality pencil sketches of. . .."

He let go of her hand, reached inside of his vest, took out a piece of paper and a number of pencils. He placed them on the table, and then he slid them over to Ann.

He looked back up into her eyes and said rather forcibly, "Draw me."

She stumbled over her emotions; she wiped her eyes and tried hard to speak.

Finally, Ann managed to speak, and some fractured words came out, "I cannot. I have not drawn anything or anyone in years. I cannot do it. It is an old life, a lost dream and a missed opportunity."

"You are incorrect, Ann. The only missed opportunities in this life would be the ones we are too afraid of in order to recognize them. The first steps for a baby to take, are the hardest ones. The first words typed for writers, are the most difficult. The first notes sung for a singer are the most strained, the first awkward glances, the first kiss, and first fumbling embraces for lovers, are nearly impossible. They are all the hardest and after we conquer those, then it all becomes easier. It becomes magical."

Ann nodded. She studied his face, took the pencil, took the paper, and with her hands shaking and trembling, she steadied herself and started to sketch him. He did not move. He allowed her to study him, to capture his features, his amazing eyes, and his every detail.

It *was* magical.

While she drew, she felt the release of the pain. Her soul returned inside of her, her creativity restored, the exhilaration of an artist suppressed, the joy of her heart, her spirit and mind lost, then regained.

She was drawing again!

She sketched, and she sketched, and within what seemed as if it were only a few moments, she had captured the image of the quiet stranger in the black hat forever on a sheet of paper.

She finished, dropped the pencil, and picked up the piece of paper. After studying it, she smiled.

It was magnificent.

An outpouring of years of suppressed creativity had created a masterpiece. She also realized that the subject material was not exactly ordinary.

She held it up for the quiet stranger to see. He studied it for a long time, and without speaking, the stranger's eyes and smile displayed satisfaction with her creation. Before Ann could even react or speak, he then suddenly and without another word, stood up. He tipped his hat, turned and walked quickly out the front door of the store, while gently closing the door behind him.

Ann reached into the jar, took out the fifty-dollar bill, and held it tightly in her hand. She jumped out of her chair, rushed to the door, and flung it open.

She rushed out to the sidewalk; she called out onto the busy street and yelled to him, "Wait! Wait! I need to know your name. Here, please come back and take your money back!"

Ann could see him walking in the distance on the sidewalk, but he did not turn around or acknowledge her cries. She watched until he left her view, lost in the maze of humanity and business upon the city street. She stood there until she could no longer see him or hear the click of the metal tips of his boots on the sidewalk.

Glancing down at the fifty-dollar bill in her hand, she realized that where he came from, and to where he was going, he most likely did not need it.

Ten months later, on a late Saturday afternoon, the Glenside Gallery and Cultural Art Center was the center of activity.

A cold February day was not ideal for outdoor activities, but in the glow and warmth of-the-art gallery, it was a perfect day for viewing fine art and inspirational collections. That is exactly what the communities of artists, art collectors, and art lovers were doing on this day. A jam-packed gallery, filled with people sipping wine and sampling cheese, while viewing the artwork, all there to enjoy the opening day of the display of pencil sketches and various other artworks, by a certain local artist named Ms. Ann Lolita.

The press releases and promotional events leading up to the actual opening of the display had been a rousing success. This long-awaited event of the unfolding of a lifetime of dreams, becoming a reality, had created quite a stir through the artistic communities of the city and beyond.

An elderly man walked up to and spoke to Ann while she stood on the sideline greeting people and watching the crowd.

"Congratulations, Ann. My goodness, what a wonderful and inspirational achievement this is for the gallery and for you. You must be so proud. I know I am! This is an even greater opening day turnout than I would ever have imagined. Some bids presented tonight for your artwork are almost unimaginable. People are bidding twenty percent over the listed prices." He was dressed in a fine suit, with a nametag on his lapel to show that he was the owner of the establishment. He shook Ann's hand while smiling broadly.

Ann stood there smiling and glowing, sipping from a glass of wine, dressed to the hilt in a fine dress, a simple gold chain hanging seductively around her neck.

She was looking as fine as fine could be. . ..

"Thank you, Mr. Jenkins. It is indeed a dream that has come true. I have you to thank, for believing in me, for giving me a chance."

The elderly man waved his hand in the air as if to discount Ann's statement.

"Nonsense, one look at your work, speaks for itself. You did this all yourself. I just gave you a vehicle to arrive in where you should have been a long time ago. In addition, you breathed new energy into my own life and in the center, too. For that, I thank you."

He turned and pointed towards a certain sketch hanging on the wall in front of them; a sketch that was the only piece in the entire gallery of which a small roped off area was set in front of in order to keep the many admirers and viewers at a safe distance from the hallowed artwork. A security guard stood in the corner near the drawing, keeping a close eye on the crowd and their behavior.

Numerous people stood around this particular drawing.

More of the crowd was viewing this piece than any other work in the entire display.

"I sure do wish that people would stop placing bids on that sketch. It is making my heart race, the amount of money they keep offering. For an old man, such as I am, it is becoming a bit precarious. We keep telling everyone that the original is not for sale, they can purchase the reproductions, but the original of 'The Quiet Stranger in the Black Hat', is not for sale at any price."

Mr. Jenkins finished his statement, took a sip of his wine, looked over the rim of the glass, and studied Ann's face for a potential change of heart.

After all, he had a business to run.

"That is, in fact . . . still true . . . right, Ann?" Mr. Jenkins asked just to make sure.

Ann smiled and placed her hand on Mr. Jenkins' shoulder, while confirming the status of the work, "Oh yes, not for sale at any price. I am sorry. Please excuse me. I need to go outside for a smoke and to take a break."

Ann excused herself and she made her way through the crowd. Along the way, she stopped many times to chat with admirers congratulating her and making small talk. Her captivating appearance only promoted her work and her image, and helped to sell even more of her work today.

Ann finally reached the side door; she opened it and stepped outside onto a small porch. There she stood, in the cool, late afternoon air.

It was cold, but the air felt so good.

She reached into her purse, pulled out a cigarette, and while she searched for a lighter in the depths of her purse, she heard the loud, distinct click of a lighter from behind her.

She turned around in haste and looked straight into the eyes of the quiet stranger in the black hat. She was not surprised at his magical and sudden arrival because in her heart and in her soul; she somehow knew that he would be here today.

He held the flame out for Ann and under the dark brim of his hat; Ann could see him smile at her. She smiled back, leaned into the flame, and drew a strong pull on the cigarette to light it.

One long drag and a puff of smoke into the air.

"I wondered if I would ever see you again. I thought today would be as good a time as any for you to return. You do seem to have a knack for timing your arrival at just the right moment," Ann said, while looking deeply once again into those wonderfully haunting eyes.

He captivated her, whoever he was.

As usual, the quiet stranger did not say anything. He stood there in silence while studying her face as she puffed on the cigarette.

"I am not even going to try to surmise who you are, where you came from, or why. I think it is best at this point, just to hold you near and dear in my heart forever. I do not suppose that I could ask you to step inside, share a glass of wine with me, perhaps, even dinner and who knows what else later."

Ann smiled. She was embarrassed at her proposition, and she waved her hand in the air as if to suggest to the quiet stranger that he should forget the entire thought.

"Please, do not answer that one. I already know what you would say. Let me dream, please, let me dream of how wonderful that would be for me, or for us."

He nodded his head and smiled.

She took one last puff and tossed the half-smoked cigarette out into the street. She reached out her hands, and the quiet stranger took them into his hands. She once again felt that warmth; his spirit projected such warmth, even on a bitterly cold day.

"Thank you for giving me my life back. I did return every penny to Miss Wainwright and then I kicked that gambling maniac to the curb. I started to sketch again within hours after you left, but I know that you already know all of these facts."

He nodded, yet remained silent.

"I now know that I have recovered what was lost inside of me, and for that, I have to thank you again. You gave it back to me, quiet stranger."

Suddenly, she hit a nerve with the quiet stranger. Something that she had said had finally caused a reaction within him.

He shook his head gently back and forth and finally, he spoke, "No, my dear Ann. You are wrong, because it never left you. I cannot return what was never gone. You see, when we become lost in a wayward life, we sometimes think that we lose parts of us along the way. All we need to find it once again, is to take the time to examine our hearts and find the true answers. I did not do that for you, nor can I ever do that for anyone. Only you can search your own heart. All that I can do is to remind you to examine it. I help people to face the truth, of which they already know within their hearts. Now, please never lose your dreams again. To lose your own heart and your dreams is as if you have died inside. Never die inside again, dear Ann. You have too much love, beauty and talent to give to this tired, old world."

He pursed his lips together, touched his fingers to them, and then gently placed his fingers upon Ann's cheek. She reached up, held his hands tightly upon her cheek, and closed her eyes.

Always, Ann wanted to remember this moment and the feel of his hands upon her skin.

She finally, reluctantly, let him go. He stepped back, nodded, smiled, tipped his hat, turned and walked briskly away.

Ann whispered, "I promise that I will never let go of my dreams again, quiet stranger. I think forever more that you will haunt me and you will always be part of them, too. No matter where I go, what I do, or when I think—I will always bring you with me. Now, until the end of all time. Thank you."

She stood on the steps next to the front door; she stood there for a long time until she could no longer see him or hear the click of the metal tips of his boots on the sidewalk.

Except in her mind and in her heart, forever more.

THE END

Love in a Pumpkin

From "The Autumn Collection"

"Now, now, twenty-seven! My dear Paul, do not become all engrossed in the hockey game this afternoon. According to my research, you still have seventy-one games remaining in the season, for you to watch." Binky, my lovely, yet forceful wife, was putting the clamps on me for sitting down to watch the New York Rovers game on the television on this October afternoon.

I felt a slight protest was in order, which I knew would be in vain, nonetheless, I needed to muster up a last gasp attempt.

"But, Binky, they are playing the Comets this afternoon in a matinee game from the garden, and the young goalie, Shambley is in the net!"

Binky stood watching me while I stood in front of the television fiddling with a blasted, new-fangled, cable box, of which I never could work correctly.

Binky dug her left foot in the carpet, and tapped her finger on top of the television, as she was about to make a forceful point, "Well, first off, I know you will need to call your seven-year-old son to come and help you tune the cable box to the correct channel. Second, the last time that Shambley played in the goal, all you did was stand in the living room and scream for him to stand up on his skates, and cut down the angles. I cannot believe that you would enjoy spending a fabulous autumn afternoon locked here in our house screaming at the television. The last and most important reason, Pastor Paul John Henson, is that your two children are already outside waiting for you to take them to pick out Halloween pumpkins, just as you had promised us this week Wednesday, after work at around seven o'clock in the early evening. I am sure you have not forgotten your promise to your children and your wife, now have you, dear Paul?"

Binky folded her arms across her chest and zoomed in for a famous Binky Hobnobber Henson stare as I stopped fiddling with the cable box. I was in trouble, when Binky used my full name, and my "pastor" title in a sentence addressed directly to me, then I was in some very serious trouble.

Oh, oh! It was time to fudge my way through this one. I clicked off the television and smiled at my wife as I said, "Nah, nah, nah, of course, I have not forgotten. Well, dear Binky, I was just about to say, how there are so many more games to watch this season and Shambley is a bum, anyway."

Binky fluffed her hair and smiled back as she quickly moved into action.

My wife was intense now as she barked out the afternoon instructions, "Oh very good, twenty-seven! Now, please take your heavier zipper jacket, and leave your favorite light vest in the closet. I am very glad that you are dressed in your No Way tee shirt and your canvas sneakers rather than your pastor's collar. I do want this afternoon to be a special family outing. Therefore, although I am aware of your obligations, just for today, I prefer not to interact with someone who requires some type of pastoral care, as tends to happen quite often, when you venture out in public wearing your collar. I must also continually remind you that with the approach of the cold weather that you need to stay warmer, dear Paul. I must also remind you that despite your fondness for the colder temperatures, you are no longer twenty years old anymore. I will meet you out in the driveway. I am so excited!"

Binky stood up on her toes and gave me a kiss on my cheek while I weakly nodded in agreement to all of her orders. She smiled and out the door, she scampered off to gather up our children.

My, oh my, she is still quite the whirlwind.

I had narrowly escaped that time since I was almost in some serious trouble, as I *had* forgotten my promise. It had been a tough week at the church office with many boring and slightly unproductive meetings, and time had run away from me.

I wanted to relax and watch the hockey game.

I knew that was a poor excuse because I did promise my children a traditional trip to the garden center for them to pick out some pumpkins for Halloween.

I was about to learn my lesson as to why these types of moments in our lives should never be forgotten.

Our son, Paul William, was already seven years old, and he had grown tall and strong already. He wore his blonde hair long as I still did. His mother would never entertain any such foolishness as to think that he should cut it all off. He loved sports, and hockey was his first love. Much to his mother's chagrin, he played goaltender, as his father did, and he had started to skate this past winter. As he was growing up, he had taken on more of my appearance, as well as some of my personality. He was quiet, smart, athletic, insightful, and slightly introverted. In the quiet way that he now stood back and studied situations, but did not say much, I could see more and more of Paul John Henson in Paul William Henson these days!

Our daughter was quite the opposite of her brother. Heather Sarah was about five years old now and she was a fireball! She was so much like Binky in her personality that there would never be any question at all that she was Binky Hobnobber Henson's little girl!

Heather Sarah's beauty was indescribable; she was just as captivating at five years old as Binky was stunning at any age. Heather Sarah had long, curly red hair, perfect features, and a dynamic personality. Just as her mother did, Heather Sarah asked a million questions, checked and dissected every angle of life into the smallest detail, and the little girl was as sharp as a tack. It was actually frightening as to how smart she was! She was a chip off the old research block for sure, and Binky was happily teaching her everything that she knew.

My wife, Binky Henson, was in my opinion, the most perfect woman in the world. I found it amazing that she had grown even more beautiful and gorgeous, as the years had passed, than she ever was. I had no qualms in saying that she was a woman who was my dream; she was my soul mate, and my love. She still researched everything in life down to the finest details and never missed a trick. It drove many people crazy as she analyzed everything, but to me, it just made me love her more! It was one of the most fascinating aspects of her quirky and wonderful personality that I loved, along with her penchant for being cute, coy, and captivating, whenever she wanted to be. Binky was one of a kind, and she was my lovely wife.

I was indeed a very lucky man.

I grabbed my jacket and the keys to my old jeep, locked the door to our house, and met Binky and the children in the jeep.

"Dear Father, you really were not going to watch the hockey game this afternoon, now, were you?" Heather Sarah zoomed in for an answer. She had inherited the staring gene from her mother and she had put me on-the-spot right away.

I started the jeep, put it in gear and said, "Well I have to be. . .."

"Shambley is a bum in the net, dear Father. He flops down too much," Paul William proclaimed as he had saved me from the wrath of our five-year-old little girl.

"I want a big pumpkin! I want one that is round and fat!

Can we find a round and fat one?" Heather Sarah had shifted gears as I pulled the jeep out onto the main road and we headed for the garden center.

"Sure, sure, sure, you guys can pick out whatever you want this year. You and Paul William can each get a pumpkin and we will get one for the family. We can put them all on the front porch."

"Now, twenty-seven, you promised us that you would show us how to carve the pumpkins this year. Grandpa Henson's method seems far superior to Popo Hobnobber's ideas. I must admit that I found the entire process disgusting as a young girl, and my brother and I would much rather to have painted the outside of our pumpkins. The juice and mushy pulp inside, used to mess my nails up for weeks, and the odors associated with the practice, were atrocious. My dear father would become frustrated with Uncle Tinky and me when we would run away when he carved the pumpkin. Dear Father would throw the carved pumpkin away and just paint faces on some new ones for us."

I laughed at the thought of my wife and my brother-in-law running away in horror at the carving of a pumpkin.

My father-in-law, Senator William T. Hobnobber, was quite the character, and famous for his absolute lack of patience that was for sure. The thought had struck our two children, funny too. They were laughing at the description that Binky had provided of the repulsive pumpkin, "mush."

As we approached the garden center, Heather Sarah asked me, "Dear Father, why did God make pumpkins?"

"Well, for food, I would think, Heather Sarah. You can make some wonderful pies from pumpkins."

I looked in the rearview mirror to see her and Paul William both shaking their heads in adamant disagreement with my answer.

"We had pumpkin pie at Grandma Henson's house last

year and it is yucky," Paul William declared and his sister agreed. "Why else? You are a pastor, dear Father, and you know all about God and these things," now my son was putting me on the spot.

"Well . . . maybe for the seeds . . . yeah, yeah, yeah, they are good. We can scoop them out, bake them, and put some salt on them. They taste good, and they are good for you too," I was happy with my answer, until I saw them both shaking their heads again.

"Uncle Harry gave us a pack of them last year. They stuck in our teeth and dear Mother yelled at him. It took her a long time to pick them out," Paul William told us. He was always hanging around my best buddy, Harry M. Redmond Jr., and in very much the same manner as I had encountered all these years; you sometimes ended up guilty by association when you hung around with Harry.

"Why, dear Father? Why? Are pumpkins in the Bible?" Heather Sarah was still digging, and even though she was in the backseat of the jeep, I could picture her staring at me with an intense gaze. "Fritzie and I need to know for sure!" She held up her stuffed doggie, Fritzie, who went everywhere with us, and pushed him into the back of my head.

Binky was chuckling now, and she leaned over and grabbed my hand, as she whispered, "On the spot dear Paul, oh thou, whose knowledge of the Bible runs so deep, huh?"

"I think I need some more time, kids. Let me think about it. Right now, we are here, so let's go pick out some nice pumpkins," I said, as I gently tapped my wife's hand in reassurance.

The arrival into the garden center parking lot saved me from any further impossible questions. We parked the jeep, the kids jumped out, and they were hopping about with excitement as they eagerly pleaded with us to hurry up to begin the search for the pumpkins.

I followed behind Binky and the children while they made their way towards rows upon rows of pumpkins set upon the ground and some wooden stands for display. There were many other shoppers and families doing the same since Halloween was just a few days away now.

It was a lovely autumn day, and the fresh clean air, set upon the backdrop of the colors in the trees, made for a wonderful setting for this type of event.

I had forgotten all about the hockey game now while we wandered in and amongst the rows of pumpkins. I watched my wife and children, as they studied every angle of the pumpkins and worked hard, to select the perfect ones they wanted for their Halloween fun.

A middle-aged man was working the garden center in the rows where Binky and the children had settled. He had spotted Binky and the children looking at the pumpkins and made his way towards them. I had bent down to study a few larger ones on the ground and my family had walked ahead of me when the man came over. I could tell by the look in his eyes and his face that he was coming over to assist Binky and the children, rather than the multitude of other shoppers, because my wife's beauty had caught his eye.

I saw his eyes go up and down on Binky as he studied my wife.

Binky was dressed in a form-fitting dress, which displayed her curves and female features in a conservative, but outstanding manner. Binky's figure was amazing, even after bearing two children and approaching middle age. She was a woman of rare and striking beauty, and she had caught this man's eye.

He hustled over as he said, "Well, hi there, pretty lady and youse kiddies. Shopping for the perfect pumpkin, I see," he smiled widely as Binky looked up at him.

Binky knew the drill.

I smiled, as I knew that the worker was about to meet

his match.

"Now sir, my children, and I are searching for the exact pumpkin for our Halloween celebration this year. Can you tell me if these are Connecticut Field Pumpkins, Big Max, or Magic Hybrids? My research this week indicated that all of those varieties, I have mentioned are the optimum varieties for carving and display," Binky finished and she zoomed in wide-eyed for his response. The children also zoomed in close with the same stare they had inherited from their mother and waited for the answer.

The worker's sudden eagerness to serve the beautiful woman in which he had spotted shopping for pumpkins had faded a bit, and he stopped and rubbed the top of his head.

"Well, lady . . . I do not really know. . .."

"You are employed here, and you do not know what type of products you sell or their origins?"

"Well, I ah can't say. Do you really research pumpkins, lady?"

All three of them, Binky, Heather, Sarah, and Paul William, stood in unison, and nodded their heads rapidly to indicate that was indeed the case. The poor worker was astounded, as he watched the nodding display, and his formerly bouncing hormones had now decided to go into full retreat mode.

I chuckled at how quickly Binky Henson neutralized the man and his ambitions to serve her.

Binky finally stopped nodding. She turned towards me and pointed, while she told the garden center worker, "Well, my husband will know. You see, he is very smart on a wide variety of subjects. I am sure that he will be able to pick out the best variety for our use."

The three of them started to nod once more as the worker looked up and saw me approaching. Now that he knew Binky was married, and she was, how should we say, "a bit of an educated shopper," and there was no "opportunity" here, he was off to plan his escape.

"I will go check for you, lady," he said, as off he quickly scampered.

"Ha! I see that you chased him off, dear Binky."

I reached over, put my arm around her as she smiled at me.

"He was most inefficient, twenty-seven. Now, do you see the perfect pumpkins? We are going to rely upon your knowledge and expertise here, you know. You will need to carve them, and show us all how it is done, while the children and I take notes."

Only Binky Henson could make Halloween pumpkin carving into a research project!

"I think that I have some in mind over here. You need the pumpkins to be round but have a flat bottom so they stand up and do not roll around. I also like to find ones that have a good-sized stem intact, so you can grab a hold of them and lift the top off easily to put the candles inside."

"Well, lead on, dear Paul. The afternoon is waning and we need to leave enough time to carve them all for our display before dark."

We wandered around a bit more, picked out three nice pumpkins as I explained the ins and outs of the world of pumpkins to Binky and the children.

We marked them all with each person's name with a small marker that Binky had in her purse, so we did not mix them up. I did not want to cause a dispute amongst the kiddies as to whose pumpkin may be whose! I remembered a few of those battles I had with my own sister.

My old man had taught me all too well.

I was surprised, when after we had picked out one pumpkin for the family, one for Heather Sarah, and one for Paul William, that my wife wandered into a row and she picked one out too.

She held it up, studied it, and she smiled.

I heard her say, "Perfect," under her breath.

"Twenty-seven, could you please get me one of those carts to carry all of these on? They are quite dirty, and I would rather not get my dress, hands, and nails dirty here."

I nodded and pulled a cart over. We placed all the pumpkins upon it and wheeled the load to a checkout register set up in the middle of the pumpkin display. Binky also grabbed some dried-out corn stalks that had caught her eye, and she thought they would look nice for the front of our porch for a nice autumn display. We paid for the merchandise and made our way back to the jeep.

The children were beside themselves with excitement as we loaded the pumpkins and cornstalks. They were asking a million questions, and I did my best to answer them all as patiently as I could.

As we drove away, I gave them each something to think about, "Now you two kiddies need to think about what types of faces that you would like me to carve on your pumpkins. Do you want scary, happy, sad, or just regular, old, jack-o'-lanterns?"

While the kids were pondering that for a moment, I asked Binky, "Say, what was the pumpkin that you picked out for, dear?"

She smiled and simply said, "Oh . . . it is mine. I wanted one too." Binky's answer was vague, which was rather unusual for her.

We arrived home, and Binky scooted into the house to bake some homemade chocolate chip cookies, a batch of my favorite peanut butter cookies, and to pour us each a glass of some apple cider, which she had bought during the week.

I set up a carving station on the picnic table in the yard and laid out some newspapers on top of the table for protection. We gathered the pumpkins together as Heather Sarah and Paul William told me what the faces should look like for each of their pumpkins.

"Fritzie and I want a happy pumpkin!" Heather Sarah instructed me.

"I want one who is scared, Father!" Paul told me as he even drew on a piece of paper what he wanted it to look like.

I drew the faces on the pumpkins with a crayon and once the children approved the designs, I went to work carving them up. Binky arrived with the snacks and as this wonderful autumn afternoon waned, I carved up the pumpkins.

Binky studied my every move, and she even took notes as to how I was carving the pumpkins. I explained, step-by-step, as I cut the top, scooped the pulp out onto the newspaper, and the kids ran away from the smell of it.

"YUCK! YUCK! YUCK!"

The two of them screamed as they ran away. Even Binky screwed her face up at the smell and appearance of the pumpkin pulp.

Paul William finally became brave enough to put his hand in the "mush" as he sorted out the seeds to give the baking idea another try.

"Paul William, ask your mother if you can get the strainer from the kitchen, and you can drop the seeds in there now, in order to make it easier to wash them off," I told our son. He nodded and once Binky approved; he ran off.

Binky smiled at me as I explained how Grandpa Henson had taught me to carve pumpkins so long ago. I could tell that my wife was enjoying this family time together. Soon enough, I completed carving the pumpkins, and I dare to say, I had done a very good job at the carving.

We all decided to make the family pumpkin, a traditional jack-o'-lantern, and it turned out rather nicely. I explained how carving the teeth inside of the mouth is always the most difficult part.

The pumpkins were perfect, and we set them on the

front porch, all together on the top step. Binky bundled her cornstalks. She tied them to a post on the porch, and we had a wonderful display on our family home for the holiday. I explained that we would find some candles to put inside and light them up tonight once it was dark. The children were thrilled, and I had to admit, it was a magical time.

We had shared a wonderful autumn afternoon together, and it certainly was a day in which I would never forget. I felt bad about my previous behavior, and I said a little prayer for forgiveness that I would have considered a hockey game to be more important than a day such as this one had been. Even Lutheran clergymen act as if we are knuckleheads, and on occasion, we need reminders as to God's plan for families.

"Come along, everyone. It is time to eat now. I have made some homemade pizza for us to enjoy," Binky waved us into the house as the display had now been finished.

"Be sure to wash your hands! Maybe later, we will cook the pumpkin seeds."

"Fritzie and I love pizza," Heather Sarah barreled into the house a million miles per hour screaming about pizza the entire way.

"Twenty-seven, do you want a Dingleberry beer or a Big Boulder beer with your pizza?"

"A Big Boulder, please dear Binky, those Dingleberries are way too sweet."

We ate, and it seemed unusual to me, but after we had finished dinner, Binky coaxed me to sit down in my easy chair. She suggested that I watch the news on television, and she was able to arouse my curiosity enough to find out who won the game today and see how Shambley had performed in the net. She told me that she did not need any help in the kitchen with the dishes and chased me away.

It almost seemed as if she wanted to get rid of me.

I heard some rustling in the kitchen, spotted Binky

gathering newspapers, while wearing an apron over the top of her dress, her long hair tied back, and she was wearing rubber gloves.

I almost got up out of my chair to see what she was doing, but the sports news came on, and I became lost in the telecast.

Paul William was now sitting on the floor watching the broadcast with me, and we both moaned and groaned as the announcer told us the Rovers had been plastered and lost the hockey game by the score of five goals to one. We were lost in the film clips and highlights of the game for quite a while.

Shambley was a bum!

"I bet he flopped all over the ice, dear Father!" Paul William told me.

"I think you're right, Paul William. He is a bum. Oh, how I wish I could get back in the net one more time! I would show them!"

Binky appeared with her coat and hat on, with Heather Sarah holding Fritzie and standing next to her. They were both dressed to go outside.

Binky told us, "Now, my dear Paul, no more talk of a comeback. Please, both of you will need to put your coats and hats on and meet us on the front porch. It is dark, and we shall see how wonderful our Halloween display is now. I have found some candles and while you two hockey pucks were proclaiming sad laments over Shambley's ineptness in the net today, Heather Sarah and I have lit the pumpkins. Now, come along. Come along, you two!"

Heather Sarah bounced along happily, and she yelled out into the cold night air, "You have to see! Happy Halloween!"

Paul William and I put our coats and hats on, and both of us followed Binky and Heather Sarah out the front door and down the steps. I could see the flickering of the lit pumpkins in the darkness, and we all stood in front of them on the front walkway to see how they looked. I could hear Heather Sarah giggling, and Binky waving at her to be quiet as we viewed them. They looked fantastic . . . one happy one, one scared one, the traditional jack-o'-lantern, and one more, all lined up on the front porch in order.

Wait!

One more?

Hello, what is this?

I smiled as Binky came over and put her arm through mine. Paul William and Heather Sarah laughed and giggled at the sight of the last pumpkin.

There on the porch was Binky's pumpkin, and it was lit up and carved with a large, "I LUV 27."

Binky looked up at me, while the lights from the candles flickered in the autumn night and reflected in her eyes, as she whispered, "And I mean it too. I hope you appreciate how hard it was for me to endure that yucky, mushy, stuff."

The kiddies moaned and groaned at first, as Binky and I started kissing, and then they giggled at our behavior.

Heather Sarah came over and she tugged at my pants as we were kissing and she said, "Dear Father, you never did answer my question, but now you do not have to. I now know why God made pumpkins."

We both looked down at her as she smiled and said, "So that Mommies could tell Daddies that they love them. I bet you now are going to say some words in Welsh that you think Paul William and I do not understand, but we know it means that you love each other. You then will put 'Dinky the Orange Teddy Bear' cartoon on the television for us, and you will giggle, and sneak upstairs to your bedroom, when you think Paul William and I are not watching."

I marveled at this little girl that our love and God's grace had given us. I scooped her up in my arms and kissed her, as I felt some very rare tears running down my cheeks.

"You know something, little girl, you are way too smart

for your age, so I am going to say to you all aloud here, Rwy'n dy garu di wastad ac am byth."

As Paul William arrived to hug us all together, Heather Sarah laughed and said, "We will love you forever too, dear Father."

We stood there hugging in the cold autumn air for a few minutes as the flickering candles cast a warm glow upon all of us.

Binky yelled out to the children, "Come along, it is now time to watch Dinky on the television, kids. We will blow the candles out for now. We can light them again tomorrow night."

She then turned towards me, fluffed her hair, and winked at me, as she whispered, "I would not want our daughter to be wrong, you know, twenty-seven."

As life marches on, we create memories in so many simple ways. I think we just have to open our hearts and minds to them and put them away for safekeeping. The best memories seem to come from the times when you least expected them to appear. Oftentimes, you do not have to shell out some large amounts of money, or travel off to some distant, far-off land, or plan some elaborate gatherings for you to create special memories.

In our lives, it is the simple times, the quiet times that mean the most. They embed in your mind forever more, now, and until the end of time.

Binky held out her hand for my hand. I grasped it, and we went back into the house.

I thought about how I was sure glad that I skipped that hockey game.

THE END

No Boiler Required

From "On the Edge of Memories
The Random Collection"

181 Belmont Avenue in Haledon, New Jersey. That was the address of what was a very old apartment building. Old; built in and around 1910 or thereabouts, constructed of red brick by artisans of a bygone era; sprawling, six floors, stacked side-by-side with long hallways, which echoed footsteps and whispers of the past and of the present.

A typical, inner-city building.

There was no elevator here. Shoe leather and stairs took you to where you needed to land. The building had a brick porch and a bluestone entrance stairway, which faced the busy city street, and it boasted concrete fresh air wells on each side of the building in order to ventilate the common areas of the building. The building had the typical metal fire escapes crisscrossing along the brick walls of each side of the building. Upon many of the landings of the metal fire escapes were folding chairs, charcoal grilles, hammocks tied between metal risers and even a few small tables. The metal monsters provided an escape route in the event of an emergency, but also a porch to sit upon, when the summer nights grew much too warm for comfort. At least sitting upon the fire escape brought some type of breeze.

The fire escapes rather strangely became places of solace, a lofty perch to look down upon the urban world, even a place to sleep when the heat inside of the apartment became unbearable.

An old boiler puffed steam from within a hidden lair in

the basement and it sent heat up through the old building, spitting and steaming inside of old cast-iron pipes. Occasionally, where the old pipes joined into each other, steam popped, spit, and drooled, a mixture of steam and condensed water out of the joints. The maintenance man packed the leaking joints of the old pipes with steel wool and coated them with a compound in an effort to minimize the steam's escape. The apartments were stifling in the summer and for the most part, despite the boiler and maintenance man's best efforts, freezing in the winter.

The superintendent, who was also the maintenance person and the boiler operator, did what he could, but old is old.

In the building's heyday, it was quite a handsome building.

The original owners of the apartment building were an Italian family, a husband and wife, and a daughter team. They lived in the first-floor apartment in the front of the building. The building's maintenance and appearance, as well as the comfort of their tenants, were paramount to the family. The pride that the family had in owning such a fine building was easily apparent. Never, in their wildest dreams, coming from the old country, would they have thought they could ever own such a grand building. Yet, years ago, hard work and dedication brought many golden rewards.

The family constructed an arbor on the side of the apartment building and planted grapes that sprawled and clung to the arbor. From those same grapes, they made homemade wine in the cellar of the apartment. A wine, they bottled in clear jugs and on summer afternoons and early evenings, the family, along with some local Italian tradesmen, such as stonemasons, and gardeners, would gather under the arbor and enjoy the fruits of their labor. The mother of the family planted rows of glorious rose shrubs along the sidewalk next to the apartment, and even though the shrubs faced a busy urban street, they presented a grand appearance. The fragrance of the rose shrubs enhanced the air between the smoke and exhaust of the many vehicles running up and down Belmont Avenue.

For many years, it was a showplace, a wonderful place to live. Then the Italian family grew older and when her parents passed away, the daughter decided to sell the apartment and move out of the old city. Off to the suburbs, where the noise of the busy city street did not reach their ears and the smoke of the exhausts of the many vehicles did not drift into your windows.

The new owner did not have much pride in the building, and as a result, he did not take as good a care of the old building as the Italian family did. Eventually, a lack of maintenance, combined with time and age, and it all caught up with the old building. It began to look worn, gritty, and old. No longer was it a showplace. Now it was humdrum, not rundown, but certainly no longer a showplace. Many things changed because nothing ever stays the same. In this life, the one thing that you can always count on is change. The new owners removed the grape vines and the arbor, in order to make more room for additional parking, and the rose shrubs were in the way of an entrance to the new driveway. No longer did the glorious scents of the roses mix in the summer breezes along the busy city street.

The scents passed away in time, as so many other things do. Yet, certain aspects of this world, and of our lives, linger forever.

Mr. Kent Lambert needed to reorganize his entire life. He needed a fresh start. The last few years had been difficult for him. To say the least. Very difficult. Kent was still very young, only forty, and he now felt as if he held on tightly to his dreams. Kent was not going to allow his dreams to escape. Now was the time to take control and redirect. Kent was sure that he was correct. On the heels of a short-lived, failed marriage, and then a bitter divorce, combined with two or three career changes, Kent felt as if his life crumbled beneath his feet. Yet, his parents taught him perseverance, and it was that lesson which carried him through the difficult times.

Kent was quiet, conservative, introverted, unassuming, and very much a man who kept to himself, and when he ventured out in the world, it was within a small circle of friends. Kent had a best boyhood friend, who he vaguely stayed in touch with, a friend who had married and moved from New Jersey a long time ago. Now, he just kept within a few friends at work. He had one friend from work that he would hang out with more than the others, but mostly, he was a loner. He was not the adventurous type and that fact might have helped to contribute to the failure of his marriage. His ex-wife sought adventure. She was extroverted, and she thought she could transform the handsome Kent Lambert into someone that he was not. Eventually, her sense of adventure caused her to look for adventures of a different type within the arms of another man.

Therefore, here Kent Lambert was regrouping and muddling through. Working a full-time job for a local supermarket as a manager in the produce department was not his idea of the ideal career. Yet, after trying his luck at sales and then a short-lived stint as an assistant manager of a restaurant, this new job had predictable hours, good healthcare benefits and while the pay was lower than his previous wages were, the work was steady. However, the major benefit of the supermarket position was that it allowed Kent some free time to attend a local community college to study what he felt as if was his true passion, which was writing. Yes, Kent Lambert was the oldest student in the class, but he did not mind.

It had some side benefits.

Kent did not look anywhere near forty years of age and since he was single and available, as well as a tall, handsome, well-spoken man, and once he opened up and became comfortable with a person, he had quite an engaging personality. Moving crates of heavy produce all day long, unloading trucks and performing physical labor, provided Kent with employment and a side benefit of an exercise program and his muscles were lean, strong, and powerful from the heavy lifting and physical labor. Despite his efforts at remaining unassuming, his classic good looks afforded Kent quite a gathering of young women, all giving him some attention and seeking his company. Kent had an occasional date or two, but right now, money was a huge issue for him, and he had little extra cash for wining and dining a young woman out on the town. Right now, he had to pay tuition, make rent, and pay his car note as well as a host of other expenses. Besides, a romantic relationship might get in the way of his plans while he pursued his passion and buckled down in his life. After all, forty is still very young, but so many things pass so quickly from us in this life.

Kent was ecstatic to find an apartment with a reasonable rent that was centrally located to both his school and his job. In fact, the supermarket where he worked was just up the avenue a few city blocks. While the location of the apartment might be perfect, it was not located in the greatest of neighborhoods. Kent did not mind because he grew up in the city and knew all too well the evils that existed here. This neighborhood was a rougher one than the neighborhood of his youth was, but Kent knew the ways of the city. He kept a low profile, remained very aware of his surroundings, and steered clear of all the trouble. For Kent Lambert, the apartment was perfect for a crash pad. He only had a small kitchen table, with one chair, his bed, and a small dresser, and in the bedroom, he set a black and white television upon an upturned cardboard box. He also had an old radio and his most prized possession, which was his typewriter. Kent bought it used for twenty dollars. It was a good one, and he felt lucky to have it for a reasonable price, even if his ex-wife scolded him for spending so much on what she deemed, "The pursuit of silly dreams."

That was all he took from his failed marriage and all he wanted. He did not want anything else; the bad memories and nightmares were enough.

The apartment house was an old building, and the apartment was stifling in the summer and freezing in the winter, but it had some advantages. It was on the main bus route for the city buses and from just a few steps away from the front door, you could find the bus stop, and above all, apartment number 602 had this wonderful fire escape.

One might question Kent as to why a fire escape in an old apartment building was so important to him. It seemed as if that would be an unusual item for a focal point for Kent.

Yet, the aspiring writer found the landing of the fire escape outside his apartment window to be the perfect, well, for lack of any other description, "escape." He found a small table in a local thrift store for five dollars and a folding chair, and armed with a piece of plywood to bridge the metal rails, he found the perfect writer's nook. A place to escape the heat of the apartment, yet a place to retreat to and a place of solitude to write in. For Kent, it was the perfect place to write. He set his typewriter up on the table and from five stories above the yakking of the busy city street; Kent Lambert recreated the world below him into his own fictional paradise.

Originally, Kent would write in his preferred genre of science fiction, or fantasy, and then as he typed away, he changed and grew bored with the tales of fantasy worlds. Instead, he began to write of the harsh realities of life, the ebbs and flows of ordinary human emotions, and gradually, stories of unrequited love crept into the pages of his work. In retrospect, Kent could say that the change in his genre was a direct result of the experiences of his own life, the breakup of his marriage, the shifts in his career and other realities. All of those factors might be true, but above all, Kent found that his writing of fantasy worlds provided him with entertainment, but it left him empty of emotional satisfaction. The best writing requires emotion and Kent ultimately found where he could uncover where his emotions were. The emotions came wrapped up in waves of reality and within the words of love, gone wrong.

At first, his professor at college judged his writing to be at a novice level, rudimentary, and then slowly, as the emotions infiltrated his words and Kent abandoned the tales of fantasy, his writing became more polished, and classic in nature.

Suddenly, his professor took notice, and he praised Kent's transformation and talents. All too soon, the semesters of school were over and Kent had more time to write, to be alone, and to be lost in his words.

On one of the first heat waves of summer, on a stifling night, after a hard day at work, Kent grabbed a cold beer out of his small refrigerator, slipped his typewriter out the kitchen window, set the writing machine upon the table on the metal deck and shortly thereafter, Kent took up his writing post on the fire escape. There he typed away, on his first actual attempt at composing a novel. At first, it was daunting, and then as he moved from the first words, to the first sentences, to finished paragraphs, Kent found it all quite easy to become lost in the world of words and most of all, lost in the waves of human emotions.

Julie Granatelli was, in her mind, just starting out. But in reality, this was a restart of sorts. Julie had just ended a long-term relationship with what she thought was the man of her dreams.

Actually, he broke off the relationship and shattered the dream.

A dream that ended abruptly and suddenly and it came to a grinding halt with what was for Julie's heart a less-than-ideal result. It all seemed, as it was a dream come true, they were high-school sweethearts; he had grown into such a handsome man, successful, from a solid family, and it looked as if they would cruise to a marriage proposal and a grand life together.

Many babies and a glorious family life. A dream.

Then, instead of a marriage proposal, came the dreaded speech, "I love you, but I am not sure that I am in love with you enough to spend my entire life with you. . .."

Recently, Julie heard he had a new love. He picked his life up very quickly, and now flaunted about town with some big-breasted, fancy woman from a wealthy family on his arm.

It all seemed as if it was one big lie.

Endless lies.

Julie grew weary of it all. Recently, Julie had lost her full-time job as a data entry clerk in a large pharmaceutical corporation, due to a work slowdown and what the corporate executives label, "reorganization." It was mindless work, but for Julie, it got her through until she could decide what her future was going to be. After all, she thought she would marry and live a happy life, perhaps two incomes, a small house, and a few children. That dream failed.

Now she was brokenhearted, unemployed and in need of a new direction in her life. Above all, in her heart, Julie sought a new life. A restart. While working full time, Julie attended school for a few evenings during the week and on Saturdays. Now, after a long grind of two years, some student loans, Julie graduated from a secretarial college, specializing in legal practices and legal administrative work. Julie's mailings of her resume, combined with placement experts at her school, finally caught the eye of a lawyer in downtown Paterson, New Jersey. A lawyer just beginning his practice and seeking an administrative assistant with which he could grow his practice, perhaps, even a person who would someday become a paralegal. It was a stretch for Julie. A small and inconspicuous town located in southern New Jersey was the town where she was born, and until now, was the only place that she had ever lived. Now, to venture up north to the Metro-New York City area, high crime, high prices, and all the things, which her family told Julie she needed to stay away from in her life.

"Oh my! Paterson! It is on the news all the time. Robberies, shootings, murders, on every street corner. It is full of gangsters and organized crime."

It was all so foreboding.

Yet, the lure was too great. In Julie's heart, it was exactly the restart that she was seeking. After all, a torn heart required some type of repair.

After an intimidating journey to the city, a sit-down interview and much discussion, Julie accepted the attorney's generous offer, and she made the fateful decision to relocate to northern New Jersey. The salary was very generous, and it was much more than she could ever imagine earning in the limited opportunities of southern New Jersey, where the large pharmaceutical corporation was the only major employer in town. A corporation where they did not rehire, they only reorganized.

Julie felt as if she had found it all. The lost city of El Dorado, the Isle of Avalon! A golden sunset on the horizon of despair.

Julie packed a single suitcase with her belongings, along with her tears, mixed with some painful memories; she caught a bus in Atlantic City and headed north. Despite her joy at a restart, her leaving town and her family still caused her a great deal of pain. The goodbyes left a rainstorm of tears behind her. Julie tried to remain positive, but she also realized there were no rainbows on the end of this rain of tears, only a lonely trail of pain. Pain over lost love can make you flee to the farthest ends of the Earth in order to escape the hurt and the tears. Julie hoped the other end of this journey was where she would find the rainbow.

Julie was the only child from a mixed-family of sorts. Her mom was Jewish and her father was Italian. Taught from when she was a young child, both the Catholic and Jewish faiths, Julie felt as if she had a unique and interesting family life, and while the family was not overly religious, Julie and her parents had their moments. With her mixed heritage, Julie had dark features and captivating dark black eyes. Julie was very cute, petite, a nice, slim figure, yet now she was full of self-doubts. She always felt her teeth were too crooked and a little brown along the edges; her hair was thin and unmanageable, her nose was too long, her breasts were too small and as of late, her mind wandered with self-doubts that her abilities at making love to please a man were lacking and inadequate. Maybe that is why he left her? Perhaps she was a terrible lover. She only had ever intimately been with one man, and he left her. It all came together to fill the young woman with self-doubts and thoughts at her own inadequacies.

When she reached the big city, reality set in and there was the stark, cold cost of rent and other expenses.

Suddenly, that high salary and all the lofty aspirations of such evaporated right in front of her eyes. It was very expensive to live here. Pounding the pavement in search of an affordable apartment eventually led her to the front porch of 181 Belmont Avenue in Haledon, New Jersey. To the place where the rose shrubs once provided fragrance and to the place where the grape arbor once stood. Now, all that remained of the past glory of the fragrance and the joy of the grape arbor was a parking lot.

If you listened very closely, you could hear the ghosts of the past. Perhaps some remnants of spoken Italian language filled the air and mixed with laughter where the arbor once stood?

Perhaps.

Every place within God's great creation has a story to tell. Some are sad, some are glorious, but there are always stories to tell.

All of this was a world away from where she came from. The whispers of the high crime and a bad neighborhood lingered, yet it was on the bus line and it was the best deal in town. Besides, the superintendent and his wife, who lived in the first-floor apartment, both seemed so pleasant. How bad could it be? They watched everything, and she had triple deadbolts on her door. In her mind, it was the perfect place for a restart.

Yes indeed, every place has a story to tell.

Mrs. and Mrs. Aviv Finkelstein lived in the first-floor apartment of 181 Belmont Avenue. Mr. Finkelstein worked as the superintendent of the apartment building. In his role as the "super," he served in many capacities. He was the gardener, the security officer, boiler operator and maintenance man. In many ways, his wife told him he also was the rabbi to the residents. His wife laughed and enjoyed when her husband would provide life advice and coaching on issues to all the tenants of the apartment. No doubt, he was a very wise man, and he willingly shared his wisdom with everyone. For the most part, Mr. Finkelstein enjoyed the job; he fought the battles that old buildings can wage upon a maintenance man, with an assortment of leaky pipes, roof drips, clogged waste lines, and electrical issues. There was not too much the wily Mr. Finkelstein could not fix. He was a very handy man and his diverse skills were an asset, because the building was not exactly new. But overall, other than kick-starting the temperamental boiler on bitter cold nights when the fire eye gave out, prying the rent out of Mr. Lansford on the third floor, chasing away street thugs and hoodlums, and dealing with the incredibly cheap owner of the building, who was also his boss, it was not a bad job.

He also could do without the Friday night celebrations of Zale McAlister and his visiting hippie friends. Their music selections wore a little thin on Aviv's nerves. Aviv loved all kinds of music, mostly big band music that the Finkelsteins would play on an old record player and dance in their living room occasionally. Yes, music was grand, but blaring rock-and-roll mixed with the pungent scents of cannabis, and complaints from all the other tenants, just did not make for fun nights. Zale was a deliveryman by day and an aspiring musician by night, and in the big picture of the apartment house tapestry, Zale and his friends were harmless. He rather enjoyed them and surprisingly, the two of them shared many interesting discussions. It was just those Friday night gatherings, combined with their music, were a pain in the ass.

The neighborhood was a bit rough, and as of late, it seemed to be turning for the worse, but the location was ideal. Mr. Finkelstein grew up in the old city, knew the evil ways of the streets and he kept a baseball bat handy, right inside his front door. In his day, the little man played a mean third base and he could really swing a baseball bat. He wanted to believe that if he had to that he could still do it.

The Finkelsteins could easily walk to the temple for Jewish worship services and other events. It was on the main bus line to downtown, and the rent was next to nothing in exchange for his services. Mrs. Finkelstein still worked as a seamstress in a garment shop in downtown Paterson. Therefore, there were additional monies earned in the household. Besides, Aviv had retired after working for over thirty years, as the head maintenance man for a production garment factory in the city, and he had a small pension to collect upon as a reward for his many years in the factory. The Finkelsteins were by no means wealthy, but they were comfortable as far as finances go and that meant a great deal to them. He was from an era when Paterson, New Jersey, was the kingpin in the silk and lace trades. Now, that was a bygone time. All the factories closed and moved production overseas. The couple raised one daughter, a daughter who married a successful real estate developer and who now lives in Florida. Recently, the family blessed them with a grandson.

Eventually, when retirement finally came along, they could collect his pension, obtain a little monthly trickle from the government and live off some savings they banked a few years ago, from the sale of their home. Yes, every job has its ups and downs, but for now, this was the perfect job to cruise with for a few more years until they both retired. Florida would be the final landing spot for the couple. Somewhere near their daughter and her family. Somewhere near Tampa.

"So, Miss Granatelli, you have a new job? With an attorney. Downtown?"

"Yes, to all three of your questions, Mr. Finkelstein. It is a new practice, just starting up. Mostly real estate law. Irving Schecter E.S.Q. Mr. Schecter is very young."

Aviv smiled, and he turned the key in the lock to apartment number 402. While the door creaked open, Aviv commented, "Please call me, Ave. Everyone does. Schecter, huh? Sounds like a good Jewish boy. Very nice."

"Yes, I do think he is Jewish. I am half-Jewish, Mr. Finkelstein . . . I mean, sorry, Ave."

The little man smiled once again, this time widely, and he handed the apartment keys to Julie while pointing at the front door with his other hand.

"I need to oil those hinges. Give me a few minutes to get the oilcan from my workshop in the cellar and I will be back. I knew that I liked you and that you were beautiful for a reason. Half-Jewish is quite good! Whole is better . . . but half works too. Let me guess, your mother is Jewish."

Julie took the keys from Aviv and laughed at his correct guess.

"Why yes, you are correct. My mother is Jewish. My father is Italian. How did you know?"

"Partly because of your last name, but mostly, because you are beautiful, and all Jewish women are beautiful. Inside and outside, too. Therefore, your mother must be beautiful. Fathers, not so much. Look at me, but Mrs. Ave . . . she is gorgeous and so is our daughter!"

"You are very kind, but I am not so beautiful."

"You are, and let's not argue the point. I can see some sadness in your heart. Mrs. Ave tells me that I am the rabbi of this building. Maybe I am, but whatever you ran away from, it was not to be. Your future would not allow it. Better things lie ahead. I know these things. I have lived a long life and seen much. Most likely, it was a young man that you left behind you. A foolish man, who does not understand the prize he lost. Someday he will. So be it. You need an older man, you are too mature for the folly of young men who cannot see past their, well, you know where I mean. Listen to your rabbi."

The little man quickly changed the subject, and he pointed to the outside wall and explained, "You are going to need some fans in here. It is the middle of June and the apartment faces into the west. The brick holds the heat like an oven does. So, listen to your rabbi and buy some fans." Mr. Finkelstein was quite demonstrative in his instructions and while he spoke, he waved his hands in the air to display the motions of many fans.

"Okay, you get it. So much for that, now you really need to listen to Ave here. Always flip the deadbolts, my dear Julie. Always. I run a tight ship here. You are a young, single, very attractive woman in the midst of a neighborhood in which you do not know yet what it can be. The tenants are for the most part, good. We do have the hippies but they are harmless. Just fun guys who smoke too much weed and drink too much beer while strumming their guitars. We also have the Lopez family on the third floor, who drink a little too much Sangria wine and dance the salsa to loud Spanish music. All of them are fun. Loud and annoying, but fun. Friday nights around here can be loud and wild."

The little man smiled as his mind must have flickered with the thoughts of Friday nights in the old building. It was plain to see that he enjoyed them.

Off he went, explaining more, "You soon will know

what everyone's favorite foods are. The hallways are samples of cuisines. Across the street, in the big green house, is the Henson family. Exceptionally, good people. They have been here forever, icons of the neighborhood. I assure you that no one dares to mess with the Hensons. If you ever are in trouble, remember they are friends. The street people, not so good. Remember, Ave always knocks three times, waits, then two knocks. I also announce that it is Ave. Always. Remember the code. If it is ever different, do not open the door, even if you look through the peeper glass and it is me in the hallway."

Julie nodded and smiled while thanking Aviv. The superintendent waved, promised to be back with the oilcan and left. Julie closed the door behind him and flipped the deadbolts.

All three of them.

When Aviv returned to oil the door hinges, he used the code. Julie quickly came to realize that Aviv Finkelstein was very true to his word. The superintendent ran a tight ship; he looked after Julie very carefully and became quite protective of the young woman. Aviv Finkelstein was a very kind man and Mrs. Finkelstein was correct. He was many things, but one of his jobs was to be the rabbi of 181 Belmont Avenue.

That job might be the most important one of them all.

It was a Friday night in June. Kent Lambert just finished a long shift at the Foodworld supermarket on the corner of Belmont Avenue and John Street. Kent did his boss a favor and covered two shifts for him, and as a result, his boss tossed him some freebies. He received a gallon of milk, some canned goods from the dent shelf and a large pack of chop meat. Usually, Kent worked Saturdays to Wednesdays, and he had off Thursdays and Fridays. In Kent's mind, the extra day was no big deal. Kent did not mind the extra work; the free items were a nice touch. He did not eat much, was a very poor cook, but he could make a meatloaf and it would last him for three meals. Kent stopped off at Trio Liquors on the corner of Cook and Belmont, bought a six-pack of cold Big Boulder beer and headed off for what he felt was going to be a productive and amazing weekend of writing bliss.

When you could allow your soul to venture into a world of words, entertainment was cheap, and it was very easy. From your own mind to your fingertips, everything is available to you. Endless romance and boundless love with gorgeous women, adventures in far-off lands, being a Wild West hero riding the range and saving towns from the bad guys, and even riding to the moon in a spaceship.

Voyages of the soul.

It was all so easy. When Kent arrived at the front entrance of 181 Belmont Avenue, he waved to the young Henson teenager, who was sitting upon the front steps of the big green house across the street. The young man appeared to be an avid reader. He sat there very often, reading what seemed to be an endless array of books.

Kent made a note that someday he needed to stop and

compare notes with the young man.

With the heat of the day, the windows were all open in the apartments and even with some road noises from the busy street; you could hear the big band music playing from the Finkelstein's apartment, a quick glance through the windows and you could see them dancing together in their living room. Even after many years of marriage, the couple was still very much in love.

High above his head, Kent could hear Spanish horns and guitars from the Spanish music playing from the Lopez's apartment. Upon hearing the telltale taps of their feet upon the apartment's floor, he knew they were dancing the salsa. Kent glanced at his watch. It was still a little early, but soon, the jam session of rock-and-roll would begin from Zale and his band mates.

The apartment house was a cornucopia of different music and cultures. It was as if you tuned across a radio dial.

Up the front steps, down the main hallway, and up the staircase, all the way to the very top. Kent always kept his eyes open and was aware of the stairways.

Sometimes evil lurked there.

A quick spin of the key; he placed the food into the refrigerator, and the beer into a bucket filled with ice. It was stifling hot in apartment number 602. Kent's apartment faced west and the sun beat upon the old brick sides of the building for a large part of the day. These apartments were, for the most part, all the same. Plaster walls with spider web cracks running in many directions, woodwork with too many coats of paint to count, old cast iron radiators tucked against walls as if they were silent soldiers of heat, wooden windows with glass that was anything but clear. No amount of cleaning and washing would restore the view. A white porcelain, claw-footed bathtub stood proudly in the bathroom, paired with an old brass faucet that spit out the water as if it were an uncontrolled roof and gutter downspout in the aftermath of a thunderstorm. The apartments had a small kitchen, an open living room and dining room combination, a bathroom off the hallway, and one small bedroom. If there were six hundred square feet here, then that would be an exaggeration and a roundup figure of the actual footprint. Kent heard that the super's apartment was larger; in fact, he heard that it even had two bathrooms.

Yet, Kent knew that the fire escape off the bedroom window provided just what he needed.

A breeze.

A breeze that would lift him off on a voyage of the soul. Six stories up in the air, on a metal fire escape, there was a glorious breeze. Yes, it mixed with some smoke, haze and exhaust from the city street below, but it also had a marvelous view of a hot summer's day sunset. A sun sinking low over the old mills and factories and the edges of the Preakness Mountains, which peaked off to the west on the outskirts of the city limits. It was not all grit and crime; even here, within the midst of a maze of buildings and congestion, there was some beauty. Kent stripped his work uniform off. He pulled on a pair of shorts, and his chest remained bare. When it was this hot, it was not worth it and since he was six-stories up in the air; no one would see him, anyway. He opened the bedroom window; he took his precious typewriter and set it out on the small table on his fire escape. Next, he took the bucket filled with ice and beer and set that out on the metal deck of the fire escape. Soon, he was at his writing post, while a hot, yet somehow glorious, summer breeze blew across his skin.

There, he typed,

"Chapter One, Put Your Hand in Mine. The snow was deep, and it was wet enough to build a fantastic snowman. Early in the morning, before anyone rose, while the snow still lay undisturbed and unblemished, he went to work. Right outside her apartment window, he rolled the first balls of the body of the snowman. Then another, and another, and finally, he rolled a snowman's head. A quick dash into the apartment for a hat, a trip to the cellar to the coal burner for the boiler, yielded some pieces of coal for the eyes and then the finishing touches, some sticks cut from the remnants of old rose shrubs for the snowman's arms. He even picked strategic sticks, which resembled hands at the end of the arms. Then, he worked hard and built a duplicate snow woman right next to his snowman. The same stacked snowballs again, but this time, he placed a woman's scarf around the snow woman's neck and a woman's hat on the head. Strategic sticks allowed the two, snow people to hold hands.

Now, the ultimate romantic touch, he pulled from his coat pocket, the red paper heart that last evening, he cut out of red construction paper, and now, he carefully pressed it into the snow of the snowman, right in the spot where his heart would be. When he returned to the apartment, he gently and silently slipped the note under her apartment's door, a note which asked her when she woke up to look out her bedroom window. Actually, he phrased and laced the instructions with some additional love."

Two floors down, in apartment number 402, Julie Granatelli tried in vain to cool her apartment down. She thought, goodness gracious. The heat of the city lingers. By now, along the Jersey shoreline, the ocean breezes would be cooling the air down and a glorious sunset would mean relief from the heat of the day was now on the way. Now, well, Julie was a long way from her hometown.

Window fans and floor fans all felt as if all they did was to move some hot air around. They pushed hot air all over the rooms, but did little more than just push hot air. Until the sunset arrived and the outside air cooled down a little, the fans were futile. Mr. Finkelstein was correct; the western exposure was just as if it were a brick oven.

Julie thought that she would move the window fan from the living room window into the bedroom and that way, when the night air did cool, she could circulate the cooler air in her bedroom in hopes that she could sleep a little. Julie made her way into the bedroom and, while opening the window to place her window fan in the frame, she heard the rattle and tap of what she thought to be a typewriter. Leaving the fan on the floor of the bedroom, Julie pushed the wooden frame of the window open a little more, lifted the window screen, and studied the fire escape. She stuck her head out and looked the metal monster up and down. Sure enough, when she looked up, she noticed a man sitting on a stool, on a piece of wood, that was bridging the metal landing of the grates, and he appeared to be typing away on a typewriter sitting on a table.

"How strange," Julie thought aloud.

Although, it was difficult to tell from two stories below, and while looking up, it appeared as if the man was in a pair of shorts and was bare-chested. Julie also noticed how there was such a gentle breeze out on the landing, and the view of the sunset was quite spectacular. It seemed as if the man working above her head had made a fine choice to escape the heat of the apartment and to enjoy the view. She also could not help but notice, albeit briefly, and from an upside-down point of view that the man on the fire escape two floors above her had a nice build and appeared to be quite handsome. From her very quick glimpse and observation, Julie noticed that there was not an ounce of fat on his lean and trim body. With a large and spontaneous smile on her face, Julie tucked back into the bedroom and stood there, thinking. Thinking, within a very hot bedroom. She put her hands upon her hips, thought about how she disliked heights and then leaned back out the window and gazed down.

With a thought and a vision of her brief glimpse of the bare-chested man sitting on the fire escape above her, she spoke a thought aloud, "It is not too high, and this apartment is hotter than twenty-seven Hells are."

Off Julie ran to the kitchen. She pulled a bottle of wine out of the refrigerator, took a wine glass, poured a tall glass of wine and off she returned to the bedroom window. On the way, she grabbed a handful of magazines, a small battery-powered transistor radio, and made her way to the window. First, she set the magazines and radio out on the metal deck of the escape, then she carefully placed the wine atop the magazines. Julie took a deep breath, ran in her mind with a few further attempts at convincing thoughts that the fire escape was not too high, and with the courage of curiosity, Julie climbed out on the deck of the fire escape. Once she cleared the window, Julie sat down as quickly as she could, with a death grip on the metal rails surrounding her. Once Julie garnered some strength over the fear of being four stories in the air, she managed to look around . . . not down . . . but around.

A gentle summer breeze drifted across her skin and the air seemed suddenly to be somewhat refreshing as the heat of the day slowly drifted away. The sunset was glorious, fabulous beauty set within a cityscape of old mills and factories as the sun licked the horizon of the mountains on the outskirts of the city.

Julie's travels and now living in the northern section of her home state provided her with a new sense of how distinctive New Jersey was. Until now, Julie had no idea of what New Jersey was actually like. It was quite amazing that northern New Jersey was so diverse, old cities, worn-out streets, yet mountains, green fields, gardens, rivers, pristine lakes, and just a little farther south from here, are endless miles of gorgeous beaches and coastline. New Jersey was certainly a unique and marvelous place. It was not only the winding asphalt of the turnpike and parkway. The serene sunset helped Julie's fear and spirit to calm, and while she admired the breathtaking colors that the heat of the day created within the rays of the sun, Julie relaxed her death grip and reached for her wine. First, a long sip of the wine and then armed with a relaxed spirit, Julie managed to lift her eyes up above her and she tried to catch a covert glimpse of the man sitting two stories above her.

Julie could easily hear the rattle and the tap of the typewriter keys, even above the noise of the city streets clamoring below her. Whatever it was that he was typing, he did so very intently!

The angles were not the best for her line of sight. It appeared as if the man sat upon a piece of wood, which he used to bridge the metal grates of the deck of the fire escape, and he placed his table with the typewriter and his chair upon the wood. If Julie tilted her head a bit and leaned her body out just a little, she could see that a metal pail with the necks of beer bottles sticking out of it sat next to the man. Julie leaned back on the metal rail and took a sip of her wine. She did not want to risk the man looking down and catching her looking up, but she did so with a coy smile. It seemed so cute to see the man sitting out on the deck, a pail of cold refreshment at his feet, enjoying the sunset and the breeze while working on something quite intently.

How had she not seen him before this? He did not ride the bus in the morning, Julie never passed him in the hallways, nor did she ever see him on the streets or even in the most frequent meeting place for all the residents of the apartment building, which is in front of the trash chutes. Did he just move in? Julie now was intrigued.

A few more sips of liquid courage brought some more relaxation to Julie, and she gathered some courage to lean out and steal another glimpse of the scene above her head. He was indeed quite handsome, dark features, thick black hair that he wore a little on the longish side, which, despite the breeze at six stories in the air, remained well groomed. He tapped away on the keys of the typewriter, not lifting his eyes, but pausing on occasion in order to reach down and take a sip of beer from one of the bottles stuck in the ice bucket. When he did so, Julie admired how his arms and chest muscles moved and rippled a little. Even sitting down, Julie could tell that he was tall, his legs were long and his chest and arms were lean and strong, and with a deep breath, Julie thought, very sexy too.

On the horizon, the sun dipped even lower, and the night stole the remaining light away. But for Julie, the scenery remained captivating. Whenever the man moved from his work post, Julie moved too. She did not want to be seen staring at him, so when he leaned in for a sip of beer, Julie sat back on the railing of the fire escape. The young woman smiled as she realized that she did not need the magazines, or the radio for entertainment, Julie instead, sipped the wine and thought how she loved her new job, and despite the grit of the neighborhood and the atrocious heat, she loved her little apartment and now, well, her horizon brightened considerably.

As darkness started to fall, Kent knew that he had precious little light remaining. At six stories in the air, the summer breeze still felt glorious, but despite the atmosphere, and a little inspiration from the beer running through his veins, Kent felt as if the storyline he had just worked on for the last hour or so, went nowhere. He leaned back on the railing, studied the words and the paragraphs he wrote and after rereading his words, he angrily tore the paper out of the typewriter, crumbled it up in his hands, and tossed it unceremoniously upon the deck of the fire escape.

He took a fresh piece of paper and loaded it into the typewriter, while mumbling, "Too quaint. Too romantic and very stupid. If someone loves a person, they should just tell 'em so. Building snow people to send a message. I need something more direct, a little edgier. Everything that I just wrote. It really sucks."

And off he started to type once again,

"There was a knock at the door and he glanced at his watch to take note of the lateness of the hour. He was not expecting anyone, and he was puzzled as to who could be visiting him. He pushed the off button on the remote control to shut off the television. It had to be his best friend, Roy stopping by. No one else would do so, and besides, it was not as if he had many friends. If it was his best friend that was stopping by for an unannounced late-night visit, he did not want to have to explain the bouquet of roses sitting on the kitchen table. While a slightly harder and more forceful knock sounded at the door, Kent pondered what he would tell Roy of his failed plan of courtship. After all, the stupid planning failed, and she virtually ignored him. Being slightly embarrassed at buying the roses and failing in his plan of asking her for a date, and not even having the courage to give the roses to her, he scrambled off to the kitchen, picked them off the kitchen table and slipped the bouquet into a cupboard."

Kent finished typing. Once more, he leaned back and read very carefully what he just composed, and once again, his frustration at his composition induced a similar reaction.

"Too contrite. More of this nonsensical drivel. I guess tonight is just not my night for creativity. Why not just give her the flowers?"

Once more, another crumbled paper ended up on the metal deck of the fire escape.

Magical things float within the summer's breezes.

Unbeknownst to Kent, the crumbled papers at his feet lifted in the gentle breeze and carried in the air. A twist of the breeze and turn of the wind currents carried the papers along until they floated in the air toward the fire escape outside the bedroom window of apartment number 402. There, they drifted and landed onto the metal deck where Julie sipped her wine and admired the last fading glimpse of the sunset. It was as if the papers were silent messengers of a magical allure.

Is fate real? Does it actually exist? Is everything predetermined and was the twist of the wind that caused the crumbled papers to float upon Julie's lap a breeze sent from another place? The wind could have moved in another direction and blown the papers away forever, to be lost in the maze of the city. Instead, fate intervened.

Julie reached out and captured the wayward papers in her hands and immediately she realized from where they came. She knew they were failed efforts of literary ventures from the handsome man who worked above her. The papers afforded Julie a propitious glimpse into what it was that he was working on up there. Rather anxiously, she opened the crumbled papers to read them. Her heart pounded, and her mind raced with thoughts. Perhaps they were technical papers or reports required for his job, or maybe he wrote a sports column, or travel brochures, or something else?

A million different ideas.

In the fading light, Julie anxiously read the few heartfelt paragraphs about the snow people and about the demonstration of love, which the character created. The handsome young man was writing fiction, and he was writing about romance! He was a writer! Furthermore, Julie could not understand why he rejected these thoughts. There were no typographical errors, and the compositions were, in her opinion, wonderful. What caused the rejection of what was in her mind, two wonderfully romantic scenes? Flowers, hearts, and a touching display of love and romance. Why did the character want to hide the bouquet of flowers from his friend? Is this character shy, insecure, introverted? Julie tried hard to piece together the two sections of the story and to figure out what it was that the handsome writer was working on in his unusual, but exclusive, writing nook.

As the sun finally dipped and disappeared below the horizon and Julie finished reading the papers, she could not help but to smile. Fate had delivered love, which escaped while on a voyage from a soul.

It floated and danced gracefully in the air and miraculously landed in her lap.

As the summer waned, Julie would often sit out on the fire escape, covertly watch, and listen as the handsome writer feverishly worked above her head. Fate did not allow any additional glimpses of what it was that he was working on up there, yet Julie had a pretty good idea.

Julie approached the superintendent one early autumn afternoon as Aviv swept down the sidewalk in front of the apartment building. Julie had finished work, and she just stepped off the bus. Despite her best efforts to cross paths with the man in apartment in number 602, he remained elusive.

Julie asked, "Ave, I must ask, there is a man. He lives on the sixth floor, two apartments above me and well, I was wondering. . .."

Aviv smiled, stopped sweeping, and before Julie could even finish her question, the superintendent answered, "Kent Lambert. He works in the Foodworld supermarket on the corner up the road here and he attends a junior college at night. Studying writing. He writes books or tries to write books. He is single. I think he mentioned that he is divorced. Regardless, he is a very nice young man. Quiet, very much keeps to himself. Pays his rent two days ahead of time. Here and there a friend of his from work comes by, some guy named Roy. They drink beer and play card games together. He is older than you are, but he will be a perfect catch for you. Love knows no silly boundaries such as age. It means nothing. He is not Jewish, half or otherwise, but my dear Julie, as you know, we cannot all be perfect."

Julie laughed and smiled, and now, in a bit of posturing, she stood with her hands on her hips.

After sharing a good laugh with the superintendent, Julie playfully reprimanded Aviv, "That is not what I wanted to know. I thank you for the information and the attempt at matchmaking, but you jumped to conclusions before I could even ask my question."

Aviv returned to his sweeping and gently shook his head while commenting, "So, what else is there for a gorgeous young woman to know about a handsome young man?"

"If you would allow me to ask, then this would be so much easier."

"Then, speak and ask."

Julie felt the superintendent had indeed missed his calling and he should have officially become a rabbi.

In a roundabout confession of sorts, Julie asked the question that she fully intended originally to ask as a covert cover-up for her ulterior motives. In her heart, because of his wisdom, she knew that Aviv knew of her attraction already, but at this point Julie chose to stay with her original plan.

"He sits on the fire escape outside his bedroom window and types his books. I guess that you allow it. That is what I wanted to know. If it is allowed or not? You know, sitting on the fire escape. I think that you would have stopped it by now if it was not allowed."

Aviv stopped sweeping again, and this time he propped the broom up under his shoulder and rested upon it. The superintendent very much tended to his flock of tenants in such a caring manner.

He gently smiled and spoke in a soft and caring voice, "Technically, no, it is not allowed. Neither is cooking out on the metal monsters, nor sleeping out there when the apartments are sweltering steam baths, or sitting on the deck, sipping wine and carefully watching a handsome man working on his literary masterpiece without being caught staring."

Julie could not help herself. She rushed in and gave Aviv a warm hug and embrace as the two of them laughed.

"I love you, Ave. You are my second father away from home and you *are* my rabbi."

"Oh my, do not let Mrs. Ave see us making whoopee out here! She will be jealous, but I do love you too and if you want to catch him, be out here early, say, around five in the morning. He leaves for work very early and returns early in the afternoon. That is why you do not ever pass by him. He has to be at work very early to unload the early produce trucks. Set your alarm, be out here early and I assure you that you will catch him."

The embrace ended and Aviv picked his sweeping back up, and then suddenly stopped. He tucked his broom under his arm and made a muscle with his one arm while playfully smiling and joking. For a brief second, Julie was puzzled as to Aviv's actions, and then when she realized what he was doing, she smiled in slight embarrassment.

"You have admired Mr. Lambert's muscles and sexiness. I will tell you that, when I retire and relax in Florida every day, instead of sweeping this dirty sidewalk, I hope to read one of his books. Something tells me the young man is brilliant, and he is constructing a great pile of material that will one day make him very famous. Until then, he unloads trucks and works very hard. I also will tell you what you already know – that the unloading of those trucks gives the young man those big muscles."

That evening, before retiring for the night, Julie set her alarm clock for three in the morning.

The morning was cold and crisp, and while there was just a slight sense of apprehension at venturing out on the city streets in the front of the apartment at such an early hour, Julie spotted the light glowing in the first-floor apartment of Aviv Finkelstein. She could also see in the driveway of the home across the street that Mr. Henson was already warming up his old car in the driveway to prepare to go off to work. Even at this hour, there were people around. In her heart, she knew the rabbi of 181 Belmont Avenue was up early watching and anticipating that his information would come into play today. Julie was in luck and she had timed her early rising perfectly. The front door to the apartment opened while Julie fiddled with her purse, searching for her bus tokens. Her plan was to go into the office and take advantage of the extra early start to catch up on work.

Early rising had some extra benefits. Even if they were carefully planned ahead of time.

Julie turned around when she heard the door open and finally, there he stood in front of her. Tall, lean, and yes, close up, he was even more handsome than she ever imagined. How could they live so close to each other for so long and not meet until now? It was worth the wait. His dark eyes glowed in the city streetlights and his smile immediately melted her heart.

"Hello. Good morning," Julie squeaked as he smiled at her and passed by. He was wearing a light jacket to offset a bit of the autumn morning's chill, so admiring his build was not to be. She wore a dress covered with a heavy sweater. She almost wished that she had opened the sweater to display just a bit of her figure, but she had buttoned it up to break the chill. In her mind, Julie thought, her breasts were not much, but right for now, they were all she had to go with. That and her smile. Since her smile and her gentle breasts were what she had, Julie went with them. She casually unbuttoned her sweater just a bit.

"Hello. Yes, good morning," Kent Lambert greeted Julie and then he stopped and stood in front of her. He seemed to be searching for words beyond the simple greeting. Words that would not come, spoken words that did not arrive easily for the fledgling writer. Within written words was where he comfortably hid. On top of his outward shyness and struggle with words, it was as if he was a bit startled to meet someone at this early of an hour on the front stoop of 181 Belmont Avenue.

In actuality, in Kent's mind, he thought, 'What a meeting that it was!'

Julie stopped fiddling with her purse. He seemed so shy and slightly introverted, yet strong, vulnerable and so very sexy, too.

Julie reached out her hand and took full advantage of the covertly planned meeting by introducing herself, "Hi, I am Julie Granatelli. I live in apartment 402. Have to go to work a little earlier than usual today. I work downtown."

Julie carefully watched while his eyes wandered, first off to the city street and then to the street lights, and finally over to the Henson's driveway, where Mr. Henson's old car stood as if it were a silent warrior waiting to go into battle, while it was warming up.

She thought about how making eye contact was not his strong point. For some reason, for such a handsome man, he decidedly lacked confidence in his own presence.

"Oh yes, downtown."

While he spoke, his wandering eyes finally locked on her face. Julie never allowed her eyes to leave his. This was her chance.

"Kent Lambert." His gentle grasp felt very warm, especially so on a cold morning as he gently held her hand and melted her heart.

Kent explained, "Well, I am lucky. Only have to walk two blocks up Belmont Avenue here to go to work at the supermarket. I work at the Foodworld as a produce manager. It is not my dream choice of careers, but it pays the bills while I go to school. Say, it was my pleasure to meet you, Julie. I have to be off. Cannot be late. There are trucks waiting to be unloaded. By the way, I live in apartment number 602. How funny, I live two floors above you and we never met until now. I will see you around. Maybe soon. I hope we can meet soon. Please, have a nice day."

Now, it was Julie's turn to become lost in words, as she fumbled and stumbled and managed to eke out a weak, "You too. It has been my pleasure to meet you, too. I too, hope to see you around."

He waved, and he was off into the early morning light. Julie sighed, and her heart melted while she admired the view as he walked away. Tight fitting dungarees and oh my, his walk did not lack the confidence that his mind, and to a certain extent, that his words did too. How she wished that she would have revealed more of what it was that she knew and that she was aware of what he was working on, but in her mind, she knew that it was not the appropriate time to do so.

Recalling the papers that she held in her purse and she kept close to her at all times, Julie had another idea.

A better idea. Julie could write a little too. She did rather well in English Literature, creative writing, and in compositions in high school and in college, and felt as if writing a little was not out of her circle of talents. She could finish a few paragraphs of a story.

She turned, bounded down the front steps with an extra spring in her step, and made her way to the corner bus stop. The number fourteen bus was due any minute now.

After peeking at the first meeting on the front porch of Kent Lambert and Julie Granatelli, while hiding covertly from behind the curtain of their first-floor apartment window, Mr. and Mrs. Finkelstein warmly embraced, and they kissed for a very long time.

When you have found your soulmate, and you have been in love forever, you often kiss and embrace for a very long time.

Julie took advantage of the extra early time in the office. The bus rolled right on schedule and she arrived hours early for work. At that early hour of the day, there were very few riders and very few stops to make along the line. When Julie arrived at her desk, she took Kent's formerly crumbled papers out of her purse and carefully flattened them out in order to remove some more of the wrinkles. Being an expert typist, Julie quickly retyped the paragraph about the snow people on a fresh piece of paper. Once she finished typing Kent's original material, Julie began to compose additional paragraphs. While contemplating her writing, Kent's dark eyes and handsome face flashed in her mind, and Julie had to admit she was feeling a little bold. It had been a long time since she faced the rejection of her longtime boyfriend and had a man in her life. Julie also had a vivid picture in her mind of Kent sitting bare-chested on his fire escape.

A very vivid picture of him.

Julie studied the words that Kent wrote and with her fingers poised upon the keys of the typewriter, she thought while she read them.

"Chapter One, Put Your Hand in Mine. The snow was deep, and it was wet enough to build a fantastic snowman. Early in the morning, before anyone rose, while the snow still lay undisturbed and unblemished, he went to work. Right outside her apartment window, he rolled the first balls of the body of the snowman. Then another, and another, and finally, he rolled a snowman's head. A quick dash into the apartment for a hat, a trip to the cellar to the coal burner for the boiler, yielded some pieces of coal for the eyes and then the finishing touches, some sticks cut from the remnants of old rose shrubs for the snowman's arms. He even picked strategic sticks, which resembled hands at the end of the arms. Then, he worked hard and built a duplicate snow woman right next to his snowman. The same stacked snowballs again, but this time, he placed a woman's scarf around the snow woman's neck and a woman's hat on the head. Strategic sticks allowed the two, snow people to hold hands.

Now, the ultimate romantic touch, he pulled from his coat pocket, the red paper heart that last evening, he cut out of red construction paper, and now, he carefully pressed it into the snow of the snowman, right in the spot where his heart would be. When he returned to the apartment, he gently and silently slipped the note under her apartment's door, a note which asked her when she woke up to look out her bedroom window. Actually, he phrased and laced the instructions with some additional love."

Julie's fingers typed as the next few lines came into her mind. With a giggle and a coy smile on her face, she inserted her namesake into the storyline.

Why not? Indeed, Julie was feeling quite bold.

Away, Julie went on a voyage of her soul. That is what happens to you when you write with emotion. You allow your own soul to go on an unknown voyage, a journey far beyond where you can actually venture. However, in your own mind, with your own words, you can venture to wherever it is that your heart desires, beyond boundaries, and fulfill your wildest dreams.

Her fingers pounded the keys.

"When the licks of the early morning light danced between the shades covering the windows in her bedroom, Julie rose, she wiped the sleep out of her eyes and the curiosity over the amount of the snowfall that the storm brought overnight, was overcome by the need for a hot cup of coffee. She tucked her feet into her slippers, shivered a bit at the cold of her apartment, wrapped her body in her robe and paddled off to the kitchen. When she crossed the front hallway of her apartment, she stopped at the sight of a piece of paper, slipped under her door, and a piece of paper that now sat on the hardwood floors of her apartment's hallway. Julie tried hard to focus, realized that she would do better with her eyeglasses, but she was too anxious to see what this strange paper was about to stop and find them.

Julie bent down, picked it up and read it aloud to the walls and her soul, "When you awaken from what I hope was a night of rest, filled with visions of joy and happiness, when you lift your gorgeous head off your pillow, please look out your bedroom window."

With the note in her hand, Julie dashed off to her bedroom. She stopped off to pick her eyeglasses off the end table and with a burst of energy; she tugged at the handle of the window shade and it rattled toward the heavens. At the sight of two snow people with their hands joined in love, the snowman wearing a red heart, Julie's eyes filled with tears of joy and her heart melted in love. He did love her! How gloriously romantic of him to announce it in such a manner. Julie sat there for what seemed as if it were forever and wondered what her next move would be. Should she rush off to his apartment, knock on the door, and fall into his arms? Should she slip a note under his door, professing her love for him? A million different scenarios raced through her head.

She prepared a cup of coffee, sat in front of the window and studied the pair of snow people in love outside her window. Julie needed to shower, dress and put her coat and hat on and visit the snow people in person. She could see them rather clearly from four stories up, but on the ground in the snow would be the best view.

Yet, if Kent saw her studying them, what would be the next move? He was so shy, so introverted, and he lacked confidence. Here, he had made such a bold move to proclaim his love. Now, Julie needed to do so too, and do so, in such a manner to boost his fragile ego and gently tell him how amazing and wonderful that he was. With a sip of coffee rimmed with a perfect smile, she knew what her plan was going to be.

Julie waited until ten o'clock that evening. She then dressed in her best dress, a black cocktail dress, slightly tight fitting, very low-cut, and amazingly sexy. She decorated her ears with her best earrings that were glowing white pearls in each ear and she framed her long neck with a white pearl necklace. A splash of perfume, and adjustment of her cleavage, and while she looked in the mirror, in her opinion, she would knock the shyness right out of this man. Until now, she had not reacted to the snow people, nor acknowledged his efforts at romance at all. She was sure that his fragile ego was now suffering.

Julie had the magic cure.

Their love would echo to the moon and back again. After dressing, she grabbed the bottle of wine, two wine glasses and left her apartment, locking the door behind her. She walked the stairs to the sixth floor, walked over to his apartment door and knocked rather gently upon his door. Behind the door, Julie could hear some noises, some reaction, and when the door did not open within a few minutes, Julie knocked once more. This time, she knocked a little harder and louder. When she heard the locks spinning and the deadbolt unlatching, she was sure he now knew it was her.

The door had a security peeper.

When Kent threw the door open, she smiled, posed, held the wine and the glasses in the air and in a rather husky voice, she asked, “If you are not planning on venturing outside and building more romantic snow people, will you join me? After all, since those two amazing snow people are holding hands and enjoying love on a cold, winter's night, then I think that we should do the same."

Kent gently took the wine bottle and glasses from her, reached out his hand, took Julie by the hand, and led her into the apartment. When he set the wine and glasses on a table in the hallway, he closed the door behind Julie, flipped all the locks, slid the deadbolt, and took her in his arms. A long kiss led to a glorious evening. Their love and lovemaking indeed, did echo all the way to the moon and back again."

Julie sat back, studied what she just wrote, and dreamed in her heart that it would be a reality. Yes, she wrote in a rather bold manner. It was worth a shot. Was this love at first sight? Maybe. No, not maybe . . . yes. She continued to type and construct pieces of the story, pieces, which when put together went through a budding romance, to a serious involvement, to a romantic proposal, all the way to a glorious wedding and then some babies. . ..

Over the next few weeks, while additional rejected pieces of his thoughts mysteriously drifted to her fire escape post and the wayward pieces of paper allowed Julie a venture into Kent's expressions within his mind, Julie took them and relished them. She knew that with the change of the seasons, her opportunities at obtaining insight into Kent's mind were escaping. Even now, Kent only worked on the fire escape on weekends, and when he did so, Julie quickly dashed out on her metal monster and hoped that fate and the wind would bring her more pieces of the puzzle. Why this man rejected such an amazing story was a mystery to her. Perhaps he was afraid of his own dreams and the pain of sharing them. On her lunch break, or when it was slow in the office or her attorney was in court, Julie worked on the story. Julie knew that she constructed what in her heart; she hoped would become a reality.

On his walk home from work on a Friday evening, Kent Lambert bought a six-pack of Big Boulder beer at Trio Liquors on the corner of Cook Street and Belmont Avenue. He just finished working another double shift at the Foodworld supermarket and it was time to relax. This had been a long week, and aside from his labors at his full-time job, his novel just would not come together. There was something missing, a vital piece of the puzzle, and despite his best efforts, for some reason, the writing just would not flow.

It was now early November and while the year waned; the darkness came rather quickly. Kent still sat on the fire escape, not to escape the heat of the apartment, but for the pleasure of enjoying the view and the wonderful, crisp air. He was very happy that the endless and unrelenting heat of this past summer was now a memory. Autumn heralded in a welcome change in the weather. It felt wonderful when the chill of the evening settled in and the sun decided to fade away and give way to the night.

When Kent approached the front steps of 181 Belmont Avenue, he turned and waved to young Mr. Henson. The young man, who looked very much as if he was simply a wayward hippie, but nothing could be farther from the truth, was in his usual post on the front steps of the house across the street. Above all, the young man was consistent. A number of times, on his way home from work; Kent had stopped and spoken to the young man. They had shared some conversations about books, writing, and reading. It turns out that Mr. Henson was a fascinating young man. He was pursuing what he dreamed would turn out to be a career in professional hockey. Kent thought that it was very unusual to run into a man playing such an unusual sport in the midst of this urban grit. Mr. Henson also dabbled in a little writing of his own, and Kent found out that he was an interesting young man. The budding hockey player possessed a charming personality, a sharp and brilliant mind and a peaceful soul. Kent was currently stuck on the novel's storyline and he bounced some ideas for the novel's plot off Mr. Henson. It seemed as if the novel was stuck in the mud. He started and stopped it more times than he wanted to count. The young man had some solid suggestions for Kent to overcome his writer's block. It was easy to see that he had a great talent for writing, and he hoped someday to be able to exchange more ideas and materials with him. No doubt Kent enjoyed his company.

After the exchanges of waves, Kent turned to walk up the steps of 181 Belmont Avenue, when he noticed Julie Granatelli sitting on the front steps of the apartment house. When she looked up and saw Kent approaching, she smiled widely. Her smile lit up the cold evening and honestly, it sent shivers up and down the spine of Kent Lambert.

She was gorgeous.

Ever since they had met in the early morning hours in the midsummer, they had run into each other quite often. Kent had to admit that he staged and planned some of his random meetings. He did so after he tapped Mr. Finkelstein for some more information about Julie's schedule and patterns. Other times, the meetings seemed as if they were random meetings. On the other hand, could it be that Julie planned them? Kent wanted to believe that Julie did so, and that she planned some meetings. As usual, Kent's usual shyness prevented him from engaging in anything other than some general conversation and exchanges on neutral subjects. The weather, the bus routes, where to shop downtown, goings on within the apartment building, the blaring rock-and-roll from the hippies. Kent wanted to ask her for a date, but he was not sure that Julie was interested in him. His past romantic adventures still stung and lingered within his soul and heart. His confidence waned too much to risk another rejection, and this young woman was too special for him to deal with a rejection from her! No, he was better off lying low and waiting for some more signs.

They were about to arrive.

"Hi, Kent!" Julie almost shouted and she was obviously very enthusiastic at the sight of him; she even stood up from the steps and waved.

Kent waved back, and as he approached, he set the paper bag filled with the six-pack of beer down on the steps.

"Hey, Julie. How are you? Been some time since I have seen you. Have you been working long hours?"

"I have been, and I just stepped off the bus and was walking up when I saw you heading down the street. I thought that I would wait for you and we could catch up a little. Nice evening . . . it sure is a far cry from those sweltering days of summer. A little chilly, actually."

After finishing pronouncing the air temperature as chilly, Julie pulled her sweater around her and hugged it tightly in a testimony of her opinion. It was a wool sweater but it might have been just a little light in fabric for the temperature on this autumn evening.

Kent sensed her chill and commented, "Maybe you need a little heavier outwear, perhaps a jacket." This was his chance. He thought how this time, Julie obviously waited for him, and so he had better not blow it. Time to make a move and shelve the shyness. This is a special woman.

He reached in the paper bag, pulled out two bottles of beer, and held them up in the air while saying, "It would be nice to chat a little. It was a long day, a long week. You want to sit out here and share a few cold ones? Do you like beer?"

Julie smiled; she sat on a step, waved her hand in the air and patted the step next to her.

Here was the chance that Julie had been waiting for,

"Sure, a beer would be great. Ave might have a rule about it, but he will yell at us and chase us away if we are breaking any of his many rules. But the beer might make me a bit colder, I might need to run and pick out a jacket from my apartment or . . . you might need to sit very close to me and keep me warm."

"I can do that and a little more, too. Here. Please, take my jacket. I have a heavy sweater on and I actually enjoy the cold."

Kent graciously removed his jacket, and while Julie sat on the steps, he gently placed it over her shoulders. Julie smiled and hugged it while noticing that the jacket had a glorious scent. It was his smell, and it was intoxicating to her soul. Kent spun the tops off the bottles, handed Julie one of the bottles of beer, sat next to her, and held his bottle in the air for a toast.

"Deal. Cheers."

It was a magical evening and the conversation and connection were magnetic. It was as if they had known each other for all of their lives. This evening, only reinforced what the two of them already knew. It had been love at first sight.

Overhead, in the November sky, a glorious full moon randomly took turns hiding behind clouds, shining brightly upon their love. The moon cast a captivating spell on the night sky and the setting.

A few times, the combination of cold beer mixed with the chilly air and Kent did slide in close to Julie, and even hugged her once to ward off her shivers. In Julie's heart, she hoped that he would stay close to her and keep snuggling with her. But Kent always drifted away after a quick hug.

The six-pack of beer slowly expired. They shared a walk to the corner to Trio Liquors for another one, and while they walked, Julie gently took Kent's hand while they crossed the busy street. His touch was warm and gentle on a chilly evening, but much to Julie's dismay, the clasp gradually faded after a few steps along the sidewalk.

Julie sensed his shyness, but she also sensed his attraction to her. A few more beers polished off, and before they even realized the time, it was very early on Saturday morning. When they finally decided to call it an evening and gathered up the empty bottles and bag, and together, while wearing a bit of a beer buzz, they walked down the hallway and up the stairs of the old apartment. There was little doubt that both of them hoped how this evening would end. However, inside of Kent Lambert, the courage to do so faded, and instead of the rest of the evening reinforcing their new love, it ended with a gentle hug, an exchange of telephone numbers and a promise to speak sometime tomorrow. Kent even mentioned something about having drinks and then some dinner. It was a rather anticlimactic end to the evening, especially so after such a magical beginning. When Julie bid good evening to Kent, smiled and closed the door to her apartment, she stood inside the door and the smile remained on her face. Yet, in her heart, she sighed. While flipping the locks and sliding the deadbolt, she knew she had fallen deeply in love, but did not exactly know how to help Kent overcome his lack of confidence and shyness.

Kent walked slowly through the hallway and then he climbed up the long flights of stairs to apartment number 602, thinking during the entire walk as to how, despite his best efforts, he messed up what was a wonderful evening. Kent simply could not make the moves that he wanted to do toward Julie. In reality, he felt as if he had fallen deeply in love with her, and that fact frightened him. Romance did not turn out too well for Kent Lambert.

Right now, the pain remains. In his heart, he never wanted to be hurt as he was with his first marriage and feel so wretched ever again.

Ever.

December brought an early winter and Julie prayed and wished and hoped that it brought with it some early snowfall. She now had a plan. A perfect plan. Finally, to let Kent Lambert know how much she cared, how much she loved him and to show him how special he really is to her. All she needed now was some snow.

A special snow, a snow that packs tightly, a snow that often arrives in the earlier parts of December and in the early part of March.

Despite Julie doing everything she could do in order to coax Kent onward, the romance between Julie and Kent progressed slowly. In defense of Kent, there were some extenuating circumstances, aside from his obviously cautious approach. Kent was very busy these days. Kent had some challenges at work, he was covering a few extra shifts while the store was short-handed, and he was still attending school, so fitting dates and romance between their schedules was not always easy. Yet they did fit in dates laced with vague hints of romance with some shopping trips, and many bus rides to downtown Paterson to catch movies and to enjoy some pizza afterwards. However, most of all, they enjoyed romantic dinners at Gabby's Cabin, which was an old restaurant right across the street from the apartment. It was next to the Henson's house, the interior darkly decorated with oak and pine wood trim. It had dim lighting and quiet music piped in for a backdrop to their romance. Gabby's Cabin served good tasting food. Nothing here was overwhelming or particularly memorable, but it was perfect for Julie and Kent and they found a quiet booth to call their own.

They even had their favorite server, who was a kind and

a gentle older woman named Mary, who understood what it was like to be falling in love. Mary left them alone to enjoy the moments. Mary had been there once, too.

A long time ago, but Mary held those memories in her heart forever. Now, Mary enjoyed watching the romance develop from her own point of view, and she could relive her own special days of her life.

In reality, Gabby's Cabin was nothing extraordinarily special, but with their limited budgets, it was very special to Julie and Kent.

Within the old neighborhoods such as this one in North Paterson, New Jersey, there are a million special stories tucked into a million special places. All we need is someone to tell us about them.

Gradually, gentle hugs turned to kisses on the cheek and then finally, one evening, a passionate lover's kiss, but it ended right there.

Julie understood there was such intense and lingering pain within Kent's soul. Kent told his story, and Julie shared her story, too. Since she loved this man with all of her heart and soul, Julie was very willing to wait. She understood his pain remained deep and to rush Kent would be a mistake. This man needed to heal his heart before his soul could voyage onward. Somehow, Julie had to convince Kent that a new love would heal his broken heart.

"A winter storm warning is in effect for northern New Jersey tonight. A fast moving, early winter, or actually, a late autumn storm will dump as much as eight inches of wet snow upon the city and outlying areas tonight. Luckily, it is arriving Friday night and will be out of the area by midmorning on Saturday, and with the weekend, storm crews will have plenty of time to clean up to prepare for Monday morning's rush."

The radio sitting upon Julie's kitchen counter spouted the weather forecast and Julie knew that it also broadcasted the answer to her prayers. Julie ran out of her apartment. She rushed to the front porch of the building and looked out upon the city. Tilting her head to the heavens, Julie could smell the snow in the air.

It smelled so glorious to her.

Leaving the front porch, she returned inside and gently tapped on Mr. Finkelstein's apartment door. The old superintendent answered the knock and smiled when he saw that it was his favorite young woman stopping by for a visit.

"Ave, so sorry to bother you. Do you have a minute? I need a favor and I will need your help. I will not be able to lift something and will need your strong back and muscles to help me. Early tomorrow morning, maybe very early. This has little to do with apartment business, but you are my rabbi. You will need to read this little story that I have co-written."

"Of course, of course. Please come inside, dear Julie. We have to read a story? Oh, my, yes, okay, Mrs. Finkelstein will make us tea. Do you want tea or maybe some red wine? We have kosher red wine. Come in and tell me what it is that you need."

After filling in Ave and working out the details later on while alone in her apartment, Julie cut out a giant heart from some red construction paper.

That evening, a very special snow fell upon north Paterson, New Jersey. It was a snow filled with dreams. Each snowflake contained parts and pieces of dreams, and when they fell individually and mixed in with the rest of the flakes, the dreams all interlocked and became one.

Aviv Finkelstein waved to Mr. Henson and his son, who were across the street working and clearing the snow from their driveway. The old car sat in the driveway warming up; even from across the street you could see the warm smoke puffing from the tailpipe into the cold air. It was five o'clock in the morning and Aviv commented to Julie,

"How nothing stopped that man from going to work."

Even Saturday snowfalls.

"We must make the snow woman have a grand smile, gentle curves and glorious breasts." Ave smiled at Julie and he continued to convey his reasoning, "It needs to be realistic."

Julie shook her head and laughed at Aviv's suggestions. They continued to work in the snow, and as they lifted the final pieces into place, and Aviv helped Julie lift the giant snowballs needed to construct the snow people, both of their hearts filled with joy. Pieces of coal from the basement coal bin, which usually fed the old boiler, now made glorious smiles and sticks pruned from the remnants of the old rose shrubs, made arms and interlocked hands. Then there was a red heart stuck into the snow of the snow woman, right near those glorious breasts, packed out of snow filled with love. Aviv hugged Julie. They kissed each other's cheeks, and Mrs. Finkelstein came out into the snow and did the same. In fact, tears ran down the cheeks of the old woman, because she too could feel the love contained in the snow.

A tap on the car horn, some quick thumbs up and a wave, and Mr. Henson and his old car rolled up the snowy streets as the previously steady snowfall gradually slowed. It was quite apparent that Mr. Henson approved of the snow people too! Young Mr. Henson finished shoveling the sidewalk, waved his shovel in the air in approval of the snow people, and the young man smiled warmly at the sight of their work.

Early morning light filtered down and the darkness slowly waned. Julie and Aviv's grand creations were finished. There, the two snow people sat in the side yard of the apartment, directly below Julie and Kent's windows. A testimony to their love. The old number fourteen bus rumbled by them, the snow chains on the tires slapping time on the snowy streets and the city snowplows followed along, carving away the snow and making cavernous paths in the streets. The bus driver waved at the sight of the snow people, and the snowplow driver gently tapped his horn in approval.

With the conveying of many warm thanks, a few final hugs, and wishes of good luck, Mrs. and Mrs. Finkelstein left Julie with just the touch needed for the final part of her plan. They handed Julie a bottle of their finest kosher red wine and bid her a final farewell. They knew Julie needed to work quickly before Kent might awaken. Julie took the envelope with the carefully constructed story lines neatly tucked inside and with joy and love in her heart; she silently slipped it under the door of apartment number 602.

Now, if her plan worked, all she needed to do was to wait until ten o'clock this evening.

This would be a very long day.

Gradually, the snow ended, and the sun peeked out from behind some clouds. Passers-by admired the amazing snow people sitting in the side yard of 181 Belmont Avenue. The old city bus chugged up and down with the glorious sounds of the tire chains still slapping time upon the asphalt. In addition, the city snowplow made a few more final passes on Belmont Avenue, with the driver now smiling at the thought of the testimony of love he saw in the side yard of the old apartment building. The driver also smiled at the thoughts of how much overtime he just packed into his paycheck.

In celebration, the driver of the snowplow lit a cigar.

In the basement of the old apartment building, the old boiler puffed steam in the basement and sent heat up through the old building, spitting and steaming inside of old cast-iron pipes. Occasionally, where the old pipes joined into each other, steam popped, spit, and drooled, a mixture of steam and condensed water out of the joints. Mr. Finkelstein did the best he could, while he fought another battle with his basement nemesis. He packed the leaking joints of the old pipes with steel wool and coated them with a compound in an effort to minimize the steam's escape.

Not too much changed here. The apartments were stifling in the summer and for the most part, despite Mr. Finkelstein's best efforts, freezing in the winter.

Old is old, but on the sixth-floor of the old apartment building, there was a change and something new was born. Inside of apartment number 602, a man's heart glowed with love, and outside, what was once a dark and snowy sky now filled with a glorious sun. The day warmed, and snow and ice dripped from the ledges and bricks of the old apartment house, and the snow people sagged in the sun, but it did not matter too much. Even when the snow people sadly melted into a spent pile of coal, along with some trimmed sticks from rose shrubs, the red heart will remain.

Snow filled with love turns into water that feeds your soul and cleanses away the pain.

Kent Lambert slipped out the side door of 181 Belmont Avenue. His plan was to work his way to the bus stop on Burhans and Belmont Avenue. There, out of sight, of the front door of the apartment building, he would catch a ride on the number fourteen bus and head for the florist. He needed to purchase a bouquet of red roses. His plan included using the side door to return to his apartment because this needed to remain a surprise and even if he wanted to knock on the door of apartment number 402, grab Julie and hold her in his arms for now and forever that plan just would not work.

In the basement of the old apartment building, from his well-worn boiler battle post, Mr. Finkelstein heard the side door open and then slam. While peeking out of the smutty window, the old superintendent smiled at the sight of Kent Lambert making his way across the snowy side yards.

Julie waited until around nine thirty or thereabouts. She then dressed in her best dress, a black cocktail dress, slightly tight fitting, very low-cut and amazingly sexy. She decorated her ears with her best earrings with glowing white pearls in each ear and she framed her long neck with a white pearl necklace. A splash of perfume, and adjustment of her cleavage, and while she looked in the mirror, in her opinion, she would knock the shyness right out of this man.

Julie had the magic cure.

Their love would echo to the moon and back again. After dressing, she grabbed the bottle of kosher red wine, two wine glasses, and left her apartment, locking the door behind her. She walked the stairs to the sixth floor, walked to his apartment door and knocked rather gently upon his door. Behind the door, Julie could hear some noises, some reaction, and when the door did not open within a few minutes, Julie knocked once more. This time, she knocked a little harder and louder. When she heard the locks spinning and the deadbolt unlatching, she was sure he now knew it was her.

The door had a security peeper.

The plan was sealed and their love was now forever.

When Kent threw the door open, she smiled, posed, held the wine and the glasses in the air and in a rather husky voice, she asked, "Since it stopped snowing and we cannot go outside and build romantic snow people, I thought that I might have a better plan. A plan for now and maybe forever? So, Kent Lambert, if we are not planning venturing outside and building more romantic snow people, will you join me? After all, since those two amazing snow people are holding hands and enjoying love on a cold, winter's night, then I think that we should do the same."

Kent gently took the wine bottle and glasses from her, reached out his hand, took Julie by the hand, and led her into the apartment. From behind his back, he handed her the glorious bouquet of red roses and after they admired them together; he set the wine and the glasses and the roses on a table in the hallway; he closed the door behind Julie, flipped all the locks, slid the deadbolt and took her in his arms. A long kiss led to a glorious evening. Their love and lovemaking indeed did echo all the way to the moon and back again.

With the arrival of the cold of the evening came the celebrations of life. On the first floor of 181 Belmont Avenue, you could hear the big band music playing from the Finkelstein's apartment. Inside, between sips of kosher red wine, the old couple danced the night away in the living room, while their love and romantic magic filled the air. Even after all of these years of marriage, they were still very much in love.

From the Lopez's apartment, the sounds of dancing feet whipping around on hardwood floors during a salsa dance echoed into the old hallways. It was just a little too early but, shortly between the echo of Spanish horns and guitars from the Spanish music playing from the Lopez's apartment, the jam session of rock-and-roll would begin with Zale and his bandmates.

On the sixth floor, in apartment number 602, well, it was a much different type of celebration. Suddenly, the old boiler chugging along in the basement was not required to generate any heat. It was certainly hot enough in apartment number 602.

No boiler required.

Within the old neighborhoods such as this one in North Paterson, New Jersey, and old apartment buildings such as 181 Belmont Avenue, there are a million special stories tucked into a million special places.

All we need is someone to tell us about them.

"Ave, it looks as if the mail brought you some kind of gift of some sort. Or a package of something, it looks as if it is a book."

"Close the door, honey. The heat is crazy today. I don't want to have to fix that air conditioner today. Not today, too hot out there. Want to relax here in my chair and drink red wine so that we can dance later. Sometimes, I miss that old sidewalk and the snow too. Not too often, but some days I do. Florida is so hot. We can't even walk to temple without sweating terribly."

Mrs. Finkelstein smiled at her husband's remarks. She closed the door and walked over to his easy chair and handed him the package. Mrs. Finkelstein knew that he loved living here in Florida and spending time with their family, but she had to admit that she missed certain parts of New Jersey too.

It did get very hot here in Florida.

One good thing was that there was no boiler required.

"A gift? A book? I have no idea what it can be," Aviv said while opening the cardboard flaps of the package with his pocket knife. With Mrs. Finkelstein watching intently with waves of curiosity overcoming both of them, Aviv peeled away the cardboard and from the inside, he removed what was indeed a book. A hardcover, with a glorious picture of two snow people sitting in a bed of snow. The snow people had sticks for arms and their sticks interlocked as if they were holding hands. One of the snow people was a snow woman and, on her chest, right near her snowy breasts, was a large, red heart. He fingered the book, opened it, and flipped through the pages. The back cover of the book had a picture of the two coauthors holding what appeared to be twin baby girls in their arms.

"Well, I'll be," Aviv Finkelstein immediately started to wipe away his tears, as his wife wrapped her arms around his neck and his wife began to cry. Between tears of joy, Aviv read the cover aloud, "Love on a Fire Escape, by Julie and Kent Lambert."

Later, on the same day, back in the old neighborhood of north Paterson, New Jersey, Mr. Paul John Henson, walked into the old kitchen at 182 Belmont Avenue. He banged and bumped his equipment bags filled with hockey gear along the way and made his way into his bedroom of the old house. The young man just returned from a road trip. Playing professional hockey and living his dream.

"Hi, Mum. I am home. We won!" He called out to his mother, while announcing his arrival home.

"Oh, good! I am in the bedroom folding laundry on my bed. Nice to have you home, Paulie. Come in here and tell me about the trip and the game. I am sure that you brought me some disgusting, sweat-filled laundry of a hockey mess. I can do a load right now. Oh, yes, you received a package in the mail today. I set it on your bed. It looks as if it is a book."

"Thanks, dear Mum. Yes, I got it. I do have laundry, and yes, it is a disgusting hockey-related mess. I am sorry, but you know how it is." Paul John called out as he picked the package up and carefully studied it.

The young man remained puzzled as to the contents. As far as he could recall, he had not ordered anything. He flipped open the cardboard flaps of the box and pulled out a book. It was a hardcover book, with a glorious picture of two snow people sitting in a bed of snow. The snow people had sticks for arms and their sticks interlocked as if they were holding hands. One of the snow people was a snow woman and, on her chest, right near her snowy breasts, was a large, red heart.

The young man smiled widely at the sight of the cover

and he read the front cover aloud, "Love on a Fire Escape, by Julie and Kent Lambert. Very cool."

He fingered the book, opened it, flipped through the pages, and studied the picture on the back cover of the book with the two coauthors and their lovely twin girls.

Many babies and a glorious family life.

Once again, he spoke aloud his thoughts, "Geez, amazing, dreams fulfilled. Good for them. He is living his dream out too and writing for a living. Writing with Julie. Can't wait to read it. What a fantastic end to their story. Good for him, he must have married her. Lucky guy, she is a stunner. I remember when they built the snow people there in the side yard."

Across the street from the Henson's home, in the basement of the old apartment building located at 181 Belmont Avenue, Mr. Jose Lopez worked in the basement of the building, fighting the old boiler, trying hard to convince it to puff out just a little of steam. He read the notes that Mr. Finkelstein gave him, he needed to understand what to do when the fire eye decided not to see the flame.

Now, Mr. Lopez danced the salsa with the old boiler.

On the front steps, Miss Rosa Lopez slowly walked up the steps while she studied the basement lights of the building. She just stepped off the number fourteen bus and by seeing the glow of the basement lights, Rosa realized that her father was working once again on the troublesome boiler. Rosa grew up in this old building and from the age of seven, she knew of the temperament of the silent monster lurking in the basement. Not too much changed here. The apartments were stifling in the summer and for the most part, despite her father's best efforts, freezing in the winter.

Now, Rosa was in her early twenties and her plan was someday to escape the confines of 181 Belmont Avenue, if she could only meet the right man.

Before she could make it to the front door and open it, it suddenly swung open and a man . . . a lean, tall, and very handsome Latino man swung the door open in front of her. Rosa jumped back to avoid the door and the young man jumped, too.

"I am so sorry! I hope that I did not scare you or that the door hit you?" The young man reached out and gently held Rosa's arm to prevent her from tumbling backwards.

She carefully studied him. He was stunning and her heart immediately melted. He might be a bit older than she was, but love knows little in the way of boundaries. Yes, indeed, the heat was on inside of her heart.

No boiler required.

Rosa gently spoke in Spanish, "Estoy bien. Gracias."

Then she smiled and gently clasped his hand.

Within the old neighborhoods such as this one in north Paterson, New Jersey, and old apartment buildings such as 181 Belmont Avenue, there are a million special stories tucked into a million special places.

All we need is someone to tell us about them.

THE END

Until the End of All Time

From "On the Edge of Memories
The Random Collection"

The train ride was a long one.

It was about four hundred-miles or thereabouts. Seemingly endless steel rails, which rolled from the city where he lived, to his final destination. He did not care; all he hoped for was that it was far enough away from here.

As he sat and thought about it, on the other hand, to be accurate, it was about a four-hundred-mile train ride to the next destination. You see, in his mind, he actually did not have a final destination planned.

He only had plotted for an escape, a way out, a way to forget. Far beyond the mountains, which separated the place that he lived from the rest of the world, far beyond the top of the ridge where he would often sit on his front porch staring at the golden sunsets dipping below the rugged ridges of the mountaintops. Staring far beyond the river valley, where the winding river that fed the valley began in the icy mountains of an unknown place.

He was off seeking an unknown place. He did not actually care where the train stopped, as long as it was far, far away.

Yes, indeed, he sought an unknown location.

An undefined future, no plans, and no commitments. He sought only an escape. An escape from many things, including life, pressure, but mostly, it was an escape from the memory of her. She haunted his days, and she especially haunted his nights. When he closed his eyes, she was there. When sleep did finally come to his weary mind, when he woke, she was there again. Right in front of him, smiling, laughing, the smell of her skin, her hair falling all around her, he could even feel the touch of her hand upon his arm.

Now, escape was his only hope.

A train of around ten very lonely Pullman cars, chugged alongside a snow-covered landscape, struggling up the side of a mountainside, the steam billowing from the stacks of the locomotives, cascading down the side of the mountain and drifting down into the valley below.

Boilers, all in high fire.

He sat next to the frosty window, in the third Pullman car from the front of the train. He pressed his hand against the glass and left an imprint into the frost. The feeble efforts of the heat vent above the glass failed to warm the glass very much. He took his finger and carefully wrote in the frost gathered on the glass, "YOU ARE MY ONE TRUE LOVE." He did not know why he wrote that sentence, but it provided him with some relief to read it.

Slowly, the heat from the vent melted the words away. He sat, while sadly watching the steam billow out of the locomotive stacks and the puffs of steam drift down into the valley. When he turned, and strained his neck, to follow the clouds of steam, he thought how it was so strange that the valley seemed as if it shone like gold in the early morning sunlight.

Funny how it never looked that way to him, and he lived there for most of his life. The other side of this mountain was where the golden sunsets always were.

When the weight of life starts to crush your spirit, the golden sunsets are always on the other side of the mountain.

He did not care; he was heading in the direction of the golden sunsets, to a place where no one knows him, where he can start over. All he had was one piece of luggage, his six-string and twelve-string guitars, and a few measly dollars to his name, but it did not matter.

She would not be there.

Only her ghost would follow him.

He sat, still staring out the window, mindlessly recalling all that had happened.

"So, you can play a little guitar and sing too, eh?" The owner of the tavern asked him, while he was looking the young man up and down and sizing him up. "You only have to keep them entertained between periods of the hockey game, once the game starts back up, ya need to pack it away and shut the hell up."

The musician nodded and went to say something, but the owner cut him off before he was able to speak.

"Oh yes, my expectations are that you help clean up the joint at the end of the night, too. Think of this as a grassroots job. Ya sing a little, ya sweep a little, and I pay ya twenty dollars for the night. On Saturday night, aftah closin' we lift all the chairs off the floor, put them up on the tables and mop the floor. That will take ya a little longer, so I will pay ya twenty-five dollars for Saturday night."

"I am in. I would love to help you clean up. "

"Ha! Ya full of shit. You just want to have a chance to play and sing, eh? Ain't no one who likes to clean and mop dirty ass, beer and whiskey-soaked floors, but your honesty got ya this far, so let's hear ya play that thing and sing. What kinda music ya play, eh? My buddy heard you and said ya were good. So, watcha play?"

"Folk rock. Well, sorta folk with a rock twist. It is mostly my own stuff, but I also do some covers too."

"Folk rock, that sounds boring. Ya better stick with covers, because this is a rough crowd, full of beer-drinking, hockey lovin' guys and hard-core chicks lookin' for hockey lovin' men. Ya might not last long with some weepy-eyed, boring ass folkie tunes."

The owner looked the musician up and down as if he was suddenly reconsidering the potential of even offering the job to him.

He blurted out rather impatiently, "Well, ya gonna play something or what?"

The young man eagerly nodded. He reached down for his guitar cases and with his hands poised upon both of them, he asked the owner, "Twelve-string or my six?"

"Oh shit, I don't really give a damn. I would not know the difference! I guess I could count the strings. Just play ya best."

"Okay, I have to go with the twelve-string then. It is a beauty. I put a capo on the second fret, kind of locked into that now since I started writing songs with it during the folk era."

"Geez, I really don't have a clue whatcha talkin' bout. Just play the damn thing, will ya. I got me a beer delivery comin' any minute now. If ya stall anymore, then your ass is hired to unload the truck!"

The owner had very little patience for the technical explanations, and the musician was awkwardly fumbling and stumbling, obviously nervous at his precarious and anything but sublime audition. The young musician fumbled a bit more, adjusted the capo on the fretboard and fiddled a bit with the tuning. He then finally sat on the edge of a table, ran his fingers along the strings, and immediately, the impatience of the owner of the gin joint faded away.

The sound of the twelve-string guitar invoked such a stir within the owner's heart that it shook him to his inner soul. It calmed the owner's impatience in a manner of which he had never experienced from music before. It was beautiful, almost magical in the resonance of sound.

The owner stuck his bar towel in his back pocket; he

tugged at a chair and sat listening. When the musician broke into a song and his acoustical magic echoed around the old tavern, the owner smiled.

He closed his eyes and listened.

His friend had been correct, this young musician was pure dynamite and his voice and guitar calmed your soul. His voice was captivating, and his guitar playing was delightful.

When the musician finished playing, the only thing that the owner could manage to do was to stand up, shake his hand and say very softly and gently, "You're hired. Ya can start tonight. Whatcha name?"

"Jack Cardin."

"That's ya real name, eh? You a Canuck?"

"Yes, my real name. I am from Ontario, but far north of here. In fact, way far north. My family is originally from Wales, but we have been in Canada for three generations. Mostly, we are or were, coal miners."

The owner nodded, smiled, shook Jack's hand and gently told the musician, "Well, let's get to work, eh?"

And, start he did, a thirty-five-year-old struggling musician, rambling on the road, going from gig-to-gig, gin mill-to-gin mill, trying hard to make a name in the music world.

It was a familiar story, which everyone has heard a few million times before. He was looking for the big break, that one magical moment. Jack Cardin was from a small town in north Ontario Province, and he left home at a young age to strum his guitar along with a group of his boyhood friends.

Despite their best efforts, they were not quite good enough for professional hockey and these days, it was either play hockey, work in the coal mines, or local lace mills, or find a poor-paying position in some retail store. The most romantic story for those musical people such as Jack was, came from those musicians, who would strike out on their own, and head for Toronto or even Edmonton and give it a whirl in the music business. They heard just enough of the random success stories to keep Jack and his little group of fellow musicians inspired and dreaming. They did not have very much, but they played some mean instruments. The little band they formed played some folk-rock covers and mixed in some of their own compositions. They called their little group, "No Need to Repent."

And they lived up to their name.

The band featured an acoustic string bass and an electric bass, an electric rhythm guitarist, a light percussionist, and Mr. Jack Cardin on lead vocals, playing lead on his acoustic guitars, and featuring both six and twelve-string guitars.

Eventually, the road wore them out; the money grew lean, the empty stomach syndrome grew wearisome and their spirits collapsed. Boiling pots of beans and sleeping in the park in Toronto were acceptable in the summer, but those long, long winters were some different stories.

You see, No Need to Repent, was in fact a very good folk-rock band, however, so it seemed as if there were a few thousand other bands.

Gradually, they grew apart. First, they lost the percussionist, then the electric guitarist, and finally the bass player returned home to a life of dreary living, while working a dusty life in the coal mines.

Now only Jack remained, and he still had no need to repent. There were many lovers along the way. He was an attractive man and musicians always seemed to attract the young women.

Attracting them was not the trouble; keeping them was always the issue.

He wandered here and there, and managed to find some work in coffeehouses, taverns, pubs, and an occasional nightclub gig or two. First in Toronto, then Quebec City, then off west to Vancouver, always finding something, but never hitting the big time.

Critics and the occasional reviewer praised his voice, his songwriting, his guitar skills, but the big contract or opportunity never arrived. In between, he worked day jobs in food stores, where he grew quite proficient at stocking shelves, and unloading trucks, and he lived in cheap flats, in shady neighborhoods that all had leaky roofs and musty hallways.

In the quiet of the flats, by candlelight to save electricity, he strummed his guitar; he wrote songs and continued to dream.

By-and-by, in this little tavern, tucked just off Yonge Street in Toronto, he grew to have a loyal following. It was not an easy place to play or to make a living as a musician. This was a hockey bar, and you had to slip a quick set in while the game was between periods, calm them down, and pick the correct song for the tempo and mood of the night. You know, read the crowd correctly and by now, Jack was an expert at doing just that.

Hockey season was busy, and in the summer, the activities centered on the outdoor seating, where the burly and rough and tumble crowds of beer and whiskey drinking men, could watch the young women walk by and dream of the possibilities of spending even one night with one of these gorgeous women. When the hockey games were a memory, and the Stanley Cup awarded, when the nights were warm and the breeze was gentle, he sat on a quiet stool set off in the corner of the outdoor seating area; he strummed his guitars and tried very hard to make a name for himself.

Every night was the same, a one-man band, and it seemed as if every night could be his last gig. He never really knew when it would end. Yet, the crowd loved him; they filled a little glass jar with tips; they slapped him on his back and some of the rough and tumble types even shed a tear at his sentimental songs. Especially the ones about lost loves.

Even the rough and tumble types knew the pain of love lost.

One late August night, when the evening breezes had shifted from the states, to the wilds of Alberta, and a tinge and whisper of the autumn to come was in the air, he spotted her. He was on his stool, under the canopy, in the corner of the outdoor seating, and she caught his eye.

She hung on his every word, his every note, and the first thing that he thought of was that he had never seen such sparkling and magnificent green eyes. The gorgeous woman had long brown hair, which hung straight and framed her long neck and perfect facial features in a manner which captivated you. She was gorgeous, and even that word did not sum it up properly; in fact, there were no words. He had seen many gorgeous women hanging upon his words with stars in their eyes, dreaming of spending a night with the handsome musician, and some had actually achieved their dreams, but this woman was different.

It was a classic case of love at first sight; it just had a twist to it, because she had a male companion with her on this night and he was one of the rough and tumble types. In addition, there was this little thing about a wedding ring upon her finger. When his set was through, she came over; her husband stayed at the table sucking down beer after beer. It appeared as if beer was his primary mission and music was not his thing.

Her voice was soft and gentle, and her smile ignited his soul, "I must say, and it might just sound a bit cliché, but what is a handsome and talented musician such as you are, doing by playing a stale, beer joint like this?"

"Thank you. I do what I have to do, in order to make rent. Well, sometimes I make rent, other times, the landlord either fronts me or throws me. Hiya, I am Jack Cardin." He extended his hand and set his twelve-string down.

"Nice to meet you, Jack, but I knew that already. It says so on the sign out front." She smiled again. It was obvious that she sensed his attraction to her.

It was impossible to hide.

"Hello, I am Leigh DuPont. Mrs. Leigh DuPont and I think that I just became your biggest fan."

She turned and pointed to the table where she sat with the beer-sucking chap.

"My husband, he does not appreciate music as much as I do, but even he said that you had a nice voice. Believe me, coming from my husband, that is quite the compliment. He does not appreciate much," Leigh said while she smiled a forced grin; that was almost a shameful smirk.

Jack knew right away that her statement had a hidden meaning. If her husband was unable to recognize this rare and precious gem of a woman, of which he was fortunate enough to have for his wife, then he was a very sad example of a man. If that was indeed the case, then it was more than just tragic—it was confounding to Jack.

They began a thoughtful conversation, first about music, then about some general subjects. The connection was immediate, and powerful, and the entire time that they spoke to each other, Leigh's husband did not even glance their way. Jack did catch him checking out some of the young barmaid's backsides, while they wiggled about, serving drinks and food.

Yes, it was confounding.

Leigh DuPont was true to her word; she became Jack's biggest fan and a lot more. After set lists, on the nights when her husband did not accompany her, she would sit at a table with him and they would talk about everything, and when they ran out of subjects to speak about, they somehow would talk some more. She made him laugh and at times, he made her laugh and his songs made her cry.

She told him about her woes, not for sympathy, but for a friendly ear.

When her husband did come along, Leigh would visit quickly, and do her best to say hello, while her husband drank down beer after beer, and was lost in his nightly haze, and flirted openly with the barmaids. It turned out that her husband mostly ignored her. He was a long-distance trucker, and he did earn a very good living. However, Leigh was sure that he made a number of "unscheduled stops" along his many roads. He was seldom home, and when he was home, he was lost in a haze of beer and a drunken stupor.

Autumn arrived, a long winter set in, and the musical activity moved inside. Once more, Jack played his music in-between periods of the hockey games. Leigh came to visit, and there was more time to chat in the winter.

Hockey was paramount, beer was second, and Jack and his music lagged far behind.

It was obvious that Leigh and Jack had fallen deeply in love. It was a forbidden love, love with no future, no hope, no right or wrong, just in love. After all, her husband, despite his faults, kept Leigh fed, warm, safe, and with a roof over her head.

Jack had nothing to offer and all the roofs over his head generally leaked.

Then one night, while her husband was away, they crossed the line, and now the magic really erupted. They were not only friends but also now they were lovers, and their love set the world on fire. Now, there was no return, no way to go back, and no way to deny what they felt in their hearts.

Jack's songs and performances became more poignant, more mystifying, more captivating. Leigh's love had transformed him into a minstrel of the night and a weaver of songs filled with depth and emotion.

Her love was the missing piece of the puzzle.

What he had searched for to bring his career to the next level. Until now, he always played his music, but now he felt each line that he sang and would write.

The crowd sensed it; they felt his transformation and his

musical and emotional peak. A solid review in a local newspaper of one of his performances brought even larger crowds. His following grew larger, and for just a few short weeks, it seemed as if they would have a future together.

He dreamed of the day when he could offer Leigh something more than broken guitar strings and smoky beer halls. In reality, he could not, he would always be a road musician. Deep down he knew it, and Leigh knew it too.

When the fog of love lifted, and the dreams became just a pile of spent wonder, the fateful night finally arrived for the two lovers to have the discussion. A discussion, of which they both knew would someday come and they would have to admit they had to have.

The painful discussion would have nothing at all to do with love. There was no question as to the depth of their love and connection, but this discussion had all to do with reality.

After a long night, together, one last night of passion, it was much to his own surprise, Jack, who first brought up his yearning to leave Toronto for Leigh's own welfare. He had become a poison to her; he was going to cause trouble; he was going to cause her to lose everything, and he was just not worth it.

In his heart, he knew his temporary success would fade; his dream, however, would never fade.

When it all shook out and reality set in, the painful truth was he had nothing to offer her. Nothing except his love. Love would not pay the bills, nor feed little children, nor keep a roof over their heads that did not leak.

Jack broke the news to her gently; lovingly, and it did not go over too well.

"No, I will leave him," Leigh pleaded, "we will find a cabin in the woods, you will write some hit songs, and I can find a job. Maybe in Winnipeg. Yes, we can go to Manitoba!"

Jack held her head gently in his hands and kissed her

hair as he pushed away the tears with his fingers. He was well grounded, and his intense love for her drove him to make the correct choice.

"I would not allow you to give your life up for a road musician without any actual future. You cannot give it all up. I would leave before I allowed that to happen. I would leave and you would never find me. I would lie and tell you all that I cared about was sharing your body!"

Leigh shook her head gently; she knew that Jack was much too kind ever to say such a thing.

She tried in vain to convince him that the hit song was right around the corner, "Jack, you will write that one special song. I know you will!"

"No, Leigh. I have yet to write that hit song. All of these years and still, I cannot write it. Fanciful dreams will only bring us despair. Here you are safe, warm and perhaps, someday, children will fill your life and help to make you whole again. They will fill the voids in your soul that your husband vacates."

She looked up at him through shipwrecked eyes and asked, "And how do I fill the void in my heart that you will leave?"

"I will always love you more than life itself. We will always be together. In some way, there will always be Leigh and Jack. Our love is more than just physical between us. It is deep within our souls. We could never solely predicate our relationship upon our bodies touching as one. That act just validated and honored our love, but it is much more than that. I know in my heart, just before I take my last breath, the vision in my mind and in my soul, will be of you. Our connection is deep, it is profound, and even if we are apart, we will always be together, in each other's heart. Until the end of all time."

There, the romance ended in a shower of tears.

Jack felt the car rock a bit as the train rolled along a steep incline. He kicked at the guitar cases under his feet. He needed to confirm that they were still there. It provided Jack with some sort of comfort, knowing that the only tools of his trade that remained, or in fact, that he ever had, were still nearby.

After what seemed as if it were ten lifetimes, the train pulled into the final destination.

Jack felt a bit foolish while listening closely when the train conductor announced loudly, "Last stop. Winnipeg, Manitoba Province!"

At least now he knew where he was.

Then again, he always knew that it was the place where those golden sunsets were always slipping behind the mountains.

He wandered about, boiled a few pots of beans in the local park, and eventually found a job stocking shelves in a food market in downtown Winnipeg.

He tried hard to crack the bar scene, auditioned hard, but it seemed as if his "Toronto label" worked against him here in Winnipeg. He was surprised when the locals called him "a flatlander from the big city scene" in the smaller city out west. It was obvious that he had crossed the line between east and west. At least his job in the food market kept him out of the park.

Leigh never left his dreams, but sadly, she entered his nightmares. She was in all of his thoughts, and she never left his heart, not for one second and not for one instant. She haunted him day and night and one night alone in a cold, dark and terribly dank flat; he wrote a song. At first, it came along slowly, and the twelve pack of beer, which he consumed, made the notes and lyrics a little clearer to him. They resonated through his twelve strings and forced tears upon his cheeks.

He entitled it, "Until the End of All Time."

Two weeks later, he answered an advertisement in the

local paper, which was advertising for a musician to entertain a bar scene between periods of the hockey game. It was a position of which Jack felt that he was well suited for, considering his experience.

When Jack finished playing, "Until the End of All Time," the only thing that the owner of the tavern could manage to do was to stand up, shake his hand and say very softly and gently, "You're hired. Ya can start tonight. Whatcha name?"

"Jack Cardin."

"That's ya real name, eh? You a Canuck?"

"Yes, my real name. I am from Ontario. From southeast of here, in fact, way southeast. My family is originally from Wales, but we have been in Canada for three generations. Mostly we are or were, coal miners."

"How old are ya? I think I see some grey creeping in on the edges of that jet-black hair, eh?"

"Forty-one. I think."

"I might need ya to hang around here and help me clean up every night. Ya know, sweep and mop. Ya sing a little, ya clean a little too. You okay with that?"

"I am. I have done it before."

The owner nodded, smiled, shook Jack's hand again and gently told Jack, "Good, good. Ya sing very nicely and that guitar has quite a sound. That is a beautiful song. Sounds as if ya lost a special gal along the way, eh? She still lives in ya heart. I know, 'bout that too. Sometimes, I think we all have. I hope mine finally found her rainbow's end."

"I think you are correct. I agree. It seems as if we all have. The rainbow's end and golden sunsets, for sure, that is my dream for her."

The owner patted Jack on the back as if to provide some type of comfort. He smiled and said, "Well, let's get to work then, eh?"

It seemed as if this were a scene, which Jack had been a participant in a few times before in his life.

In the wintertime, during the hockey season, he played in between the periods of the game, but in the summer, he moved outside to a familiar stool under a canopy in the corner of an outdoor seating area. It all reminded him of a time that now seemed as if it were so long ago.

It was late on an August night, and it was a night when autumn loomed so close that you could smell it. The gentle summer breezes had changed from the south to the north and no longer blew over Minnesota and Michigan, but instead, the breeze came down out of the Yukon and out of Alberta.

On this special night, Jack Cardin sat on his familiar stool and he played, "Until the End of All time." For some reason, this evening, he played it extra well.

When he finished, the crowd politely clapped, and some cheered. Most of the crowd tonight was regulars. They had heard the song before and it was familiar to them. For some patrons, it was the first time they had heard it, it was a new song, and it seemed as if overall, they appreciated it.

That was the final song of his set and while Jack bent over his guitar case and carefully packed his twelve-string guitar away, a gentle tap came upon his shoulder. Jack looked up, and he saw a short, round, and balding man staring at him.

The man smiled, handed Jack a business card, and he spoke, "Say, Mr. Cardin, pardon me, but I would like to speak with you for a few minutes. Please, first, I need to introduce myself. My name is John Castile. I am a music and talent agent as well as a music executive with a publishing company. That last song was amazing. Is it your own composition?"

Jack stood up, shook Mr. Castile's hand, and answered, "It is. I call it, 'Until the End of All Time.' I wrote it about three years ago."

Mr. Castile smiled again, and he explained, "Well, it is fabulous. The woman who tipped me off to your talent was not exaggerating at all. This was certainly worth the long trip to listen to your entire set. That one song is spectacular, but you have an entire list of great stuff. All your own too. No covers. Impressive body of work, for sure. I would like to speak to you about coming down to New York and maybe we can discuss a recording contract and lay a few tracks down in a studio or two."

Jack's heart skipped a few beats when he realized that this might finally be his big break.

Finally, his chance.

His euphoria over what Mr. Castile was telling him suddenly became overshadowed, because over Mr. Castile's shoulder, he saw her. . ..

At first, he thought it was his mind playing tricks on him. Then, he felt weak in his knees, but strengthened in his spirit. There she stood. Once more, she returned to his life, only this time it was different. Very different. She stood with her green eyes sparkling, her smile, and her long hair hanging down all around her. His heart melted, and he had to think that hers did, too.

Between what Mr. Castile was saying and offering him, as well as once again seeing her golden smile and magnificent green eyes, Jack knew that this time, she would never leave him and he would never leave her.

Not now, not ever, not until the end of all time.

The young couple slipped into the seat on the Pullman car. They sat close together, shared a kiss or two and they smiled. It was very exciting to be leaving on an adventure to visit Toronto. They were very much in love and when you are young and in love, the world is full of rays of golden joy. While the train slowly chugged out of the station, the young man noticed how the sunlight reflected onto the glass of the window of the car.

There in the glass, he could read the words, "YOU ARE MY ONE TRUE LOVE" written on the dusty window, and now the remnants of the words reflected in golden sunlight. He reached over, pulled his lover in tightly, and pointed to the words.

Upon seeing them, she laughed and smiled, then kissed the young man very deeply.

After kissing, she gently whispered to her lover, "I guess that someone else feels the same as I do! I wonder how long ago they wrote those words on the glass?"

The young man smiled and said, "I think they have always been there and always will. Now, and until the end of all time."

THE END

Nightcap

From, "Nightcap and Other Stories
The Fantasy Collection"

The Weary Life of Jacob McCabe

Jacob "Jake" McCabe trudged through each day in a mindless and bored stupor. Why not? All the days seemed to be the same. He viewed the world through an opaque window. He could see the motions and hear the muffled words, but it was so mundane and boring that he seldom really paid attention. He was present. He smiled, went through the motions, but after all of these years and all he had been through, he seldom took it very seriously.

Jake was a traveling salesman, and he often sat alone on the edge of a bed in a hotel room, flipping through channels on the television, never stopping to watch a show for very long, just flipping and thinking. Thinking about how he should consider himself lucky. That is lucky, in a roundabout way. He earned a very good salary, and most people would consider him a highly successful man in the business world. Jake held a lofty position within his company. Sure, he lived on the road, out of a suitcase, but he earned a nice salary. After all the years of selling whatever the hell it is that he sold, he could perform the sales pitch and work with his eyes closed. And therein was the trouble. It was mindless, and the glory of the road had worn thin. Very thin. In fact, after doing this for close to fifteen years, all the hotels appeared the same, and the restaurant food tasted the same. As of late, the gin joints all watered down his cocktails in the same manner, and they priced the drinks ten times more than they should cost. Most of all, all the people whom he met along the way were all the same.

Same old, same old.

The company that employed Jake sold extremely high-quality surgical tools, medical supplies and precision medical instruments and equipment, everything from scalpels to microscopes to syringes to glassware. Products used in hospitals, laboratories, and universities, and Jake swore that after fifteen years, he had made a commission by peddling his wares to every hospital, university research center, and laboratory in the United States. There were not too many locations that he did not sell to, or call upon, or had visited. Now, with the internet, he did not even have to carry brochures of the product lines with him. Just a laptop, a smile, an order form, answer a few questions, take the customers to lunch or dinner, drop a few bucks on cocktails and hop a plane for the next stop. The commission money rolled in, and Jake banked it all.

However, commission dough did not buy happiness, nor did it always buy excitement. At least, not the type of excitement or happiness that Jake McCabe sought.

Yet, Jake knew in his heart that the end of the road was near . . . it was closer than anyone could ever imagine. Jake gave it a year to two more, and then it would be over.

The rumor mill within the company that Jake worked for was that the plans were to move all the manufacturing of their products overseas. Jake had seen it before within his industry. The lure of inexpensive labor was far too great for corporate accountants and executives not to succumb to these days. The bottom line was all too important and large profits and successes are never enough. They always want more and more.

The company had formed right after World War Two and it was the byproduct of retooling military production lines into goods for use in the civilian world. The company had now been in business and thriving for close to fifty years. Presently, the company manufactured premium products in the United States with skilled and dedicated workers. The products were the best of the best, and Jake had no trouble at all in peddling his products, because of their reputation for outstanding quality. When the inevitable move to overseas manufacturing occurred, Jake knew that the production would shift to some haphazard and poorly managed manufacturing plant with poorly skilled workers in some dump overseas.

Who cares?

And that would be the deathblow.

It was, in Jake's opinion, all very predictable. Perhaps Jake's mundane world and his now skewed view on life had tilted him toward cynicism. On the other hand, perhaps Jake was overly factual. In his mind, he could envision the press conferences with the announcements of the plans.

Despite assurances that quality would not suffer but the profits would increase, the result will be cheaper products at the same, or in fact, inflated prices. The company's reputation for making the finest products would be gone forever and they would fade away like so many other American businesses. Inferior products at top dollar are not a winning formula.

It seems as if in God, we trust and everyone else must pay cash.

Predictably, the deathblow would come in the words muttered by another clueless, high-level executive, "We have a duty to our shareholders to increase our profits. Our bottom-line is dramatically suffering due to the high wages and costs of medical benefits to the current line-up of employees and while we certainly appreciate all their hard work and dedication. . .."

Oh yes, indeed they do, but in their distorted view and mindless greed, they feel as if they have no duty to the factory workers or the employees who helped the company earn the reputation they now have, or the loyal customers who shelled out top dollar for a top-notch product for so many years. No, not in this modern world of business populated with countless clueless jackasses. Clueless, overly educated jackasses, posing as executives, all of them with spray tans, expensive overlays on their teeth and alcohol on their breath at ten in the morning. Executives, who are all, dishing out buckets of alimony dollars to their unceremoniously ditched high-school sweethearts, whom they married when they were still poor, still too young, but still somewhat honest and untainted by perceived fame and real money. Now with money in their bank accounts and stars in their eyes, they have lost all their wives and sweethearts as they thoughtlessly tossed them all aside in favor of the cute chicks sitting on the third floor with the tight backsides, loose lips and overly exposed chests.

None of these executives has a clue about the real world. They obliviously sit in their fancy offices and could give two shits less about anything but themselves. Now, there are some important things on clueless jackasses' agendas! Yes, golf dates are important, and the chick's tight ass is important, as are the covert or in some cases, advertised liaisons with the cute chicks, but not too much else matters in their worlds. After all, they just keep telling themselves that it is all about the duty to the shareholders and in making sure their bonus money ends up in their bank accounts. Because of these selfish decisions driven by business avarice, the now-unemployed schleps of the company would crawl away from their well-paying jobs, which are now overseas, and they would replace those jobs with lower-paying service jobs. Good honest jobs, which by their nature, paid lower wages. The executives do not care. They walk away with bonus money and move over to another corporation to wreak havoc upon others in much the same manner. How these jackasses continue to thrive and find jobs remained in Jake's mind, the real puzzle. Yet, they blame it on the economy and walk away filthy rich and unaccountable for their previous performances. Then the talking heads and the politicians will shake their heads and finger point as to the reasons of why the economy never really recovers.

Friggin' geniuses.

Yet, Jake had another year or two selling what it is that he sold, banking the money and waiting for the death spiral. Then, he might actually have something to brighten his days, a little excitement, or even a challenge. Maybe an end to the boredom.

Jake spent about three hundred days a year traveling, and honestly, he did not know what to do when he did return home. Home, for Jake McCabe, was a small five-room townhouse in south Jersey, in the same township where the corporate office for his company was located. On a clear day, from his deck, he could see downtown Philadelphia.

Whippy-doo.

It was not much, but it was carefree, maintenance free, cheap, had a few, cute young women for neighbors, who occasionally added to the view when they sunbathed topless on their decks in the summer, and for Jake, it was perfect. Not that he was home often enough to enjoy the view.

Of Philadelphia, that is.

He had an agreement with the property manager for monthly visits to check on his place, to knock the cobwebs down, oversee a housekeeping crew, adjust the heat and air conditioning and inspect the home for him. The electric bill and other utilities all were on auto-pay as were all the other fees. Jake paid the mortgage off years ago.

One month, his electric bill was seven bucks.

Jake threw the property manager a monthly management fee. When he returned home, he tossed him a few bucks on the side, and gave him a bottle of expensive booze for Christmas, and all was well.

It all wrapped up in a tidy bow for Jacob McCabe.

Sort of.

When he was home, other than gazing at the cute neighbors, Jake had one or two co-workers at the corporate office that he hung around with here and there. One of his coworkers, Mr. Wayne Hampstead, could be the closest person to a friend that Jake had. He always went out for a few drinks and shared dinner with Wayne whenever he returned home. They often went out shooting pool together or to a hockey game in Philadelphia if it was the hockey season. Jake liked Wayne. He was a good man, honest, a hard worker, he had been with the company for ten years or so, had two children and an attractive, pleasant and cordial wife. Wayne's wife worked hard at her own job and she seemed very loyal and did not seem to nag or harass Wayne. Amongst the female world, those types of women are difficult to find these days. His friend had a happy marriage, great kids and a good life.

Wayne was a very lucky guy.

Jake was so rarely in the corporate office that when he did appear, it was a major event. He was something of a celebrity. Not only was Jake McCabe the highest grossing salesperson in total sales, Jake was now the longest tenured sales employee within the company. Yet, for Jake, he could do this all with his eyes closed. He checked in with his direct boss via the telephone once a week, participated in conference and video calls and of course, the plague of modern business these days; he answered countless texts and endless email.

In his personal life, Jake had been alone now for about ten years or a little more. His wife grew bored with him, his lifestyle, and with Jake being away for so long. No doubt that she loved spending the money and the young guy, just out of prison, with all kinds of tattoos, who lived with his parents down the street from the McCabe's expensive home. Jake returned home without notice from a long road trip one day, and found them wrapped up tighter than tumbleweeds, making love like wild baboons, and decided that they deserved each other. Their two children were all grown, all long since off on their own, so he took off and let them have it all.

In the big picture, Jake couldn't care less. Let the loser have her. She was a pain-in-the-ass. He will find out quickly enough. It was a speedy divorce. Painless and uncontested. He gave his ex-wife half of everything, and the entire house. Half was all he required in this life, and he felt a sigh of relief at never having to pay the outrageous taxes and high maintenance on a house that he seldom even lived in or visited. It was a grand home, set in the finest neighborhood, and to Jake it meant nothing. It was just a big pain-in-the-ass and a money pit. He was happy to let them have it all. Jake sure as hell never had the chance to enjoy it. To hell with fancy subdivisions and status in society. In Jake's mind it all sucked big time.

Jake kept himself in good physical condition, nowadays, most of the hotels had fitness centers, he was not a bad-looking guy, still lean, still tall and dark and he caught the eye of more than just a few ladies along the way. Jake could have his pick of most of them. Young and old. The one-night stands were not the greatest, but what the hell.

Ah yes, a dubious lifestyle, not too much changed for Jacob McCabe. Yes, the money rolled in, but the boredom went on and on along with him. Then, on a February evening, in a hotel in Boston, Massachusetts, Jake's seemingly endless run of boredom came to an unusual and abrupt end. A remarkable end. An end that he could never have imagined, or even years later, figure out or describe. His greatest dreams and his wildest fantasies could not explain it, but then again, was it all a dream?

This world is full of great mysteries, unsolved, and

perpetual and they remain mysteries that the greatest minds can neither solve, nor explain or understand. Perhaps, of all of these mysteries, the greatest of them all is love. Does love guide us, steer us, mold us and lead us? Does love do all of those things and even more? Can love conquer the greatest pain while simultaneously being the cause of it too?

Then, there is this little matter of this thing that we call time. What really is time? How do we define it? Where does it come from? Can we say that time is man-made, and that humankind created time as a tool to chart our lives and years with, in our human world?

Perhaps.

On the other hand, is time something deeper?

Much, much deeper.

Jacob McCabe Begins to Tell his Story

My best, and more accurately, perhaps, my only friend in the entire world, Wayne Hampstead fiddled with his beer mug, and while trying hard to attract the attention of the bartender he told me with some concern in his voice, "So you are looking a little shook up there, Jake. I have to say that in all the years that I have known you that I have never heard you quite so rattled as you were on the telephone when you called me. When you called me to meet you here after work, I could hear the quivering in your voice, and now that I see you, I can tell by the look on your face and the lick in your eyes that something is really bothering you. Usually, everything in your world is so controlled, sort of humdrum and commonplace."

I nodded my head and went to speak, when the bartender finally scooted over to us and waved his hands in an indication for us to order quickly, especially if they were just refilling of the brews. A lively Friday evening crowd packed our favorite gin joint this evening, and the bartender was running hard.

I saved the bartender a few steps by waving to him as I told him, "Yes, please, the same . . . for both of us. Keep the tab open."

Seemingly within seconds, Wayne and I had fresh brews in front of us. The bartender was efficient and very good at his job.

Over sips of the cold brews, I told my friend, "Wayne, my man, I have to tell you that, I am a bit rattled. I have no explanation for what happened to me on this last trip. A trip that started out just as ordinarily as all the thousands of others. A stop or two in lower Massachusetts and then off to my usual stop in Boston and that is where things became strange."

Wayne leaned back on the bar stool. He took a handful of some bar snacks from a small dish in front of us, and popped a few crunchy snacks in his mouth.

While he chewed and crunched them, he mumbled, "I see. Strange, huh? How so?"

"Well," I shook my head; it was going to feel good to get this story out of my head and off my chest. Maybe someone else could make some sense of it.

"Sit on back there Wayne, enjoy those beers, and let me tell you my incredible story."

Wayne nodded and smiled while sipping his brew, "I got all night, Jake. Wife and kiddies are off to her mom's house for the weekend, so go ahead. I am interested in what has a normally cool, calm and collected, Jake McCabe so damn worked up."

"Okay, it is a long story, but you said you have all night."

Jacob McCabe's Testimony

Here we go then.

It started out much the same, as all of these trips tend to do. The weather was a bit of a pain-in-the-ass. I had a delayed flight out of Atlanta, unusually cold for late February in Atlanta, had to wait for the stupid-ass deicing truck and then we made our way up to Connecticut.

I drove the rental car first to Worcester, there I made a quick sales call, filled out the usual order with a hospital that I have been calling on forever, and took the clients to lunch. Showed the customers a new product line, flirted a bit with a cute woman who just came on staff with them, and then drove the rest of the way into Boston. I checked into the hotel that I usually stay at, The Grand City Marquis Hotel. It has a fancy-ass name, but let me tell you that it is nothing special. It is just a typically overpriced bullshit hotel stuck in the middle of the old city, but I rather enjoy the parking arrangement. The parking is in a garage adjacent to the hotel, easy in and easy out, and the hospital that I call on is within walking distance of the hotel. No hassles at all, with traffic or parking.

It was cold and let me tell you for late February; the wind whistled through those buildings and I froze my ass off just walking from the parking garage to the hotel. There was no way that I was going to venture out into the city streets to eat. The hotel lounge would work just fine for me. Besides, despite the fact that the hotel is nothing special, the food there is very good. Exceptional in fact. They have a magnificent spinach and cheese ravioli dish and the chef has known me for years. He takes extra good care of me. Certainly, it was a better choice than freezing your ass off walking to some restaurant that charged you fifty bucks for a meager pile of spaghetti and meatballs that are more breadcrumbs than they are meat.

I checked into my room, set up the laptop, answered a few million emails, all of them the usual bullshit. I washed up, dressed for dinner, and wandered down into the hotel lounge and restaurant. The hotel had a high occupancy and I think that everyone in the entire hotel felt as I did, and no one else wanted to wander out into the cold city for a meal when you could eat here. After these many years of staying here, the night manager knows me quite well, and despite the evening dinner crowd, she managed to seat me at my usual table in a far corner near the kitchen door. I had gone out on a date here and there with her over the years, nothing serious. We never spent the night together or anything like that. We just tested each other to see if there might be a match. She wanted to date on a more serious level, and while I enjoyed her company, I always kept it friendly with her. We shared some general chit chat; she is a cutie, a very nice person, and while she still seemed to hope that I would take our relationship to the next level, she did not seem overly miffed at my desire to be only friends. After we caught up a bit, she brought me my usual Scotch on the rocks; I ordered the ravioli dish, and all was going rather well.

Honestly, when the hotel, bar, and restaurant are this crowded, I always scan the crowd for some women who I might want to meet or share some general chit chat with, you know, pass some time with. Not everything is always about sex. Often, you meet interesting people who are just fun to chat with and to discuss things with on evenings such as these. Tonight, however, despite the crowd, there did not seem to be any women around, at least none, who caught my eye. It might just have been *too* crowded, if that makes some type of sense, or I was just too tired and uninterested in anything, but having a few drinks, enjoying a good meal and hitting the sack early. Long travel days combined with business and long drives suck. No doubt that the trip had tired me out. I bid the manager good evening; the chef came out to check on me and the quality of the meal and with a tiny bit of a buzz on from three Scotches; I made my way to my room.

While I passed by the bar, I leaned in and said hello to the bartender. His name is Bradley. He is a very pleasant guy, a helluva bartender too, and he has worked at the bar for as long as I have been staying in the hotel.

"Too crowded to sit with me tonight, Jake? Missed yah."

"Hello, Bradley. Yes, I picked my corner table. Just a little quieter. Have you been doing, okay?"

"Yes. I've been okay, working, living the dream. You?"

"Same. Living the dream, earning the wage. Why, I do not know why, but I am earning the wage. Nuthin' to spend it on when you work all the time."

Bradley nodded, waved, and as he hustled off to the other end of the bar, he told me, "I know that you usually stay two or three nights. Occupancy goes way down tomorrow. Maybe, we can catch up tomorrow night."

I nodded and told him, "Yes, I am here for a few nights. That sounds like a plan." With that, I wobbled towards the lobby elevators.

This hotel is a high-rise; it towers endlessly into the sky and is stuck in the old section of the city. The view from the room was spectacular. After undressing and lounging around on the bed in my underwear, I grew bored stiff. My mind was uneasy, restless, and even though I was tired, sleep, for some reason, was not easy to find. After flipping through all the channels on the television, I checked my email once again and then officially gave in to the captivating view of the city. Restless, I sat in a chair and mindlessly stared out at the view through the window, and before I knew it, I fell asleep in the chair next to the window. When I woke, it was just a hairpin past midnight and as so often occurs when you are sleeping on the road, a catnap steals all the sleep from your mind and your body too. Now, I was not the least bit tired, and I grew even more restless. Why I was so restless, I could not quite place my finger on, but there was little doubt that sleep was going to be hard to come by now.

Looking back on all of this, it might have been for a reason. After pacing the floor, I finally conceded defeat and dressed. Casual dress, a pair of khakis, a long sleeve mock neck shirt and on the way out the door, I grabbed the room key and a few bucks in cash from a stash in my carry-on bag. I am not sure why I did that because I usually charge road expenses on a credit card or to my hotel room. I never carry much cash on my person when I wander on the road. It was strange, but something told me to have cash on hand. Anyway, I knew the bar was open until two in the morning. Walk-ins off the city streets often crowded the hotel bar when the nightlife of the city wound down. Bradley would be pissing and moaning at the action and between moans, he would pocket a ton of dough in tips. The guy made a killer of a living here.

Oh yes, a nightcap would do it. The Scotch was now a process in my worn-out liver and its influence was in the past. I needed a nightcap and I would sleep like a baby.

Yes, indeed. Like a baby.

Rode the elevator down from the nineteenth floor and when I walked into the bar area, I must say that I was amazed. Strange was a word that did not quite describe the scene that played out in front of me. There was not a single patron in the entire place. I glanced at my watch with the thought that perhaps I had made a mistake and lost track of time. My watch told me the time and the date. It was twelve-thirty-five in the morning on the 29th of February. I chuckled at the fact that it was Leap Day. A day that man created to fill a void in a calendar and a day that only comes around every four years.

I had to wonder, does this day even actually exist?

The bar remained lit with the back lights gently and gracefully illuminating the colors of the bottles and broadcasting their promise of a delectable, yet temporary, escape from your realities. The taps for the various brews sat happily in the dispensing handles; the bar was still open, but no one was home.

Except for the bartender.

I did a double take. No, honestly, that might not be correct; I did a triple take, or maybe even more. This bartender sure as hell was not Bradley.

No, it certainly was not Bradley in front of me. I settled into a bar stool on the far end of the bar and studied the glorious rear view of a woman, who was preoccupied with washing glassware in the glassware bath on the opposite end of the bar from where I decided to sit. She was a goddess, perfectly shaped, her tight black pants gripping her fantastic backside like a glove, her gentle hips swaying as she washed the glassware, oblivious to me studying and frankly, lusting after her. She had shoulder length black hair. Hair that was so clean, shiny, and jet-black that the lights from the back lights of the bar and various colors of the liquor bottles reflected off her hair. Her hair was gorgeous. It hung rather straight, and it moved and chased about her body as she moved. All I could do was to sit there and study her, while remaining mesmerized at her beauty, and now that I had admired her attractiveness from the rear, I immediately longed for her to turn around. I thought how if the front view was as amazing as the rear view, then I might just fall off this damn bar stool.

Finally, the impatience inside of me rose to a new level, so I leaned over the bar and waved in the air while saying, "Ah, hello there. Sorry to tear you away from such a riveting job, but . . . good evening. Or should, I say, good morning?"

When she turned around, I did almost fall off the barstool. Wish I had more of an ass, at least a big enough of an ass to have anchored me firmly in the bar stool. I am not kidding, nor am I exaggerating, when I tell you that her beauty was such that I held onto the edge of the bar to prevent myself from toppling over when she spun around and faced me. Yes, indeed! A goddess! Perfect facial features, a wide smile, and her perfect breasts, perfectly shaped and enhanced by a black pullover blouse that neatly tucked into the waistline of her black pants. Sorry, Bradley the bartender, but I ain't gonna miss you at all!

"Oh, I am so sorry!" She loudly spoke as she picked up a bar towel, wiped her hands and tossed it aside as she hustled over to where I sat. As she walked closer, her beauty surrounded her. Suddenly, this ordinary road trip had turned very extraordinary.

"Were you sitting there for a long time? I was washing the glassware, and to be honest, I was daydreaming and did not see or hear you there. It is so quiet in here right now, unusually so."

Her eyes displayed a shimmer of green in the light of the bar, a green color, which danced and twinkled at me. Her smile and beauty went through me and as she stood in front of me now, my eyes went from her smile to her breasts to her hips, and I am quite sure that she noticed me checking her out. Surely, a woman who looks as stunning as she does, might be used to such a gaze from a man. Yet, I did not want her to perceive me to be a typical lust-driven businessman asshole on a road trip. Even if, as of right now, after seeing this gorgeous woman, I was a typical lust-driven businessman asshole on a road trip. Despite my best efforts at trying not to gawk at her beauty; I failed rather miserably and I could not help myself. I answered her rather vaguely, with one of those stupid-ass dumb coy answers loaded with double meanings. Stupid flirting.

"Oh, no trouble. I did not mind at all . . . the view was

quite intriguing."

To my surprise, she did not frown or show any sign of disgust with my silly comment. Instead, she softly smiled and I caught her eyes carefully studying me. First, her eyes went to my face, and then her gaze lingered on my hands as they sat on the polished finish of the bar top. I displayed my hands neatly in front of me, my fingers purposely outstretched in front of me in an outward and unabashed display. Yes, no wedding ring, and no there, gorgeous; I do not take it off for road trips. I dumped her sorry ass years ago, and as far as I know, her tough-guy, mean-ass prison boy ended up back in prison on more felonies. Rumor had it that my ex-pain-in-the-ass was now married to her third husband and he, too, was finding out what I did so long ago. She was indeed a pain-in-the-ass.

My eyes studied her hands and no wedding ring existed there either.

My guess would be that she might have been a few years older than I was, but it was difficult to tell with a woman of this level of beauty. Age was not a factor in my attraction to her. Judging by her initial reactions to me, I think she felt as if I was not a bad-looking man, and that might have been dreaming or supposition on my part. Yet, I hoped it was true, and now, I felt some pangs of regret at not taking more time in front of the mirror before wandering down here. At least, I had a fresh shower; it was a close shave that I was lacking. Usually, women found me attractive, if not with overwhelming Hollywood good looks. Perhaps I landed just a cut above the average Joe. I dunno. It was not as if I had to beat the women off with a stick, but I attracted my share. But this woman was not the average woman.

No, no, no, I damn sure wish that I had shaved.

"Oh, I see. The view, huh? I must say that things have picked up considerably with your arrival. Suddenly, the atmosphere has improved around here. And yes, technically, it is morning. So, good morning."

Sparkly comments, followed by a wickedly sexy smile. A glorious pose, with a bent leg, a tilt of her head, a flip of her hair and a flash of her green eyes. I shivered at her golden voice and words.

"What will you have? A nightcap? A nightcap in the morning?"

"Yes, please. A nightcap. I dozed off for a few minutes in my room. Now, sleep is a lost cause. Dozed, while sitting in a chair, gazing like some idiot looking out at the city. I am on the nineteenth floor. The view there, as it is here, is quite spectacular."

She nodded with the smile still upon her face and offered, "Might I suggest a snifter of brandy. Warm, brandy. It always works for me. Manages to somehow, send a trickle of warmth and a touch of magic through your veins."

"Sounds perfect. Works for me. Pour it, please. Say, I was here tonight, or actually, last night, for dinner . . . what now seems as if it were a lifetime or so ago. I would have certainly noticed you, but I only saw Bradley working at the bar. Am I incorrect?"

I tried hard to read her nametag, you know, the little brass or plastic tags that the hotel staff wears on their lapels, but she had turned so quickly away from me to prepare the drink that I could not catch more than just a fleeting glimpse of it. Within a flash glimpse, I thought the first letter was an M . . . but I thought that I was wrong.

As she searched the multitude of bottles behind the bar, she explained, "No, you are correct. I relieved him at midnight. I will work until two and then close the bar down. I am just so amazed that you have been the only customer, it seemed as if I chased them away."

She found the bottle, took a brandy glass, unscrewed the top and poured the drink for me.

While she did so, she laughed a bit at her statement,

"Seems as if we are the last persons left on Earth. Even the lobby traffic has died down."

She walked over, placed the drink in front of me, and leaned in a bit. When she did so, it was difficult not to gaze at the hint of cleavage she revealed to me. I smiled, picked the drink up, and then placed it gently back on the surface of the bar. Now, I could clearly read her nametag, and I did so under the false pretense of also catching more of a glimpse of her amazing breasts.

"I doubt that you could have chased any person away, unless they are blind . . . ah, hello, Michelle. It is a pleasure to meet you this morning. I am Jacob McCabe. Most everyone just calls me, Jake."

I reached out my hand and Michelle stood up straighter and gently took it. While she was neither tall nor short for a woman, she had tiny hands. Yet, her touch was soft and her hands were warm, especially so on such a cold evening. We held each other's hands for an unusually long time. It was not a handshake. Instead, I rather describe it as a gentle grasp. I cannot describe the feeling when we touched; it was magical and the best that I can do to capture the moment was that her touch sent some type of wave of overwhelming joy throughout my body. I have never experienced a feeling or anything quite like it. There actually are no words to describe it.

"Please, surely the pleasure is mutual, yet, in some way, I feel very lucky to have you wander down here and keep me company. On second thought—the pleasure is all mine. Nice to meet you, Jake. Certainly, it is mine. What do you do for a living, or entertainment or both, to bring you in here for a nightcap on what has turned out to be such a strange evening?"

Now, I could feel that the conversation changed to a different level. I sipped the drink and it indeed immediately floated some warmth and additional magic in my veins. I leaned in and so did Michelle.

"By the way, you might be, Jake, rather than Jacob, but most everyone calls me, Shelly. Shelly McDermott."

Without hesitation, I took the opportunity to make the conversation more informal and more relaxed, "Shelly it is then. I am a salesman. I travel the entire country, on the road three hundred days a year, until tonight every stop looked the same, felt the same and smelled the same. I sell bullshit. What salesperson could tell you something different? Technically, I sell medical tools, surgical devices, instruments and laboratory equipment. Yet, I imagine that I am the same as every other salesperson is. I guess that I sell bullshit. No matter if you are selling furniture, magazines, appliances, or religion, you are selling bullshit."

She smiled widely at my statement. She leaned back in, put her one foot on the inside railing of the bar and gently grasped my hand. Our eyes locked, and her beauty overwhelmed me. Something connected between us and I cannot say if it was love at first sight or some other type of feeling, but it was a very powerful feeling and connection. Right now, as I try so damn hard to figure this out, I am not actually going to try to dwell upon corny nonsense and clichés.

"Damn, Mr. Jacob McCabe. I have seldom heard such true words or honesty from a man. I agree that when you stop and study it, I think you are correct and all that I sell are drinks and conversation, so I specialize in bullshit too."

"Sorry, I didn't mean to imply to you, that what you do here in any manner might relate to what I do."

"You didn't. Never say sorry to, Shelly. Truth is hard to find in an absurd world, Jake. And for sure, this bullshit world is absurd. Please, no one in management is around, in fact, no one at all, is around. Therefore, I might steal a brandy and join you. Meeting you will give me a good enough reason to break some rules."

"Please, do. Just pour it and put it on my tab. Room 1962. I sell bullshit to an absurd world, but damn sure make a ton of dough doing it. In a nutshell, Jake McCabe lives a boring and simple life. I have no wife and my children are all grown and on their own. I send them money here and there, but until grandchildren come along, I have no grand reason to spend too much money on them. My children all have good jobs and make a solid living, too. When the grand kiddies come along, then I can spoil them. I only have a small townhouse in New Jersey, and I am never there. Drive a company car, no fancy cars, shit, I will end up being dead and rich and so the kids will get it all, anyhow."

Michelle walked over to the bottle and poured a drink for herself.

As she poured the drink, she spoke, this time, with her back turned to me, her glorious rear view in full display, "Room 1962, huh? Very interesting number and coincidental too. Then, Jake, what the hell. Let's spend just a little of it today. I will join you for a sip or two and take you up on your tab offer too. We deserve it. Today is my birthday. I am a Leapling. Born on Leap Day in 1962. Is that screwed up or what? I only have my birthday every four years or so. Maybe, I never age or better yet, maybe, I do not even exist at all. Who the hell knows . . . right?"

She turned around, and with a brandy glass in her hand, Michelle returned to stand opposite to where I sat. Leapling? Never heard of that term, but I guess it makes sense. Wow, I must say that I now recalled that it was Leap Day and my previous thoughts on how strange this day was.

"Wow, interesting. I must tell you, Shelly, that until now . . . I never met anyone born on Leap Day or even thought about how unusual that is. That is what they call people born on this day, huh? Leaplings. Very cool. Well, I for one can testify that you do exist. I have some magic running in my veins now, mixing with some expired remnants of Scotch from dinner, so I will venture on the bold side and say, my goodness you do exist, and are one gorgeous woman."

I recalled thinking, what the hell, right now; I needed to be bold because this was a rare woman in front of me.

Now or never.

Therefore, I gave it my best try, lifted my glass and touched her glass while saying, "Cheers. Happy birthday. Seems as if I should give you something else, something special for your birthday. I think that you deserve something more than just buying you a drink or two."

She touched my glass and spoke in almost a whisper, "Thank you for the compliment and the well wishes. I must say that you are quite the handsome man. I love the sparkle in your eyes. Therefore, perhaps, you are correct and I do exist. For what reason, I am not sure, but perhaps, you are correct."

I thought how that was such a strange thing to say, but as she took a sip she smiled, so I dismissed the words as her teasing me a bit.

After our sips, she placed the glass back down upon the bar top and told me in quite a matter-of-fact manner, "I do want something for my birthday. I need new shoelaces."

With that statement, she lifted her leg and held her foot up to show me her shoes. I stood up from the stool, leaned over the bar top, and checked out what it was that Shelly was showing to me. Shelly's shoelaces were broken and too short to make the rounds of all the eyelets. The laces all were too short and tied off into a small loop on the tongues of her shoes. She started to laugh, a golden and hearty laugh and I burst out laughing, too.

Sometimes, you search the entire world for a soulmate and you think that you find them. You share sex, lust, kisses, life, pain, and conversation and they are all wonderful, but when you find someone that you can truly laugh with, then it lifts you to a higher place. I do not mean a few jokes or random silliness. I mean laughs and I mean to share heartfelt joy with in your life.

That is a true soulmate. A person who you can share and honor every range of emotion with during your lives together. It is a profound connection, when you share the mutual joy within your lives, when joyful emotions surround your love, and when your lover and you hold them close to your hearts. When you lock your minds, bodies and your hearts forever. When, no matter what happens, you believe in each other. That is the definition of a lover.

"Okay? Wow! Shoelaces. Really? You only have your birthday every four years and you ask for a pair of measly shoelaces. I am sure that someone special in your life will buy them and some other special presents for you."

The smile quickly faded from her face. She shook her head to indicate no.

She whispered just loud enough for me to hear, "Until tonight, there were no special persons in my life."

Her statement floored me. The look on her face and the lick in her eyes when Michelle spoke those words sent me into cold shivers.

I managed to squeak out some drivel, "Damn. You are not a woman with very high demands. I can tell that, to you, materialistic things do not matter very much. It seems as if you deserve a hell of a lot more for your birthday than shoelaces. I can write you a check and you can go and buy a sports car or a new wardrobe."

Once again, Shelley shook her head, and she spoke softly to me, "Why? What do they mean in this life? You just met me, and already you can see into my heart and see certain things such as those, which you just mentioned, are not important to me in this world. Now, life is long, or is it too short? Jake, honestly, I am not sure which it is. I do know whom it is that you love along the way, and how you treat them is all that really matters. Love is the most important thing and it will overcome the greatest sorrow and be the cause of it, too. Material things pass away. Even measly shoelaces. They all mean nothing. Yet I do need shoelaces, in order to help to hold me up and to propel me through this world. We live in a replaceable world where only love and respect mean anything. When we have the courage to peel off the layers of all the human emotions and press our face against the windows of our lives and force our eyes to view what we have done, we see that only love and respect are important."

She then shifted moods and returned once again to waves of humor and with a coy smile, she lifted her foot and pointed at her ragged shoelace, while telling me, "We all need to try to walk along rather proudly through our lives. As best we can, you know, as we make our way. Therefore, I have with some profound and wonderful insight, determined that shoes, Jake, they are important too."

When she said that, I looked at my watch, jumped off the bar stool and told Shelley, "Please, pour me another drink. The magic is amazing. I will be right back. I promise that I will be right back."

With that, I dashed out the side door of the bar, sprinted into the freezing cold air, and ran along the city streets. Hell no, I did not need a coat or hat. Something else was keeping me warm. I knew there happened to be a twenty-four-hour drugstore on a nearby corner, and I knew what I needed to buy. I do think the store clerk in the drug store thought that I was some type of lunatic. There I was, on a bitter cold night, a whiff of booze on me, no coat, and no hat, while bursting breathlessly into the store in the early morning hours of the day, asking between huffs and puffs where the shoelaces were and then asking where the stick-on birthday bows were.

Red bows.

I threw the cash at the clerk. I now understand the strange cash urge because all of this was fate. The clerk insisted on writing a receipt . . . something about his cash register not working because of Leap Day. I was in a hurry so I gave him a huge tip and ran out of the store. In a few short minutes, I returned to the bar. When I pulled the "present" of a pack of black women's shoelaces adorned with a red bow out of the bag and handed it to Shelley, it was then that I felt love. Therefore, to revisit the clichés and corny bullshit, yes, now, I do believe in love at first sight. In a few minutes, she had new laces in her shoes and I might have been incorrect or misjudging, but she had new shoelaces and perhaps a touch of love in her heart, too.

"Here, Jake. Please take the used shoelaces. Maybe someday, when you are desperate and down on your luck, you will find that they come in handy. You might need them to stand upright and propel Jake McCabe through this absurd world."

She handed me the used laces. I laughed and stuffed them in the pocket of my pants.

"I will keep them. You are correct. In this crazy life, you never know when used shoelaces will come in handy."

All too soon, two o'clock and closing time came. I signed the tab slip to charge the drinks to my room and mustered up some courage to ask for her contact information, and if I could see her again. Sitting there on the bar stool, sitting like some love-struck jackass, while holding my stupid-ass smart phone in my hand, I waited for her to take out a cellphone and we could exchange numbers.

It was more than just a grand disappointment when she told me, "Now, Jake. You just gave me shoelaces for my birthday. You have seen into my heart. I do not own a smartphone or a cellphone. Sometimes, I do think that I own nothing at all."

Michelle must have sensed my disappointment. She walked over to me, reached out her hands and told me, "You will see me again, I promise. Soon. I have to close out the bar. Good things come to those who are willing to wait.

Nightcaps are worth it. Will you wait?"

"I will."

She leaned over the bar, motioned for me to lean over too, and she kissed my cheek.

I heard her say, "Good."

With that one word, she pulled the drawer out of the cash register, closed off the lights of the bar, and she disappeared through a door behind the bar. I sat there in the darkness for a few minutes, not too sure what all of this meant, and when I finally realized that Michelle was not returning, I pulled my sorry ass off the stool and made my way to the elevator. Once again, it seemed so strange not to see another person in the hotel. Thinking about it now, I should have walked out to the front of the lobby to see if the nighttime security officer, bellhops, and desk clerks were on duty or not. I did not do that. Instead, I just pushed the elevator button, stood like a disappointed and lovesick teenager with my hands in my pockets and stared around me while waiting. Not a soul in sight. In fact, other than the store clerk and Michelle, I had not seen another person since dinnertime.

Here we are in a huge hotel, in the bustling city of Boston, and not another person in sight. Not a person on the streets when I dashed to the store. There were no cars, no taxicabs, any pedestrians, or police cars screaming down the main streets.

Friggin' bizarre.

I returned to my room. For some unknown and strange reason, I sat motionless on the edge of the bed for a long time. Did not move a single muscle. I can recall those moments very vividly. Even now, after all of this time. It was as if I froze in time and space. Unable to move. I could hear my own heartbeats. I swear to you that I could. After reflecting on all that happened to me, and trying as hard as I could possibly try in order to forget how gorgeous Michelle McDermott was, I took my shoes off and tossed them aside. I drew the curtains closed to prevent another gaze at the beauty of the city below and decided that since it was now close to three in the morning, I should sleep now.

After all, I had enjoyed a nightcap.

I was just about to undress for bed, went as far as pulling off my shirt, when to my shock, there was a gentle knock at the door of my hotel room. I would be a shitty liar if I told you that I hoped, wished, and dreamed it to be any other person on the face of this Earth other than Michelle McDermott at my door.

My heart told me that it was Michelle. Without a single hesitation, no apprehension, no viewing through the security viewfinder in the door in order to check who it was out there. I did not care if it was Jack, the friggin' ripper on the other side of the door. I flung the door open and there she stood. Glowing, seductive, her smile a mile wide, her green eyes flickering in the dim light of the hallway. She had changed from her work attire and now wore an amazingly tight-fitting black cocktail dress, a dress, which if she walked by them, any man on the face of this world would faint at the mere sight of her in.

I smiled.

She did the same.

In her hands, she held a bottle of brandy and with a seductive growl, she told me, "I told you that I would see you soon and that your nightcap would be worth it. Good things come to those who are willing to wait. I am so happy to see that you waited."

"I did."

"You bought me more than just shoelaces and a few drinks for my birthday. You bought me this bottle too."

"Good. Works for me. I love this stuff. Only just had it tonight. Never had a drop of it until tonight and already it is my favorite."

I grabbed her hand and gently pulled her into the hotel

room, took the bottle from her hands, and placed it on the top of the small shelf of the wardrobe. Her appearance and her dress mesmerized me in such a manner that I did not realize that I was bare-chested until she placed her hands on my bare chest. I turned and held her while kicking the door to the room shut.

It slammed with a positive latch.

Good.

I reached over, and with one hand, flipped the deadbolt and slid the door security lever tightly down upon the door.

A door closed on that absurd world, which lies out there on the other side. If it only was so simple to close it out forever. Goodbye, bullshit. Goodbye, deadlines, and numbers and sales quotas, and all the other things that in the end will not or never will have actually mattered. Yet, for just a few hours, we have this moment. I knew that the absurdities of the world no longer mattered. They were on the other side of that door. Now, it was just Michelle and a love-struck fool.

Alone. Uninhibited. New shoelaces and green eyes.

Her eyes gazed at my chest and she gently moved her hands up and down my chest while intently studying me.

"You are well built. No doubt, lots of hotel fitness rooms. A road warrior who takes care of his body. You are quite the man, Jake McCabe."

I did not answer her; instead, I had waited too long for this. In essence, I only just met her a few short hours ago, but it actually might have been a lifetime that I had waited for this. We kissed, long, deep, and wet. No doubt, I had waited for this kiss an entire lifetime and maybe a few more lifetimes.

No doubt.

In mere seconds, my hands explored her body, and she willingly allowed me to hike up her dress and slowly and gently remove her panties. She stepped out of them. She almost laughed as she bent over and undid her new shoelaces and forcibly kicked her shoes aside. With the same magical glow in her green eyes, she turned her attention to me. She worked with the belt of my pants and she fumbled a bit with the stupid-ass button that held the two sides of my pants together.

I helped her.

My excitement was rather obvious, and I gasped as she held me in her hands.

She whispered, "You feel glorious in my hands. Amazing manhood."

I answered, "And you are a goddess."

When I pulled the glorious dress over her head, and she undid and dropped her brassiere to the floor, she stood naked in front of me, and I stood naked in front of her. Nothing mattered any longer. Only love at first sight. Her breasts pressed against my chest, her glorious nipples were bursting with love, and they were hard. Yet somehow, if this makes any sense, they were soft too. Her body was more than glorious. It was a temple, and she was shaven clean. Not a whisker of hair lay upon her, no blemishes, no cracks in her heart, there were only openings to her soul, openings, which revealed her exposure. An exposure, without any regrets or worries, just an exposure of her endless search for love. She was soft, naked, and clean. Untouched and unfettered. Just the smell of her skin and the smooth touch of her hands upon my body sent shock waves of love into my heart. We made love uninhibited for hours. Explored every inch of each other's bodies, and nothing went untouched or unexplored. I am not ashamed to say and use the word, nothing.

When the first hints of the early morning light stole our precious darkness away, and it filtered and danced through the drawn curtains into the corners of the room, I knew that this glorious and magical time was ending. While exhaustion had long since overtaken our bodies, our love remained unfiltered and just as powerful as any force on Earth and perhaps in Heaven too.

In a haze of sleep, combined with ecstasy, I heard Michelle whisper to me, "Soon, I have to go. We need to make love one more time. I will need to climb on top of you and lock my eyes with yours while we make love. It is how I want to remember you. For now, for always, our love shared with locked eyes. We will make love one more time to last us until we can meet again. We might not understand all of this. You will be confused about our love. I will be too. Promise me, Jacob McCabe. Promise me that you will wait. Will you wait? No matter what, no matter the confusion or the doubts, or the mystery of this, please, promise me that you will wait. I have waited for you forever. Will you wait for me?"

I did not know what to make of her statement and when you considered that other than my catnap, I had been awake for thirty hours or thereabouts, consumed a lot of alcohol and made love for hours upon end, to the most gorgeous woman that I had ever seen or known, well, now that might be understandable.

"Yes, of course, I will wait. I promise, with all of my heart and soul. I, too, have waited a long time for love such as this."

She smiled and gently shook her head while saying, "Not as long as I have. You have no idea how long I have waited for you."

I was confused and asked, "Why? Where will you be? Where are you going?"

She did not answer me, instead, she smiled, placed both of her hands upon her glorious breasts to support them as she swung her legs over me and then she allowed her breasts to go free. While she climbed on top of me, we locked our eyes forever and for the last time, we made glorious and amazing love.

Never knew that I had such stamina and manly

fortitude. I lost count now as to exactly how many times we made love.

Afterwards, when we both had finished sharing our love and joy, I must confess that I rolled over, Shelley did too, and to my recollection, we both fell fast asleep. When I woke up, it was midmorning and Michelle was gone. My cellphone spit out angry texts and obnoxious voice mails at me. Luckily, for me, I only had an afternoon meeting and appointment to make. I still had time. I jumped out of bed. My head was clear, and another frank and honest testimony to the wildness of the evening, was that the male parts of my anatomy hung limp and withered.

I had worked them extra hard.

It seemed very strange that no sign of Michelle remained. There were no notes on the desk, no sign of her anywhere. There was a faint, yet a glorious odor of her perfume upon my chest, and in the room, and her scent remained very strong in the bed. I scampered over to the shelf in the entry area of the hotel room and the bottle of brandy sat upon the shelf of the wardrobe. No, it was not a dream, it might be Leap Day, her birthday, and a day that might not actually exist, but it was not a dream. Friggin' bottles of top-shelf brandy do not magically appear in hotel rooms. I had a bit of a chuckle at the fact that we never even touched it.

When I climbed in the shower, I had dull thoughts in my mind of struggling through another mindless day. In an attempt to boost my spirits, I then countered those thoughts with glorious hope and joy mired within the promise of seeing Michelle later tonight. I was not sure, but somehow, I remained confident that she would be working the late shift again. I had nothing to base that upon, except for my heart and our love.

Let me tell you how difficult it was to concentrate on selling medical instruments when you had experienced what I experienced. Looking back, I am sure the customers knew that I was a bit preoccupied. I had been calling on them for many years now, and they knew me quite well. Somehow, I successfully pulled off the sales call, and I wrote up a ton of orders. I managed to use some dumb excuse of a lingering headache and not feeling too well, in order to explain my inattentiveness and to beg out of dinner and cocktails. Besides, these were longtime customers, and they had milked me for many dinners and gallons of booze over the years. All that I wanted to do was to return to the hotel, to see and to hold Michelle. Tomorrow, I had to drive back to Connecticut and catch an airplane flight to the next horrible stop, which, as far as I knew, would be in Milwaukee, Wisconsin. I wanted to corral Michelle, tell her how much she meant to me, stop all of this traveling, and make plans for our future. It was time to stop the daily madness.

After the sales call, I quickly returned to my hotel room. I showered, dressed for dinner and made my way to the bar. Just as Bradley had explained last evening, the hotel occupancy dropped off considerably and the restaurant and bar were quite sparsely populated. I kept telling myself that was why no one was around early this morning. It seemed as if it was a valid explanation for why the hotel was so lonely for Michelle and me, but it did not explain the empty streets.

At this point, I tried hard not to dwell upon too many of the facts. Strange facts or otherwise.

I slid into a bar stool and Bradley spotted me right away; he waved and quickly grabbed a bottle of my usual Scotch off the shelf and a glass.

"Hey, how goes the day? Sell lots of very expensive widgets and fidgets to unsuspecting customers?"

I laughed and told him, "I did. It was a good day. Not as good as last evening, but it was a successful day. Last evening was the most magical and wonderful night in my entire life."

Bradley carried my drink over and he set it in front of me while saying, "Good, glad to hear it. I told you this place would clear out. Gonna be more manageable tonight. Say, why was last night so special? When you left last night, it seemed to be under control and quite ordinary."

I lifted my drink and smiled while taking a sip. Looking over the rim of the glass, I winked and continued with my long smile. A dopey ass, sly grin locked upon my stupid face.

After my sip, I placed the glass back down on the coaster and while Bradley stood in suspense, I decided to whisper a name to him. "Special . . . because of Michelle. Michelle, or actually, Shelly McDermott. Some credit has to go to catnaps, sleepless nights and enjoying a nightcap too."

Whispering her name provoked absolutely no reaction with Bradley. He stared at me and remained stoic, and actually, his face changed to a somewhat puzzled look.

Finally, he said, "Uh, okay, there Jake, if you say so. Catnaps? Who? Michelle, who? Shelly? Is that some chick that you met? Am I supposed to know her? I do not know Michelle McDermott. Never heard of her."

For a few seconds, I ran a number of different scenarios through my mind, but it was not as if I knew Bradley well enough to decide if he was joking with me or not. I mean I knew him for many years, but hell, in the big picture; he was a bartender on one of my regular stops. All he really did was to pour me drinks, and we made small talk. I played with a few different scenarios in my mind for a few seconds. Okay, you know, perhaps, Bradley spoke with Michelle and she told him about me and after hearing about our meeting, Bradley then decided to play dumb and catch me in a joke. On the other hand, perhaps, he was not actually paying attention to me and did not fully catch the drift of my conversation or hear her name correctly. While studying his face and reaction, either Bradley was one helluva damn good actor and he should be on the big screen, or something was really friggin' weird and strange here.

After the thoughts left my mind, I decided to pursue the idea that Bradley was messing with me here, "You know, geez, Bradley, she is kinda unforgettable. You know, the bartender, the gorgeous woman who relieved you at midnight last night and took over until closing. You know, c'mon man . . . Michelle McDermott."

After listening to me, Bradley smiled faintly and waved his hand at me while he laughed a bit.

At first, I thought, okay, he *was* joking with me here. When Bradley followed the wave with some additional comments, then the smile that appeared on my face quickly faded.

"Oh, shit, man. You musta had some good Scotch up in your room after you left here. You had me for a second or two. Did you have a bad hangover this morning or what? If you did, then I am happy to hear that you did not miss your appointment. Gotta, admit that it was weird closing up last night at midnight." Bradley then glanced at a regular patron settling into the bar to my right. He knew ahead of time what the order was that the patron wanted, and quickly grabbed a mug and started to pour a brew from one of the taps.

While he poured the brew from the tap, Bradley leaned in my way and he continued to speak, "Leap Day. What the hell is that, exactly? A friggin' day we make up time with, in a year where we elect a president. Anyway, technically, it is the only day other than Christmas that we close at midnight. Christmas is on purpose. This day is because of some local laws and bullshit about not having a valid liquor permit for the day until four in the afternoon. Ya know, we gotta close the bar at midnight on the twenty-eighth and we can't open until four in the afternoon today. Not sure that it makes much sense. Who knows? It only happens every four years, so no one knows, cares, or gives two shits less about it. It seems as if the day does not actually exist. . . ."

Bradley smiled and carried the full mug over to the thirsty patron, and I sat there stunned. My mouth hung open, shivers went up and down my spine, and I began to tremble and shake. Bradley was sincere. There was no doubt that he was not messing around with me. Michelle's words echoed in my head, a head that I now hung over the bar top and held tightly in my hands.

In my now aching head, her sweet voice resounded, clearly and distinctly, "No matter what, no matter the confusion or the doubts, or the mystery of this, please, promise me that you will wait. I have waited for you forever. Will you wait for me?"

What the hell is going on here?

I thought for a second or two that the explanation was that I was nuts. I had gone raging mad and crazy out of my mind. The loneliness of the road had finally taken my sanity from me. In my loneliness, I invented a magical lover to spend time with and we escaped to a special place. Yes, that was the answer. This crazy situation was because I now was stark raving mad. On the other hand, was I, as Bradley suggested, drunk, and I dreamed all of this and blacked out? Was Michelle an invention of too much Scotch? No, no, I only had three drinks. I swear that I did! I then decided to try to take deep breaths and calm my nerves. I gave up right away, because it was not going to work; the deep breaths made my body tremble even more. I knew that earlier today, I held the most gorgeous woman that I ever made love to, ever saw, or fell in love with. There was no love like this love. It was once in a lifetime.

No way was I going crazy.

I took the Scotch and swigged it down. My hope was that the drink would stop my body from trembling. It did not.

That was a real love. Profound, powerful, deep love

from a different place, from a different world. Perhaps that is where the answer lies. In a different world.

Bradley looked over when the now empty Scotch glass hit the bar top with a loud thud. He bent his eyebrows at me and glanced at my face. After some small talk with the other patron and delivering his beer, he scurried over to me.

"You okay, there, Jake? You look like ya been seeing ghosts or are feeling sick. Not like you to toss drinks, ya usually a slow sipper. Were you hungover? Rough day recovering?"

I bent over the now empty glass and did my best act in order to hide the shock and horror that were rippling through my soul. It was an effort to conceal my struggle as I tried to put all of this madness together and decide if I were crazy, drunk, dreaming or if in fact, as Michelle and Bradley and even I mentioned, did the 29th of February actually even exist?

"Please another Scotch. Double. Neat. Screw the ice." Bradley still stood looking at me as if he, too, was now in shock.

"Okay, sure, sure, sure. Are you going to be, okay? You are not going to keel over on me, are you?"

"No, I am okay. Not sure, what the hell is going on right now, not hungover, but it is going to be all right. I think. Right now, things are mixed up."

Bradley nodded, still watched me carefully out of the corner of his eyes and prepared the drink for me.

He set it in front of me and gently told me, "Look, this is on the house. Maybe you should eat something. Alternatively, better yet, maybe go to your room for some room service and relax. This Michelle that you mentioned . . . she . . . is real?"

"Hell yeah, she is real. If any one person on the face of the Earth is real, then in my heart, I know it is, Michelle McDermott. Please, charge me for the rest of that bottle. I will head to my room, and yes, room service is a good idea. Please charge me out. Put it on the room tab. 1962 is the number."

Bradley looked at me very suspiciously; he nodded his head, turned to the cash register, filled out the paperwork and then turned back toward me.

"Jake, are you sure that you are, okay?"

"I am. Just a little change in plans, but I will be fine. Thank you."

The bartender pointed at the bottle in his hands and offered some worldly advice, "Okay, if you say so. Be careful with this amount of Scotch now. Ya leavin' out 'morrow, eh?"

"Yes, thank you for everything. See you in six months or so."

"Yeah. See you. Please take good care of yourself. Not sure, what this Michelle stuff is all about tonight. Sorry that I do not know her and shook you up a little. Here you go,"

Bradley handed me the tab and the bottle. I signed the tab, shook his hand, and picked up the bottle.

I was acting the entire time because I actually felt like passing out. I knew that I needed to head to my room and examine the proof, try to regain my thoughts and myself. No way could I entertain any thoughts of eating. My stomach was in such terrible knots that I would toss it right up. The Scotch ran around in my veins and dulled some of my senses. Yet, the pain of Bradley's words and his sincerity turned my life upside down. I hustled to the main lobby and while pushing the elevator button, I hashed out the events of last night, replayed the conversation, studied the entire scene, and tried desperately to figure out a sound and reasonable explanation for all of this.

The elevator door opened, and I walked in the car and I was relieved that there were no other riders. I could lean on the wall of the elevator car to prevent my collapse. Let me think. The 29th of February, Michelle's words when she asked if this day actually exists, her birthday on the same day, no one else around in the entire hotel, the entire weird and surreal scene. Her beauty, our endless lovemaking, her gorgeous body, her passion, the taste of her body, her lips, the smell of her perfume. She was, by far, the greatest lover I have ever known.

This shit was real. I was not crazy. Shelly was and is, real. The elevator stopped on the nineteenth floor and I stepped out. Let me tell you that it is difficult to walk when your knees are knocking and your legs can hardly support you, but I made it to my room.

It was not the Scotch making me wobbly.

When I went in the room, I headed straight to where I left the bottle of brandy on the shelf and yes, it was still there. The housekeeper had cleaned the room and changed out the bed linens, so there was little hope of detecting any remnants and whiffs of Michelle's perfume on the pillowcases or bed sheets, but I sure as hell knew where to find the other evidence that I required. As if the bottle was not enough evidence. That is how strange and unexplainable this entire encounter is and was! Bottles of brandy do not just friggin' show up and materialize. Or do they? Does the 29th of February even exist?

I headed straight to the casual khaki pants that I wore last evening. In a furious and frantic effort to find the last pieces of confirmation that I required, I found the pants in my luggage, grabbed them, and dug into the pockets. Sure enough, my hand pulled out used shoelaces and a deep dig into the other pocket, pulled out a receipt from the corner drug store for a pack of new laces and a red bow.

The receipt had neither time nor a date stamp on it.

Of course, I should have known that would be the case. Damn!

Once more, the question remains, does the 29th of February even exist? Perhaps it was all quite explainable with some very simple explanations, such as the cash machines or the store's computers were not set up for Leap Day.

On the other hand, could I even explain it at all?

I smiled and held the used shoelaces tightly in my hand. While still holding them, I reached for the bottle of Scotch, unscrewed the top and did not even bother pouring it into a glass.

Top-shelf Scotch straight out of the bottle.

Damn, not exactly a proper way of drinking fine whiskey and it might be a wretched waste of very expensive Scotch and years of aging efforts, but right now, it works for me. I took a long swig, sat on the edge of the bed, and thought. Shelley's words floated in the air all around me. I reached into the air and grabbed the words; they were as if they were the seeds of dandelions in an open field that blew away in a wind. I captured all of them and held them along with the shoelaces.

I heard her soft voice say to me, "Here, Jake. Please take the used shoelaces. Maybe someday, when you are desperate and down on your luck, you will find that they come in handy. You might need them to stand upright and propel Jake McCabe through this absurd world."

I smiled as Michelle's prediction came true. Right now, I required used shoelaces to keep me upright. I stopped shaking a little, my heartbeat no longer raced, and I knew it was all very real. I kept the smile still frozen on my face and at that special moment, our love impaled forever into my heart.

More of her words escaped my hands and once more echoed inside of my head, "Today is my birthday. I am a Leapling. Born on Leap Day. Is that screwed up or what? I only have my birthday every four years or so. Maybe, I never age or better yet, maybe, I do not even exist at all. Who the hell knows? Right? Promise me, Jake. Promise me that you will wait. Will you wait? No matter what, will you wait for me?"

I held the words in my heart. Not that I understood what she meant or what this was all about, but I trusted and, above all, respected her honor. A great deal of true love involved large amounts of respect and trust.

Even upon reflection of the words, I did not know what to make of her statement and when you considered all of what had transpired for me, for us, well, now that might be understandable.

"Yes, of course, I will wait. Why? Where will you be? Where are you going?"

No answer. Perhaps, in looking back, there was a very good reason that Michelle did not answer me; then again, she did, because after I asked her that question, with our eyes locked forever, she made love to me as no other woman ever had.

Therein was my answer.

I might add, when you find that one special person, you will wait a million years, a hundred lifetimes, or even more for them.

Therefore, the answer is simple.

Why dwell upon it?

In my mind, Michelle asks me again and I answer in less than a second.

Yes.

I will wait for you.

Yes, indeed.

Jacob McCabe Finishes his Testimony

"That is, it. Wayne, my friend, I have told you the entire story. Strange, bizarre, beyond weird, but I swear to you . . . my old friend, upon my honor, that this is real and is all the honest truth. Still, now, five weeks or so later, I have no explanations for this. An internet search for Michelle McDermott turns up a few, and I called the ones that I could find and even searched the social media sites and sent emails to various Michelle names that I found. Even tried just using Shelly McDermott. No luck, just some nasty replies and countless hang-ups on the telephone. Believe me when I tell you, Wayne, I have poured over the internet, crawled through old-fashioned white pages, exhausted every idea to try to find her. People that I call and inquire of her, they think I am nuts. Even ventured out on the limb and called the management of the hotel. They reported that they did not have an employee by that name and, in fact, never had one. They confirmed the fact that the bar closed on that evening after midnight. I say, no way. But, shit, let me tell you that I am not nuts. This does sound crazy, but Michelle was too real not to be real. Even hired a private detective. He exhausted every angle of the investigation, too. The investigation cost me a small fortune, but I would spend anything to find her. He even dusted the bottle of brandy for prints and only my fingerprints are on it."

While I rambled on and recanted this wild tale for what seemed as if it was half of the evening, the bartender had refilled our beers countless times, and he once more filled our empty mugs. As he grabbed the mugs for a refill, I leaned in and assured him that we both were going to call a cab. He nodded, with an obvious sign of agreement on his face, at my decision. Wayne and I both were wasted. Being wasted made this slightly easier to deal with.

I watched as the only person in my peculiar and strange world, who I could tell this crazy tale to, Mr. Wayne Hampstead, leaned back and shook his head.

Wayne, while still shaking his head, commented, "Shit. Wow. Beyond wild. You have evidence. The laces, the bottle of brandy. Geez, I do not know what to tell you or even suggest. Seems as if you have tried everything to find her and figure this all out. It is like some damn paranormal movie. A mind-bender. Yet, honestly, I believe you. Other than our friendship and having known you for many years, I do not know why or how I believe you—but I do. Please know that I believe you with all of my heart and soul. I can tell that you fell madly and deeply in love with her. It is all over your face and in your eyes. At this point, what do you think? Who is, Michelle?"

I answered Wayne as honestly, and factually, as I could, "To tell the truth, I have no friggin' clue as to who she is, where she went off to, or what happened to me . . . or to us. I only know that I am deeply in love with her and that the plan was for us to meet. Thank you for believing me and not thinking that I am a nutcase or a raging drunken fool. You are an honest friend and a good man."

"Of course, of course, Jake. There is no need to thank me. We are good friends and I care about you. So, once again, I ask. Who is Michelle McDermott?"

"I cannot say, for sure, I just do not know. I have been running around the country for years, lost my wife, my family seldom pays attention to me. Maybe, this was all meant to be. Maybe, Shelley is that one true love that you wait an entire lifetime or many lifetimes for to arrive. I just dunno. My life was a boring ass mess, a humdrum shell, an existence. Michelle gave me my life back, restored my soul, filled my heart with love, and gave me a purpose. Damn well, if I will allow this to pass by me or to lose her after finally finding joy in my existence."

Wayne nodded in agreement to my comments, and he spoke after a long sip of brew, "Let me tell you, of all the people in the world that needed to find a special person, well, my friend, you have my vote. The shit ya been through in your life. Living as if you were some damn vagabond traveling from city-to-city. Catchin' your wife in bed, rolling around with some punk-ass hoodlum. You gave the company everything, sure, you made lots of dough, but you gave it your all. I cannot suggest anything concrete or of value, but there has to be some reasonable explanation. There just has to be. Now, what are you going to do?"

Wayne leaned in and looked deeply into my eyes.

I answered without a second of hesitation, "I am going to do just what Michelle asked me to do. What I promised her that I would do. I will wait. She said that we would not understand all of this and it would be a mystery. That we both would be confused. While that might be one of the world's greatest understatements, I trust her. Above all, I love and respect her. In four years, if the good Lord grants me a few more years, then I know exactly where I will be. I will be back in her arms."

Four Years Later

Four years later, on the 28th day of February in a Leap Year, Jacob "Jake" McCabe checked into The Grand City Marquis Hotel in downtown Boston, Massachusetts. Jake waited day and night for four years for this event and for tomorrow to arrive. Finally, it was time.

It was all he could ever think about every single day. Four years of waiting is a long, long time. He endured countless sleepless nights and dreamt endless dreams.

He no longer had sales calls to make, nor did he have appointments to keep or boring sales meetings to conduct. He no longer had to buy cocktails, dinners, or lunches to sway customers into purchasing the products he sold. Most of all, Jake did not have to travel everywhere and laugh at stupid jokes and comments that stupid and obnoxious customers would speak. He did not have to flirt with washed-up prunes of female customers to lure them into making a purchase. It was now all over and Jake began a new era in his life. Jake's prediction of the demise of the company became a cold reality and when he saw the company begin the predicted spiraling down the proverbial drain, he took his pension, his 401K and his bank account full of money and retired. He now dabbled here and there with a small internet company that he began as a startup, selling widgets and some small items. The company provided some play money and allowed him to buy a new car every year without ever touching his savings. He also took good care of his grandchildren.

He was now a proud grandparent.

Jake had a Midas touch. He was a smart businessman and a salesman, with no equal. All the side business and money worked out well enough, but it did not settle his soul. Money was not an issue for Jake McCabe. He had more money than he could ever spend or ever want.

What he desired most of all was something that you could not purchase.

Jake did not find it even slightly unusual when the desk clerk handed him the card key for room 1962 and told him the directions to reach the nineteenth floor. Of course, it would be the same room. Jake smiled when the desk clerk proudly told him about the spectacular view from his room. He had no doubts at all of what was going to happen after midnight tonight. None whatsoever. Not a single one. True love was all about trust and respect. When Leap Day began, he knew that he would be at the bar in the hotel and there would not be another person in sight, all would be quiet; yet, he knew that he once more would stare into the lovely eyes of his true love. And her name is, Ms. Michelle McDermott. He had faith that their love would endure now and forever.

True love has no equal in this world. It has no measure, no rules and no doubts.

Things had changed around the hotel since his last visit. The cute restaurant manager had left her position, Bradley was no longer working the bar, the faces all changed, Jake was just another patron, he no longer was a celebrity around the establishment. Four years is a long time and all good things pass in this world.

Most good things.

Jake ate a pleasant dinner in the restaurant in the hotel, had his usual Scotch, the ravioli dish was no longer on the menu, therefore, he had a salad laced with some grilled chicken. It was a superb dinner. There was now a new chef, new staff, and a new direction here at the hotel.

Jake finished his dinner and the cocktails and headed off for his room. He had a few hours to kill. In his room, he listened to some music on his MP3 player; he showered, lounged around the room, and gazed out the window at the old city. The same room.

On purpose, he did not shave. Jake found it quite strange that he was not nervous, he was not uptight, and instead, he was confident. If he lingered too long on the thoughts, then yes, his heart raced a little at the thoughts of what this evening and in fact, the new day at midnight would bring to him, to his heart, to his life, and to his soul. Yet he tried his best to remain calm.

A few minutes before the hour of midnight, he changed into a casual pair of khaki pants and a long sleeve mock neck shirt, no use in changing the formula. Watching repeats of old movies is often more enjoyable than the original viewing.

It was now Leap Day.

It was time for a nightcap.

When the time came around and the new day arrived, the midnight hour found Jake riding alone down the elevator, entering into the hotel lobby and walking to the bar in the hotel lounge. He already could predict that no other soul was around. He passed no other person, no one in the lobby, no one in the hallways, no other riders on the elevator cars. Outside of the hotel, without even looking out the windows, Jake knew that there were no cars on the streets outside, no police sirens, and no pedestrians. Yet, this time, it did not cause him any thoughts of how strange it was that there were now only two people in this entire world.

He knew that right now, there was only going to be one person in the entire world that Jake would see. Now his heart ached and raced all at the same time.

It was time. In fact, it was way past the time. Only true love tested by separation could withstand the passage of time. It is the ultimate test.

Maybe true love will always remain a mystery, one of the strangest and most powerful of all the emotions, a feeling, which transcends time, space, and all other feelings. Once you find that special person, your one true love, then truly nothing else matters. Not time, not space, not the distance between you and your love, nothing. All that matters is what you both feel in your hearts. It is all that will ever matter, now until the end of all time.

Jake climbed onto the same bar stool at the end of the bar and he noticed how the back lights all looked the same, the glow, the feelings, and the atmosphere. Predictably, it all was the same. He knew it. He knew that nothing would change. Most of all, Michelle stood at the end of the bar, in the same location that he first saw her. Her back was facing him while she washed some glasses out. This time, despite how his heart raced at the mere sight of her, his body ached for her, and all he wanted to do was to run and hold her in his arms, he instead, resisted the urges and allowed the scene to play out all over again. He knew that nothing would change; he was . . . mostly correct.

Michelle reacted to Jake clearing his throat and when she turned around, she looked as radiant and as gorgeous as she did on that night and glorious day four years ago. She stopped in her steps, wiped her hands on the bar towel, tossed it aside, and smiled. Remarkably, there was no sign of shock on Michelle's face. Rather, she displayed peace and an outpouring of joy at the fact that Jake returned.

"You waited."

"Of course, I waited. Happy birthday, Shelley. This time, I will not bring you new shoelaces. I only bring you my heart and me. I love you with all my heart and soul. What did you expect? Time and the absurdity of this world could not come between us. Nothing can come between us ever again. Nothing."

"I guess that in my heart I expected you to wait, Jake McCabe. I really did." Sparkly comments followed by that wicked smile. A glorious pose, with a bent leg, a tilt of her head, a flip of her hair and a flash of her amazing green eyes.

With a coy smile, Michelle asked, "What will you have? A nightcap?"

"Yes, please. A nightcap . . . and you."

Michelle took a few more steps toward Jake and it almost seemed as if she would run into his arms, but she stopped and said, "Of course, a nightcap and I will join you. Join you now and forever. Now, in thinking about it, I must honestly admit that I am not sure what I expected. I know what I wanted, and it is as if a dream has finally come true. I dreamt of you day and night for four years."

"As did I too, Michelle. A lot of things changed in four years, but my love for you only grew deeper."

Michelle smiled and said, "Mine too. I love you too. With all of my heart and soul. It is just that in my long past, no one ever returned before . . . none of them ever waited. You are the one that I hoped, dreamed, and prayed that would come back, the one that I wanted to wait." She looked down, then back to Jake, wiped some tears from her eyes and spoke just above a quiet whisper, "Now I know for certain what I felt in my heart and body. You are the one. You are my one true love. We will now go together, off to live the rest of time, somewhere away from all of this absurdity. Somewhere forever. Do you want to know where we will go?"

Jake smiled, stood up from the bar stool, walked around behind the bar as Michelle rushed to greet him. The two lovers embraced, and they shared a remarkable kiss, a kiss that waited for four long years, or actually perhaps eons of immeasurable time to occur.

Jake whispered as they finished the long kiss, "No, I do not know or care, as long as you will be there with me."

"I will. Forever. You and I forever together. Jake, you have to understand that I too have waited a very long time for this day and for you to appear. Now that you are here, we will never be apart. We will have each other forever."

J.J. Duffy

Jeremiah James Duffy reported for his shift as the nighttime bartender at the main restaurant and lounge within The Grand City Marquis Hotel. He was in a bit of a rush, he scooted in a side door of the hotel, tried his best to avoid any of the wait staff or his coworkers, and especially, he wanted to fly under the radar of the night manager of the restaurant and lounge. He was a few minutes late, and he only had fifteen minutes to prepare the bar area for the opening.

He did not want to face any grief for a late opening.

"J.J.," as his close friends and associates affectionately called him, had assumed this shift and position when the longtime bartender, Mr. Bradley Laurent took a position as the Head Bartender over at a fancy, high-end hotel on the other side of the city. Bradley was here forever at the Grand City Marquis Hotel, and J.J. had big shoes to fill. So far, he did rather well. He was young, but experienced. Good-looking, smooth talking, efficient. He knew the buttons to push. J.J. was happy to have the position. It paid him handsomely. J.J. closed the bar at midnight of the previous evening. It was one of only two days of the entire year that the bar closed before 2 A.M. The bar closed early on Christmas and today, which was Leap Day. Christmas was on purpose, Leap Day was some nonsense about the liquor license not recognizing the date or some other bullshit that J.J. did not pay much attention to, or was of great concern to him. All he knew was that right now, he needed to shake his ass, get the bar in order, and open on time. As J.J. approached the bar and started to unlock cabinets and put items in order, his eyes focused upon two brandy glasses and a bottle of expensive brandy sitting on a stainless-steel counter next to the wash sink.

"Shit, damn! I hope no one else saw this. I must have blown it last night and missed this. How the hell did I miss this?"

J.J. spoke aloud to the walls as he quickly scooped up the evidence, dumped the glasses in the wash sink and tucked the brandy bottle away in the proper cabinet.

"Shit, I gotta stop sneakin' hits of hooch. Must have caught a buzz and missed that bottle and those glasses while locking that up for the night. The last thing that I need is to lose my job for not lockin' up stuff. I swear that I cleaned everything up. I swear that I did."

Wayne Hampstead's Testimony

"Yes, it is a little strange, but more power to him. He worked hard for a long, long time. Jake decided what he really wanted out of life, and he took it. Shit man, the guy never stopped working, traveling all over the place. It must have grown wearisome. When he packed it all in and retired, then I guess the townhouse no longer fit into his plans."

I was with the property manager and we were showing a realtor the townhouse property that my best friend, Mr. Jacob McCabe, left entrusted to me to take care of. The realtor looked all around, and within a few minutes of inspection, the realtor could easily see that the home was in pristine condition. I could tell in the realtor's mind that there was little doubt that the home would sell quickly.

I was not going to tell them the strange details of his wild story, nor mention the letter that Jake left for me before he went to Boston. A long letter detailing his wishes for me to sell the townhouse. This was after Jake, for the most part, and quite honestly, virtually gave the property to me for the meager sum of one thousand dollars, and for lack of any other description, Jake sold it to me. All that Jake asked in the letter was to give half of the proceeds of the sale to his two children and grandchildren, and I was free to keep the rest of the money. The only other condition that Jake requested of me was for me to run his internet company for a few years, and when his grandchildren were old enough, I was to sell it to them for a few dollars. In the meantime, I was free to take some profits from the company. Good thing I had this business, since the corporate jacklegs running the company where Jake and I had worked together had run the company into the ground. Yes, a grand business, gone. They had to move the production overseas. Some bullshit about, "Duty to the shareholders." Now, the shareholders have stocks they can wipe their asses with and that is about all. Jake was correct because it was all absurd. Now, I needed the money, so the internet gig was perfect. Jake McCabe was one helluva nice guy. Exactly as Jake had specified in his letter, I worked the details out with his attorney. Jake had made it legal and meticulously planned every detail of all of this ahead of time.

As the two men looked around, and I knocked a few cobwebs down with my hands, I thought to myself, that this was certainly one of the strangest and most unexplainable damn things that I had ever heard of, not to mention that I had actually experienced.

No doubt.

I was a happily married family man, so I needed to remind myself never to go for a damn nightcap in a hotel in Boston.

On the other hand, it might be interesting.

"I guess so, Wayne. Sure, I will miss him. Helluva nice guy. Not that we saw him that much anyhow. In my next life, I want to come back as Jake McCabe. He is a cool dude," the property manager said as he fiddled with the sliding door, which led to the deck. The property manager opened the door, and I stepped out on the deck, along with the anxious realtor.

"I can turn this over quickly, especially with that view of Philadelphia," the realtor drooled as he snapped a few photos from the deck.

He sensed an easy commission, a quick sale.

I heard the door to the deck open and turned my attention to the property manager.

While standing on the deck, with one foot remaining in the living room of the townhouse, the property manager asked me, "Do you know where Jake went off to, Wayne?"

I thought about it for a minute or two and then decided it was best to remain vague in my answer. Not that anyone would believe the story anyhow.

Why even try?

I shook my head and smiled, while I told them both, "Nah, not really. I just know that wherever he is, or whatever time of the day it is, that knowing, Jake McCabe, he is enjoying a well-deserved nightcap right about now."

THE END

Red Wine and Autumn Memories

From, "The Autumn Collection"

I have always felt that I have an awful lot to be thankful for in my life. I think that God granted me a full time of it in this world. I will repeat just a tad more emphatically that I have an awful lot to be *very* thankful for in my life. I have experienced more things in my life than most people could ever have dreamed of experiencing. I have met such an array of wonderful and fascinating people over my lifetime that I truly feel blessed.

Now, I do admit; I have had an unusual combination of careers that have contributed to where I am now in my thoughts, but nonetheless, I have still been very lucky to be where I am right now.

First off, playing professional ice hockey early on in my life brought me to visit places that I had only ever heard of in schoolbooks, or I had spotted on maps. I started out on the gritty streets in good old Paterson and then Haledon, New Jersey, shooting sawed off ends of Christmas trees that were acting as hockey pucks, around on Geyer Street with my best friends, Harry M. Redmond Junior and Jeffrey Porter. I then made my way to the outskirts of Canada, and then wandered around New England, the southeastern United States, and even the Midwest.

Playing professional ice hockey, then afterwards, becoming a Lutheran pastor, sure made this apple roll far from the tree!

That statement brings me to clichés and idioms. I for one do not find them annoying or contrite. I use them in my sermons and my writings all the time. Oftentimes, I wonder why some people frown upon them and discourage their use. I feel another one coming on, as the old, "you cannot judge a book by its cover," has come to mind for me this afternoon. Then again, my writings never follow proper rules of grammar or structure. In true Harry and Paul tradition, I would not have it any other way.

My mind wandered back once more to the past, on this clear, wonderful, autumn afternoon, and it alerted my memory banks to turn on and dial up a few old memories. It never does take too much to flip me back in time these days. A word, a commonly spoken phrase, a sunset, or a cold day, and the ghosts of the past, which I believe that until the end of my time will always follow me around, come roaring back into my mind.

On this perfect autumn afternoon, it was my wonderful wife, who triggered the memory.

My wife, Binky, and our two children, Heather Sarah and Paul William, were off on a mission to pick up some supplies for school projects. That left me alone to handle some household chores. I planned to rake up the leaves in the entire front yard of the parsonage this late October Saturday afternoon, gather, and then bag up all the leaves.

It was a perfect October day. It was the kind of October day, where the world is on fire in a once a year, colorful and awe-inspiring display. Where the hillsides, the roadsides, and in this case, our own backyard, exploded in colors that reminded us that God is indeed the greatest artist of us all.

I love the autumn weather, and this cold and wonderfully crisp afternoon was the perfect day to tackle the project. It was a golden day here in northern New Jersey. The sun filtered down through the leaves, and the wind gently shook some more leaves from the branches above my head. The spent leaves fluttered to the ground like rain in front of me. The front lawn of the parsonage of

Reunion Lutheran Church was a carpet of spent, dried leaves and I was determined to clean them all up. Besides, not only was it great to be outside, but also raking leaves was a great exercise too!

As I was leaning on the rake, waving goodbye to my family, watching them pull out of our driveway, my wife set off the memory trigger.

We were planning to have our best friends, Harry and Rose Redmond, and their little girl, Blue Cloud; over to our house for dinner tonight, and as Binky pulled out of the driveway, she stuck her head out of the jeep and asked me, "Should I pick up some red wine for tonight for Rose? Rose has been drinking wine as of late, instead of her usual Purple Pirate beers. I think that we may be out of red wine, twenty-seven!"

I thought about it for a moment and answered her, "I think you are correct, please go ahead and pick some up on your way home." Binky had nodded, waved, and they were off.

That was it. I was off to another time and place, as I leaned on my rake, and thought about red wine, not judging books by covers, and apples rolling far away from trees, or something like that.

"Great game, twenty-seven. You played great. That glove save on that shot during the power play in the third period was something special. Were you screened just a little, or what?"

"Hey, Coach Davis. Thanks for the kind words, I got lucky on that save, the screen just moved in time."

Coach Davis shook his head in disagreement of my statement. He looked at me, while I finished dressing into my civilian clothes, in the locker room of the Albany Flying Dutchman in Albany, New York, in October 1980.

"I don't think so there, Paulie. I think that luck had very little to do with it. You are quite a goalie and as the head coach here, I sure am happy that we managed to sign you for this season. You will not be here for long. You will be in the big time soon, number twenty-seven. I can tell. I have been around this game for more than thirty-five years."

I nodded my head and said, "Thank you," as I reached down to tie the laces on my shoes.

Coach Davis sat down on the bench next to me. He was from Ontario Province in Canada. He was about fifty years old, with a thick head of hair and a torn-up face. When I describe his face as torn up, I really mean it! He wore the scars of a lifetime of hockey without helmets, face shields, and mouthpieces.

He had made it to the big time, he played in the big league for about ten years with the Boston Bears, and the word was that he had a reputation as a tough defenseman with a fearless approach to the game. He was one big, strong, tough player, and looking at him now, he looked as though he could still play. I knew from practices that he could still skate well, and his slap shot was a rocket from the point.

I had a few bruises to prove it.

I could also tell that he was a hard drinker, and he had lived a rough life, but deep down he loved hockey, and working with the young players, more than he did anything else. I had only been on the Albany team for about a month or so, but I really liked him, as well as respected him. He knew the game, and although he was tough on his players, he was fair.

"You know, twenty-seven, I cannot quite figure it out, but for a nice, polite, young man who actually looks like a hippie . . . you have an edge. You are fearless, and play at times so hard, I swear you are going to eat that puck! I cannot even recall knowing more than a handful of persons from New Jersey, let alone a professional goalie from there. In retrospect, you know, I have to admit, when I first saw a picture of you, I chuckled."

Coach Davis leaned his head back on the wall of the

locker room and smiled as if he remembered his comical reaction and shock at my appearance.

Coach Davis continued, "Some, long-haired hippie kid, with a beard, and all that facial hair, I thought to myself, this is a joke, eh. This kid is a hippie, not a goalie, eh! The scout who was showing me the film clips of your play, had told me to laugh now, but once I saw the film, then he assured me that I would stop laughing. He was right, Henson, he was right. I have seen a lot of goalies, but at your age, I cannot think of one who was better." Coach Davis continued as he then asked me, "Say, Henson, if you do not have any plans, can I buy you dinner and a few beers? We can talk a little strategy, but we can just, well, you know, talk. We can walk to that little bar and grille close to the arena here. Hopefully, not very many people recognize us and we can eat and drink in peace, eh?"

"I would enjoy that, Coach Davis. Thank you," I said as I stood up and shook his hand.

Coach Davis whistled, and he commented while shaking his right hand in the air, "I often forget how tall and strong you are. Big chap, for a goalie too. Man, you are one strong, young man."

We left the arena and walked together to the bar, which was a short distance from the hockey arena. Downtown Albany, New York, was very pleasant. It was a very clean city, with well laid out city streets. For a smaller city, it really had everything that you could ever need, or want, without being overwhelming. I really was growing accustomed to the city, and I was certainly enjoying my time here. The bar was crowded, and a few patrons who were Albany Flying Dutchman fans recognized the two of us right away.

We greeted them, signed some autographs, and thanked them for being fans. After the fanfare died down, the two of us settled down at the bar and ordered a few beers. Coach Davis joked with the barkeeper, who did not know a thing about hockey, but he turned out to be a good sport about the situation.

It turned out that I was correct in my analysis of Coach Davis and his drinking habits. He chugged the first beer, ordered a shot of whiskey, and by the time that it took me to finish one beer; he had already downed two more.

We chatted about hockey, my skills, things that I needed to do better, things the team needed to improve upon, and a myriad of other hockey related subjects. I had the feeling that this was a threefold mission to teach me some things, get to know me better, but also to pass some moments in time for Coach Davis.

Deep down, he seemed to harbor some inner sadness, some kind of painful loneliness. Those were feelings that I also knew so well, and I shared.

As we sat there downing our beers, a young, and very pretty woman walked over and sat down a few bar stools away from us. She had selected a stool close to my right side, and while she sat down, she made a point of smiling and winking her right eye at me. She had shoulder-length brown hair, wide green eyes, and a wonderful smile. She had a perfect figure, and she was dressed in a white pullover sweater, with tight, blue jean dungarees on.

She was indeed gorgeous.

She was only sitting there for a minute or two when the barkeeper came right over and took her order. He smiled at the young woman and made small talk; it was obvious that he was not going to allow such a pretty young woman to fly under his radar for very long!

Coach Davis had watched the scene unfold, and he leaned over to me and spoke in a low voice, "Nice-looking young woman there, twenty-seven, eh? She sure has her eye on you, eh? It must be all that hair, and that beard. I imagine you could have your pick of them, Paulie. I like how you decide to stay away from all of that romance and allure, even though these young women are drooling over you all night long in every stop we make. This is admirable, Paul, but I cannot help but think there is more to it than that, eh? Is there a woman back home? I never hear you mention that there is."

Coach Davis seemed as though he was looking for an answer, and I was sure the drinks were finally affecting him, because he was rambling a bit in the conversation, and he then leaned in close to me for an answer.

I was suddenly uncomfortable, because I didn't really want to share with my head coach my true inner feelings, and the fact that the love of my life, Ms. Binky Hobnobber, had up and left me, and without any notice, suddenly and abruptly ended our relationship. Her sudden departure had sent me into a tailspin, a downward spiral of emotions, filled with pain and loneliness that I did not want to face, or even to admit.

Hockey was my release, my comfort. I hid behind my goalie mask, where it was safe, and not one single person knew the real Paul John Henson. I could hide there and Coach Davis was correct. I did have a hard edge since Binky left me, and it was in the playing of my position that it manifested the most.

I loved playing the position of goaltender; it was so unique. I could be the hero, and the bad guy at the same time, and it perfectly fit my present state of mind.

I was sure that I could have struck up many relationships with all the attractive gals that came along, smiled, winked, and flirted, and even took it to the next level. But the trouble was that I could never forget, Binky. She was in my heart and mind forever, and there was no escape.

I decided to stall and whip up a little smokescreen, "Well, she sure is pretty, Coach Davis, but I want to keep my mind on hockey. I need to stay focused."

As soon as the words came out of my mouth, I could detect that Coach Davis knew that they were insincere. I took a long swig of beer and I could feel some numbness from the alcohol creeping in now. We had ordered some sandwiches, and the barkeeper came over, set them in front of us, and brought us both another round of beer. Coach Davis did not answer me, but he stared as the barkeeper sat a long, stemmed glass, filled with red wine in front of the gorgeous woman.

The woman crossed her legs, glanced over in our direction, smiled at me, flipped her hair, and took a slow, seductive sip of the wine, while she coyly watched me over the rim of the wine glass.

She was a classy woman, and she knew how to work her assets well.

Coach Davis sighed, and I could see him lean back on his stool. His mind suddenly seemed to be far away, perhaps, to another time or place. It was then that I knew the smoke screen had not worked, as he said to me in his thick Canadian accent, "Lost a young love along the way eh, Henson?"

I did not answer him, but I intently stared right back at his face and eyes. I had not fooled anyone, and certainly, I had not fooled this very intuitive, sharp, and perceptive man.

"Is she as pretty as that gal there drinking that glass of red wine, twenty-seven?"

Perhaps it was the beer or the emotions, but it all was coming back to me now, and I no longer held back, "A lot prettier, Coach Davis."

I spoke softly, and the tone of my voice was sad, almost forlorn. Would be a more accurate description.

"Really? What color is her hair, the same as this gal?"

"No, she has blonde hair. It is long, down past her shoulders. She has blue eyes that sparkle like little stars when the light hits them. I still see them in my mind every day, Coach Davis. Every single day, I see her eyes, hear her voice, feel her gentle touch on my body, and I remember every kiss and incredible moment of passion that we ever shared. Every, single, day, I am haunted by her, Coach Davis."

Coach Davis nodded as if he understood. He took a big bite of his sandwich, and so did I. We sat in silence for a few minutes while enjoying our meal and we chased the bites down with sips of our beer.

Suddenly, Coach Davis leaned back on his stool, folded his arms across his chest and said softly, "Me too, twenty-seven. I lost a woman along the way. It was a long time ago. She was from Toronto, and I was from a little town out in the pucker brush that no one ever heard of. She was a big city woman, how would you say, a sophisticate, or a socialite, eh? She traveled in fancy and wealthy circles."

Coach Davis smiled and he took a long sip of his beer. He folded up his napkin, tossed it on top of his empty plate, and pushed the plate away. The drinks had set in heavily now on Coach Davis, and he now must have been feeling the same as I had just felt because his guard was down.

Who knew?

Here was this rugged, tough, former professional hockey player, now turned coach, who was now full of emotions and sadness as he became lost in his romantic past.

He was a book whose cover certainly did not match.

He looked straight at me with bloodshot and watery eyes and spoke once more, "I was not always this carved up, stitched up, ugly mug. Before I played hockey for so many years, I actually was a good-looking chap, and she was, for some unknown reason, smitten with me. We met at a hockey game that was so long ago that I could not remember or even guess what the name of the team was, or who I was even playing for. Nonetheless, tell you where it was. She was special, with long, brown hair down to her waist, brown eyes, perfect face, a perfect figure, and features. Her smile was something that I will never forget. It was like a golden ray of warm sun, and her voice was soft and kind. Like your beautiful woman, she was even prettier than this young woman next to us is."

Coach Davis looked away from me for a minute. Then he stared back, and his eyes had a far-away look upon them. He had traveled back in time to face the ghosts that also followed him around.

"We met at this time of the year, Paulie. In the autumn, when the leaves were turning golden yellows, reds, and beginning to fall, when the cold air would whip down out of Alberta and Manitoba, and Toronto began to turn cold. The autumn of the year is very special, eh? It is when you say goodbye to the heat of the summer, and the world changes into a maze of color and refreshment. Changes of the seasons are so profound, it is as if another page in your life has passed, and you have turned another corner. We would sit on gorgeous autumn afternoons in those wonderful, street-side seats and tables at the outdoor bars and cafes on Yonge Street in downtown Toronto. You have been there. Have you not, Paulie? You know how special it is there on Yonge Street, eh?"

I had been listening very carefully, and I was amazed at the depth of his emotion, the profound descriptions, and the range of this tough man's insight and personality.

I nodded and replied, "I have, Coach Davis, and I agree that it really is very special. Our first road trip was there, and the guys on the team who know downtown Toronto, took me around when we had spare time."

Coach Davis nodded and finished off the last of his beer. He signaled the barkeeper to take our plates away and bring us another round.

"We would sit at those outdoor tables and talk for hours upon hours on those, wonderful, autumn afternoons, with the colors ablaze in the trees above our heads, and the cool breeze would blow wisps of her hair all around her. She elegantly drank red wine out of long-stemmed glasses, just like that young woman here tonight does. She wore pullover sweaters just as she is wearing tonight, too. Strange, eh? It is sometimes very strange, how life is really one big circle and memories come roaring back in your mind, from such simple situations. Then, she was gone, I cannot tell you why or how, but the last memory that I have of her is her walking down a sidewalk on a late October afternoon, kicking the dried leaves out of the way, her smile as wide and as beautiful as anything on God's good creation. Our love was real, and then it all disappeared. It is funny, twenty-seven, but as hard as I try to remember the reason that she left, I still cannot. It is very strange, but I am just not sure to this very day, why it all ended."

Coach Davis paused a long time, and he fiddled with his beer mug. He was obviously in pain and searching for an answer. An answer that had never come to him, despite the many years that had passed.

I stared at the man, and then out of respect, and to take some pressure off, I grabbed my mug and took a long sip of the beer.

He then turned to me as his mind must have settled on a thought and he said, "Red wine and autumn memories, eh, twenty-seven. That is all I have left of her."

The barkeeper set the new beers down in front of us. We both took long sips and stared straight ahead.

Coach Davis leaned back on his stool once more and his eyes rolled back in his head a bit. He then leaned forward and hunched over his mug.

I could see in the dim light of the bar, some tears in the edges of his eyes, as he turned to speak to me, "I wonder where she is now, Paulie? Perhaps, somewhere in Canada. I guess. I wonder if she ever married, if she had children, what our lives would have been like. Maybe someday, I will find out."

He looked at me while remaining hunched over his mug, and he spoke very quietly, "Maybe someday, your lovely woman will come back to you too. That big circle of life may roll back for both of us twenty-seven, you never know, eh?"

"I hope so, Coach Davis, I hope so," was all I could manage to say without choking up. We both were the same. We were both hiding in our hockey worlds and trying in vain to purge the memories from our hearts and minds. The two of us sat in silence the rest of the time, both of us lost in a stupor of beer and booze, and dreaming of our women so far away.

The common trouble was that we did not even know where they both were.

"Well, I think it is time, twenty-seven. Thank you for the time and the chat." Coach Davis motioned for me to keep my wallet in my back pocket; he reached into his wallet and plunked down a wad of bills on the bar top.

He leaned over to me as we both landed on our feet; we teetered and tottered a bit from the influence of our drinks until both of us caught our direction.

Coach Davis then spoke low, so no one else could hear us. He was enjoying this moment, as he said with a big smile, "That young woman is about to be very disappointed. She had her sights set on you, Paul, and all of her hard work is about to go to waste. A woman who looks as she does, she is not used to rejection, Paul, but I guess we both have our red wine and autumn memories, eh?" Coach Davis put his arm around me and gave me a playful shove.

"We sure do, Coach Davis. We sure do."

We walked out of the bar, out onto the main street, and headed back to the hotel, pulling our light jackets around us as the cold wind whipped down the city streets. I remember that we walked most of the way together in silence, and enjoyed the cold, autumn night air in Albany,

New York.

A gust of wind blew, and it unleashed a barrage of leaves from the trees above my head. I stopped leaning upon my rake, and came back to reality, as I watched the leaves fly through the air towards me. The leaves blew all around and chased one another into a pile that stopped at the base of a hedgerow on the side of the parsonage's front yard.

I grabbed the rake and started to gather up the carpet of leaves.

As I worked the rake, I thought about where Coach Davis was right now. I received a Christmas card from him last year. He wrote that he had finally retired from the Boston Bears organization, and was living on a lake up near Orillia, Ontario. Lake Couchiching, if I remembered correctly, or maybe it was Lake Simcoe. I could not remember now which one it was.

He had invited me up to go fishing with him and talk about the old times. He had also paid me a warm compliment in a note that he had written inside that card, which meant an awful lot to me.

He had written inside the card that, "Paul John Henson was still the best goalie that I have ever seen. None better ever, then the long-haired hippie from New Jersey, who wore number twenty-seven."

Those were special words, especially coming from a man who had spent a lifetime in ice hockey. Let me tell you that they were something very special.

I stopped raking the leaves again, and I leaned upon the rake once more. I stared out at the trees that lined the property of Reunion Lutheran Church and smiled. It was such a gorgeous autumn afternoon. The colors of the leaves provided a display of a once-a-year testimony to nature's beauty.

I never asked if he ever found her, and he never asked me the same question. I had this dream that he somehow, or someway, did find the woman with the golden smile. I hoped and imagined that, right now, he was sitting with her in some chairs lined up on the edge of the lake, while enjoying this amazing afternoon. They were relaxing together, watching the sunset over the lake, and admiring the fantastic tapestry of autumn colors in the mountains that lined the water's edge.

I bet you that they both are sipping red wine from long-stemmed glasses, and talking about autumn memories, eh?

THE END

Stunning, Through the Lens

Previously unreleased

The large, pudgy man leaned back in his chair and blew a large exhale of cigarette smoke into the air. His thick joules shook and waved while he blew the smoke around the room, and his beady eyes followed the smoke as it floated in the air. He seemed proud of the exhale; as if he produced something short-lived but artistic. He was the Chief Editor of one of the world's premier photography magazines and despite his sloppy appearance, his obnoxious habits and his overall disgustingness, the editor was considered an expert at judging photography. He had a knack for picking great photographs and putting them in the correct slots at just the right time. His skills in the business were legendary, especially so for a man who never took a damn photograph in his entire life. Unless a point and shoot shot of the ocean with a drugstore, disposable camera while on vacation at Wildwood Beach counted. His skills allowed him to do whatever he wanted, wherever he wanted, and to accept and reject and to underpay and to do all sorts of despicable things and get away with it. Even smoke inside a building. In his office. A plush downtown office in midtown Manhattan. When other print magazines were struggling, the editor's magazine was thriving.

Yet, he was obnoxious and disgusting. All rolled into one blob. Moreover, he held the keys to the present and possibly the future for the nervous photographer sitting opposite his desk. The editor wore a suit jacket that was too tight on his body. He resembled a stuffed sausage. Even under the suit jacket, when he moved, you could see the pools of sweat leaking into his shirt under his arms and the photographer swore that the sweat was now visible on his dark suit jacket. Maybe. His necktie was loose, and it remained tied, but it hung as if it was a life preserver around his neck. The editor took another drag of his cigarette and then ground out the cigarette into the ashtray on his desk. An ashtray already overflowing with stinky, spent cigarette butts now added one more to the ranks.

The photographer clutched at his necktie and loosened it just a little. He felt the heat of the office and the cigarette smoke burned his eyes. He loosened the necktie around his neck but stopped before he feared that his tie would resemble the editor's necktie. The photographer was very uncomfortable now and the more this meeting lingered without words, the more uncomfortable the photographer became.

The editor's nicotine-stained finger tips ground out the cigarette and he turned his attention to the prints on his desk. Prints that the photographer presented to the editor just a few minutes ago. Prints that the photographer hoped would sell and make his rent this month. Prints that seemingly held his career in the balance. The editor peered in with his beady eyes and focused on the photographs. Suddenly, he was serious and deep in thought as his skills dove into use in a careful study of the photographs. He shuffled them around on the surface of the desk, while his eyes darted back and forth and scanned across them. Then picked one up and examined it closely, then another, and he quickly scanned the rest scattered out upon the desk.

The editor had a smoker's gruff voice with a sound that emitted along with the words that resembled pebbles stuck in his throat, "These are good. Very good. Beddah' than your last batch, and that sunset picture that I paid you a lot more than it was worth, a few months ago." The editor's New York accent prevailed on a few words here and there. "Yep. Got good feedback on your work. Ya landscape shots are wonderful. You have some talent there. I do like this one of the Tri-Borough Bridge with the sunset hanging above it." The editor nodded his head, picked up the print of the bridge, and studied it carefully. "Helluva shot. Filtered? Cokin? Did ya take this here shot on da Minolta? That old one you still use."

"No. It is unfiltered. Yes, on the Minolta. I feel comfortable with it. However, no filters. I think that I was just lucky with the timing of the day and the shot to give it that golden hue. It is just the way the sun was reflecting off the river."

The editor nodded. He belched just a little and tapped at his chest with his fist while mumbling, "Damn, chicken salad. It gives me disgusting gas, every time. Wait until it comes out the other side."

After mumbling, the editor then pulled out the desk drawer on the left side of his desk and fished around in the drawer for a few seconds. By the sounds the editor was making during his search, the photographer surmised that he had a ton of junk piled in that drawer. It made sense, given his other habits. The editor produced a bottle of anti-acid pills and unscrewed the top of the bottle, shook out two pills, popped them in his mouth and began to chew them. With a quick toss, the editor threw the bottle into the drawer and pushed it closed with his knee. While chewing, the editor continued to speak. Small particles of half-chewed anti-acid pills slipped out of his mouth and fell upon the desk and a few of the prints. The photographer slid his backside deeper into the chair in an effort to create distance between them. The editor picked up the photograph of the bridge and shook it in the air to shake free the blobs of the pills and said, "Yeah, this is a great shot."

The photographer smiled, and now he leaned in a little more. He never worked so hard for a few hundred bucks in his life.

"However," with that word and the ensuing pause from the editor, the photographer felt his spirits collapse, ". . . I am going in a different direction for a next month's edition and maybe even a few after that. Not sure yet. Gotta feel the heartbeat of the trends and the sales and stuff. I might buy this guy . . . this bridge photo . . . in a few months. Not now. The rest of them . . . I am not interested in them. Not that they are not good work, but ya can only have so many sunset pictures. Do ya know what I mean?"

With those words, he opened the desk drawer on the right side of the desk, pulled out a whiskey bottle and stood it on his desk. He swallowed the rest of the pills and then smiled. With a quick swoop of his hands, as if he was gathering a deck of cards, the editor gathered up the photographs, formed them into a haphazard pile, and rather abruptly handed them back to the photographer. The photographer reached out, took the prints, and felt his heart ache at the pain of the rejection. The photographer knew that the bridge shot was the ace in the deck, and a great shot, maybe even worthy of a cover shot, but he felt as if the rest of the work was exceptional too. Perhaps some of his best work ever.

"Do ya want a drink? Bourbon will steady ya nerves. Ya look like ya dog just died. Here," the editor removed two glasses from the same drawer, held them up to the light and mumbled, "a little dirt won't hurt ya ass. The whiskey kills anything. It might even kill me. I will take the dirtier one."

He set the glasses on the desk, uncorked the cap, and poured three fingers deep of whiskey into the glasses. He slid the glass across the surface of the desk over to the photographer, who nodded and picked up the glass. Yes, indeed, the editor did anything that he wanted to do on the job. Drinking, smoking, rejecting, and who knows what else? There seemed to be very few limits. The editor downed the glass of whiskey in two long gulps and two heavy swallows.

The photographer mumbled, "Thank you" and he took a gentle sip and nursed the rest while he spun the glass and swirled the whiskey. The editor pointed at the actions of the photographer and commented, "That ain't no fine wine, there chum, it is one-step above rot gut."

He poured three-fingers more of the whiskey into his glass and took a quick sip but did not down the whiskey as he did with the first glass. The editor reached for his cigarette pack on the desk, tapped out a cigarette. Plucked his lighter out of his pocket and leaned into the flame. Another long drag and a swirl of smoke enveloped the editor's head. "I'd offer ya one, but I know ya don't smoke. Nicotine on a camera is a no-no. Dog hairs and cigarettes are the enemy of photographers. Booze is ya friend." The editor studied the acknowledging nod of the photographer and with the cigarette dangling from his mouth, the editor spit out the words, "Look, cheer up. Here is what I need. I like ya. Ya, a quiet guy and not a smart-ass cocky bastard like some of those photographers that I deal with. Free-lance is good work for youse creative type of guys . . . guys who are into the art aspect of photography, but it is a hard sell."

The photographer spoke, "It is a very hard sell. I received some exposure from that publication, and I thank you for it. It is short-lived, though. I guess that you cannot be a one-hit wonder, and I have to find a way to sustain the momentum. I sold some other prints, some consignment work, but I am starving now. I gave up my full-time career to pursue this dream of mine and the art and my love of capturing images, but it is difficult. I had just a taste of success, but now . . . it is hard. Really, really hard, and I don't want my love of the art to become lost in the reality of money. I thought that bridge shot was a slam-dunk. The rent is due and my savings are now depleted."

The editor nodded and said, "I git it. Ya might need to take a part-time job until it rolls for you. Anyway, I do like ya work. Every photographer has to fall in love with their subject. Be it a tree, or be it a bridge, or be it a beautiful woman. It needs to be intimate. Those are where the marriage between the subject and the lens takes place. You are almost there, chum. Almost. The bridge shot is great. Told ya that already. It is just not what I need right now. Don't wait on my ass to write ya a check for it. Sell it now. Sell it on consignment. Make some money on it. No promises, but I might even republish it after you sell it because it is that good. I know ya got some exposure from that shot we bought and printed, so . . . gonna give ya this to ponder."

He waved his hands for the photographer to down his drink, he picked up the bottle to indicate a refill and when the photographer downed the whiskey and slid the empty glass over to the editor, the joules shook once more while he poured the whiskey, and explained, "It's almost football season here in America. Almost hockey season. Basketball playoffs. Over in the U.K. we got soccer going on . . . I want sport shots. Action shots. I want pretty young gals in hockey sweaters and football jerseys." He finished the pour, exhaled a long exhale, and then he slid the glass over to the photographer. He ground the butt out early, with over half of the cigarette remaining, after another quick drag and exhale. "Yeah, for this up-coming issue, I want gals in skimpy hockey sweaters and football, basketball and soccer jerseys. We ain't no girlie magazine, but it draws the male audiences in along with the sports action shit. Play with ya shutter speeds and capture some action shots of athletes, but do some studio work too. Do some backdrop work, enhance with some cool and different lighting, and recruit some beautiful gals for a photoshoot.

Now, mind ya, not fully naked bullshit. Any dope with a camera can zoom in on a gal's private parts and take a photo. I am looking for something different, maybe a gorgeous gal wearing a hockey sweater, frozen with a perfect pose and with a seductive look on her face, a hint of a tilt to her body, with one little ass cheek exposed or the top of her fun jugs hanging out. Just a little. Just a hint and a little sneak and peek more of 'em. Don't give it all away. The sexiest shots leave most of the truth to the viewer's imagination. When you give 'em everything in one shot, it becomes boring. Let's face it . . . naked chick's bodies, no matter how glorious they are, all have the same stuff. Ya seen one smooth ass, ya seen 'em all."

With the ending of speaking those words, the editor leaned in over the desk and his voice dropped to a whisper. A great deal of the usual gruffness was missing from his voice, and his New York accent was not as pronounced. His voice, while hardly gentle, had a hint of airiness to it. Perhaps, his love of the art of photography invaded his senses and the lit of his voice broadcasted that love. He stopped in his speech and seemed deep in thought, as if a vision of the photographic work that he required floated in his mind and he was working hard to find the words to describe his vision to the photographer.

It was then and there that the photographer realized the depth of the editor's talent. It was not all about the money with the editor. It was about the art.

"It's the mystery of the barely exposed body parts, the lean of her body, the smile, the focus on the eyes, or the pose, or the crossing of her legs, or the glimpse of a shadow, a dash of light, combined with gentle, innocent, natural beauty, not artificially enhanced plastic parts and pieces that makes a special photograph of a gorgeous woman. The beauty of the body, the structure of the curves, the focus on the muscles, the skin and even the bones. That is art. Not exposed hoo-has." The editor blinked. He mumbled, "Oh well, what the hell." He poured another glass of whiskey and took a long sip.

The photographer sipped his whiskey too and said between sips, "I have no actual experience in portrait shots. Just some shots we did in an advanced photography class with nude models. I am not experienced in portraits. Landscape photos and still shots are my bag."

"I git it, but I already told ya what I need. Take some shots, make a name, and then ya can do whatever the hell ya want in this business. Ain't like selling ya soul to the Devil. Ya just got to take some photos of pretty gals."

"I understand, but I barely have money for food for me, nonetheless pay for a model."

The editor waved in the air and pointed at the photographer's hand and said, "Ya, not too old. What, maybe forty-five at the most? No wedding ring but, c'mon, now, a handsome guy like you . . . must have a girlfriend?"

The editor held back a smile while the photographer answered, "I am forty-seven. Nope. No gal. Can't afford one."

"Well, here is my suggestion, drink some large amounts of whiskey for inspiration, be careful of crazy women, looking to roll you for whatever, and figure it out. I am bettin' on ya to bring me a winner. The money shot. As I said, I like ya."

With those words, the editor raised his glass, smiled over the rim of the glass, and downed the rest of the whiskey.

It was a stainless-steel diner on the corner of the city, just a block or two away from the photographer's apartment in Hackensack, New Jersey. You can find them on every street corner in New York and New Jersey and Connecticut. The windows were a little grimy from the city bus that pulled away from the street corner bus stop in front of the diner, countless times per days, the glass and stainless-framed entrance doors opened to a hostess booth next to a glass display case displaying fresh-baked cakes and pastries and other goods for the daily desserts. There was a counter with a line of red-leather-covered stools for seating in front of the grille area, cocktails for sale in the afternoon, along with beer and wine. Booths to the right and booths to the left. Some booths with coin jukeboxes, some without. Restrooms in the rear. The sign hanging from the ceiling above the counter, on two lengths of jack chain with just a hint of dust on the links of the chain, pointed the way.

The daily specials were in chalk on the chalkboard easel. Leading the way were two eggs any way you want 'em, toast, bacon or sausage, coffee, and orange juice for three bucks. Usually, Greek families owned these diners, sometimes, Italian families too. Occasionally, Spanish. This one was Greek.

"Why so glum today, Mr. Camera Guy?" The young woman working as a server asked while she topped off the photographer's coffee mug with some piping hot coffee. "Lemme, guess that the meeting yesterday with the gruff, sweaty, editor guy did not result in a sale?"

The photographer sighed and nodded, and said, "You are right on. Thank you for the top off on the coffee. Lord knows that I need it. Did not sleep very much last night. He loved one of the shots and liked the others, but it is not what he needs right now. Just my luck and timing. He wants something different for a vision that he has. And I was sure that I had great shots. The money shot. My feelings were that they all were good photographs that I brought to him today, but one of them was superb. Awesome. Might be one of the best shots that I ever took. Ever."

The young woman nodded, and she stood poised, with the coffee carafe in her hands while she studied the lines of disappointment on the face of the photographer. The photographer studied her for a few moments, too. The young woman was in her mid-to-late twenties. She had dark features, an exotic face, with a perfect facial structure that hinted at her mixed heritage. The photographer supposed her to be of mixed race. Somewhere between Spanish and, perhaps, Native American. Her olive skin glowed, her dark eyes sparkled, and her black hair hung straight and it shone brightly in the overhead lights hung above the counter. Until now, the photographer might have stolen a glance or two at her backside, or checked out her figure as many men innocently did, but right now, he focused upon her figure in an entirely different manner. Her figure flowed gentle and curvy, from a long neck to the swell of her generous breasts hidden under her server's apron, and the tie around her waist hinted at the glorious and generous curves of her hips and a nicely shaped backside. Two beauty marks near her mouth added to the interest in her facial features, and her smile suddenly invaded the photographer's senses. He had been coming into this diner for over two years or more, the young woman was usually his server, they always made small talk, got along well, and if the photographer studied his heart intensely, and honestly, he always sought her out for service and conversation. There was little doubt that he appreciated her personality, as well as her attractiveness. However, right now; the photographer saw the young woman in an entirely new light. Perhaps it was because now he remained focused on shifting gears from taking photographs of sunsets and landscapes to beautiful women, or perhaps he always noticed her. But not until now did he appreciate how truly beautiful she actually was. The young woman was a glorious natural beauty. There was nothing fake or made-up about her.

"Be right back. I want to hear more," the young woman said, while she swayed off to serve a middle-aged man who settled into a counter stool on the opposite end of the counter from where the photographer sat. The photographer tried hard not to stare, but his eyes wandered to her backside as she walked away. No doubt, she had all the parts and pieces in the correct places.

He mumbled, "This is just the same as scouting out a spot to take a sunset shot."

The photographer worked hard to convince himself and remove some of the guilt of checking out the backside of a beautiful young woman, a woman who was a good number of years younger than he was. This was a huge change of direction and attitude for the photographer, and it would take some getting used to. The photographer sighed and leaned into his coffee. She was back in a flash and she rested her foot on the inside of the counter and leaned into the void of the counter in front of the photographer. The early morning rush was over. Lunchtime loomed. For now, the diner quieted.

"So, this editor guy," the young woman said while leaning over and displaying a hint of her ample cleavage, "he liked the photos, but has a different agenda. Lemme, ask, what is that all about?"

Her eyes flickered with interest and excitement.

The photographer averted his eyes from her cleavage for just a second, but the lure of her beauty was too powerful, and he still stole a few glimpses at her hidden attributes. Two of them.

The photographer set his coffee cup down and he nodded, "Don't get me wrong . . . the editor is still gruff, grimy, and slightly disgusting, but I saw a side of him that I never saw before in our previous encounters. He is a genius in recognizing quality photographs and has an appreciation of the art of the photograph and of what hard work that it takes to capture a fabulous image. What he wants is. . .."

The photographer leaned forward and reached into his back pocket for a folded piece of paper that he had made notes on and, after unfolding the paper; the photographer read his notes aloud.

"He is looking for something different, maybe a gorgeous gal wearing a hockey sweater, frozen with a perfect pose and with a seductive look on her face, a hint of a tilt to her body, with one little ass cheek exposed or the top of her fun jugs hanging out. Just a little. Just a hint. Don't give it all away. The sexiest shots leave most of the truth to the viewer's imagination. When you give 'em everything in one shot, it becomes boring." The photographer looked up at the young woman and he cleared his throat before finishing reading the notes. The young woman was intensely listening to his reading of the notes.

He continued reading from his paper while turning slightly red in his face and embarrassed but relating the words of the editor honestly, the photographer said, "here is what else the editor said, ah, ah, let's face it . . . naked chick's bodies, no matter how glorious they are, all have the same stuff. Ya seen one smooth ass, ya seen 'em all."

Upon completion of reading his notes, the photographer immediately looked up at the young woman and studied her face and quickly added, "His words, not mine."

Her beautifully dark eyes narrowed and she asked, "And do you agree?"

"Agree with what?"

A hint of a smile formed on the young woman's mouth as she admired his genuine naivety. "That all naked chick's bodies all look the same?"

The photographer leaned back on the stool.

Carefully. He needed the distance, but not an embarrassing and ill-timed fall.

He was now on the spot, and from the gleam in her eyes, he knew that those gorgeous eyes demanded an answer. Not only did they demand an answer, but eyes that held such remarkable beauty and mystery deserved an answer.

"Not necessarily," he said, just above a whisper.

She smiled, waved a gentle breeze in the air, and scooted off to assist the man at the opposite end of the counter.

The guest was finished eating. Time to settle his tab. The photographer welcomed the break. Her return seemed instantaneous.

The photographer, while he welcomed her presence, seemed to beg for more time because he required more time to think.

"There is more," the photographer added.

"Oh?" Her perfect mouth formed a perfect letter o with the words.

The photographer nodded and felt a little empowered as he touched a finger to his forehead to indicate that this part of the editor's words was from memory. No notes.

"The editor told me that he liked me and was rooting for me, so he gave me some of the inside scoop for what he was looking for to publish photos for this issue. He shared a vision, and it is typically bold, powerful, but beautiful too. He said that it is the mystery of the barely exposed body parts, the smile, the focus on the eyes, or the pose, or the crossing of her legs, or the glimpse of a shadow, a dash of light, combined with gentle, innocent, natural beauty, not artificially enhanced plastic parts and pieces that makes a special photograph of a gorgeous woman. Not exposed hoo-has. The guy is grimy but talented."

The young woman stood silently for a few moments and, after a pensive pondering of sorts, she leaned back in over the counter, glanced around the diner to check for new patrons, and asked, "So, there is exactly what you need. The guy likes you. He laid it all out for you. You have an in. What's the problem?"

"I am not a portrait photographer. I have very little experience there. Only some shots in school. Besides, I don't have any models on hand, or in mind, and cannot afford to pay any to pose for me. I have no wife, or a girlfriend, or any female friends to help me out here and pose and model for me. Lord knows that I appreciate his honesty and assistance and such, but it is so much more than just. . ..”

The young woman stood up. She folded her arms across her chest and, in doing so, her generous breasts closed together and the top of them almost popped out of her shirt.

The photographer swallowed.

Hard.

Hard swallows are generally painful, but this one remained laced with glorious appreciation and some elements of anticipation enveloped within an intense allure. The swallow was as if there was a rock in his throat. Her eyes caught his glance. Their eyes met. Some emotions do not require words.

“So, Mr. Camera Guy, I know shit about photography, but you had to take a sunset shot for the first time, and a bridge and a mountain and all the other things that you focus your lens upon in this amazing world. Do you, by chance, have these rejected pictures with you?”

The photographer nodded, and he leaned into the camera and the messenger bag that he set at his feet and with a laugh said, “I never leave home without photos or a camera.”

In a few seconds, he produced the stack of photos and handed them to the young woman. Her eyes darted over them while she thumbed through them and studied the photos individually. Of course, she, as everyone always does, paused on the bridge photo. She whistled and smiled and then handed the stack back to the photographer.

“So, these are great. I love them all. You have mountains of talent and just need to change up a little. Now, you need to venture into new waters. Big friggin’ deal. I served my first customer and poured my first cup of coffee while never doing it before. This your dream, right? You have been coming in here for years and if I recall the story correctly, you gave up your job as an accountant to do this . . . right?"

"I did. Yes."

"So, are you gonna give up now? I only know you for these years with some passing of words, some coffee and breakfast and such, but I don't think you are a quitter. Nope. Too big, too bold, too strong. Quit now? C'mon. When this guy, this editor of the biggest and the baddest-ass photography magazine, just gave you the keys to the castle?" Her dark eyes flickered, and she smiled, then leaned in and said in a whisper, "You have a dream. You came this far. It would be very stupid to quit now. Dreams are the whispers of our heart invading our minds. Never ignore them. They deserve our full attention. Dreams never go away. They return endlessly because they come from our hearts."

Her words held tremendous power, and they penetrated the photographer's soul. He stumbled with excuses.

"I don't even have a studio or lights or backdrops. I only have my apartment. The walls are white, but it all would be so makeshift."

"Excuses really suck. You are too classy and awesome to use excuses as a crutch. Ya need some positive vibes in your life. Move on from the negative energy." She paused and her next words fell out of her mouth in a perfect tumble, "Besides, you are too amazingly handsome and sexy to make excuses. It does not become your perfect face. You are perfect."

The photographer wanted to mumble a thank you for the compliment, but when he went to speak, the words escaped his lips. Instead, he blinked hard under her careful study; he now narrowed his eyes and stared at the young woman. He knew what was coming next. He could feel it. The vibrations in the air were too intense. Too overwhelming. There were no other persons present in this entire diner, other than the photographer and the young woman. There might not have been any other persons in the entire world. At least for a few seconds. Was this a last gasp at success? Perhaps. Fate? Perhaps. Love? Could be. Her young heart had no limits. Age had not yet suppressed her aspirations, and life had not yet beaten her spirit down. She was what the photographer needed in his life. And he was the same for her.

Mutual aid.

"I will pose for you. This is not pornography . . . this is art. I am in."

"I can't pay you."

"I don't need any money," the words flowed out of her mouth effortlessly and with a duality to the meaning, "unless you think that I am not pretty enough to grace your lens."

The photographer almost choked out the words, "I assure you that . . . you are pretty enough."

Another hard swallow.

Pebbles.

The photographer reached for his camera bag. He unzipped the bag and reached inside to pull out his faithful Minolta. He lifted it to his eyes, flipped the lens cover off with a knack practiced a million times. He fiddled with the lens as he aimed the camera at the young woman. She posed a loose pose and made a silly face, but there was no denying how gorgeous she was.

"In fact, you are stunning, through the lens. Absolutely stunning." He pulled the camera away and snapped the lens cap back in place and, while replacing the camera in the bag, he added, "Not only through the lens. Always." Their eyes met.

A smile. A glorious smile. It made his spine shiver with her beauty.

"Okay. C'mon now. Lunch crowd is flowing in. My boss is giving me the stink eye. Here is your tab. Write your phone number and address on the back of the slip. Wednesdays are my day off. Be ready. Nine in the morning. I will be at your place, ready to go. I have absolutely no experience—so, it is all very cool, because we will learn together. You dance with me and I will dance with you. I do have a hockey sweater. It fits me rather big. Very cool, though. Rangers. An old boyfriend was a fan-boy. He was a ding-dong, but I got a cool hockey sweater out of the mess. Wednesday. Nine in the morning. Be there or be square."

Her optimism filled his world. It might have filled the entire world.

The young woman slid the paper tab along with a pen to the photographer, and he nodded. He picked up the pen, filled in the numbers, reached into his wallet and pulled out some green stamps. He dropped the tab amount, and an added generous tip of what might have been his last cash on Earth. The photographer then flipped the paper over and wrote down his information. He slid it back and studied her face.

She picked up the paper, studied it, winked her left eye and said, "Once more, Mr. Camera Guy. Be there or be square."

It was a dingy apartment. On a corner. Two down, side-by-side and two up, side-by-side. Brick front. Hot in the summer and cold in the winter. Close to the bus stop. Nothing fancy. Paupers cannot be too fussy. He had three days to make rent. He could tell when the bus pulled away from the corner because the fumes filled the living room with hints of diesel. He knew that it was not healthy.

The photographer spent the last few days preparing everything in a strategic corner of the living room for the photoshoot. He repurposed an old stool; it was what he used to sit on to eat. The apartment was void of furnishings. He carefully set the old stool in place and studied the light and measured the lumens with his light meter. The photographer studied shadows at different times of day. He studied his cameras, and in the end, he picked the old Minolta. He knew that he would. After all the fussing, the photographer knew that he would just wing it. The best shots are when you wing it.

"Hi there, Mr. Camera Guy," the young woman said, while she flashed a shy smile and while she stepped into the apartment and allowed her eyes to travel around the interior of the apartment. The photographer followed her eyes and studied her thoughts. Her eyes captured and settled upon the lone chair in the room, and then she spotted the small folding card table acting as a dining room table with one steel folding chair as a seat at the table and paper and pen sitting on top of the table. In one corner of the living room, there was a black and white television with rabbit ears sitting upon an upturned cardboard box for support. One end table near the chair. An old table radio sat on the lower level of the end table. A bottle of whiskey sat on the upper level of the table with two shot glasses for company. Chains of dust danced in the sunlight through the front window. The window facing the street. She pointed at him as she ran her tongue over her upper lip.

"Okay, Mr. Camera Guy, I see that you don't dress up for these photoshoots. Black tee shirt, black jeans and black canvas sneakers."

He shrugged his shoulders.

"Not too much in here," she commented as her eyes returned to scanning the voids within the apartment.

"I know," he said as he ran his hand through his thick black hair and rubbed the stubble on his jaw, "but it's all I have in the world. Cameras and this and some clothes on my back. I burned up my savings like a damn bonfire. Oh, and I have that bottle of whiskey on the table there, too. Editor guy said to drink whiskey and loosen up when I shoot."

The young woman nodded and smiled but did not comment. Her long black hair hung perfectly straight, and it shone like the sun. She wore a loose white blouse, tight-fitting jeans, and a delicate gold chain necklace around her neck. She carried a small bag in her left hand. With a point of one finger, the young woman focused upon the stool in the corner of the living room, with a reflector light clamped to a makeshift stand and a tripod standing a few feet away from the stool. The window shades were drawn open on the front windows, just enough to cast a hint of light and create some interesting shadows across the stool.

"Wow, I guess that is where you want me to sit?" She asked and then blinked a few times and admitted, "I am nervous. Does my make-up look okay? I recalled the editor's words. Natural beauty. I did not want to overdo it."

The photographer studied her gorgeous face, and he wanted to blurt out that she took his breath away, but instead, he said, "It is perfect. You are perfect and yes, the old stool over there is where we will start." He walked over to the card table, picked up the piece of paper on it, walked over, and handed it to the young woman.

"This is a photo release form. It gives me permission to take photos of you, that you are of legal age, and sound mind and all of that stuff and it is kind of mean, but I have the right to use the photos as I please, sell them and you only get prints. Cuz, as you can see, I am on the balls of my ass."

He caught his words as she took the paper and pen and glanced at it.

"I promise, though, if I sell them that I will give you some dough."

She walked over to the end table, moved the whiskey

aside, and signed the form.

"I already told you that I don't want any money. I am twenty-eight years old. I want to help you."

She handed him the paper and the pen, and her eyes begged for a reply.

"I am forty-seven. I will turn forty-eight in the fall of this year. In November." She nodded but did not comment, so the photographer continued while he set the paper and pen on the card table, "I have some visions of the poses and shots and I made some notes on the poses. The light right now, is perfect. We are lucky for a bright, clear day this morning. We have about two hours before it moves away from the front windows and things will get tricky. The reflector light is for enhancement of . . . parts of you." He swallowed and almost took a gulp of air before admitting, "I am nervous, too. So much hangs in the balance. I have just enough money to have the film developed. I have three rolls left. Two color film rolls and one black and white roll. No rent money. I predict it is one week until the first eviction notice arrives." He cleared his throat and added layers of nervousness in his stammering voice, "I really appreciate you helping me out and I cannot thank you enough. . .."

The young woman waved in the air and cut off the photographer's words.

"Wow. Okay, the pressure is certainly mounting, then. I see why the editor prescribed shots of whiskey. Pour yourself a shot and pour one for me, too. No thanks needed. Glad to help. Only three rolls of film and a few hours of light. Well, now, let's get going and make every shot count, Mr. Camera Guy. Is that the bathroom over there?" She asked while pointing to a small room off the edge of the kitchen.

"It is."

"I will change into the sweater and be right back. I need to touch-up my makeup too." She picked up her bag and quickly made her way to the bathroom, flipped on the light, and gently closed the door behind her. The photographer took a deep breath, walked over to the end table, and poured two shots. Her soft voice behind him caused the photographer to jump so high that he almost spilled the whiskey.

"Cheers. I guess to a blessing on three precious rolls of film."

He recovered and turned to face the young woman. She only wore the hockey sweater and the delicate golden chain. She also wore her smile, her delicacy, and her beauty. That stole away all of his breaths. For a few seconds. His breathing was halting for the next minute. A full minute.

"Indeed. Cheers and blessing," the photographer said as he handed her the glass. A lift, a tilt, and down the whiskey went. She smacked her lips and set the glass on the end table and glided over to the stool.

"So, Mr. Camera Guy. Let's go. Tell me what to do. I have no idea what to do here."

He stared at her long legs. Beautiful.

'Damn,' the photographer thought, 'she has amazing legs. They go on to infinity.'

"Over here?" the young woman asked, and the photographer nodded and pointed at the stool. "Sit or stand?"

"Stand for now. Maybe place your hands on the stool and stare me down. I need to set the camera settings first. Gonna go with the tripod for a few shots and get a feel for what we have here and then we might hand hold. I need to feel this. It has been forever since I did a photoshoot with, ah, ah, a person." She nodded, stepped to the stool, while he circled over to the camera and he set the tripod height and fiddled with the adjustment levers.

"Oh, yes, I guess, I need to lose these," the young woman said, as she reached under the sweater, tugged at her panties and wiggled out of them. She tossed them aside while the photographer stood up and watched. He swallowed hard and his eyes went to the panties, now sitting on the floor in a seductive heap.

Black. Lace.

A hard swallow. She rolled her hockey sweater up and the Ranger's logo folded and disappeared as she revealed a delicate lace black brassiere. She held the front of the sweater with her arms and deftly reached in front and unsnapped the brassiere and wiggled out of it. A front hook. Her perfect breasts fell out, and they stood in glory. Her nipples were pale and delicate and reflected her mixed-race heritage. Her shaved body was perfect. Her olive skin glowed in her perfect nakedness. Every inch of her. She was a goddess. Her eyes flashed at him and they glowed. Not in embarrassment, but in a hint of love. Her eyes followed him as the photographer walked over to the whiskey and poured two more shots. These were both for him. The young woman chuckled as the sweater fell down all around her and she tossed the brassiere next to the panties. Both black. Both lace.

"Are you doing, okay?" She asked.

"I am," the photographer answered between gulps. "Let's do this. Look over here, but don't stare at the lens. Stare beyond my shoulder. Look at a space beyond us. A void. Give me a look as if you want me to run over to you and hold you and, well, kiss you. Give me a come and get me look."

Now the young woman swallowed hard.

She added, "Mr. Camera Guy. With you, that is easy to do."

The photographer smiled at the duality of her words.

His heart jumped, too.

"Be sexy," he added.

"I am not used to being sexy," was her retort.

The photographer peered into the viewfinder, and his

heart nearly pumped out of his chest as he stared at the young woman as she leaned in, and the hockey sweater opened just enough to catch the top of her breast. Her dark eyes glowed in the sunlight, her body fell loose, and her hair enveloped all around her entire body. Her beauty filled the room. The air. The shadows and the sunlight.

"Bullshit," the photographer mumbled, "you can't be anything but sexy. Stunning, through the lens."

He adjusted the focal length, checked the ISO and the shutter speed, locked the settings, and locked the tripod.

He stood up, ran over to her while saying, "Don't move. Please." He adjusted her hair a little, tugged at the sweater to conceal her breasts a little to show just a hint of the top of their glory.

"Sorry. I fiddle with shots."

He repeated the editor's vision softly aloud, "It's the mystery of the barely exposed body parts, the lean of her body, the smile, the focus on the eyes, or the pose, or the crossing of her legs, or the glimpse of a shadow, a dash of light, combined with gentle, innocent, natural beauty, not artificially enhanced plastic parts and pieces that makes a special photograph of a gorgeous woman. The beauty of the body, the structure of the curves, the focus on the muscles, the skin and even the bones. That is art. Not exposed hoo-has."

The photographer returned to the viewfinder and mumbled, "This sure as hell ain't no sunset. However, this sure as hell is beautiful art. Beyond description."

He squeezed the camera trigger and nailed the first shot. After that first one, it was a helluva lot easier. The whiskey helped. Then he coached her, and she moved, she stood, she sat, and he shot. She posed, she tilted, and he made endless adjustments to her hair, to her body, to her poses, to her arms, to her hands, to her angles. The photographer was an artist at work. Not in clay, or in fine oils, but he was feeling it. It was magical. He removed the camera from the tripod and held the camera in his hand. He sat on the floor, he stood up. The photographer measured the distances, and he endlessly fiddled with the camera settings. One roll of film gone. A reload. A new pose. A new angle. He checked his notes of proposed shots. They both took more shots of whiskey. She giggled, and he laughed. The photographer was sweating, his tee shirt was damp and his sneakers squeaked on the floor as he moved and studied the angles of the shots. He lifted his tee shirt up and wiped his face with the end of the shirt. Her eyes focused on his abs and the hints of his chest and the trickle of sweat running along his skin near the waistband of his pants.

"Two color shots left," the photographer said as he walked over to the discarded undergarments. "I have an idea. I long since ditched my notes. Winging it now." He picked up the brassiere and handed it to her. "Please, turn around with your back to me, but you will coyly look over your shoulder at me. Hold this bra in the air with your right hand and let it tumble out to a full length. Put your other hand on the sweater and slowly pull it up until I tell you to stop. The panties go here."

He set the panties at her feet and adjusted them so they were perfect in his mind's eye. He stepped back and framed the shot with his hands and then turned on the reflector light and adjusted it to shine on her backside. Another frame of the shot.

A few steps away, another framing, and he heard the young woman mumble, "Damn, this is hard work."

He laughed and nodded his head in agreement, grabbed the camera, went down to one knee, and adjusted the shot. Now, just give me a hint of a bare cheek. She giggled and lifted the edge of the sweater, and the photographer carefully studied the scene. "Stop! Perfect spot. Right there! Please, hold that pose."

Bang, bang, the shutter clicked and the camera stopped.

"End of the roll." The photographer stood up and he

smiled and said, "Relax. Please take a break while I load the black and white film. Last roll. Thirty-five more shots. There is a pitcher of ice water in the fridge, or," he pointed to the whiskey and added, "more whiskey."

The young woman nodded and said, while she wiggled away, "I will have both, and I have to pee."

He executed a perfect black and white reload in the darkness of the hallway closet. The photographer could do this blindfolded. The Minolta hummed in his hands. Color rolls carefully tucked away. Those rolls held his life and future in the balance. Perhaps hers too.

"Ready?" the photographer asked. She nodded. He took a deep breath. Last roll. Last chance.

They repeated the scenes and poses and the sunlight began to fade from the front windows, and the photographer studied the lights and the shadows and let the camera hang from the neck cord and it dangled down his chest as he walked over to her.

Two shots left. Did he have the money shot already? Perhaps.

"Let's do this."

He placed his hands on her body as she studied his eyes and he gently turned her and, with a deep breath, set her sideways on the wall. "Here. Damn, the shadow is perfect right here. We only have a minute to take this shot."

She felt his haste.

He stepped back.

He took an airframe of the shot with his hands. He was intense. He was working the vision in his mind into reality. More of the editor's words spun in his mind, "Every photographer has to fall in love with their subject. Be it a tree, or be it a bridge, or be it a beautiful woman. It needs to be intimate. Those are where the marriage between the subject and the lens takes place. You are almost there, chum. Almost."

The photographer felt that he arrived. He was there. He

was in love.

"Roll your sweater up but don't, ah, ah, ya know, turn so that you don't show me anything."

He made a demonstrative move in the air. Her eyes studied his hands.

"You mean don't show the lens anything," the young woman said and then lowered her voice and said with such a delicacy to her voice that it sent shivers down his spine. "Mr. Camera Guy, I will show you anything that you want. Or need."

He smiled.

She rolled the sweater up, turned to the side so that no bare parts showed, only hints of their gloriousness. The sweater stopped on the underneath of the mounds of her breasts. She stuck her finger in her mouth, flipped her hair over her shoulders, and narrowed her eyes at the lens. No correction. She narrowed her eyes at the photographer. He stopped breathing. The photographer focused and snapped the shot. He knew it was a money shot. He knew it. He just knew it.

"Now, let the sweater hang down, throw your arms and head back, stick out that amazing chest, let the hair hang down behind you, and show me that hockey logo. It's hockey season! That's the title to this shot."

He snapped the last shot. Another money shot. Maybe it was the best shot of all of them.

A smile and a return of the same. His eyes caught some of the whiskey remaining in the bottle and he pointed while explaining, "Let me unload this film and we can finish off that bottle in celebration."

The young woman nodded and said, "I think I am tipsy. As in very tipsy but yes, let's celebrate."

He went to turn away and unload the film. When she gently grabbed his arm and asked as their eyes met, "Did I do well? Do you think the shots are good ones?"

His eyes sparkled, and the photographer gently placed

his hand over hers. The warmth of their touch filled the room and their souls.

"You did amazing. Are the shots good? I think they are more than good. They are great. Be right back."

He disappeared, and she wandered into the kitchen, found larger glasses in the cupboard and held them up to the light. Clean as a whistle. He was poor but squeaky clean. She poured two fingers into each glass. He reappeared, wiped his hands on his shirt, and she admired the veins in his arms and the lean muscles of his arms and his frame. He was lean, tall, and gorgeous. Magnificent. She recalled the first day that he walked into the diner. She could never forget it. His shy smile. His quiet and introverted demeanor. His loneliness, with only sunsets, bridges, and photos for company. The young woman had fallen in love with him on that first day. The young woman lifted the glass and smiled at him as she handed his glass to the photographer.

"Woaaahhhh. No shot glass, huh? Big boy glasses and big girl glasses."

"No shot glass, Mr. Camera Guy," was her answer.

They touched glasses, and while studying each other's eyes, downed the whiskey.

"Well, thank you. I guess you can get dressed and maybe, I mean, I don't have much money but I want to drop this film off for development and perhaps, I can find a few coins in the chair over there and manage to buy you lunch."

When he finished speaking the words, the photographer felt the air change in the room. It was heavy with love, laden with some lust.

The young woman set her glass down on the end table and shook her head.

She took a step back and said, "I don't want lunch. I am not hungry . . . for lunch."

She reached for the edges of the hockey sweater, pulled

it over her head, and tossed it aside while the photographer swallowed hard. Hard swallows were becoming a habit. The young woman swayed over to him, displaying her glorious naked body. She took the hem of his tee shirt and pulled it over his head in one quick move. They locked eyes. Within an envelopment of passion, their heads tilted and their lips met and the power of the kiss curled their toes. After kissing, he buried his mouth into her neck and tasted the salty taste of the remnants of their work. It was glorious.

She took his whiskey glass from his hand and seductively ran the edge of the glass up and down his bare chest. She ran the edge of the glass from the very inside of the waist of his jeans, all the way up his chest to the base of his neck. All while her breathing changed to a set of heavy gasps. She took a sip of the whiskey, set that glass down next to her glass, spun around, reached for the button of his jeans, unhitched the button, and slowly worked the zipper of his jeans down.

"You are magnificent, Mr. Camera Guy. Your kindness, your passion, your honesty, and your spirit. Not to mention you're the sexiest man alive, and you're so handsome that you take my breath away. Honestly, I locked my heart with yours and fell in love with you the first time that we ever met. So, Mr. Camera Guy . . . lunch later. Love now."

"But I am so much older than you are."

Her eyes filled with light and with love, and their joy filled the room.

"Exactly."

They made love for hours. On the floor. In front of the old stool. And in front of and on the chair. On the old stool, too. Once.

The day waned and the sunlight left. So did the dust chains in the air. Only their love remained. It hung in the room above them as if it was all the stars in the sky on a clear winter's evening.

Exhausted, they rolled on their backs and while gasping for breaths, the young woman looked over at her lover and asked, "If we were cold and in a cabin in the woods and you had a choice of wood for a fire or planting a seedling of a tree, which one would you pick?"

The photographer seemed puzzled at her question, but he admired the depth of her thinking. He loved her intelligence and the power of her soul. Suddenly he realized what he knew in his heart a long time ago, perhaps, all the way to the first time that their eyes met; he was madly in love with her.

He rolled on his side and studied her naked body. He gently ran his fingers over all of her glory.

"So lemme get this straight. A cabin in the woods. Would you be with me?"

She nodded yes.

"Then, I would pick the seedling because it will grow up into magnificence. The tree would provide shade, it would capture the snow and hold it on its branches, it would give birds and other animals a home, and it would clean our air and add beauty and majesty to this weary world. This tree would be our tree. At our cabin. It would become a home for a family of owls. Generations of them would live in our tree. I love owls." He studied her eyes and lowered his lips over hers while gently explaining, "After all, fires are overrated. Our love would keep us warm."

Okay, so they made love on the old stool twice.

The editor leaned back in his chair and blew a large exhale of cigarette smoke into the air. His thick joules shook and waved while he blew the smoke around the room, and his beady eyes followed the smoke as it floated in the air. He seemed proud of the exhale; as if he produced something short-lived but artistic.

The prints lay out on his desk in front of him. He ground out the cigarette and then turned his attention to the prints in front of him. His eyes narrowed and his eyes focused. The photographer leaned forward in the guest chair and his eyes went from the prints to the eyes of the editor. The photographer's confidence in the greatness spread out on the desk in front of them, brimmed to the point of overwhelming.

"Damn," the editor mumbled, "these are magnificent. Un-friggin' real. The shadows, the light, her looks, her facial structure and her body, she is stunning. Absolutely stunning and your poses are glorious. I knew you had it in ya, but damn, ya went for the brass ring of works of art." He tapped the tops of four of the prints with the tips of his nicotine-stained fingers and, as he did so, he said, "I want them all. All of them, right now. Top dollar plus. Gotta tell ya though, these here ones are going into publication with the sports issue. This one, with her holding the bra and with the panties on the floor, this black and white shot with her totally naked but turned sideways, this stool shot with that look on her face of come here and git me baby, and this one. . .." The editor lifted up the black and white shot with the young woman throwing her arms back and her head back and her hair hanging down and sticking out her chest with just a hint of her glorious nipples showing through the hockey sweater, "This one, is the first black and white cover shot we will publish in many, many years. Black and white is stark, open, and so wonderfully special. Amazing. They are all outstanding. We will work them all into money for ya ass and for us, but lemme tell ya, those three photos are all mega-money shots, but this cover shot is friggin' gold. What did ya call it?"

"It's hockey season!" The photographer answered.

"Yeah, sure. Damn, I love hockey. Gonna be a whole lot of new hockey fans after they spot her on the cover. She sizzles."

The editor picked the photos up as if they were precious gold, and he carefully stacked them into a neat pile. He leaned back, folded his hands on the desk, and looked at the photographer with intent.

"I want them all. All of them. I want you too. No more free-lancing. Gonna draw a contract up. Lead staff photographer. What do you say to that offer?"

The photographer leaned back, and he blew a breath to steady his nerves and control his emotions.

"I say thank you, sir, and I say that this is a dream come true."

"No thanks needed. Ya earned it. I gave ya mission, and ya pulled it off. That's the kind of photographer that I need. That our magazine needs. Ya gonna be gold, ya do realize that. Don't ya? Anyway, damn straight it is a dream come true. For both of us. It calls for a drink. Ya went from pauper to a wealthy man in a week's time. By the way, I want that bridge shot too. Let's celebrate."

The editor pulled out the whiskey bottle and the dirty glasses and poured them drinks. The photographer couldn't care less about dirty glasses. As they celebrated the success, all he could think about was the young woman. Not the money, not the future, not the cover shot or his name and her name there underneath the prints. Her. Forever more, it would be her. Forever.

"So, where did ya find her? Is she a pro? Did ya hock ya life away and sell ya soul to the Devil to get her to pose in order to pay her?"

The whiskey burned going down, but the photographer loved it.

"No, it was her first photoshoot. She is or was, an amateur. In reality, she was right under my nose."

The editor paused in taking a sip. The shock enveloped his face.

"First shoot ever. Damn. Luck was on your side. She is gonna be a superstar when the magazine hits. Ya do know that, don't ya? Can ya hold her?"

The photographer leaned back and downed the rest of the drink.

He smiled and answered, "I can and do one better. I am gonna marry her."

"Damn. Lucky bastard," the editor said with a laugh. "I guess it is true. The handsome stud photographer always gets the hot chicks. That is why my fat ass is an editor. I guess that ya ain't going back to landscape shots?"

The photographer stood up and extended his hand, and the two men shook hands. "Only with her in them."

"Gotcha. Smart move. Our attorneys will be in touch and ya need to sign ya life away. It will be worth it. Thank you."

"No, I need to say thank you to you. By the way, you were right on many things but wrong on one thing."

The editor downed the rest of his drink in one tilt.

He hunted down his pack of cigarettes while asking, "What's that? Drinkin' whiskey durin' the shoot?'"

"No. That was great advice. You were wrong when ya said that when ya seen one smooth ass, ya seen 'em all."

The editor glanced at the pile of photos and he smiled.

"No doubt. I was wrong. As in, very wrong. The first half of ya life sucked, but somethin' tells me the rest of it is gonna be glorious."

The young woman squinted in the sunlight as she looked at the photographer while waiting for him to exit the building. It was a bright, beautiful, and glorious day. The sun shone with a special brilliance.

Her heart was beating out of her chest as she tried to read his face.

"Well?" she asked. "C'mon, Mr. Camera Guy, I am dying here!"

The photographer smiled and said, "Start looking for that cabin in the woods, baby!"

She squealed and jumped into his arms and kissed him all over as passers-by clapped and cheered their celebration without even knowing why they were celebrating. It was that kind of joy. It was that kind of love.

"Now, I need to ask you . . . what about that tree?" The photographer asked.

The young woman slipped one finger over his mouth and gently whispered, "Hush. First, we take the train back to Hackensack, we buy some food to last us a few days, and we buy some bottles of wine and whiskey, because first, this is about that old stool, and the floor and the chair, and maybe, just maybe, we will eventually discuss the tree."

They turned and walked hand-in-hand to the train station.

It was a bright, beautiful, and glorious day.

The sun shone with a special brilliance.

The glow of their love was even brighter.

THE END

A Question of Mathematics

Previously unreleased

Mathematics can be very tricky. Even simple addition has hidden pitfalls.

They had been married for sixteen months. She thought the honeymoon period ended three months earlier.

Apparently, she was wrong.

"Is my husband in his office?"

She asked his assistant and then added, "He forgot his cellphone. He would forget his head if it was not attached to his body."

"Oh yes, well, I work for him, so I better not comment. He is in there. Please go in."

"Thank you."

Two strides, a gentle knock on the office door, and she swung the door open.

He was tapping away on the keyboard of his computer. He looked up and smiled.

"Hiya, honey. I guess you got my message."

"I did. Very funny, but not really. I guess you sent it from here. The buzzing woke me up. It sent a ripple up my ass to my back."

He leaned back and smiled. "Well, now that sounds interesting. So, honey, did you figure it out or what?"

"I did. Simple math and that is not going to happen."

She reached into her purse, grabbed the phone, and tossed it to him.

"Here. Catch. Don't leave your cellphone under the

covers anymore."

He caught it with a sly grin on his face.

"But it added up."

"It did. Despite that, not going to happen."

"Why not?" He playfully frowned and added, "It did when we were dating and on our honeymoon."

"That was then, and this is now. Nice try. Be safe on your trip and text me. Ah . . . text me . . . normal stuff."

"Normal? Okay. I will bring you red roses and wine when I get home. I will pick it up on the way home from the airport. Will that make the math formula agreeable?"

"Nope. Only text me normal stuff. I love you. Be careful."

The buzzing of the incoming text on her phone woke her up. At least it was not a phone in bed with her this time. She rolled over, reached for the phone and, after some probing, found it on the end table. She also found her glasses and put them on her face. It was too early for this.

Much, much too early.

A swipe at the screen and the text appeared.

"40 + 60," She read the text aloud.

She smiled and typed back:

"That adds up. Be sure to bring the roses and the wine. I get the 60 side."

THE END

Echoes within the Stillness

From "Flashes, Sparks, and Shorts
Book One"

The house was quiet and still, yet; there were echoes within the stillness.

It was late on a Saturday afternoon. Just before six o'clock. His usual dinner hour. Their usual dinner hour.

The old man took a deep breath, placed his hands on the wooden arms of his old easy chair, pushed off with a loud groan and he painfully and slowly stood up. He carefully shifted his feet to measure his balance and picked each foot up to gain control of his stance.

To think how many of the simple things in life we take for granted. Then, we grow old and everything is difficult.

He thought, 'Nothing is easy now.'

His eyes glanced at the easy chair next to his as he squinted at the details. He moved his feet a few steps in the chair's direction, then leaned forward to hold on to the wooden table centered between them.

'Steady now,' were his thoughts and once grounded, he moved again in the chair's direction. He reached up and ran his hand along the wooden arms of the chair.

The chair was empty.

With a gentle pat on the arm of the chair, he turned and slowly shuffled off in the kitchen's direction. On the way, he stopped and grabbed two sweaters for the hallway closet. His and hers.

It took the old man and his old legs what seemed as if it was a lifetime to make it to the kitchen. Where the second hand of the old clock on the wall kept time with a halting second hand. An audible click measured the seconds. Of a lifetime of audible clicks. More echoes with the stillness.

First, he lovingly draped her sweater over the back of one chair and he put his sweater on. Then he moved the candle to the center of the table and lit the wick. With a flash and a spark along with a whisper of smoke, a gentle light broadcasted on the old wallpaper on the walls above the table. The wallpaper that his wife picked out. Some of the seams peeled now. Six months ago, he used some glue on the edges and seams.

Then he shuffled to the stove and lit the flames under the water and under the saucepan. He just needed to heat the pasta up; it was left over from a day ago . . . so was the gravy. This would take only a few brief minutes to prepare.

Not as it was years ago when the gravy simmered for hours and hours.

Now it is store bought.

He set the plates out on the table, carefully folded a dinner napkin and gently placed it next to the dinner plate on one side of the table, then he set out the silverware and the wine glass. After preparing the first table setting, he set another on the opposite end of the table.

The table was small.

With a careful shuffle of his feet, while the clock struck the top of the hour, he opened the refrigerator and lifted the red wine from the door ledge. He had uncorked it earlier and then chilled it. The corkscrew gave him troubles these days, and he did not want to delay the dinner.

The pasta boiled and the steam rising from both of the saucepans signaled to the old man that it was time. While carrying one dinner plate from the table, he shut the flames off, grabbed the colander and set it inside the sink. With a careful motion, he plopped the pasta into the strainer as the steam rose all around in the kitchen. It fogged the inside of the windows.

It was early November, and the kitchen was cold. Fixed

incomes meant that you always wore a sweater.

First, he loaded one plate with pasta and then shuffled to the saucepan and dished out the gravy on the pasta. Then, after setting the plate on one end of the table, he repeated the task for the other dinner plate. Now for the grand finale. Just the same as they did together every Saturday evening for such a long, long time. Why change it now?

The old man shut off the lights and only the candle remained. Romance and candlelight and pasta and wine. The glow captivated his old eyes and warmed his heart.

And the clock ticked, and it danced in time within the quiet stillness.

'Steady now,' were his thoughts while he carefully tugged loose the cork on the wine bottle and with careful movement of his arms, he tilted the bottle over and carefully filled one wine glass, then after steadying his feet, he shuffled over and filled the other glass. He set the wine bottle in the center of the table, pulled out the chair and with a loud groan, the old man finally collapsed into the chair.

"Now, my dear, please, a toast to us," the old man said as he lifted his wine glass in the direction of and in the worship of the empty seat on the opposite side of the table. The old man tilted the glass over and took a long sip.

He set the wine glass down and a single tear rolled out of his eye and landed on the table.

When the tear fell, it landed with an audible sound that mixed in with the rest of the echoes in the quiet stillness.

The Silver Locket

From, "The Chronicles of Henson"

For some weird and strange reason, wandering around stores always stirs up my memories. The only explanation is that I, too, am rather weird and strange! It does not matter the type of store, it could be a department store, a food store, a sporting goods store – it does not matter.

It seems as if the ghosts who constantly haunt me shop there, too.

Even if I have a purpose for shopping, in order to pick up an item for a specific need, I find my mind wandering away from the mission. You would think that I would remain focused, but it is a constant struggle.

Today, there were powerful memories that came over me. Emotional thoughts that ravaged my soul and my mind to recall, yet, in the end, the thoughts provided me with joy in my heart when I revisited them.

I walked by the jewelry counter strategically seated in the center of a large department store. I was on my way to the men's clothing section to pick up some packs of socks and while I cruised past the jewelry department, a glass display case full of women's jewelry caught my eye. Now, mind you, dear reader, I was not in the market to purchase any jewelry for any woman. There was no valid reason for me to allow my eyes to wander there, except for the fact that strange experiences such as this always seem to happen to me. Then, the words flow afterwards as I detail my memories and experiences.

I slowed in my steps and my eyes glanced over the

jewelry selection. When my eyes met a display of elegant and graceful gold and silver lockets, then the flow of memories overwhelmed my mind. I found this one particular memory both glorious in content and painful too.

Oh, so glorious and oh, so painful.

Since my wife passed, the painful memories rolled over me far too often.

I fought back, and sometimes I won.

Other times, I did not win. They were bittersweet defeats. As of late, it seemed as if every memory had a taste that was bittersweet.

The silver locket sat gracefully on the hints of her remarkable cleavage while clinging to the end of a thin and elegant chain. A chain and locket that exemplified beauty. The chain seemed as if it consisted of tiny threads of precious silver that an angel wove with love and with the power of Heaven. Surely, no human hands could create something so intricate, so tiny, so elegant, and so delicate. On the end of the chain, the locket dangled, held by a single loop of polished silver. The chain was too tiny to glisten very much, but the locket, oh how it glistened. It gloriously glistened and I am not sure that I can find the words or the phrases to describe the appearance. I can try, perhaps, with stars twinkling in a clear evening sky, or perhaps diamonds reflecting sunlight. Surely, they both work as an accurate description, but let me tell you that it glistened like no other piece of jewelry that I ever saw. Sitting there, shining, glistening, and the glowing silver offset with elegant grandeur, the black blouse that she wore so gloriously.

Until now, even though I had met with and spent countless hours with Maria Tooteroni, and I remain quite sure that Maria often wore the same silver locket during our meetings, I, for some reason, never noticed this amazing piece of jewelry before this meeting. It was strange to me, because I am not sure why I never noticed it, except for the fact that today, my view of Maria was different.

Very different.

Then again, this was a very different Maria Tooteroni and a very different Pastor Paul John Henson.

Ever since a chance and rather weird encounter of what is now many years ago, in a local supermarket where my best friend, Harry M. Redmond Junior and I ran into Maria and her husband Salvatore, while they shopped in a local food store, Maria and Salvatore had been on and off attendees of church services at Reunion Lutheran Church. A church, where I had served for many years as the Senior Pastor before my promotion and assumption of the office of the Bishop of the Northeast District. Although they were members of a local Catholic church, they often felt the need to visit and share in the services at Reunion Lutheran Church. For many years, Maria would make appointments and come in to speak with me in some counseling sessions, where we would speak of religious topics, share scripture, but we would speak of general subjects too. Occasionally, Salvatore would attend our sessions, but most of the time, Maria would come by and visit without her husband. I enjoyed meeting with her. Maria was deeply thoughtful in a wide variety of conversational subjects, both religious and otherwise.

The remarkably wide variety of topics in which her mind would roll through, made me, at times, quite exasperated. She was difficult to keep up with, and to describe Maria as high energy and fast-talking did not even do justice in describing her.

Maria was a very beautiful woman. She had short hair that she often dyed into wild colors, always vibrant colors such as green, or pink, or blue, and a lean neck and perfect facial bone structure. Her figure was perfect, with generous curves and perfectly shaped breasts. Maria had an engaging and captivating personality, with keen intelligence, and a good sense of humor. She also was rather forthright, and the counseling sessions were, well, how shall we say, at times, rather, "honest" and open in nature. There were not too many subjects of which Maria did not cover, from her wild thoughts after consuming too much red wine on a recent Saturday night, to her past adventures, to her up and down sex life and relationship with her husband . . . it was, at times, a bit difficult!

I enjoyed her company, and I felt as if over the years that I did an acceptable job of assisting Maria with not only her personal issues but also answering her religious questions. Maria and Salvatore never joined Reunion Lutheran Church as full members, but I felt as if they gained from the experience and from our discussions, and somehow, somewhere, they found a comfortable place within their own beliefs.

I had not seen or spoken to either Maria or Salvatore in many years. Time passage was difficult for me to measure because my life often felt as if it was a blur, but my best guess was that I had lost track of them between fifteen and twenty years ago, or thereabouts. Despite my counseling and their best efforts, their marriage always remained a rocky one, and when Salvatore had an offer of a generous promotion and combined the promotion with an opportunity to relocate to California with his employer, they felt as if it was the restart and change that they required for rekindling their relationships and their lives. Salvatore worked in management in a huge retail corporation with stores coast-to-coast and Maria worked as a paralegal. Maria felt as if she could find work anywhere and with her husband given such an outstanding opportunity, Maria was supportive and willing to relocate and leave their lives in New Jersey behind in an effort to begin over once again. If I recalled correctly, Salvatore was from California and his parents and the majority of his family lived there, and that fact was part of the issues in their relationship. In my heart, I felt as if Salvatore suffered with major feelings of homesickness. I never recalled Maria ever mentioning her family. It seemed to be a sore spot and after I brought the subject of her family up in our sessions and was met with a vague answer or a lukewarm response; I decided that Maria had little or no family on her side, or the relationship was strained.

There was always a very special connection between Maria and Pastor Paul John Henson. My beloved Binky told me that Maria had a hopeless crush on me and with that fact in mind, I always remained keenly aware of Binky's observations. I made a supreme effort on my part to manage as best that I could to keep our meetings and conversations strictly on a professional and religious level. There was about fifteen or so years between us, but in all those meetings, the way that Maria spoke so frankly and openly and the way her eyes glanced at me, all combined to convince me that Binky was right on target in her assessment of Maria's feelings.

Now, many years later, it seemed as if the connection remained just as strong. I was quite surprised when I received a phone call in my office a few weeks earlier, and it was Maria Tooteroni not only checking back in to say hello but also requesting if she could stop in and see me again. Of course, it was a voice from the past for me. Now, in looking back on it all, there are so many voices from the past that drift in and out of my experiences and my life that it seems as if it is part of God's mysterious plan for my life. Somehow, Maria had kept track of my life and my career, as well as read many of my books and work. Maria knew of Binky's tragic passing and that of my dear best friend and in fact, as I called him, my brother, Harry M. Redmond

Junior, had also passed on and she was keen to the fact that I remained a widower.

Even though we only spoke for a half an hour or so on the telephone, she expressed genuine and deep condolences as to Binky's passing as well as Harry's death too. Maria was always deeply emotional, and she wore her extensive feelings outwardly, as if they were part of her clothing, or, specifically, part of her own body.

On the telephone, Maria could still speak very fast and cover many subjects quickly, but there was something in her voice that seemed very different to me. Maria's voice had deep elements of sadness to it; it was a slightly subdued tone tinged with an element of heaviness. During our telephone call, when I asked about Salvatore, her voice stalled, stopped, and when she spoke again, there was more than just sadness in her voice because there seemed as if there was a vast emptiness to her soul.

For an explanation, Maria only told me, "That is why she was in New Jersey alone and she would explain more when we were able to meet."

It was a Friday in early September.

The prelude to Labor Day.

A special holiday to me because Labor Day had many powerful memories associated with it. The thought of the holiday was wondrously uplifting to my spirit for me to recall the world-famous Labor Day picnics and parties in the Redmond's backyard during my youth, and my teenage years, to my early manhood and to recall the joy of celebrating the good times at good old 20 John Street. Every Labor Day flooded my mind with other memories such as my own family's getaways, to memories of summer romance with the gorgeous and captivating Maureen Zipperelli during a special holiday getaway. Yes indeed, Labor Day always had spectacular memories associated with it for me. It seemed as if it always would be so.

Labor Day, in many ways, is the summer's last hurrah, and in keeping with our usual summer practice, my faithful assistant, Ms. Martha Wiggins, had left work at noon. It still was our summer schedule and Fridays were our "goof-off-days" and our get-away days too. Especially so for the long holiday weekend!

Now, it was just Maria and Pastor Paul John Henson in the office. There was no way for me to know that I was soon to undergo a life-changing experience with Maria.

Life is full of twists and turns.

Maria now sat in front of me, while sitting gracefully in the desk chair in my office in downtown Newark, New Jersey. She wore a black, button-up blouse, open to reveal just enough of her chest to make a man's heart skip a beat or two, and her black dungarees clung to her shapely figure as if they were painted upon her body. Her pants were tighter than tight.

While she had gained a few pounds since we last met, so many years earlier, and her face was fuller and her skin flusher, Maria Tooteroni remained an incredibly attractive woman. For the first time in our many meetings and knowing each other, she did not dye her hair into some extraordinary color. Surprisingly, her hair was a rich and breathtaking black color; with some gentle licks of gray along the edges. Maria now wore her hairstyle a little longer, still on the shorter side, but longer than I recalled, and the black color was what I surmised was her natural hair color. Her brown eyes, somehow, reflected the glow of her face. Brown eyes, almost round in their shape. Usually, brown eyes caused no glowing casts. I am not sure that I was accurate in my description of their influence on me. A glow is the best that I can do.

Maria was truly gorgeous and stunning.

Then there was that amazing silver locket hanging around her neck. A silver locket that, honestly and frankly, I found difficult not to focus upon, as it not only dangled over the pathway to Maria's glorious breasts but it advertised the silver locket's profound beauty, and in a loud and clear manner, the silver locket broadcasted Maria's beauty too.

Not that either of them required any broadcasting to notice!

After a very warm greeting with many even warmer hugs and some gentle kisses, or two, or three, on our cheeks, we ended our joyous reunion and now, we sat opposite each other and began our discussion and recapturing of so many lost years.

"I must say, Pastor Paul, in fact, no, that is over now," Maria gently shook her head and said, "too many words, too much time, too much pain and way too many lost and crushed dreams. I missed you, I really did. Your quiet insight, your handsome face, your amazing voice and hard New Jersey accent, your quiet wisdom." She then continued, "I mean . . . I am not here for conducting any religious business or for more scripture or Biblical counseling, no, I am here strictly as a friend to catch up for so much lost time, so for the first time, I will simply call you, Paul."

While speaking, Maria nervously fingered the silver locket; she picked it up and then allowed it to drop once again onto her chest.

The ripple that Maria speaking my name caused up and down my spine is still a feeling that, even to this very day, I can feel and recall. It had stirred some intense feelings within my soul. An exciting vibration of some sort that is difficult, in fact, it is impossible for me to define. In my life, only the persons closest to me, ever called me by my first name of Paul. Generally, even with those persons, they always called me, Paulie or Pastor Paul, or by my hockey alter ego of my uniform nickname, which became a common label for me as everyone simply called me, "Twenty-seven." Harry, Rose, my sister, my dear Mum, the old man, and of course, my wife, Binky, would use my first name, but even they often used the other names to address me.

Binky always called me, Paul, in our most precious times together, in moments of passion and in some of our most intimate moments and perhaps, hearing my name whispered from the lips of a gorgeous woman such as Maria Tooteroni was, caused my mind to whirl with the memories and the raw sentiments. It stirred such vibrant and incredible memories and layers of emotions.

Now, I snapped back into reality by the sound of Maria's soft voice, and I realized that the emotions and the ghosts captured me and brought me to a different but a wonderful place. How I wish that these memories did not haunt me as forcibly as they did.

On the other hand, did I?

"Paul? Are you there? That is okay, is it not? Otherwise, if you are uncomfortable, then I will call you, Pastor Paul, and I will. . .."

I cut her off, partly in defense of my spirit, because if she used my name again with that gentle and honestly, sensual voice, then I might break down and sob, and partly because I needed to hide the fact that such a simple whisper of my name had touched me so deeply. We were still so early in this conversation.

"No, please, I am so sorry, Maria. Please, of course, call me, Paul. Thank you."

Maria slowly and gracefully leaned back in the chair and she smiled widely. The silver locket stirred against her chest. She smiled a golden smile full of the elements of the deep depths of her spirit. No doubt, this was a very special woman.

The thought seemed to please her, as if she needed to establish the fact that this was not a meeting for purposes falling within my professional duties, but more as if it was exactly as she defined it to be. This was simply a meeting of two very good friends, in order to catch up on lost time.

"Good. I am so glad. It sounds so wonderful to call you by your first name. Very sexy," Maria said as she giggled.

Her voice came out as a happy, little chortle that came from not her throat, but from deep within her. From the depths of that same spot that produced the golden smile.

"I mean your actual name. It warms my soul and sends chills up and down my spine. A bishop, my goodness it sounds so important."

"Not really. I am just a manager of budgets, real estate, mission work, and pastors and processes."

"Ah, the power and the plan of God are so mysterious. How ironic, the unconventional and reluctant hippie pastor, and former professional hockey player still wearing canvas sneakers and rock-and-roll tee shirts, now moved by the Holy Spirit to be a bishop. The leader. Do you preach very often or conduct any worship services?"

"Very seldom."

"You are still ordained, though, correct?"

"I am. Ordination is for life. In my opinion, it can be renounced but never removed."

Maria nodded and continued, "Interesting. I must say that the years have treated you so remarkably well."

With those words, Maria smiled rather seductively, put her finger to her chin, and pointed her eyes to the ceiling, as if she was deep in thought.

Then Maria's golden voice rolled the words along her tongue, "Age is just a measuring stick, a barometer of some sorts, the true age of a person, lies within their heart, in their soul, and in their mind."

Recognizing the words as my own, I laughed and said, "I see you still have that remarkable memory and that you have been reading my books."

"Of course. Your wonderful books allowed me to own pieces of you, no matter the distance between us. As far as your handsome appearance goes, I really had no doubt that would be the case. You are just as handsome, if not even more handsome, and sexier than you were twenty years or so ago. The long hair, the beard, it all remains the same, if not even better than my memory recalled, just some licks of gray here and there, which only adds even more to your incredible sexiness and smoothness. You do not even have any wrinkles around your eyes. Do you have a time machine hidden away somewhere, Paul? Ha! Look at me. No time machine here. I have wrinkles around the edges of my eyes now. Has it been that long, Paul? I mean, since we have seen each other?"

I thought how in many ways this was still the same Maria Tooteroni that I knew so long ago. She spoke her mind, frankly and openly. I admired that fact. No covers, no dancing around with innuendos. Direct and honest.

"I think it has been at least that long, Maria. All of twenty years. I am very poor at measuring time. No time machine here. Thank you for the compliment. . .."

"Sorry, Paul, but I have to cut you off. Compliment? Really? You can make a woman's heart stop beating!" Maria's eyes blinked a number of times and her mouth turned up on one side in a rather sultry grin. Her eyes then wandered across my face before she spoke once more.

"I must say that your body and build remain amazing too. My goodness, the muscles, as if you still play hockey. In fact, I heard about your involvement in professional hockey. A few more legendary chapters, to add to the ever-growing legend of, Paul John Henson. It was on the news, even in California. I watched that interview on the television with that hot chick host of the entertainment show and watched with some jealousy while she drooled over you. I followed that part of your hockey career with intense interest and I would not even consider myself a hockey fan. Of course, unless the hockey story is about you. Do you still skate and work out?"

"I do. Yes."

"It shows. Most men of your age would die to look as you do. I confess to catching a glimpse of it, so let me say that the rear view is amazing too. Goodness gracious!"

It was not easy to suppress a laugh at the same old Maria, but I did and then said, "Thank you. Okay, well, since we are being so open, you look simply amazing too, Maria. Gorgeous and captivating. Despite your testimony of the lack of a time machine, I swear that you turned back the clocks."

"Oh, Paul," Maria said while grabbing playfully at her mid-section, "look at this flab. You are too kind, but my body has gone wayward as of late. A victim of late-night snacks and munchies while watching old movies alone on the sofa."

Here we go now.

The root of the conversation. No more messing around with compliments or rehashing of the past.

I leaned back in my chair, folded my hands and gently asked, "Alone, dear Maria?"

The golden smile left, and her eyes went down to the floor, then back to my face.

Her glow changed to a frown.

In a low whisper, Maria managed to say, "Yes, Paul. Alone."

I did not answer because I could tell that she had more to say, so I held my thoughts.

"Before I get to that, I have to say once again, even if we discussed it at length on the telephone, how sorry I am about the loss of your wife. To lose a spouse to an accident like that. My goodness and you look so strong and still carry on with your mission. A tower of strength and courage you are, Paul."

She looked away for a few moments while she studied some pictures on the wall of my office, her eyes darting and capturing as Maria caught a glimpse of each of them. Pictures that were as if they were newsreels of the various phases of my life. Pictures of Binky and me, pictures of Harry and me, and of Rose, and of our children. A picture of the old man, Mum, Dottie, and me. Glorious photos in transparent wooden frames of me playing hockey and of me standing with Bishop Von Houten and Rabbi Goldberg and Father Mark O'Brien. A photo of me preaching in the pulpit on Christmas Eve at Reunion Lutheran Church. Photographs capturing parts and pieces of my life and of all of our lives.

Streetlights along the walkway of life for all of us.

After an inventory of them all, Maria gently said, "And you are a tower of faith."

"Thank you. It was horribly difficult for a long time. Beyond description. I was a mess and even now, I am very good at hiding the pain. Had a bit of practice. You see, my dear Maria, you never get over the loss of loved ones. You just come to some type of cold acceptance. Some type of bizarre understanding of the fact that they are gone. No, no, no, it is not emptiness, which dwells in your heart forever more, and beyond. It is a void of such a deep depth that nothing can ever fill it. Nevertheless, thank you."

"And then, Harry too. What a grand man and a spectacular life lived."

I mouthed another, "Thank you," and then I very softly whispered, "Harry is my brother. Our souls remain forever interlocked. We are never far apart. Ever. The saints in Heaven guard our closeness. Binky and Harry are simply our loss and Heaven's gain."

"Heaven's gain, huh? It is very typical of you to spin such wretched events into some kind of glorifying proclamation to God."

I did not comment, nor did I answer. Maria could tell that I now wanted to hear her sad tale of woe, and the reason she was now in New Jersey without her husband.

Alone. As I was alone too.

Once more, she fingered the silver locket and although

Maria's heart was heavy and the golden smile had faded, the silver locket still glistened with overwhelming glory. Her fingers grasped it. She picked it up and then dropped it again while her mind searched for the correct words and her soul grasped at the remnants of whatever remained of her joy.

She, too, was very good at concealing the pain. With a lick of tears in the rims of her beautiful brown eyes, Maria finally spoke, "By the way, my name is no longer, Maria Tooteroni. My name is now, Maria Grace Ellsworth. That is my birth name. Salvatore decided that California's life was very good. In fact, too good. Back in his home stomping grounds, he decided that screwing every available woman and actually, every unavailable, young woman and a few older ones in our neighborhood suited him just fine, well, and good. I, however, apparently, did not make the cut. I guess, as usual, for some reason, I fell short of his expectations. I am never good enough for anyone. Anywhere. Anytime. Thank goodness that we never had any children."

With those words, Maria buried her head in her hands and she sobbed aloud. I immediately jumped up from my chair and walked over to her, knelt down beside her, and consoled her. I wrapped my arms around her and tried my best to absorb her pain. While doing so, I prayed silently in my head for The Lord to help me absorb what had been years and years, and countless events of pain that Maria endured. Bring it all into me, Lord. Let me share her burden, let me hold her pain, and let it cause me to weaken and then be strengthened by you, dear Lord. Strengthened in a testimony to your power and your glory.

"C'mon now, Maria, it is going to be all right. I have you and, more importantly, God holds you tightly in the grasp of Heaven. Let it out."

She sobbed in great gasps of air, heaving uncontrollably as the pain left her. I felt my prayers answered as I held her tight and the pain left her and entered into my body. It made my knees weak to feel her anguish, but The Lord gave me strength. I gladly accepted her pain and suffering.

After all, Jesus wept.

Jesus felt the anguish, too. It always gave me strength to know that Jesus traveled these same roads too and felt his knees buckle under the weight of despair.

When she caught her breath for a moment or two, she looked up and managed to tell me, "I found him, in our bed, with a neighbor, making love to her in great heaves of passion, after he told me the night before that he was too tired to make love to me. Yet, there he was, in our own bed, with another woman."

More sobs, more pain.

Then a shout of, "I always fall short. I never feel adequate. He told me that I was too much work to love anymore. Too difficult to love. Too much of a project. I was reduced to a project."

I remained stunned that Salvatore would cast aside such a gorgeous, rare, and precious woman, as Maria was. But who the hell knows what goes through certain men's minds? There remained not too much that I could do, besides to hold her and ride this one out. I felt her pain leaving her body. It was something that I had felt many times before, and I determined that it was a gift from God to me, to be able to absorb pain.

Now, I needed to take control of this situation. I could no longer allow the pain to reduce such a perfect woman to a pile of rubble by an incredibly foolish and selfish man's actions and stupid-ass decisions. I gently grasped Maria by her waist and used my considerable strength to coax her out of the chair.

"Okay, I heard enough. I can guess at the rest of this horrible story. Paul can connect the dots on this disaster board. You divorced him, left him to sort out his harem of women, and to choose one woman over the other. How long have you been divorced?"

"About two years or so. Around the same time that I found out about my. . .."

Maria did not finish the sentence, and I sensed that for some reason, I should not pause to allow her to expand upon it, so off I went to finish my supposition.

"Okay, so after struggling for a few years with emotions and life in California, you gave up and came back to where your heart is. You needed to return home to New Jersey. Now, the wretched mess is in the past, in the rear-view mirror of your life and you can begin your life anew, as Maria Grace Ellsworth."

Maria stood up and nodded in approval, and then inexplicably, she strongly nodded her head the opposite way to indicate some type of denial. I was not sure why she did so, but I handed her a tissue from the box of tissues on my desk and she cleaned herself up. Maria wobbled a bit, but I steadied her. Then it might have been the intenseness of the moment, or the reason for the denial, or the pressure of the immenseness of the entire situation, but she looked at me, reached up, grasped my face in both of her hands, and kissed me, long and deep. Honestly, it felt more than glorious, because it felt indescribable.

After kissing me, she buried her head into my chest and said, "Oh, Paul, how I wish that I could tell you how long that I waited for and dreamed about that kiss. A kiss that was beyond glorious but I have to tell you that, no, Paul, unfortunately, I did not return to start over with my life. I finally came home to find you and to find what might be left of me, too. Yet, I have to tell you that there is no starting over, or beginning anew here. I am afraid there is only an ending."

The statement puzzled me, and I was about to ask Maria what she meant when Maria lovingly looked back up at me. Despite her pain and the flow of tears, I studied and admired her beautiful and alluring brown eyes. I felt the glorious beauty that she radiated out of her magnificent body and soul. Maria was beyond gorgeous! My heart felt as if it would jump out of my chest at the sight of her. She blinked her eyes free of tears, but the tears ran from the edges of her eyes and slipped down her cheeks. I took my fingers and gently wiped them away; she reached up with her hands and gently grasped the sides of my face and pulled me towards her glorious lips. I leaned down until our lips met and we kissed once more.

In a gentle whisper Maria said, "Paul, please, I do not want to be alone this long weekend. I have only been in my apartment for a day. I only flew in yesterday morning and I ate in a restaurant and slept in a hotel last evening. Did not want to deal with the mess the movers made when they dropped what is left of my disastrous life on the floors of some lonely and unfamiliar apartment."

Her eyebrows furrowed together in a sign of pain, and then I watched as her eyes darted around as they captured my face.

"Paul, I cannot stand the thought of being alone and now that you are in my arms and I have tasted your love, I cannot endure these upcoming days without you close to me. Not this weekend. No, no, no," Maria said while she shook her head no to state her desire. More tears, her head buried hard into my chest in an effort to hide those same tears, followed by a muted question hinted in more than just the want and need for companionship, but the words danced with desire, "Paul, will you stay with me?"

I looked down and the silver locket glowed with such brilliance that I thought it would damage my eyes.

Instantly, love filled my soul and washed away any of my fears.

Without any hesitation at all, I said, "I will, of course, I will. I will never leave you alone. You are never alone, Maria, you know that God is always there with you."

Maria looked up. She smiled, and with her smile still

frozen on her beautiful face and with deeper intentions . . . she powerfully and purposely pulled me tightly into her own body. Very tightly. I could feel every curve of her body and the swell of her breasts and then the resulting increasing hardness of them while they pressed against my chest. I am quite sure that Maria could feel the reactions of parts of my body, too. It had been a bit of time since my body reacted in this way to the touch and feel of a woman.

The emotions of her sobbing began to clear from Maria's voice and in a rather different voice; a voice laced with some huskiness. Maria said, "I know God is always around us and with me. Paul, I did not travel from the left coast to the right coast of America in order to know God. I came to see, and to love, you."

I nodded, kissed the top of her head, and then gently separated from her hug. My thoughts raced and my mind spun, but Maria's well-being was now foremost in my mind.

With great power and fortitude, I managed to ignore the raging in my loins, yet I made no effort to conceal it from Maria. Her eyes darted over my body and focused on certain areas, and I rather easily read her thoughts.

Somehow, I managed to overcome the pounding of my heart and I found the power to speak, "C'mon, let's go and get something to eat. Have you eaten anything today?"

She shook her head, to indicate, no. I took her by the hand and led her out of the office.

"Okay, I have only eaten lightly today, too. We will go. First, we need to eat and have a few drinks and try to relax a bit. We need to chase away some of these ghosts hovering over and howling at the misery. Then, you need to have someone tell you the bloody truth. As my old man said and preached, to tell it as it is. Please, leave your car here. I will drive. We can pick up your car another day. Let's leave everything behind us. After we eat and drink and shake off the ghosts, I need to tell you how glorious you are and more importantly, I need to show you too."

That is what I did. First, I told her that she was rare, precious, and glorious amongst women.

Then, I proved it to her.

Given our past and current circumstances, this evening was inevitable.

When she came to me, later on that same night in her apartment, naked, innocent, exposed and glowing, wearing nothing but that silver locket around her neck, I absorbed her once again. She was beyond gorgeous. In fact, Maria was an immaculate woman.

Flawless in every way.

Yes, her natural hair color was black.

We made love for hours on end.

Once again, I told her that she was rare, precious, and special, too. I told her how beautiful she was inside, and outside, and how she did not make any mistakes; the burden was for Salvatore to weigh. Not Maria.

When we paused for a few moments during our long night of seemingly endless passion, I noticed and then carefully fingered a long scar along her naked back. In the heat of passion, I had felt it on her back, but now I examined it closely. Something inside of me was telling me that this was something important. Even in the dim light of the bedroom, I could see it rather clearly. It was deep and long. Nasty. I held it in my fingers and then gently glided my thumb along the outline of it. I had my share of hockey scars on my body, but this one was different. It was surgical, concentrated, and with a purpose. It was still red and slightly puffy, so I knew that it was an operation that occurred within the last few months or within a year or thereabouts.

"Okay, what is this? Sorry to be abrupt and nosey, but when I touched this scar right now and when we were making love, something tingled inside of me and told me that this was very important."

At first, Maria ignored my question. Instead, she sat up in the bed and quickly turned to me, with the covers and sheets slipping down below her glorious breasts. The silver locket glowing and glistening on her chest. Maria was captivating beyond description. It took very little light to illuminate this stunning piece of jewelry. I now surmised that God illuminated it with the glory of the power contained within Maria's soul. Maria was breathing heavily and her eyes were intent on my body. She ran her hands seductively up and down my chest.

"You are as if a marvelously skilled artist cut a sculpture out of marble. The most remarkable man that I have ever seen, not to mention, having been lucky enough to have shared my love with."

"Maria? You are not answering my question. You are avoiding it and trying to change the subject. Please. . .."

She sighed and then leaned forward, away from me.

I heard her mumble with a slightly shaky voice, "It was a malignant melanoma that surgeons removed out in California about two years ago. I am a New Jersey gal, remember?"

"Ah, huh, yes, of course, the Jersey shore, suntans, and nasty sunburns. Right?"

"Right. Well, it was serious. An aggressive form of skin and tissue cancer. After they carved it out, the doctors made me undergo chemotherapy and waves of tests. It wore me down and made me so ill. It was disgusting."

I sat up and slid closer to her and put my arms around Maria as she explained some more, and in my mind, I replayed the timetable. 'Okay, around two years earlier . . . about the time of the divorce. Geez, my goodness, no wonder she harbors such pain. What Maria had endured was incredible.'

I had to ask to confirm it.

"Correct me if I am wrong, but Salvatore was out of the picture by now. You went through all of this alone with no support?"

Now, Maria began to weep. Even in the dim light of the bedroom, I could see her tears, so I held her tighter as she wiped them away and nodded to confirm the fact that it was after they divorced.

"How about a church? Did you ever join a church out there? A priest or a pastor?"

"No, Salvatore had it with churches and, as he told me, my ever changing, and wacky ideas on religion. I went to a Lutheran church on occasion, but honestly, without Pastor Paul, it all meant very little. There is only one Paul John Henson. After tonight, I am even surer of that fact."

"Maria, geez, why did you not call your family, or friends, or me?"

Maria then turned and gently pushed me back onto the bed, and when she sensed that I was puzzled, she used a little more force. Maria guided me to rest my head on the pillow, and when I did so, she slid in next to me. Maria placed one hand on my head and ran her fingers through my long hair and her other hand, she ran up and down my bare chest. It was obvious that she did not want to speak with me being able to look into her eyes. Maria and I had spent a huge amount of time together, and she was brilliantly intelligent and conscious of the fact that I focused on a person's eyes during a discussion.

It was an old habit of mine.

While gracefully gliding her hands up and down my chest, she finally mumbled, "Because, I have no family. No real friends. Now, I only have you. I am an orphan. My birth mother was an unwed teenage woman when she gave me life and dropped me off at a Catholic orphanage run by nuns. No one ever adopted me. Instead, I grew up in various foster homes. But no one ever wanted Maria. I know nothing about my mother or my biological father. Nothing, except for this silver locket."

My heart sank, and my mind spun. In all of our time

together, all the sessions, all the discussions, Maria never told me, nor did her former husband. Geez, I blew it! It was a major error and an epic failure on my part. I should have probed deeper and asked. Maybe I could have helped more. She never mentioned family, but this was beyond my wildest imagination. An orphan.

She now sat back up and looked down at the locket, and then to me.

"Please, Paul, remove it for me. I want you to see."

I sat up and nodded while Maria spun around and leaned over for me to work the connector on the delicate chain. In the dim light of the bedroom and using my huge fingers, it was not easy to unhook the delicate chain, and I sighed, while I fumbled with the hook. Realizing that it was not easy for me, Maria laughed as I fumbled a bit more with it. It was nice to hear her laugh.

"Sorry, God made me a little oversized. This hook is so tiny."

Her voice changed and in a seductive whisper, Maria said, "Oh, don't, I know it. All parts of you are gloriously oversized."

I did not comment on the actual meaning of her statement, partly because I finally opened the hook and Maria sensed it and she grabbed the locket and chain and held it in her hands. She slid over to the light on the nightstand next to the bed and turned the light on. The light was still dim, the lamp must have been set on the lowest setting, and even though I had just handled every inch of her body, I still admired the fact that her body in the increased light was like the body of a goddess. The sight of her nakedness in the light made me shudder, and as she turned and held the silver locket in her hands for me to take and examine, I felt as if my world was turning over endlessly. If it makes sense, even while sitting in a bed, I was weak in my knees.

God created volcanoes so that every once in a while,

they cough up diamonds. In my life, I have been lucky enough to catch some of them and hold them in my hands and close to my heart.

Maria is one of those diamonds.

I took the silver locket and carefully studied it, the power and glory of the piece combined with the significance of it, and it felt as if it exploded in my hands.

"Did you always wear this, Maria? I never noticed it before today?"

"I did, Paul. Well, maybe, because that is all that I have been wearing."

I smiled and said, "No, even before, in the office, when you were, well, you know. . .." Maria finished the sentence for me with a laugh and with the licks of her golden smile. Her incredible humor remained intact.

"Dressed."

"Yes. Dressed. Thank you. I mean, until today, I never noticed it, but when you walked into my office, I saw it right away. I think God opened my eyes to you in a very different way. I think this is all part of the plan. I really do. I mean, we crossed a few questionable lines here today, but love is all around us."

Maria nodded and whispered, "It is. All around us. Obviously, I am fine with all that has happened. It was always my greatest desire. Since we first met. I fell in love with you right away. My goodness, what woman has not? No doubt that I always wanted to feel all of you and to know every inch of you. Of course, years ago, for obvious reasons, I hinted at my feelings and I kept my distance, but my feelings never changed. Now, it is all different for so many reasons, with your situation and mine. There is no reason not to share love. To share and prove my love and feelings for you. Especially right now."

I studied her carefully in the improved light of the bedroom. Maria's eyes were full of love, and she was very confident and determined. Besides, Maria was so matter of fact that this was what should have occurred between us on this day. Yet, for some odd reason, I had no response to her comments. Perhaps it was because I could not argue with her reasoning. No doubt, some lust was involved here, but there was a serious connection between the two of us. A serious connection that existed so long ago and continued to this day. It was undeniable and very real.

Yet, I was not exactly sure of what she meant by the comment of, "Especially right now."

I could not help but to think that there was so much more to this story than loneliness, mutual comfort, and succumbing to attraction and falling into each other's arms in an incredible evening of love and passion. So much more.

"Maria, what do you mean by especially right now?"

Maria deliberately ignored my question and instead, she pointed at the silver locket and said, "Please, Paul, open the locket."

Sensing her intense focus upon the silver locket, I nodded, looked down and gently opened the snaps, and the locket opened, revealing a tiny picture of roses in a garden. Magnificent red roses, framed upon glowing green stems, surrounded by the supporting structure of leaves of hope and joy. Such a tiny picture, yet it was full of detail. I swore that angels must have painted the picture.

"It is captivating. From another world, it is. Who or what we cherish the most in our lives is where we always hide our heart, Maria."

Maria snuggled up closer now. Her bare breasts rested upon my chest, she placed her legs over mine, and her right arm wrapped tightly around me and with the other arm and hand, we held the locket together in our hands.

Maria spoke in a low whisper, full of all the emotion that the world has within it, and gently explained, "I always love your words. Glorious words. My heart is there. Inside of the silver locket. The nuns told me that it was my mother's locket. That my mother wanted me to have it and to know that it was my grandmother's locket before my mother received it. It is the silver locket. The only piece of my family that I know of, Paul. That is all there is to me. I think you are so correct, about hiding our hearts. I think my mother hid her heart inside of that silver locket for me to cherish."

Maria gently placed my hand over the top of hers, and we both held the silver locket in our clasped hands.

"Now, I hide my heart inside of it, too. I used to dye my hair all kinds of wild and different colors and honestly, act a little crazy, in order to hide behind the pain and make myself into someone other than what I am. A disguise. I think that you understand what I mean. You only occasionally reveal hints inside of your mind and unveil parts of your own soul, Paul. Yet, now, I felt your soul inside of me when we finally joined our bodies as one. Generally, you are very private and concealing. I know that when you played hockey, your goalie mask hid the real, Paul John Henson. When you wore it, you became number twenty-seven and no one could find the real, Paul John."

Her insight into my soul and deepest secrets absolutely floored me. There remained profound and glorious reasons that I was making endless love to this remarkable woman tonight.

"I completely understand the disguise part, but as far as this glorious silver locket being all there is of you, no, Maria. You are incorrect. There is so much more to you than just this. Your beauty, your love, your brilliance, and your presence, fills the entire world. Why did you not call me? I would have come out to be with you during all of this."

"Oh, Paul, I almost did a number of times. However, you have had so much in your life. You were lost in a little of your own world of horrible madness. Think about it. All that you had to deal with—I love you too much to have added to your burden."

"Maria, I care and I love. It is my mission. Even before tonight, we shared an awful lot over the years."

"We did. Nevertheless, it is your mission to care for yourself a little too. Besides, it is what it is. I have faith and now, I need to go with the plan. In my heart, I know that tonight is part of that plan. I know that it is. For many reasons."

Once more, the tears returned, and I placed my other hand over hers as we gripped the locket together.

Maria looked up and now, we locked eyes as she said, "And now, you need to know the entire story. The painful truth because I have no shame in saying that you are my one true love. Always and forever. I love you, Paul. More than any words can ever convey. I need to tell you that I am here to not only reunite with you and my soul, but to check into St. Bartholomew's Medical Center to begin more cancer treatments. I check in on Tuesday after the holiday. The cancer is back, and it is in many other parts of my body. The doctors picked it up on a follow-up scan a few weeks ago, before I left California. My prognosis sucks. Very little chance. Even with treatments, maybe, a twenty percent chance to live for three months or so."

Upon hearing her words, with a horrified shock rippling throughout my body, I somehow mustered enough strength to whisper, "So that is the reason for the especially now."

Maria nodded and between tears and in a low whisper Maria answered, "Yes."

That was it for me, now; I worked as hard as I could to hold back the tears. I failed miserably. I grabbed my mop of hair and pushed it all back on my head while my stomach twisted and turned. The room spun in unison with the entire world. The entire world spun, and I could not stop the spinning or hold on any longer. Instead, I reached out and held onto Maria. We held each other tightly and exchanged sobs. As we cried, I replaced the silver locket around her neck.

"That is why I did not want to be alone. That is why I had to be with you, Paul. Just once before I left this world. To honor and prove my love for a real man. A glorious soul, a man, who knows love in his heart, who honors a woman with his love and does not destroy her. It is you, Paul. It will always be you. I needed you to love me just once, for us to be one and to share love, share our bodies and exchange our deepest levels of passion. Just one incredible session of love with you. That is all I ever wanted or needed."

Maria leaned in and once again, she ran her hands gently and seductively up and down my chest while we shared a hard and then a deep and passionate kiss. After kissing, Maria rested her head upon my shoulder while she still ran her hands over every inch of my naked body, exploring and gently touching, as she studied me carefully. We were silent and void of words except that I could hear her breathing change to a low growl that kept time in an alluring rhythm.

Finally, Maria spoke, "Oh, Paul, our age difference means nothing. How I wish, this all could be so different. You are amazing. If I judge our love by the intenseness of our lovemaking, and the level of passion between us, then, I have to say that our love could have been epic and forever. On the other hand, maybe, I should say that *it is* epic and forever because we have these moments to share now and forever in our hearts. I have never had a lover like you, Paul. Never. Even. Close. Your stamina is remarkable. Epic and forever, but I guess the timing was just wrong. Maybe in the next world, my love. Maybe."

"Maria, you are beyond glorious. There are no words to describe you and your love. I love you too, and your love fills my soul with joy. Remember that love is God's greatest gift to us."

Maria smiled her golden smile, but said not a single word. She did not have to speak.

"You hold me in such honor and I am humbled, but I am just a man. A very weak man, who makes many terrible choices. Nothing special."

Suddenly, the world stopped spinning and many strong thoughts resounded very clearly inside of my mind. I knew what I needed to do now.

Rather forcibly, I said, "I need to pray."

I climbed out of bed and dressed.

"Excuse me, Maria."

I left the room, found the door to the hallway just as Maria shut off the light and I heard her soft voice call out, "Do you want to pray together? I can dress and join you."

"No, not right now, Maria. Soon, but not right now. This is between God and Pastor Paul John Henson. The pattern repeats in my life and I need to know why."

In the darkness of the living room of Maria's apartment, I knelt and prayed. To understand, to hope that my faith could and would reveal some type of answer. The answer came back to me as it always does, the same answer, loud and clear. Love her, Paul. Love her as you did Binky, Harry, Sky Blu, Renee, Maureen, and all the others in your life that left you alone. Love them with all of the immense love that I placed into your heart when I allowed you into this world. This time is different, it has to be love of both body and soul. Honor her and extend the faith through the pain. Do not waver and do not give up now. I, your Lord and your God will sustain you, Paul. Now you need to allow Maria to steal your faith and strength. I rose from my knees, returned to the bedroom, and undressed. I climbed back into bed and held Maria tightly.

"Well, Paul?" Maria asked, while sitting up in the bed and carefully studying my eyes. Her beauty, combined with the silver locket's elegance, filled the entire room with glory.

"Paul, what does God tell you to do?"

"To stick with the plan," was my answer. "I will love you with all of my heart, body, soul, and my power. We will cling to our love and to our prayers and hope for healing, together."

Maria said not a word, but she smiled and then kissed me deeply.

A salty kiss, laced with the bitter taste of her tears that flowed and rested upon her lips.

Maria whispered to me between the waves of passion and with tears in her eyes, "Will you always be here, Paul? Just as you have always been for me?"

"I will always be here. In the dark and in the light. The happy times and the sad times, the desperate times, always and forever, I am always here. God will not allow me to be anywhere else."

Maria smiled and off we went to a very special and unique place.

During that long, yet overtly short, holiday weekend, we only stopped making love to shower together, to eat and drink and to walk to the corner store in order to pick up supplies of wine, beer, and some snacks. At times, it became so hot in that apartment's bedroom that it is a wonder that the paint and wallpaper did not peel off the bloody walls.

We ordered a helluva lot of pizza too.

I stood in the corner of a hospital room in St. Bartholomew's Medical Center in my old home city of Paterson, New Jersey. It was a much-respected hospital. I kept telling myself that fact. As if I felt that the doctors and nurses here could overcome God's plan through their skills and tools.

A medical procedural expert sat in a chair and she explained the plan and procedures, while a nurse prepared Maria for chemotherapy treatments.

The woman, who was explaining the treatment plan,

finished with her explanation of the treatments. She then paused and studied me.

Our eyes met for what seemed to be a long time and the woman asked me, "Are you the emergency contact for Maria, Pastor Paul?"

"I am."

"Oh, okay, got it. Please, her next of kin, can you help me with that?"

"I can, it is me."

The worker looked up from over her glasses at me and nodded her head while she took some notes. I glanced over and watched Maria grimace as the nurse poked an I.V. needle into her arm.

Now, the horror begins. Lord, give us strength.

"You are obviously her pastor, so we have her religion as Lutheran."

"No, I am not her pastor, but Lutheran is correct. Yes, it is." I leaned in, glanced at the medical worker's name tag, and caught her name. "Honestly, since you are all sworn by medical secrecy rules and laws these days, Ms. Davison, I am Maria's best friend and I am her lover. I love her with all of my body, heart, and soul."

Ms. Davison dropped her papers and her pen on the floor. The nurse's head spun around, and the nurse's eyes stared long and hard at me. I watched her eyes go from my pastor's collar around my neck, to my black suit, to the wooden cross hanging by a lanyard around my neck, to my beard and long hair. Her eyes studied my fingers for rings and seeing none, she smiled, as did Maria, who, despite the pain in her arm, gloriously laughed at the immenseness of the situation.

The nurse looked at me again, then to Maria.

The nurse then said to Maria, "Hoowee. My goodness, girl, you are one lucky gal. I need to take your temperature and I might need to take mine too. That man is hotter than seventeen Hells."

Maria winked at me and smiled that golden smile. The silver locket never shone so brilliantly.

"He is. No doubt that he is. I am lucky. I really, really am. The luckiest woman in the entire world because God's greatest gift to us is love."

I smiled back at Maria and proudly announced, "Love *is* the greatest gift. And, no, I am the lucky one here. I am a lucky man in so many ways because Maria is beyond beautiful. Her beauty is beyond words to describe. Maria is gorgeous, inside and outside too and she fills my heart and this world with love and with joy."

Maria never left St. Bartholomew's Medical Center alive. It was not part of the plan. Despite the aggressive treatments, the cancer was too powerful, too far spread. At the end of three months, it ravaged poor Maria. She withered before my eyes from a vibrant woman into emaciation. Her hair fell out, and she vomited blood every day. Enough of this! I cried to The Lord for mercy and pleaded with The Lord to stop the agony. My heart was breaking into so many pieces that I was not sure that I could gather the strength to watch and endure this wretchedness any longer.

Maria decided to end all the treatments and enter into hospice care. Despite the pain and the agony, her gorgeous beauty remained.

Beauty, inside and outside, beauty beyond words or comprehension.

I visited her every day and every night. Often, twice a day and even more. Due to my clergyman's status and not because we were lovers, the night-shift nurses allowed some bending of the rules and looked the other way, while I spent every night in a chair next to her side.

Endless tears and painful discussions. Precious little time we had together.

So precious.

Maria was very brave, full of love, and full of faith.

Truly, she *is* an amazing woman.

Maria desired cremation and to have her ashes spread in the ocean at the Jersey shore. She was quite specific and adamant and made me promise that there would be no notification to Salvatore. None whatsoever. She donated all of her worldly possessions to Lutheran Social Services.

However, the silver locket was forever my own silver locket to keep. On the day she asked for hospice care, Maria gently placed it in my hand and closed my fingers around it while kissing me very deeply.

I planned to give it to our granddaughter, when and if she marries or upon my passing away, it will be in my will for her to receive it. My son-in-law adopted our granddaughter after her biological father abandoned her and signed her adoption papers over to my daughter and her second husband. Considering the circumstances of her life and of Maria's life, it seemed to be an appropriate gift. Until then, the silver locket will remain safely locked within my safe.

Heed my warning, with all my power and honor and my swearing to both Heaven and Earth, that I will guard the silver locket with my own life.

The day before Maria slipped into a doctor administered pain medication-induced coma to relieve her terrible pain; I brought to her three dozen red roses and placed the roses in a huge vase right next to her bed. She loved them and we compared the roses in the vase to the picture in the silver locket. I held her hand all day and all night, too. I stayed next to her bedside, managed to stay awake with God's help, and I read scripture aloud and prayed the entire night. The next morning, all that remained were closed eyes and a slow but relaxed breathing. But thankfully, the pain and suffering were over. After I lost my wife, and I fell into the depths of ruin and finally crawled back to this world, I vowed and made a promise to my loved ones, and most importantly, to dear Rose that I would never allow grief to overcome me ever again and allow the defeat of grief to invade my soul. Grief tramples life and it drowns out the happiness and glories of love. Yet, with God's Grace, love overcomes all the pain. Grief was not going to win this one. I kept my vow when Harry left us, and I intended to keep my vow now. Maria was full of life and love and nothing would trample that in my heart.

Maria passed away three days later, on a glorious day full of sunshine and gentle breezes. One deep breath and then she was gone from me and from this world. I felt her love fill my soul as I held her hand during her last breath.

I swear the scent of those magnificent roses surrounded me as if they were a cloud of testimony of her love when she passed.

Heaven's gain.

Alone, standing on the sand, I spread her ashes into the ocean at the Jersey shore on a day very similar to the day in which she entered Heaven. With a gentle prayer and a kiss on my lips, I tossed three dozen red roses into the waves; I stood there and watched the waves carry them to and from the shore. Waves of emotions, filled with love and red roses, and Maria too. I held the silver locket in my hand and honestly, the glory of the silver locket filled the entire world and I was quite sure that the locket's radiance crept into Heaven, too.

"Can I interest you in purchasing one of our gold or silver lockets, sir? They are all on sale today. I can give you a wonderful deal on a special gift for that special woman in your life."

A very attractive saleswoman with long red hair and a wonderful smile spoke to me, and her voice snapped me back to reality. I felt like an idiot because I had no idea how long that I had zoned out in front of the sales display.

"I am sure such a handsome and stunning man as what you are, has a very special woman in his life."

Ah yes, a little touch of charm along with the sales pitch. Hey, everyone has to make a living.

"Oh yes, thank you, but I was just browsing. I actually have a fabulous silver locket already. It is full of love and glory. Someday, I am going to give it to our granddaughter as a very special gift."

"Oh, okay, then your wife and you have shared it, and you have a plan. I guess."

I shook my head and said, "Well, no. It was actually a very special person's possession. She willed it to me. I am a widower. My wife passed away a long time ago."

I thought how it was silly to reveal so much information to a sales person. The emotions rolled over me and made my mouth too loose. Oh well.

"Oh, I am very sorry to hear of your loss. Well, if you change your mind, here they all are. Besides . . . I am here too," she said with a wink and smile.

I waved and thanked her and walked away. I took a few steps, then stopped and turned and returned to the sales counter.

The sales woman seemed surprised at my speedy return. She looked over at me, smiled and said, "Wow! That was a fast change of your mind. I would like to think that it was my wonderful sales pitch or my pretty smile."

"Both. Say, which one of these silver lockets is your favorite? I mean, which one, would you wear? I am not too swift at this kind of shopping."

I smiled and pushed all my long hair out of the way while I leaned over and stared at the sales display.

"Oh, well, that is easy. This one. The one with the diamonds. The most expensive one, of course. A piece of advice, handsome man, you should never ask a woman for her favorite. It will always be the most expensive one."

No mirror handy, but I am sure my face grew very intense.

The passion rose in my soul and it reflected in my words, "I guess, but money does not really matter. Does it actually matter? Am I incorrect? In the end, what does it matter? Only love really matters. Love is God's greatest gift to us. When everything is dust, only love remains. The money becomes the dust sifting through the fingers on our hands."

I watched her face break into a slight smile, and her eyes studied me. Her eyes went from my eyes, to my long hair, to my beard, to my face, to my faded rock-and-roll tee shirt, to my black dungarees, to my canvas sneakers. I am sure she had no idea that I was a Lutheran bishop. Maybe some wayward hippie, but never a clergyman.

With intention, I broke the spell and asked, "Say, how many of these exact silver lockets do you have in stock?"

"Ah, ah, okay . . . I will need to check in the stockroom and yes, I agree with you about money and love. Honestly, your words caused my spine to tingle. They went right through me and for a few seconds, I could not speak. I needed to regain my thoughts and, honestly, my soul. My soul almost escaped with your words." She paused, shook her head, and breathed very deeply before continuing. "Anyway, thank you for those glorious words and amazing thoughts. Please wait. I will be right back."

I watched her disappear behind a wall and within a few minutes, she returned holding jewelry boxes.

"Handsome man, I have four and the one on display."

"Good. In fact, perfect."

I quickly figured it in my mind—one for Rose, one for Heather Sarah, one for Blue Cloud, one for Dottie, and an extra one.

"I will take all of them. Please gift wrap them and keep one for you."

She almost dropped the boxes, and I laughed.

"Please, tell your manager to come over here and I will explain it. I mean—do you want one?"

She smiled and said, "Of course, but it is very strange and I am sure that it is not really allowed."

"As I said, I will explain it to your boss. Please ask the manager to come see me and I will work the deal. I am from the north side of Paterson in New Jersey and I am very good at working out deals."

"Well, okay, but this is kind of amazing. Shocking! This is a six-hundred-dollar locket. You are a special man and I have to ask. Are you going to ask me out on a date? I am available and I assure you that I am not married or dating anyone seriously right now."

I laughed and said, "I am hardly special at all. Just a man. A man who simply wants to honor someone that filled this world and my heart with love. That is all."

"Oh, yes, the original owner of your silver locket. The person who gave it to you. I understand. How wonderful of you, she must have been special."

"Yes, incredibly so. Beyond words."

"Ah, about the date?"

"No, sorry. Nothing personal. But, please know that you are gorgeous, inside and outside too."

"Oh, too bad, because I would go out with you in a second." She extended her hand and said, "Anyway, thank you for an amazing gift from an amazing man. My name is Claire Dawson."

I shook her hand and said, "You are welcome, Claire. I am Paul John Henson. Thank you."

For some reason, of which I was not immediately sure of why, I left off the pastor title, and certainly, I left off the bishop title to my name and introduction. After some pause, I think that I wanted to leave this all here on Earth and exclude the power and the glory of Heaven. I think that sometimes, God expects us to take up the mantle on our own.

After explaining the purchase to the perplexed and dazed store manager and receiving strange looks and eventual approval, as well as a covert slip of the sales woman's telephone number written on a small piece of paper, "In case that I changed my mind," I walked away with the gifts in my hands, wearing a terrifically broad smile.

I recalled that I still needed to pick out the socks. Oh well, the hell with them.

My thoughts overwhelmed me.

It felt so good.

I felt renewed.

Yes indeed, renewed once again.

While I joyfully exited out the store, I spoke aloud, "I will always be here. In the dark and in the light. The happy times and the sad times, the desperate times, always and forever, I am always here. God will not allow me to be anywhere else."

THE END

Epilogue

From, "Christmas Cocktails"

A gentle calm settled in over the town of Wayne, New Jersey, on this Christmas Eve. There was no snow falling, but it was very cold and the calm signaled peace. Indeed, it was a quiet, gentle calm and in the home of Fred and Marlene Kelleher, there was some Christmas magic settling in too.

The home was a typical suburban New Jersey home found in a quiet suburban town. A modest, split-level home with a nice backyard, located on a quiet street tucked in off a main drag. A home filled with glorious memories and glorious love, too.

Fred had not earned a fortune in his career as an accountant, but he earned enough to raise a family, provide a college education for both of them and to give to Marlene the life that he promised to her. While the home might be too large now for just Marlene and Fred, it was a home that had too many memories attached to it to sell it and move away. The Kelleher's raised two children here, and it was a home that had seen too many Christmases, Thanksgivings, birthdays, anniversaries, and other celebrations, to count them all.

Remember them, yes; however, to count them all was impossible.

Tonight, on this quiet Christmas Eve, there was to be one more celebration. Fred planned it all out very carefully and he lovingly banned his wife from the dining room of their home while he prepared for the celebration. Fred slowly and gingerly shuffled back and forth from the kitchen to the dining room. His back was not too good these days and arthritis crept into his legs and ankles. Yet Fred kept moving. First, the red tablecloth, then the candles with the holly and berry Christmas centerpiece. Then, some quiet Christmas music for the backdrop and as Fred checked his suit jacket pocket a few times or so on this Christmas Eve, he felt no nervousness.

Only joy.

After all, sixty years ago on this very night, the love of his life accepted his proposal and while there were ups and downs, some good times, and some bad times, and Fred was quite sure that Marlene wanted to wring his neck a few times along the way, their love remained strong and powerful.

Fred put his eyeglasses on. First, he checked on the roast beef in the oven. The meat was cooked, and it was just on a warming setting now. Perfect mashed potatoes (right out of the packet) as well as perfectly cooked turnips along with a helping of hearty green beans. Slices of chocolate cake waited for dessert, but first Fred needed the prelude.

The all-important prelude.

The magic.

Fred stared into the pages of the "Bartender's Guide to Amazing Cocktails" and while he certainly was not Hal, the amazing and gloriously skilled bartender, Fred Kelleher remained determined to give it his best shot. Earlier in the day, he had picked up all the ingredients for the Christmas cocktails at the corner liquor store, and now it was time for the mixing magic to occur. With crossed fingers and perhaps some toes too, Fred carefully selected the glasses and mixed the drinks. First, a bourbon Manhattan in a cocktail glass with ice and then a rye whiskey sour. Fred studied them and he had to say that they looked perfect to his old eyes. He slowly shuffled off and delivered the drinks, set them at their places at the table, and lit the candle. The candle flame flickered and danced, and combined with their small tabletop Christmas tree, along with the music, Fred felt as if he created a perfect Christmas Eve setting.

Satisfied, Fred checked his suit jacket pocket once more to make sure it was still there.

It was.

Fred pulled at the lapel of his jacket and mumbled, "Not too bad for an old coot. No lumps in those potatoes, either. I love those premixed packets. Fred Kelleher, you are indeed, a very lucky man." He then turned and called for his wife. "Okay, Marlene! Honey, you can come down now! Dinner is ready. Along with some Christmas cocktails."

Fred heard the door close to their bedroom, and he stood at the base of the stairs and watched as his wife appeared. Fred was a little wobbly in his knees from old age, but his wife's beauty just about knocked him over. Marlene wore a black dress and those same amazing white pearl earrings and that glorious white pearl necklace from so long ago. Fred swore that she was more beautiful tonight than she ever was before in their sixty years of marriage.

Stunning!

Marlene floated on Christmas magic. Fred met her at the base of the stairs, held his hand out, and she took it as the old couple teetered and tottered their way to the dining room table.

"You are the most beautiful woman in the world, Marlene," Fred said while Marlene smiled. He held the chair out for his wife and Marlene sat at the table and admired the amazing setting.

"Oh my, Fred, this is so glorious! You are a remarkable man. The meal smells heavenly!"

Fred smiled as he too sat at the table and said, "It is not our quiet nook at our favorite restaurant, with a view of the city and the snow falling down . . . but I guess it will do."

Marlene smiled and said, "It is even better."

"Please, let's try the Christmas cocktails. I bought a silly recipe book and I would like to think that I did my best. A toast," Fred said as he lifted the glass and Marlene did the same. "Merry Christmas, my love, and thank you for sixty glorious years."

"Thank you, Fred. My darling, Fred."

They each took a sip and Fred had to think that he did a pretty good job on mixing the cocktails.

"Oh, Fred, this is delicious! Thank you. Honestly, this is the best sour that I have ever had. There is just something magical about Christmas cocktails! I have to say that Hal would be very proud of you, my dear. Perhaps, you will get me tipsy and take advantage of me later tonight," Marlene said with a coy wink and a smile.

"That's part of my covert plan, my dear. Besides, I put some magic in that Christmas cocktail, and now, I have just a touch more." Fred reached in his suit jacket pocket and pulled out the box. "I am too old and too stiff to get down on one knee for too long. Therefore, I will stand up and hand it to you. Here, Marlene. Merry Christmas and I will love you forever and just a little more too."

Fred stood up, walked over to Marlene, slowly opened the lid to the box, and then handed it to his wife. Marlene gasped at the diamond necklace inside, and she burst into tears as Fred gently took the box and removed the necklace. As he motioned for his wife to stand up and Marlene tried hard in order to gather her emotions, Fred gently removed the pearls and replaced them with the diamond necklace.

"Oh, Fred, it is gorgeous. Thank you for the gift and for this wonderful and remarkable evening. I will love you forever, Fred Kelleher. Merry Christmas."

They kissed, and as they did so, a gentle snow began to fall outside. The snowfall began very slowly, and the flakes drifted silently to the ground. The peace and the calm remained; it simply received a coating of white.

Yes, indeed, there was some extra magic in those Christmas cocktails.

It was a glorious Christmas Eve and a peaceful evening. The snow covered the land in layers of white beauty and the moonlight of the cold, crisp winter evening reflected the diamonds hidden within their white magic while it flickered upon the freshly fallen snow. On this peaceful night, the magic of Christmas slowly unfolded.

We must always believe and allow the magic of Christmas, and in fact, the magic of every day, unfolds in our hearts.

Along with the peace and the calm and the love.

ABOUT THE AUTHOR

Way back in time, when the dinosaurs first died off, at the ripe old age of sixteen, Paul John Hausleben, wrote three stories for a creative writing class in high school. Enrolled in a vocational school, and immersed in trade courses and apprenticeship, left little time for writing ventures but PJH wrote three exceptional and entertaining stories. Paul John Hausleben's stories caught the eye of two English teachers in the college-preparatory academic programs and they pulled the author out of his basic courses and plopped him in advanced English and writing courses. One of the English teachers had immense faith in Paul's talents, and she took PJH's stories, helped him brush them up and submitted them to a periodical for publication. To PJH's astonishment, the periodical published all three of the stories and sent him a royalty check for fifty dollars and . . . that was it. PJH did not write anymore because life got in his way. Fast forward to 2009 and while living on the road in Atlanta, Georgia (and struggling to communicate with the locals who did not speak New Jersey) for his full-time job, PJH took a part-time job writing music reviews for a progressive rock website, and that gig caused the writing bug to bite PJH once more. He recalled those old stories and found the old manuscripts hiding in a dusty box. After some doodling around with them, PJH decided to revisit them. Two stories became the nucleus for the anthology now known as, *The Time Bomb in The Cupboard and Other Adventures of Harry and Paul.* The other story became the anchor story for collection known as, *The Christmas Tree and Other Christmas Stories, Tales for a Christmas Evening*. Now, many years and over thirty-five published works later, along with countless blogs and other work, PJH continues to write. Where and when it stops, only the author really knows.

On the other hand, does he really know?

If you ask Paul John Hausleben, he will tell you that he is not an author, he is just a storyteller. His mission is to continue to write and tell stories to warm your heart, make you laugh, and sometimes make you cry, just a little. Most of all, he deals in memories, and helping you to remember the good times of your own life, and the special people who touched you along the way. Paul was born and raised in Paterson, and then nearby Haledon, New Jersey, and began writing at an early age. He revisited a writing career later in his life, and he now is the author of a number of novels, compilations, short stories and audio and video works. Most of his work, touches upon nostalgic remembrances of simpler times, and tells the stories of heartfelt, humorous, and special human relationships. Other than writing, among many careers both paid and unpaid, he is a former semi-professional hockey goaltender, a music fan and music reviewer, an avid sports fan, photographer and amateur radio operator. He now resides in Somewhere, U.S.A., but his heart always remains along Belmont Avenue in good old Paterson, and Haledon, New Jersey.

Other Work by Mr. Paul John Hausleben

The Time Bomb in The Cupboard and Other Adventures of Harry and Paul

The Night Always Comes, Another story from the Adventures of Harry and Paul

Reunion, A sequel to the Night Always Comes and Another story from the Adventures of Harry and Paul

The Miracle Tree, Another story from the Adventures of Harry and Paul

The Chronicles of Henson

Heaven's Gain
The Final Adventure of Harry and Paul

Geyer Street Gardens
Beneath the Mask of a Hockey Goaltender
Another story from the Adventures of Harry and Paul

Where the River Bends and Curls

And a few others too!

You may write to the author at ctte27@gmail.com

Published by God Bless the Keg Publishing LLC
Henrico, Virginia, U.S.A.

You may write to the publisher at
Godblessthekegpublishing@gmail.com

"Life's simple pleasures are so often the best ones!"

www.ingramcontent.com/pod-product-compliance
Lightning Source LLC
LaVergne TN
LVHW041108080826
845145LV00007B/1727

* 9 7 8 1 7 3 3 0 9 2 7 1 5 *